THE *HOLT FAMILY* SERIES

This Time
you

T.M. CROMER

ISBN 978-0-9965720-3-3 (EPUB)

ISBN 978-0-9965720-5-7 (PAPERBACK)

Cover Design: Deranged Doctor Designs

Edits: Trusted Accomplice

This is a work of fiction. Names, characters, businesses, places, events, and incidents are either the products of the author's imagination or used in a fictitious manner. Any resemblance to actual persons, living or dead, or actual events is purely coincidental.

For Joye and Jannaya:
You've waited long enough for this one!

CHAPTER 1

he slamming of multiple car doors jolted Margaret Holt from a light sleep. The second the fuzz cleared from her brain, she registered the source—the new neighbor to the west.

"It must be moving day," she said aloud to no one.

The house had been empty since the death of her elderly friend, Opal. The old woman had been a pistol, cracking jokes and keeping active despite gnarled joints from rheumatoid arthritis. Margie sniffed and blinked against the sudden onslaught of tears.

Margie missed their morning routine the most. She'd send the kids off to school, grab a second cup of coffee, and trot over to hang with Opal on her front porch for exactly forty minutes. One of them would always have a baked treat to share. Afterward, Margie would return home to prepare for her workday. Not that she needed to do much other than comb her hair and sit down in her home office, but it required a change in her mindset.

Her mornings seemed empty now. They stretched long and were packed with monotony. Same routine day after day.

Margie reached out with her foot and set her hammock in motion.

The frame took up an entire corner of her upper deck, but she

1

didn't care. The stand was out of the way enough to allow the kids free run of the pool deck at their standard mach-5 speed. No matter how many times she yelled, *"No running!"* her boys ignored her as if she didn't exist. And some days, she felt as if she didn't. They only needed her as their personal alarm clock or when they arrived home from school as ravenous little beasts, gorging on everything in the fridge and pantry. She was expected to drop everything to feed the black holes they called stomachs.

As for her daughter, Kaley, well, most of the time Margie didn't warrant a second glance. More often than not, she received an eye roll for bothering to speak at all.

Kids. Pfft. If only her ex-husband were a hands-on dad, maybe she wouldn't worry about her kids becoming little hoodlums.

"Excuse me. I'm sorry to bother—"

She screamed and sloshed what remained of her lukewarm coffee on the deck. When she met the contrite eyes of her visitor through the mesh of the screen enclosure, she almost tumbled from the hammock.

Holy hell!

For a second, she thought she was seeing a ghost.

"Sebastian?" she croaked her shock.

He frowned. "No. Gabriel."

She gave herself a mental forehead smack. Of course he wasn't Sebastian. He couldn't be. Sebastian Harwick had died over a century earlier. Margie needed to get her mind out of the past and into the present. Still, the resemblance between the two men disconcerted her. It was madness. Like looking down the wrong end of a telescope. Seeing down a tunnel of time.

In fairness, he must get reactions like hers a lot. The man was divine from the top of his chestnut-colored hair to the tips of his... *flip-flops?* Her eyes trailed back up over the long length of his legs. He wore designer duds with a pair of canvas flip-flops that had seen better days. *Huh.* Yeah, even his large feet were flawless. Of course, large feet led her down the path of large—*nope,* she wasn't going there. She'd sworn off those after her divorce.

With an attempt to corral her thoughts and get her wayward blush under control, Margie dropped her gaze from his person. With a little luck, he'd assume her flushed skin was a result of the hot Florida sun. Nevermind it was mid-October and the sun wasn't as fierce at eight a.m.

The silence had gone on way too long, and she needed to say something. But damned if she knew what. "I'm sorry. I..." She glanced over his shoulder toward the street in hopes of finding the words, only to discover her daughter was at it again.

"*Aww, fuck.*"

His eyebrows shot up.

Dismounting from a hammock was harder than imaginable, especially when Margie was fumbling to sit up with a coffee cup in hand and was in a hurry to stop Kaley. The wind whipped up at her moment of dismount, and with it, her indignity at fighting her way free of the swinging death trap.

His hand appeared in her line of vision, offering assistance.

How the hell he'd moved so quickly was beyond her. With little to no pride left, she allowed him to haul her to her feet. As she stood next to him, she gawked at his height and build. He made her five-foot-six frame look positively petite. A small thrill swept through her at his nearness, and she tamped down a girly sigh.

"Hi," he said. "I'm Gabriel James. Opal's nephew."

His voice hit her like the first sip of coffee in the morning. A perfectly concocted mocha with a hint of yumminess underneath woke her right up and was absolutely delightful. Her body shuddered in appreciation of the rich sound.

They stood a hairsbreadth away from one another with their gazes locked. The sunlight turned his eyes to a sparkling silver, or maybe it was the laughter lurking in their depths.

Yep, he was definitely Sebastian—in two-hundred-dollar jeans and a pricy brand-name t-shirt. It should be impossible, but her eyes, her nose—shit, all her senses—were telling her this was him. *Unless she'd finally gone off the deep end and conjured him.* For years, she'd dreamed of Sebastian, and now here stood his clone. She wanted so badly to touch him. To reassure herself he was real. To *prove* her mind hadn't snapped.

"My daughter," she blurted. "I... she..."

Margie was becoming seriously pissed at her inability to form a coherent sentence around him. *What in the world was wrong with her?* She cleared her throat and tried again.

"I just saw her walking toward... a jeep. Down the block. She should be at school. I have to... go." Yeah, babbling was no better. If she didn't get control of herself soon, he'd think she was a total spaz. Which wasn't far from the truth.

She shook her head to clear her thoughts. "Excuse me. I really have to stop them before they leave." Proud of herself for managing a full sentence without stuttering, she stepped around him.

"Just a sec." Gabriel held up a hand. He shifted to observe the teenagers locking lips in the front seat of the vehicle. "I'm assuming those two are the delinquents you want stopped?"

At her nod, he put two fingers to his mouth and released an ear-piercing whistle. The two men unloading boxes from a pickup in Opal's driveway swiveled their heads toward Gabriel at the sound. He jerked his chin. They immediately caught on to what he was asking them to do. The taller of the two trotted toward the jeep and yanked open the door.

Kaley jumped out of her side. Her red face promised to give him hell, and with hands on her hips, she made good on her promise. A loud, heated discussion ensued.

When her daughter took a swing at the tall man closest to her, Margie inwardly winced. Violence had become Kaley's go-to reaction when angry lately.

Taking a step back, he cast an inquiring look their way.

Of course, Margie might've mistaken disgust at the situation he found himself in for inquiry. At a chuckle from Gabriel, she glanced upward.

"Setting your friends up to feel the wrath of a demon posing as a fourteen-year-old girl amuses you?" she asked dryly.

"They're my brothers, and you have no idea." He grinned down at her, his silvery eyes twinkling with mischief.

She bit her lip to prevent a laugh.

An outraged cry from her daughter brought Margie's head snapping back around.

Kaley swung both fists as one of Gabriel's brothers held her off, his arm outstretched with a hand on her head. Her face was quickly approaching scarlet—a direct contrast to her pale-pink hair color—as her frustration grew from being unable to reach him with her shorter arm span.

Margie groaned and raced toward the mayhem. The last thing she needed was an assault charge against her hot-headed daughter. Before she cleared the screen door, the harried but bravehearted man swung Kaley up over his shoulder in a fireman's hold. His long, purposeful strides ate up the distance to where Margie and Gabriel waited.

The foul language Kaley showered on him could be heard the neighborhood over. Margie cringed. Who knew her child had such an extensive vocabulary? She couldn't even be mad at the guy for manhandling her daughter. If it were her, she'd have dragged Kaley back by her ear.

As he got closer, the resemblance to her grinning neighbor became more obvious. He stopped, grimaced, and arched his back like he'd been shot—or stabbed—before charging forward, a black look clouding his features.

She rushed to open the screened door as an apology formed on her lips. Any other time, she'd rip the arms from someone manhandling her child, but he'd done what she couldn't and had stopped Kaley from whatever nefarious plans she'd concocted for the day. Cleaning up her last day of hooky had cost five-hundred dollars and a month of community service.

Gabriel's brother reached the edge of the pool and tossed Kaley in the water. As he turned to leave, he growled, *Chase your own hell-cats next time, Gabe!*

There might've been mention of antiseptic needed for the bite on his back. Margie couldn't be sure, and she missed her chance to thank him as he stalked past her.

The whole unbelievable incident lasted less than five minutes, and she struggled to process what had just happened. She turned her gaze to a laughing Gabriel, who lounged against the stucco wall. She couldn't decide whether she wanted to kiss him or hit him. He'd unknowingly set her up for weeks of hell because Kaley carried a grudge like it was nobody's business.

Margie settled on gratitude. "Thank—"

"You ruined my life!" Kaley came out of the pool like an angry water sprite. Long pink hair streamed down either side of her pissed-off, red face. She sputtered her outrage.

Wow! Straight to the ruined-my-life stage. *Typical teen drama.*

"You're fourteen!" Margie yelled at her retreating back. "There's no kissing boys at *fourteen!*"

Kaley stormed away, dripping water all over the pristine tile floors. It also didn't matter she could've easily used one of the towels hanging over the rack by the back door to dry off. No, Kaley had a point to make. She had to prove to her mother she didn't give a rat's ass about all the hard work Margie had put into cleaning the house yesterday.

Margie put her hand to the back of her neck and attempted to rub away the knots forming there. "I'm sorry. Kaley's hit that age..." There was no excuse for the type of behavior her daughter had exhibited today. Instead, she went with, "Thank you. I appreciate all you've done."

Butterflies fluttered low in her abdomen as he continued to gaze down into her face. What must he be thinking? It surprised her he wasn't already running for the hills. He had no idea of the hornet's nest he'd kicked.

"If you'll hand over the key to my house, we'll call it even."

If he'd picked *her* up and thrown her in the pool, Margie couldn't have been more surprised.

. . .

GABRIEL STARED DOWN AT HIS NEW NEIGHBOR. HER DEEP BLUE EYES were large in her heart-shaped face, and she'd forgone mascara. Those thick, dark lashes were all her own. Natural beauty appealed to him, and he appreciated her lack of cosmetics.

If he were being objective, he would've said her nose might be a tad on the long side, but it didn't affect the overall symmetry of her face or her girl-next-door prettiness. Gabriel dropped his gaze to her mouth. Her full lower lip was held captive by her straight white teeth. As he watched, she released it with a puff of breath.

"Key?"

"Was I wrong to assume you had the spare? I could swear Aunt Opal mentioned you had a copy. That is, if you're Margaret Holt."

She closed her eyes and rubbed a spot between her brows. "Right. The spare key. One sec."

Margaret rushed away in a flurry of movement, and Gabriel smiled. She was amusing without trying. He found it difficult to resist the temptation to check out her shapely ass, encased in a pair of capri-style yoga pants.

"Uh, Gabriel?"

He jerked his attention away from her backside and lifted his gaze to her flushed face. She twisted to hide her butt from view, and he bit the inside of his cheek to curb his laughter. A lot of women were self-conscious about their body, but she should be proud of her assets. The woman had a mighty fine ass.

"I can bring it over in a few minutes if you don't want to wait."

"I don't mind waiting for you, Margaret."

"Right," she said in her breathy voice, ducking into the house.

"You going to stand here and flirt all day, or are you going to help us unpack the truck?"

Gabriel spun around to see his brother Greyson standing on the other side of the screened enclosure, with his arms folded across his muscled chest.

"Seems you and Gordie have it handled." Gabriel glanced back through the kitchen window and at the dark-haired woman who'd captured his interest.

"She's pretty in that messy-mom kind of way. The topknot and yoga pants are the crowning touch."

Even though he'd had a similar thought, Gabriel scowled at Grey. "For a messy mom? She's beautiful regardless."

"Oh." Margaret's soft, startled voice wrapped around him and squeezed. The one breathy syllable shot straight to his groin.

He narrowed his eyes at his grinning brother. The bastard had set him up. Grey must've caught a glimpse of her returning and decided it would be fun to mess with him.

"Here it is. Your key." She held it out with a barely discernible tremble.

A small surge of electricity shot up his arm as his hand touched hers.

Their gazes connected, and the air grew charged.

"Thanks." Gabriel didn't mean to sound terse, but he didn't want to give Grey any more ammunition. The teasing would be merciless as it was. He softened his tone. "Nice meeting you, Margaret. I'm sorry I interrupted your morning."

She tilted her head sideways toward the sliding door. "No, you and your brothers did me a favor. I'd never have reached Kaley before they drove off."

He gave her an impersonal smile and followed Grey across the lawn. Maybe he was being fanciful, but he imagined her eyes burning into his back as he walked away. A quick check behind showed her zeroed in on his ass. He chuckled to himself. Life was about to get more interesting in this Palm Coast cul-de-sac.

CHAPTER 2

argie saw brief glimpses of Gabriel over the next few weeks. Sometimes when he lounged on his front porch and lifted his mug in a friendly salute. Sometimes when he left or returned from work. And a few times when he tinkered in his garage, organizing tools or carting another box inside his house. He always gave a friendly wave and a knee-weakening smile.

Today, she once more reclined in her hammock and did her best not to glance his way, failing miserably. A leggy blonde in a form-fitting dress sashayed up his driveway where he met her halfway and caught her as she flung herself against him. The woman's seductive laughter floated across the lawn, and Margie wanted to gag on her yogurt.

As if he sensed her stare, Gabriel glanced her way. She averted her face so fast, she popped her neck. How embarrassing was it for a thirty-seven-year-old woman to be caught spying on an intimate moment? She pretended fascination with a raft in her pool.

"Mom! Scotty's hogging the remote again!"

Of course he was. Scotty could be a little shit, like his namesake, Scott Senior.

"Owww! Mom, he hit me!" There was a slight pause. "Cut it out, jerk!"

The tension headache tightened the muscles at the base of her skull, and Margie eyed the rope attached to her hammock. It probably wasn't long or thick enough for her to end it all.

"Mom! Aaron's kicking my chair!"

Dropping her chin to her chest, she sighed. God, she hated her life some days. At least days that ended in Y.

"Margaret."

A wealth of warmth was in that one word, and she instinctively turned her head toward the seductive sound of Gabriel's deep voice. She didn't bother to open her eyes. If she did, she'd probably cry. The squeak of the screen door basically gave her no choice, and she lifted her lids. The up-close and personal view of his wide, t-shirt-clad chest was a nice consolation for her crappy morning.

"Are you all right?"

She managed a slight shake of her head without speaking.

"Mom! Scotty still won't let me play!" Aaron screeched from their living room.

Margie lifted weary eyes to meet Gabriel's concerned gaze.

"Want me to handle it?"

"What are you going to do? Sell them to the traveling circus?"

His lips twitched. "If that's what works best for you."

"Mmm. Be my guest." She gestured toward the door. "But if there's bloodshed, I'm claiming I know nothing when the police arrive." Margie peeked behind him, but didn't see the blonde. "Where's your friend?"

"Friend?" He frowned down at her and glanced back toward his house. His expression darkened. "Yeah, you mean my wife."

Margie lost her grip on the yogurt cup. Gabriel wasn't quick enough to avoid the strawberry spatter on his bare shins and flip-flops.

Wife? Opal never mentioned a wife!

"I didn't realize you were married." She willed the shock from

10

her features and tried to play it cool. It would be nice if her face played along.

"It was a mistake." He bent to pick up the plastic cup and ran two fingers up his leg to remove the goo. "One I hope will be rectified soon. We've been separated for the better part of two years."

"Let me get you a washcloth." Avoidance was easier than discussing emotions or other people's problems. There was a dark quality to his voice when he mentioned his marriage, and she wanted no part of that mess.

Gabriel followed her into the house, and Margie was sure he missed nothing. Not the arguing boys on the gaming chairs in the living room. Not the pile of breakfast dishes on the table. And not the surly pink-haired teen who walked out of her room, looked at her mother, and did an about-face.

"Yes, this is my life," Margie muttered as she handed him a damp cloth. In exchange, she took the trash from his hand and dumped it into the sink to rinse later.

He studied her in silence for a moment before bending to scrub his shin.

She had no idea what rested behind his inscrutable expression, and she found her inability to decipher his look bothered her. Mainly, because she felt she came off severely lacking.

"Hey, guys, time to shut that off and go pack a weekend bag. Your dad's going to be here soon."

"Aww, Mom!" was accompanied by the groans of two boys.

"*Now.*"

The gaming remotes were thrown down in a fit of pique with no care as to the replacement cost should they break. Scotty stomped to his room, and Aaron folded his arms across his chest.

His lip quivered. "I didn't get a turn."

"Come here, bud." Aaron was her sensitive soul and needed a more careful, loving touch. When he stood in front of her, she leaned down to kiss his smooth forehead. "I promise, the next time the game is fired up, you'll get to go first. But right now, I need a break from the sound and screaming, okay?"

Aaron wrapped his skinny arms around her middle in a quick hug. "Can I invite Tuck over to go swimming?"

Margie glanced first at Gabriel and then at the stove clock. "Your dad will be here to pick you guys up in about a half hour. I think you should get ready to go."

"I don't want to go to Dad's. Why can't I stay with you?"

When his begging blue eyes looked at her as if she were his entire world, she wanted to bundle him up and tell Scott to go screw himself. It wasn't fair to her kids that they had to be shuttled back and forth this way, but custody guidelines were custody guidelines.

"Because it's your dad's weekend. Go get ready. Be sure to tell your brother and sister I said they have twenty minutes to have a bag packed and their rooms cleaned."

Aaron raced off, happy to be in charge.

"You didn't need me to sell them to the circus after all."

"Let's keep that idea on the back burner." She turned to find Gabriel watching her. His warm eyes were locked on her face, and for a moment, she wondered what he could possibly see that he approved of. Her life was a train wreck. Why had he come over today? *And how did she prolong his stay?* "Coffee?"

"If it's no trouble." Gabriel collected dirty dishes from the table and brought them to the kitchen. "I don't want to make your morning harder." He tilted his head and studied her with shrewd, all-seeing eyes. "Besides, it looks like you could use a break."

"I'll get one if Scott doesn't cancel at the last minute. He has a tendency to forget he sired children."

"Ouch."

"Sorry. I know I sound bitter."

"No, you sound like a woman who has a lot on her plate."

He got her. Right away. No explanations or excuses on her part needed. He'd seen and summed up the situation in an instant, and he just *got* her. She smiled with genuine warmth. "Tell me again why you're getting divorced? You have to be the most understanding man on the planet."

. . .

GABRIEL AVOIDED ANSWERING. THE TRUTH WAS, HE COULDN'T RECALL why he'd married Tamara. She'd been high maintenance even before their grandiose wedding. Could he say he'd ever loved her? Looking back, probably not. Mostly, he'd been attracted to her confidence and hot body, and he failed to realize they were accompanied by a shallow personality. After enough time had passed, he began to feel the pressure from both her father and her to take their relationship to the next level. Since Jerry Silverman was a senior partner in the law firm where he'd worked at the time, it seemed like the right thing to do. However, her spoiled-little-princess routine with the temper tantrums and continuous pouting when Gabriel refused to cater to her demands sealed the fate on their short-lived marriage. Their separation coincided with his departure from Silverman's law firm.

"Tamara thought so. I guess that's why she assumed it was okay to spend every dime I made and to have affairs when I wasn't paying her enough attention. She figured I'd be 'understanding.'"

Christ! Overshare much?

Margaret's jaw dropped open, and her eyes rounded in horrified wonder. "She cheated on you? Is she stupid?" Her gaze swept his body. She shook her head and turned back to brew a cup from the single-serving coffee machine.

Margaret looked over her shoulder to ask his flavor preference.

A pale-pink flush rode high on her classic cheekbones, and a sparkle had entered her magnificent eyes. Gabriel's breath caught in his throat. Although she was vastly different from anyone he dated in the past, she'd haunted him since their first meeting. Every day, he found a reason to linger outside to catch a glimpse of her. If he could capture her eye and receive a shy smile, his day became brighter.

"Coffee preference?" she asked a second time.

"Dark roast, please."

A strange desire struck him as she turned away to busy herself

13

with the coffee maker. He wanted nothing more than to wrap his arms around her and bury his face against her long, graceful neck. The urge to touch, to breathe in her unique scent, gripped him.

The doorbell interrupted his private thoughts—and none too soon. Another minute, and he'd have probably given into his compulsion to touch her.

"Fucker's early," she muttered. "Figures."

Gabriel sputtered a laugh. It wasn't the first time her swearing surprised him, and she had a tendency to catch him off guard in moments like this.

Color surged into her cheeks. "Crap. Did I say that aloud?"

"You did," he confirmed with a grin. *And didn't her colorful language add to her appeal?*

"I'll let you fix it the way you like it." She indicated the machine. "Be right back."

Since he preferred his coffee black, he picked up the ceramic mug and read the front: *I try to act nonchalant, but inside I'm actually chalant AF.*

He chuckled. Margaret Holt possessed a sense of humor he could appreciate. Gabriel's desire to smile died a sudden death when she returned, followed by the man he assumed was her surly ex-husband. The guy even looked like a prick. Buzz cut hair and what looked to be a perpetual scowl.

"Who the fuck are you, and why are you in my house?"

Gabriel's brows shot up along with his irritation at the asshat's belligerent tone.

"*My* house, Scott, and none of your damned business," Margaret snapped.

"It *is* my business if you're screwing this guy while my kids are under the same roof."

A decision had to be made. Gabriel could either chew this guy a new asshole or leave Margaret to deal with Scott's aggressive attitude. Since leaving her alone to face Scott's nastiness didn't sit well, Gabriel chose to stay.

He casually sipped his coffee and swallowed. "You're doing

Margaret a disservice when you throw around accusations. You really should get your facts straight before your diarrhea of the mouth gets the best of you."

Margaret smirked, and a modicum of the weariness left her eyes. He felt confident he'd made the right choice.

"Tell the kids I'll be in the car. If they aren't ready in five minutes, I'm leaving."

Scott stalked toward the front door, and Margaret was quick to chase after him. "Scott!"

Not above eavesdropping, Gabriel leaned back, away from the counter, to get a better view of the couple in the hallway.

"You can't show up twenty minutes early and drop ultimatums. If you'd have called or texted, they'd have been ready."

"Then you keep them. I have shit to do."

"You're being unfair—*again*. I have plans this weekend that don't include children."

"With the asshole in the kitchen?" Scott demanded.

"Oh, knock it off. We've been divorced nine years. I don't answer to you. But if you don't want the kids on your scheduled days, perhaps we should go back to court to increase your child support. I'll have to pay for care on days I want to have a life."

Gabriel wanted to applaud Margaret's fierceness. He imagined he could hear the grinding of Scott's teeth.

"Whatever. Tell them to hurry." Scott beat a hasty retreat.

Margaret rolled her shoulders and rubbed her neck.

Gabriel allowed her two deep, cleansing breaths before he joined her in the hall. "You okay?"

"Yeah, but I'm sick of his behavior. It's always his way or the highway, and I'm done."

"Anything I can do to make it better?" It was the second time the urge had overtaken him. And why he wanted to when he had a busy day ahead was questionable.

"No, thank you for offering though." She finally faced him, and the hardness in her eyes softened.

Now he knew why he'd offered. He found himself volunteering

his services for another of those same soft looks. "If you need free legal advice, I'm your man."

"You're a lawyer?"

"Criminal, but I know a thing or two about family law. Plus, I have a good number of friends who specialize in that field."

"Tamara was an idiot to lose you, Gabriel James."

He grinned. "I'd like to think so."

"Let me round up the kids, then we can enjoy our coffee on the deck." She bit her lip. "I mean, if you still want to hang around for a while."

"I'm happy to."

Margaret hurried down the hall and peeked her head into a room, urging the occupants to "speed it up." She then knocked on the farthest door from him. "Kaley? Your dad's here, and he's in a rush."

"I'm not going!"

"It's his weekend, and yes, you are."

The girl whipped open the door and glared at her mother. "I said, I'm not going."

"What's this about, sweetheart?"

Kaley's pale eyes focused on Gabriel. "What's *he* doing here? Is he the reason I have to go?"

"He popped in for a neighborly chat. And, no. He has nothing to do with the guidelines your dad and I set for you kids."

"Can't I stay home, Mom?" Kaley's sullen expression eased into pleading. "Please?"

"You're old enough to make the choice if you want to stay or go. But you'll need to be the one to tell your father."

Margaret handled each minor crisis with admirable calm. If Gabriel hadn't witnessed the exhaustion on her face mere minutes before, he'd have never guessed she found all this emotionally wearing.

"Thanks, Mom."

Kaley ran past him on the way out the door and gave him a curious look. The hostility from a minute earlier was gone.

Margaret gave the smallest boy a hug and a kiss on his upturned face, but when she tried to do the same with her older son, he shrugged her off and wiped her kiss from his cheek. She still managed a tight smile. "Have fun, boys."

"Love you, Mom," the younger one called.

"Love you, too, sweetheart."

As soon as the door closed behind them, the silence in the house became deafening. Margaret's busy household was a sharp contrast to his own calm and quiet home. Her ability to smoothly transition from one situation to another within the chaotic storm of activity made him aware he'd be a complete amateur in the parenting arena.

Gabriel cleared his throat. "Is it always this... busy around here?"

"Busier on a school day." She laughed and crossed to the coffee maker. "Are you still good, or do you want another?"

"I'm good."

They settled into the lounge chairs positioned outside the sliding doors, and sipped their drinks in companionable silence. No awkwardness hung in the air, and the feeling of contentment Gabriel experienced was like nothing he'd known before.

"You know what I do for a living," he said. "But I know next to nothing about you."

"I'm an artist. Commercial stuff and cartoons mostly, but I sell the occasional landscape or sketch of someone's beloved pet here or there."

He smiled at the image of her, sketchpad in hand, concentration total on her current project. "Would I have seen anything of yours?" A half smile played on her lips, making Gabriel curious as to what was amusing. "Okay, how famous are you?"

"It's not like that." She shrugged and gestured toward his house with her mug. "There were one or two hanging up when Opal was alive. She also commissioned me to paint a few landscapes for her nephews." A smile teased the corners of her mouth. "Since I'm assuming you and your brothers were her only relatives, one of you must've received my work as a present."

He sat up straighter. "Athena's temple! She gifted me that one for my office about two years ago. I couldn't make out the signature. One of yours?"

"Yep."

"I love that painting."

"You don't have to say that."

"I'm completely serious. It speaks to me."

"I'm glad you like it."

"Love it," he corrected, leaning back. The mug was inches from his mouth when he remembered the paintings in his brother's restaurant. "The Italian landscapes Opal gave to Grey—you did those, too, didn't you?"

"Guilty."

"They inspired me to take a trip last year."

It was her turn to stare at him in surprise. A horrendous crash from inside the house aborted her response. She bolted, Gabriel right on her heels. They found Kaley, lying on the floor in a pool of blood.

CHAPTER 3

*G*abriel wasn't entirely certain how he found himself sitting in a hospital room with his new neighbor, other than the fact she'd become unglued the second she saw her daughter on the floor—and rightfully so. The sight of the blood flowing from the girl's head had left *him* a bit queasy.

Because Margaret had rushed to help Kaley, he'd been the one to call for an ambulance. The first responders arrived with the usual fanfare of lights and sirens, and Gabriel had needed to physically restrain Margaret to keep her away from her child long enough for them to treat the girl. Although the paramedics were able to stop the bleeding on-site and their patient had regained consciousness, they recommended a trip to the ER to make sure nothing more serious was going on in the girl's brain.

Gabriel shifted in the hard plastic chair and stretched.

A radiology technician had come and whisked Kaley away for a CT scan about a half hour ago, and now here Gabriel sat with Margaret, waiting for news. She retreated into her own little bubble, chewing her lip and sending out texts to God only knew who. Scott perhaps? Gabriel couldn't really see her ex-husband caring all that much. The guy didn't seem the hands-on, fatherly type.

As for Gabriel, one glimpse of her haunted sapphire eyes, and he'd been a goner. The need to ease her suffering wouldn't be denied. The feeling had never happened before, or if it had, he bailed. But not this time.

To gain her attention, he touched her knee.

She jumped and released a little "eep!"

He pressed his lips together to bite back his laughter. In her flustered state, Margaret was cute as hell and damned near irresistible.

"Are you going to be okay, Margaret?"

"You don't have to wait with me. I'm sure you have better things to do with your time. I'll be okay."

Her brave façade didn't fool him. She didn't have the art of pretense down, and her every thought showed on her face.

"I have nowhere to be. I'm happy to wait with you." Actually, he had a shit-ton to do, both at work and home, but oddly, he preferred to remain here with her.

She opened her mouth and snapped it shut again. Perhaps she'd intended to argue but came to the conclusion she didn't really want to be alone. He was okay with that, too.

"She's going to be fine." Gabriel curled his fingers around her delicate wrist and gave a light, reassuring squeeze. He doubted it would help, because until Margaret saw with her own eyes that her daughter was going to be okay, she wouldn't completely believe anything he said or did.

"So I know you are Opal's nephew, but not much more."

He gave her props for attempting conversation when her mind was elsewhere. "Opal was my aunt on my mother's side. She actually left me the house. I'll never understand why she didn't will it to my brother Greyson since he was her favorite. For whatever reason, she wanted me to have it, and because I fancied an actual house, I sold Grey my condo at the beach."

She sucked in her lower lip, and Gabriel's attention was drawn to the fullness of her mouth. A mouth he desperately wanted to taste. In the short time he'd known her, he learned the biting of her lip was Margaret's nervous tell. She would be shit at cards. Maybe down the road, he should engage her in a game of strip poker. He was sure to win. With a slight shake of his head, he pushed away all thoughts of a naked Margaret Holt. A hospital emergency room wasn't the appropriate place to fantasize about the woman he'd so recently met—especially when her child was hurt.

"So that explains it."

"Pardon?" he asked.

"Hmm?"

"You said, 'So that explains it.' Explains what?"

"I did?"

"Yes. You did."

"Hmm."

"Explains what?"

"I couldn't say."

"Can't or won't?"

"Mmhmm."

Gabriel was beginning to feel this was a game of "Who's on First." Because he was a sucker and his aunt was adept at emotional blackmail, he had allowed himself to be conned into repeatedly watching Abbott and Costello reruns. Now, he practically knew it by heart.

As he sat beside Margaret, trying to decide if following this line of discussion was worth the mental strain, a raucous group charged down the hospital corridor. In the lead was a petite blonde woman with a distinct look of determination stamped firmly on her features. Other than the hair color, she bore a striking resemblance to Margaret.

"Your family, I presume?"

MARGIE WHIPPED HER HEAD AROUND. "YEP, THEY BELONG TO ME."

They'd spotted her and their questions flew fast and furious.

"Margie! Thank God! How is she?"

"What happened?"

"Is she going to be okay?"

"Any news yet?"

She jumped up to field their questions—at least that's the excuse she told herself. The reality? She needed a break from her disturbing companion.

Gabriel's presence overwhelmed her, and every time she looked at him in all his gorgeousness, her brain cells malfunctioned. The result made her feel dumber than a rock. If she stared long enough, she feared she'd go blind, much like staring at the sun. All his yummy sexiness short-circuited her wiring. Their last little exchange could be used as a prime example.

When she learned he was the nephew to whom Opal had left the house, Margie understood *exactly* why Gabriel inherited. The elderly woman had been trying to get him to come for a visit in the months preceding her death, but Gabriel had always been too busy.

At the time, Margie couldn't understand why Opal continually sang the praises of her nephew when he couldn't be bothered to give her the time of day. But she went on ad nauseam about how wonderful the oldest "boy" was and how perfect he'd be for Margie. Without a doubt, that little she-devil was trying to set them up from beyond the grave.

At this stage in Margie's life, pushing forty with three children, a small stomach pouch, and a network of stretch marks to show for it, she would be too embarrassed to do the bump and grind with Gabriel.

Ugh! Why did she have to go there? It wasn't like he'd expressed interest.

Or had he?

She snuck a peek at him.

His intent silver gaze followed her as he cocked his head, expression akin to a hawk scoping out its prey. The heat of embarrassment swept from her toes to her hairline. Although he didn't outright smile, his eyes crinkled as if he suppressed one. Margie knew his expressions well. She had seen that particular look on his face at least a hundred times before. Not much changed lifetime to lifetime. He was amused by her and her antics. If she concentrated enough, she could hear the long-ago echo of Sebastian's full-bodied laugh.

With considerable willpower, she ripped her gaze from his and returned her attention to her family. Heat flooded her face as she belatedly registered her mother's softly spoken question. "What happened, sweetheart? How did Kaley get hurt?"

Kaley!

For a brief moment, Gabriel had distracted her from her daughter. Stricken, Margie glanced up to see her sister's boyfriend observing her. Michael brushed past the others to gather her close into a tight hug, offering up a kiss on her forehead.

"Sammy's on her way. She was in Port Orange and got stuck in traffic." His low Southern drawl soothed her. He had a special way about him. An ability to recognize someone's hurt, and with quiet consideration, he provided a comfort they weren't aware they needed. He continued to keep her tucked against his side as he rubbed her back. "Any news yet?"

"No," she said tearfully. "She's still in radiology. You didn't have to come. I would have texted you when I found out anything."

"Don't be ridiculous. You know I have to be here for my best girl."

The air around her altered and became charged. Only one person ever had the power to make her feel such a sensation, and Margie watched Gabriel as he approached their group. She moved closer to Michael to allow room in their small circle.

A dark frown lent a menacing quality to Gabriel's face. Michael must've recognized Gabriel's agitation, too, because he squeezed her tighter.

Gabriel's frown deepened as he pointedly stared at the arm draped over her shoulder. His possessive reaction was enough to make a normal woman giddy, and she bit her lip to hold back a laugh. Silly she should feel euphoria when he likely viewed her as little more than a stranger, but deep down, she knew this man.

When Michael had said "best girl," he was referring to Kaley. The man absolutely adored her daughter. He loved to tease about cloning Kaley so he and Sammy could have a child exactly like her. However, Gabriel didn't know that.

She shrugged off Michael's arm and placed her hand over Gabriel's. As she was about to introduce him to her family, she heard her sister speak to someone in the hallway, and Margie rushed out to greet her.

"Ohmygod, Margie! I'm sorry I couldn't get here any faster. How's Kaley? Michael said she was hurt. What the hell happened, and where were you?"

And like that, Margie felt judged. Why was it Sammy had the ability to make her feel like a shit parent at every turn? "She's in imaging. You really shouldn't have come, because you're not needed."

Sammy jerked as if she'd been slapped, and her eyes narrowed as she stared at Margie. Her shock and hurt stamped plainly on her features.

"Let's go outside." Michael stepped in and ushered her away. Likely preventing the eruption of World War III with his quick thinking.

Sammy's tearful words floated down the corridor. "Why does she have to be such a bitch all the time?"

Margie closed her eyes. Once again, the blame was hers. She couldn't recall a time when she wasn't at odds with Sammy, but as the older sister, she was expected to be the one to suck it up. The one to bite her tongue and cater to her little sister's every whim. As the baby of the family, Sammy had been allowed to run wild, and it still rankled after all this time.

A hand came down on her shoulder, and she reached for it like a lifeline.

Gabriel.

Had he witnessed her ugliness? She snorted. Likely the whole hospital did. She turned to see her parents and brother crowded in the doorway, staring as if she'd lost her damned mind. Perhaps she had.

Gabriel crowded closer as if to protect her from her family's censure, and the sweetness of the gesture warmed her cold insides. He'd retained the same hero quality throughout the centuries.

"Margaret!" Whenever her mother scolded using Margie's full first name, the reprimand was going to be harsh. Did it matter that she was a grown-ass woman? *Apparently not.*

The hand on her shoulder tightened.

Anything Margie would've said was aborted as Kaley was wheeled down the hallway. She was holding her head as if she was in excruciating pain, and Margie's heart lurched to see Kaley hurting.

Margie squeezed Gabriel's hand tighter. It was telling of her life that she found this man, with whom she'd only spent a sum total of three hours, a hundred times more supportive and understanding than her own family.

After the tech assured her the doctor would view the scans with all due haste, Margie perched on the edge of Kaley's bed. "Can I get you anything, sweetheart?"

"Nah, I'm good. Mom? Did you see the guy who hit me?" Kaley toyed with her hospital wristband, and real fear was reflected in her solemn gaze.

Unease stirred in Margie's belly. If Kaley was hallucinating, perhaps the scans weren't as clean as the radiologist assumed. Either that, or this was another of her daughter's bids for attention. "Honey, what are you talking about? There was no one else in the house. Only *you*."

"No!" Kaley winced and pressed her palm to her bandage. "I saw him. He came at me when I walked into the kitchen. Mom, I'm not making this up. I swear."

Margie's gaze snapped to Gabriel's to see what he made of Kaley's baffling comment. His dark scowl was impossible to decipher, so she transferred her attention back to her daughter.

Listen to her. The thready voice flitted through Margie's mind and brought with it raised gooseflesh. Long ago, she'd learned to heed the warnings. While not psychic like Sammy, Margie had a healthy respect for her inner voice.

"All right. Can you describe him?"

"He didn't seem very tall. Definitely shorter than Uncle Jamie and Grandpa. But his face was covered. He might've had light hair. I'm sorry, Mom. I..." Kaley swiped a forearm across her face to dry the start of her tears. "He shoved me. I can't remember anything after hitting my head."

One question after another rolled through Margie's mind. She feared Kaley wasn't telling the truth, but putting her on the spot in front of everyone wouldn't gain Margie the answers she sought. Instead, she hugged Kaley, taking great care not to jar her. "It's okay, sweetheart. It's okay."

"Do you believe me?"

Margie hesitated. She hated lying to her children if she could help it, but she doubted the truth was worth the drama. Biting the bullet, she said, "I don't see how it was possible for anyone to be in the house when we were right outside, Kaley. I'm not saying I don't believe you, but perhaps you imagined it. I think we would've heard something with the slider open."

Kaley reared back and shoved her away. "You never believe me! I don't know why I even try." She grabbed her head again. "Go away."

"Kaley." Margie chose her words with care. "Gabriel and I came running as soon as we heard the crash. *No one else was there.* Can you entertain the possibility, for a moment, that you dreamed someone up when you were unconscious?"

"Whatever." Kaley's look of loathing singed her.

With everyone witnessing the exchange, Margie wanted to curl in on herself. She'd never done anything to deserve fierce hatred from her child, and she continually felt like a failure because she was unable to bridge the gap. If she zigged left, Kaley did the opposite and zagged right.

She rose and crossed to the small sink in the connecting bathroom. After she turned on the tap, she soaped, allowing the water and the cool glide of the hand soap to soothe her. As she lathered between each individual finger one by one, she ran through the scene in her mind.

Was it possible someone had been in the house? No sounds or movement to indicate otherwise, but Kaley's insistence couldn't be ignored. Yes, she was a rebellious teen with a hair-trigger temper. Yes, she snuck out on occasion. But she'd never been one to make up stories, although there was always a first time.

Margie dried her hands and returned to the room as her mother wiped the last of Kaley's tears away. Her mom had an easy way about her, and everyone gravitated to her.

Once again, feelings of being an abject failure rose up and nearly suffocated Margie. She could admit to a smidgen of jealousy. Kaley adored everyone *except* her, and every time Margie spoke, she sent her daughter into a rant about the unfairness of being her child.

The arrival of the doctor was a welcome break from her own mind.

He explained Kaley's scans were clean, but she would most likely suffer from the effects of a concussion for a few days. He detailed her care and suggested a date to remove the stitches.

When the doctor met her gaze and tilted his head toward the hallway, Margie's gut somersaulted. "Whatever you have to say, you can say in front of my family. I'll only have to relay it to them anyway." God knew they were an interfering bunch.

"Fair enough. I have concerns. I received two very different stories as to how Kaley's injury happened. Your daughter told me she was shoved, and yet on the admission form, you stated she slipped." The doctor paused, and his eyes met Margie's squarely. "I'd like to hear a more detailed explanation of the events that led to her injury. I'm sorry, but returning a child to a home where her safety is in question isn't an option."

Stunned speechless, Margie could only stare at the doctor.

"My mom would never hit me. *Ever.*" Kaley voice was hard and left no one in doubt as to the truth of her words. To say she surprised Margie by speaking up was an understatement. A grateful warmth spread throughout her chest, and she wanted to wrap Kaley in a fierce hug.

Once again, Margie took comfort in Gabriel's presence as he stepped closer and brushed her fingers with his. "Margaret and I were sitting outside when Kaley was injured. I promise you, nothing untoward happened on anyone's part."

She met his stormy gray eyes and smiled softly to relay her thanks.

Gabriel nodded, and his steely gaze softened. "I need to make a phone call. Are you going to be okay if I step out for a few minutes?"

"Of course. If you need to get going, my dad or brother can drive us home."

He shot her an irritated glance, shook his head, and strode from the room. Margie was left to interpret his look, but after being single for the better part of a decade, she was likely to be way off base.

CHAPTER 4

*G*abriel's irritation built with every step toward the hospital doors. Why exactly Margaret's easy dismissal annoyed him, he couldn't say. Honestly, he should be grateful to return home and get on with the million and one things he needed to do to put his stamp on the new place.

Shrugging off his pique, he placed a call to his friend Dr. Stephen Montgomery. A stellar psychiatrist, Stephen could offer a lot of insight, and Gabriel wanted his professional opinion on the situation.

Kaley's plea for Margaret to believe her had been heartfelt. Genuine. It made him uneasy to think they might have missed a stranger in the house. Maybe Stephen could provide insight on why Kaley would have made something like that up.

If she did make it up.

When Gabriel's call went straight to voicemail, he disconnected and shot off a text instead. He wouldn't have long to wait. His next call was to Grey. Gabriel gave him a rundown of the situation and asked, "Can you double-check the locks on Margaret's doors and windows?"

29

"You think someone was bold enough to break in while you were right there on the deck?"

"I don't know. It's more of a feeling I have than anything else. Her ex had just left with the boys, so the front door was most likely unlocked."

"I'll see what I can find."

"Thanks, Grey. Also, can you have your staff whip up an order for pizza? Four large, any variety, should do."

Gabriel strode back to Kaley's room. Resting his shoulder against the doorframe, he watched the Holts. Based on their inter-actions, he could tell they were a close-knit group. What bothered him the most was the way Kaley treated her mother. The girl had a lot of pent-up hostility. He knew it wasn't unusual for kids to be disrespectful, but he had no way of knowing if this degree of anger was the norm. What he *had* come to realize was that raising kids wasn't for sissies. For the brief minute when Margaret had held Kaley, Gabriel thought he imagined the tension between the two. He hadn't. It became more obvious after Kaley tossed accusations at Margaret. For both their sakes, Gabriel intended to get to the bottom of the alleged intruder.

His gaze was drawn to Margaret.

The younger guy, who he assumed was her brother due to the similarity in coloring, said something to make her laugh. Gabriel had thought her striking before, but when she flashed the full wattage of her smile and amusement lit her tired eyes, she glowed. For a moment, she was carefree and beautiful. In the course of a week, she'd become the flame to his moth, and he wanted to bask in her glow.

Previous to meeting Margaret, he would've freely admitted his taste ran to model-thin, professional, and blonde. But then Margaret turned her sapphire gaze his way. She was a hot mess. Her spandex yoga pants and baggy t-shirt hid what he suspected was a mouth-watering figure, and the hair escaping her topknot had an unfortunate tendency to kink. Yet somehow, this one woman made others pale in comparison. It confused him. Gabriel didn't like the sensation of being off-balance. Yet, the tentative smile she sent him required an answering grin.

He shook his head slightly to clear it. In the short window of time he'd known her, he became obsessed. It took effort, but he dragged his gaze away to look at the girl on the bed. It startled him to find Kaley staring back. A calculating gleam entered her eyes, and he could almost see the wheels turning in her brain. He fought a smile. Sending her a quick wink, he straightened and walked farther into the room, telling himself he'd be better to run, not walk, in the opposite direction as fast as he could.

"Who's up for pizza?" he asked instead.

Five hands went up.

SINCE KALEY HAD ELECTED TO RIDE BACK HOME WITH HER UNCLE, IT afforded Gabriel the opportunity to talk to Margaret about her daughter's attack.

"I'm not sure she was lying, Margaret."

For the span of five beats, she said nothing, then she sighed and shook her head. "I don't know what to believe. She thinks she's an adult but acts like a kid half the time, and she has yet to prove herself trustworthy."

"There was a quality to her voice and expression..." He was unable to define what he'd witnessed. "Like I said, I don't believe she was lying. In my line of work, I see plenty of liars."

"Do you suppose I should have the police come investigate?"

Gabriel debated telling her he'd already had his brothers check out her house. On one hand, he didn't want it to appear he'd crossed a line. There were plenty of females who would get up in arms about assumptions of that nature. On the other, being a single mother, she might appreciate the fact someone was looking out for her.

"It's strictly up to you. However, when Kaley told us she thought she saw someone, I went ahead and spoke to Grey. Our other brother, Gordon, has a friend who knows something about security. They checked out your place and could find nothing."

"Why would Kaley make something like that up?" Her voice shook, and it didn't take a genius to understand she was upset.

"I don't know that she did." Gabriel was going on pure instinct, and his gut screamed something about this whole situation was off. "But it begs the question, if someone was in your house, who was it, and how the hell did they get in and out with no one being the wiser?"

"I have a neighbor who owns a local security company. Maybe I should ask him to put in an alarm?"

"It wouldn't be a bad idea. It would probably make you feel safer. Also, it could help keep your wild child from sneaking out at night."

His teasing grin faded when he heard her gasp and saw her sickly shade.

Vomit was his kryptonite. If she yakked, he would be yakking right next to her in sympathy. Perhaps he should refrain from teasing about her kid in the future if this was the type of reaction he was going to get.

Gabriel eased onto the road's shoulder. "Are you okay?"

"I'm fine. Thank you."

"You'll tell me if you are going to be sick?"

The sharp tone of his voice brought her head around to stare. He wasn't a freak about his car interior. Lest she think he was, he confessed to a weak stomach where vomit was concerned.

She giggled.

"You think it's *funny?*" he demanded with mock outrage.

"Don't have any children," she said. "The first time one regurgitates his or her food on you, you'll lose it."

Gabriel put on a display of dry heaving.

Her burst of laughter was lovely to hear, and he basked in the sound.

"I promise you, I was never going to vomit on the precious interior of your Lexus."

"You looked pretty green there."

"It was the idea of Kaley sneaking out. Or rather the thought of going through it two more times with Scotty and Aaron." Her eyes flared wide and she grimaced.

"Valid point and reaction, I'd say." He eased onto the road, and his smile stayed in place the entire ride to their street.

Their arrival home coincided with the pizza delivery.

"Ah, perfect timing. I think I could eat a whole pie by myself."

"Seriously? You can eat a whole pizza?" When he acknowledged he could, Margaret snorted her disgust. "Awesome. I eat one damned slice and gain five pounds. I hate people like you."

"We all have our cross to bear."

"Pfft! Bite me."

"Oh, Margaret. Don't toss out a phrase of that nature unless you want me to take you up on it."

MARGIE SUCKED IN A BREATH AND ALMOST CHOKED. WITH ONE SIMPLE suggestive remark, the air around them became sexually charged. It didn't matter she hadn't had her morning shower and now smelled like hospital antiseptic; Gabriel seemed to find her attractive. Maybe he hadn't gotten laid in a while.

She snuck a sideways glance his way. Yeah, no. The man had never suffered a dry spell in the entirety of his life. Men who looked like Gabriel James could have their pick of women whenever and wherever they wanted. All he had to do was snap his fingers at some unsuspecting female and she'd drop her panties on the spot. Margie included.

She hadn't realized her quick glance morphed into an all-out stare, but he returned her look with an open, honest interest. The heat radiating from his silvery gaze seared her.

Oh, damn.

Right when Margie was sure she'd give in to the impulse to drag him across the console and suction-cup her mouth to his, a hand slapped against the driver's side window.

They jumped like guilty teens.

The brother Margie had yet to meet peered through the window. He had a shit-eating grin on a face meant to grace a magazine cover. Gabriel's good looks brought to mind the powerful gods from Greek folklore, but this man, with his perfectly chiseled features, sparkling almond-shaped eyes, and wind tossed dark hair, brought to mind the Prince of Darkness himself. Those blue-gray eyes lit with an unholy light as he took delight in his prank. He had a seductive quality any woman would fall for. Well, any woman but Margie. She only had eyes for the man sitting next to her.

Gabriel powered down the window. "What is it, Grey?" he bit out.

Margie clamped down on her lip. It was flattering to think he was irate at the interruption.

Grey's dark brows shot up to his hairline as he looked first at Gabriel then to her. Containing her laughter was impossible. Growing up a Holt, she knew all about family dynamics and hijinks. If she didn't miss her guess, Grey was just about to have serious fun at his expense.

A loud smack against her window elicited her bloodcurdling scream. Really, she didn't know she had it in her to make such an ear-splitting noise, but her nerves were still shot from the idea someone might've been in her house.

Her brother, James, lurked on the other side of the door, grinning like the tool he was.

"Asshole!" She'd been unaware of blurting it aloud until all three men laughed. "Not funny, you jerks." Margie whipped open the door, only missing her brother's man parts by a mere inch.

"Hey!" James cupped himself. "I'm the only Holt with family jewels. Careful."

She flipped him the bird over her shoulder.

Gabriel's "She's incredible" drifted to her and eased a smidgeon of her irritation. She looked back in time to see him narrowly miss his own brother's privates.

"Jesus, Gabe. *Watch it!*" Grey cried out. "Oh, and you're welcome for the pizza!"

Gabriel, not to be outdone by Margie, threw up both middle fingers and ate up the distance between them. Grinning, she took the hand he offered and entered the house.

As she rounded the corner of the foyer, she stopped in her tracks, wishing they'd gone anywhere else. The quantity of family was daunting, and chaos ruled.

Gabriel's grumpy brother, the one who'd thrown Kaley in the pool, was going out of his way to be solicitous to her, handing her pizza and soda where she reclined on the chaise. If he wasn't careful, Kaley would make him her servant for life.

His relieved expression when she and Gabriel entered almost made her laugh. With a brisk nod, he exited out the back door.

"I think your brother is happy to be off nurse duty."

Gabriel laughed. "Gordie is the poster boy for disappearing acts."

Margie's sister Annie sat at the kitchen island and stared intently at Kaley. A deep frown marred her otherwise smooth forehead. Whatever emotions she was picking up on had to be heavy.

Margie's curiosity on the matter would have to wait to be appeased. Right now, she needed to confer with her family where they gathered around Sammy in the kitchen.

Margie whirled around, blocking Gabriel from fully entering the house. "Um, would you mind..." She gave a half-hearted nod back the way they'd come. "I have family stuff about to go down, and I don't—"

He stared at her for a long moment; his eyes seeming to miss nothing. "I can go if you'd like."

His steady gaze made Margie fidgety. She wanted to tell him not to look too closely, because there was nothing worthwhile to see.

"It's not that you aren't welcome, I... my sister..." She shrugged. What could she say? She wanted him—a complete stranger—to stay and offer her comfort, but to embroil him in the crazy was asking too much of him.

"Keep your secrets, Margaret." Gabriel tucked a strand of her wayward hair behind her ear. "I'm sorry we didn't get to finish our coffee. When things are settled, how about a rain check?"

She gave him a non-committal half smile.

His lips twisted, and he nodded. "I'll go until you've had a chance to settle things a bit. If you need to talk later, my door is open."

As Margie regretfully watched him leave, eyes locked on his jean-clad butt, she overheard Sammy say, *"Someone was in here with her."*

The blood in Margie's veins turned to ice. Essentially, her daughter had been in serious danger, while *she* lounged on the deck, ogling her neighbor. Stricken with guilt, she rushed to Kaley's side.

"I believe you." She squatted and rubbed a hand along Kaley's calf. "I'm so sorry for—"

"You only believe me because Aunt Sammy saw what happened."

"Kaley, you're not being fair to your mom." Sammy's stern words came from behind Margie.

She whirled to scowl at her. "I don't need you to defend me to my child."

"What the hell is wrong with you?" Sammy's blue eyes, normally so bright and happy, held resentment. "No matter what I do, it isn't good enough. I show up at the hospital in support, I try to have your back, but what do I get in return? Not a damned thing."

"Here we go again. Poor Sammy—always so misunderstood. Maybe if you'd have called first instead of reacting, I'd have saved you a trip to the hospital. And as for having my back, I can talk to my own child. Did you ever think I'm tired of you trying to tell me how to raise my children? You can barely manage your own life, and yet you are constantly trying to tell everyone else how to behave."

"That's rich, coming from you, Margie. You order everyone about constantly. If you aren't micro-managing someone else's life, you aren't happy."

"It's called a schedule. I have four people I'm responsible for. Five, if you count the fact I have to always consider Scott's social life. But yes, let's twist this back around on me. You do what you want without any consideration for anyone else, and you're teaching my daughter to do the same. Did you know she's been skipping school? It's not acceptable."

36

"Whatever. I'm done. When you can learn to be a civil human being, give me a call."

"Don't hold your breath."

Sammy pivoted on her heel and stormed out through the garage door, followed closely by Michael.

The silence in the room was painful.

Expressions ranged from shock to outrage to disappointment.

Gabriel, who stood in the entrance with the door halfway open and Grey at his back, gave her a look of quiet understanding and concern. *Was it wrong she wanted to run to him and sob out all her frustrations?* She drudged up a tight smile instead.

Drawing on the last vestiges of her strength, she said, "Well, since I've ruined the mood for everyone and embarrassed myself in front of virtual strangers, I think I'll leave you all to salvage what you can of lunch. I apologize for any ugliness. Please, stay as long as you'd like." She bussed a kiss on Kaley's cheek only to have her daughter wipe it away.

Nine years she'd put up with attitude because she left her no good husband. Nine years of blame by Scott and the children. Only nine more to go until Aaron was off to college. Then she could think about herself.

Tired to her very soul, Margie beelined for the sanctuary of her room.

Her mother intersected her. "Margaret..."

She held up a hand. "Not now, Mom. Please? I know I've behaved badly. I'm tired and stressed. I promise I'll apologize to Sammy later when she's had time to calm down. Do you mind staying to keep an eye on Kaley? I really need to get a shower and lie down."

"Of course, dear. Get some rest. We'll talk later."

Her mom must've seen her exhaustion, because she hugged her tight. Margie closed her lids, accepting the much-needed comfort. Even disappointed in her children's behavior, Violet Holt was caring and generous.

The perfect role model.

Maybe her kids wouldn't be such little shits if Margie could channel the Zen like her mother.

Remembering her manners, she drummed up a lukewarm smile for Gabriel and Grey. "Thanks, guys. I appreciate everything you've done for us today. Please let me know if I can ever repay you for all your many kindnesses." She looked from brother to brother and back again. "Who do I owe for the pizzas?"

"They're on me," Gabriel said kindly, crossing to her. "Go get some rest. I'll help clean up here."

"But you were leaving. I—"

"No buts, Margaret. You've had a traumatic experience. Let someone take care of you for a few minutes, okay? I don't expect it happens often."

Understatement of the year.

She stretched on her tiptoes to drop a light kiss on his cheek. "Thank you, Gabriel."

CHAPTER 5

One thing Gabriel was sure of as he watched Margaret weave her way toward her bedroom: Margaret Holt had the weight of the world on her shoulders. Yes, she'd been reactive, but it only took one glance to see she was barely holding it together. For as tough as she pretended to be, below the surface lurked a fragile quality. Maybe that's why he'd turned around and come back. Leaving her when she seemed so troubled didn't sit well with him.

Gordie would call it his "do-gooder complex."

"Well, I never thought I'd see the day." Grey chuckled and lowered his voice. "The great Gabriel James has been felled like the mighty oak."

"Suck it." Gabriel moved to the kitchen to get cleaning supplies to remove the last of the blood from the tile.

James Holt blocked his path.

At six-foot-four, there weren't many men who stood as tall as Gabriel, and Margaret's brother was no exception, standing roughly four inches shorter. However, the guy possessed a larger-than-life presence and he was hard to ignore. With shoulders befitting a linebacker and an impressive display of bulging biceps.

James focused to the left over Gabriel's shoulder.

Gabriel turned to see who was behind him.

No one.

James's hyper-focused intensity caused the hairs on the back of Gabriel's neck to lift. A compressed smile teased the other man's lips, as if he was fighting not to laugh.

"Care to share the joke?" Gabriel moved around him to forage under the sink.

"Joke?"

"You seem to find something funny, but there's only the two of us in the room."

"Ah." There was a wealth of meaning in the one syllable, but Gabriel was damned if he could figure it out. "Yeah, no joke. I...uh, I was thinking about Opal, and how much I enjoyed her company."

He twisted to meet James's amused stare. "You knew my aunt?"

"You could say that." The statement was cloaked in mystery, as if he knew something others didn't.

James cocked his head to the side as if listening, then he rolled his eyes.

Had Gabriel not been watching him closely, he would have missed the barely discernible nod. Again, he looked behind him.

"Why do I have the feeling you're communicating with someone who isn't here?" The startled look on James's face brought with it a feeling of unease for Gabriel. "*Are* you communicating with someone who isn't here?" The sensation of cold fingers danced along Gabriel's spine, and he shivered.

"That would be ridiculous now, wouldn't it?"

He formed his next words carefully to appear open-minded. "I'm a lawyer. I deal with facts and the here and now. But I'm also aware not everything can be explained."

"True enough." James grinned. His resemblance to Margaret was much more pronounced. "I have a message from your aunt. There's a false bottom in the last drawer on the left of her old bedroom dresser. Apparently, you marked it as a garage-sale item? She said it's important you find what's hidden there."

James laughed at Gabriel's dumbfounded expression, gave him a jaunty salute, and grabbed the bucket of cleaning solution. As he exited the kitchen, he said, "I've got the tile. You're on dish duty."

What the actual fuck? Gabriel suppressed his desire to dash home to verify James's weird statement—but just barely. With one last wary glance around the room, he turned on the faucet to fill the sink.

THE IMPROMPTU PIZZA PARTY BROKE APART, AND GABRIEL COULDN'T say he was sorry. The day had been exceedingly long, and it was only three p.m. He was replacing the kitchen can liner when he noticed Kaley had joined him.

"You look pale, kid. Should you be up and about?"

"What's the deal with you and my mom?"

Now her reason for seeking him out became clearer. Talk about cutting to the chase, the girl was as direct as they came.

"We met the morning you skipped school. About two minutes before my brother Gordie dumped you in the pool to be exact. Today's the first time I've spoken to her since."

She frowned.

The paleness of her skin bothered him, and he pulled out a chair. "Sit before you fall down."

Leaning back against the opposite counter, he crossed his arms and waited for her continue. It didn't take long.

"Why did you go with her to the hospital?"

"When we heard you fall, we came running in. Your mom was pretty torn up. I couldn't, in all good conscious, leave her alone."

"Do you believe me?"

"That someone was in the house?"

She nodded, and he studied her, looking for signs of falseness or guile.

He nodded in return. "I do."

Tears crowded her eyes, and she ducked her head.

Again, he waited her out, staring at his feet to give her time to regain her composure.

"What about my mom? She thinks I'm a liar, doesn't she?"

"No, she doesn't." Margaret's voice startled them both.

Gabriel straightened, and Kaley slipped on a rebellious mask. He couldn't fail to notice Margaret's heavy sigh. The woman was at a complete loss as to how to communicate with her daughter. Whatever had happened to cause the tension must've been a doozy. If he'd have been better acquainted with them, he'd have sat them down and had a come-to-Jesus meeting. These two needed to get out of their own way and resolve whatever their issues were.

Margaret shuffled in his direction. As she stood in front of him, all kinds of inappropriate thoughts crowded his mind. First and foremost was the desire to ease her burden and kiss her worry away.

"Do you mind?" She gestured to the single-serve coffee machine.

With reluctance, Gabriel shifted sideways.

A giggle sounded, and Gabriel looked to the source. Kaley was about ready to bust a seam in her effort to contain her laughter. The kid hadn't missed his interest in her mom—unlike her oblivious mother. Because his large frame took up a good portion of the room, he moved to stand beside Kaley. He bumped her shoulder when she snorted.

"Pathetic," she whispered.

"Ya think," he whispered back.

"Dude, you need game. She's never going to acknowledge you exist."

"That's what I'm afraid of."

Their whispered conversation brought Margaret's head around. "What's the secret?"

Kaley, the little fink, spilled the beans. "Your not-so-secret admirer is super into you, Mom. You totally dissed him without even realizing it."

Color flared to life in Margaret's cheeks, and Kaley burst out laughing. Her laugh turned into a groan of pain and brought Margaret rushing to her side.

"You okay, sweetheart? Is it your head? Should I call the doctor?"

The girl waved her away. "I'm fine, Mom. My head hurts a little if I move too fast. And if I laugh."

"Such is the curse of a concussion," Gabriel inserted. He leaned down and murmured in Margaret's ear, "She's fine. Try not to worry, okay?"

"I can hear you. I have a headache. I'm not deaf."

He snorted and decided coffee sounded like a great idea. Anything to occupy his hands, or he was likely to flick the kid's ear. He opened one other cabinet before he found the one containing the mugs. Like the contents of the first cabinet, the shelves were extremely organized. All the coffee-cup handles were on the right, shifted about a half-inch forward. Equal amounts of space separated them. Like little soldiers.

Curious, he spun in a slow circle. For a house with children, no papers or art projects rested on the counters, and not one thing was out of place. Canisters were lined along one wall, an inch spacing between them. The magnets on the fridge were all the small, round black kind. No ornamentation of any type.

He couldn't recall seeing anyone's kitchen this clean and organized. Or at least not anyone who legitimately used theirs. He turned his incredulous gaze to Margaret.

Embarrassment flushed her cheeks and parted her lips. The tinge of pink highlighted the blue of her eyes.

Damn, the woman was beautiful.

Kaley held her head with one hand and had the palm of her other pressed to her lips to fight her laughter. She must see his kind of reaction often.

He opened his mouth and closed it twice not quite sure what to say. "I didn't notice before because of the pizza boxes, plates, and people, but is your whole house this... um... organized?"

"It was messy this morning when you arrived." Margaret's color deepened.

Yes, it had been, but the remains of a morning meal was to be expected, and apparently someone had cleaned it up before they arrived earlier.

"You should see my Aunt Annie's place," Kaley volunteered. "She has her whole pantry alphabetized, and all the labels have to be facing forward. My brothers like to mess with her by mixing everything up when she's not looking. Oh, and Aunt Sammy color-codes everything. We'd screw with her, but she's threatened to cut us if we do."

His brows shot up. "Should your sister go around threatening to harm your children?"

Margie waved a hand in dismissal. "She'd never really do it. Threatening violence is the Holt way."

"I think your family frightens me."

MARGIE LIKED THE WAY GABRIEL JOKED WITH KALEY. HER DAUGHTER blossomed under his attention. Normally, Kaley didn't respond to any adults outside the family to any degree. She always held herself in reserve, and Margie suspected it was the distinct lack of fatherly affection.

"I'm going to make a cup of tea, and then I want to discuss what happened this morning. Kaley, are you up for it?" Margie filled the brewer's water reservoir.

The sullen-teen attitude was back.

Of course it was. Margie had only to open her mouth for her daughter to hold her in contempt.

"I'll leave you two to talk alone." Gabriel moved toward the door.

"Will you stay?" Kaley's tentative question surprised her.

Gabriel's silvery gaze met Margie's across the distance, a brow raised in question. Since he'd been here from the moment the attack happened, she inclined her head in agreement. Why not? He'd probably never return after today anyway. *And didn't that make her sad?*

"Absolutely. How about you and your mom go get comfortable on the couch, and I'll fix the tea?" Gabriel paused, a slight frown tugging at his brow. "Should I make you a cup, too? Do teenagers even drink tea?"

Kaley's wide grin warmed Margie's heart. "I'm good."

"Right. I'll be out in a sec."

In an effort to keep the conversation light until it was time to get to the meat of the discussion, Margie asked, "Where did everyone go? I thought Mom was going to stay with you."

"Dad brought Scotty and Aaron home. He said he couldn't keep them overnight." Kaley's anger vibrated in her tone. Her large blue eyes were clouded, and her cheeks were flushed.

The hurt Margie understood well. There were many times in the past when Scott aborted their plans for an agenda all his own. His continued inconsideration affected her children and infuriated Margie. If he was in front of her now, she'd show him the Holt family violence for real.

"Gram said she was going to take the boys for ice cream to keep the noise down. She didn't want to make my headache worse. And you know Aunt Annie."

Her sister always sought isolation when she could.

Margie nodded. "What about Jamie? Did he head home?"

"He said he'd be back tonight after he took care of a few things at work."

"Back?"

"Yeah, he's staying until you get a security system installed. His words."

"I don't know about you, but it makes me feel better to think he'll be here," Margie confessed, although she probably shouldn't have shown her anxiety.

"Me, too, Mom."

Margie could have been knocked over with a feather. This day, this very moment, needed to be marked down in her calendar for posterity. Unsure where to go from here, she sat on the sofa and patted the seat next to her.

Kaley took the armchair.

So much for bonding.

Gabriel poked his head around the corner. "How do you take your tea?"

"Black, one sugar."

In another minute, he joined them and settled in the spot Kaley had ignored. He stretched one arm along the back on the couch and covertly caressed the back of Margie's neck. The gesture was quick and oddly reassuring. Probably exactly what he'd intended, but his light touch woke the butterflies in her belly.

Smoothing her features to appear unflustered, she addressed Kaley. "I want to start with the fact that I do believe you were attacked this morning, sweetheart." At the skeptical look, she emphasized, "*I do.*"

A small portion of the attitude disappeared from Kaley's face, and Margie thanked her lucky stars. The next few minutes would be a challenge. "The first thing we need to do is to figure out who would've wanted to hurt you. In order to do that, I need you to be upfront with me. Can you?"

"Yeah," Kaley said, looking forlorn.

Margie wanted to go to her and cuddle her close, but for the moment, they needed to discuss this as if they were all adults.

"Lies aren't going to help this time, Kaley. If you're in trouble, I need to know."

"I'm not! I swear!" Her earnestness was plainly visible, and her wide eyes begged for understanding. "I know I've lied in the past, Mom, but it was only because I wanted to have some fun. You..."

Margie forced herself to remain calm. The accusation was on the tip of her daughter's tongue, and it was only one of many always being thrown her way. Conversing with Kaley was exhausting lately. "I what?"

"I feel like you never want me to have any fun. You never like my boyfriends. *Ever.*"

"Skipping school was your answer?" If her voice rose a little, it couldn't be helped. Again, Gabriel brushed her neck. A warning of sorts. One designed to encourage her to focus on the matter at hand. "I'm sorry, sweetheart." Margie sighed, moderated her tone, and continued. "You're too young for boyfriends. And your generation isn't the first to feel the sting of rules, Kaley. Can I be honest with you?"

A sullen nod was her answer.

At least the lines of communications were *somewhat* open.

"I was your age when I started dating your father. I snuck out constantly. At fourteen, you think you know what love is. You don't. In high school, those feelings are purely infatuation. Until the pressures of the real world have had a chance to take a toll on your relationship, and until both people can step up to the plate as equals, working for a mutual goal, love can't happen."

The lost look on Kaley's face was disheartening. Resentment was sure to follow. By now, Margie could recognize the signs. Frustrated, she stood to pace. From the corner of her eye, she saw Gabriel bite back a grin. She halted in her tracks and shot him a glare. The jerk was enjoying her predicament. Wait until the day he had kids and had to deal with this crap.

She turned her back on him and paused before Kaley. "Okay, let me put this another way. Boys in high school want pretty much one thing. Girls your age put out because they want the boy to like them in return."

Margie ignored the choking sound behind her. Gabriel was going to get an earful when this was over. Her cheeks burned hot. Like Chernobyl-meltdown temperatures. *God, this was embarrassing.* It wasn't as if she hadn't discussed the birds and bees with her child before. Her ire rose up, and she decided to throw her nosy neighbor under the bus. "I'm sure Gabriel can confirm what I'm saying, right?"

Knocking the ball in his court didn't cause her one second of guilt. However, it appeared he was smarter and more prepared for her tactic. *Damned lawyers.* He stretched out his long legs in front of him and crossed his arms behind his head.

Margie's mouth went dry. Good grief, the man was smexy. Smart and sexy all rolled into one—her personal catnip.

"As fascinating as we're all finding this conversation, is there a point in there somewhere, Margaret? I thought we were going to discuss the break-in."

He smirked.

She fumed.

"Yes, dammit." She glared one final time before facing Kaley. "Bottom line is this: at your age, it's difficult to weed out the asshats from the good guys. And now, I'm worried you've attracted the wrong type of person."

Two shocked pairs of eyes stared up at her. *Shit.* She'd ventured way off the reservation.

"Ah, fuck." Margie plunked down on the ottoman in front of Kaley. "I'm sorry. It's not you I don't trust. Not completely anyway. Kaley, what I'm trying to say is this: you are beautiful and vibrant like the rarest butterfly. Others want to capture your uniqueness for themselves. But sometimes, people don't know how to do that without destroying what makes you special. And if you've attracted someone who wants to hurt you or is threatening you, I need to know so I can protect you."

Thin arms grabbed her neck in a stranglehold, and she barely paused before returning Kaley's fierce hug. The two could have been fused together, so tight was their embrace. Her daughter hadn't hugged her like this since she was a small child, and fierce emotion clogged Margie's throat. She had to clear it twice before she could speak.

"I love you, baby girl. I just want you safe as long as possible. Can you understand I only have your best interests at heart and I'm not trying to be a fun miser?"

"Yeah."

"Good. Let's get back to figuring out who the scum bucket was that attacked you. I have to know whose ass I need to kick."

As expected, Kaley giggled at her mother's profanity. Teens loved it when their parents did things like swear. "Um, Mom? No one says scum bucket anymore."

"Shut up, you ungrateful punkass." To belie her words, Margie lovingly smoothed back Kaley's colorful hair.

Gabriel suggested writing down names of potential threats, and the three of them spent the next twenty minutes listing anyone Kaley thought might fit the bill. It frustrated Margie to see the list was practically nonexistent. In the end, no one person stuck out.

Gabriel called a halt to their little meeting. "You're looking tired, kid. Why don't you go lie down for a bit? Your mom and I need to talk."

Kaley didn't argue, and it was a testament to how poorly she must've been feeling.

"I'll be right back." Margie gave in to the overwhelming need to see her daughter tucked safely in bed as she'd done when Kaley was a small child. The two of them were on the same wavelength because she hugged Margie tightly before she rolled on her side to sleep.

Gabriel was in the kitchen, washing their dirty dishes, when she returned.

"Something occurred to you, hasn't it? Care to share?" she asked.

He took an exceedingly long time rinsing the mug he was holding. He set it in the rack, dried his hands, and finally shifted to face her. "You've been going on the assumption the attacker was after your daughter. What if he wasn't? What if he's just a random stranger who took advantage of the house being empty while we were out on the deck? Or perhaps it was someone who's been watching your house for a different reason."

Margie sagged against the counter. *Dear God!* She'd never even spared a thought to any other explanation.

"Not to scare you, but let's take this one step further. What if the intruder was waiting for *you* to come back inside? Anyone who knows your schedule would know Kaley was supposed to be with her dad. She could've surprised your would-be attacker, and he panicked."

"That's the more likely explanation, isn't it? Ohmygod, Gabriel! I've been so oblivious. Here I am, lecturing my daughter on attracting unsavory characters, and it probably wasn't even her."

"Do you tend to attract a lot of unsavory characters?"

The teasing glint in his eye warmed her. She offered him a half smile. "Sometimes."

"Come here, Margaret."

The intent behind those words was clear as crystal, and she'd be a fool to miss it. Nervous and a bit giddy, she approached where he lounged back against her counter. He separated his legs when she got close, and tugged her to stand between them. Due to his half-slouched position, they were nearly the same height. His face was mere inches above her own.

"I want to do something unsavory to you. Have since the moment I saw you relaxing in your swing."

Oh, hell yes!

Her gaze dropped to his full, smiling mouth. All the unsavory acts he could perform on her with those lips flitted through her mind. Her deep inhale brought his pure male scent, clean with a spicy aftershave and a hint of deliciousness. It felt like a million years since she'd experienced any type of desire. But one searing look from him, one touch, and her girls puckered along with an ache starting low in her abdomen.

She leaned into him. Welcoming. Encouraging.

He lowered his head.

The front door slammed open. "Mom! We're home!"

She wanted to beat her fists against her chest and scream her disappointment. Instead, she backed away and put distance between herself and Gabriel.

His disappointed sigh made her feel marginally better.

In the instant when he'd almost kissed her, it all became clear. This was her Sebastian. Her Marcus. Her Hugh. And now her Gabriel. He was always the same—bold, beautiful, and commanding. She'd loved him in every lifetime and, in all probability, would continue to do so.

CHAPTER 6

*G*abriel sat with his feet propped on his porch railing, listening to Gordie prattle on. He tuned his brother out and concentrated on his neighbor's house. The light from Margaret's master bedroom taunted him. He hadn't stopped thinking about their aborted kiss since he left her alone that afternoon.

"Are you even listening to me, Gabe?"

He whipped his head around. "Sorry, man. I…"

There was no excuse. Well, no good one other than he'd been bewitched by a single mother of three in less time than it took for her to bat an eyelash in his direction.

"I'd never have pegged you for the ready-made-family type."

Irritation flared. "I'm not."

"Hmm, could have fooled me."

"What are you still doing here? Don't you have a concert to perform or something?"

Gordie threw back his head and laughed. "Typical Gabriel. Don't want to talk about it? Deflect."

"Okay, you want to open up and share our feelings like a couple of girls? Here goes. From the second I saw her, I've felt like I was in over my head. It's as if I already knew her. Knew how she's going to taste, how she's going to feel. When I tease her, she responds exactly as I envision in my mind. The carefully controlled mother is gone and, in her place, is a woman with a wicked sense of humor and a zest for life. I've never experienced anything like it."

"Sheesh, that's a lot to dump on a guy."

"Screw you."

"Seriously, you got all that from one day with her?"

Gabriel returned his attention to the bedroom window. A shadow passed in front of the curtains, and his heart gave an extra-hard thump. "Yes."

"Well, say goodbye to the bachelor life."

Gabriel nearly dropped his beer. "Whoa! Who said anything about marriage? I'm still dealing with my last mistake."

"You don't make time with a single mom unless you plan to get serious. It's not cool, man."

"Shut up. Who asked you anyway?"

"Does this mean we're not best girlfriends anymore?"

"Why couldn't I have been an only child?"

"On that note, I'm going in to crash in your guest room. Later, loser."

For a long time after Gordie left, Gabriel watched Margaret's bedroom window. His brother wasn't wrong. He should keep a safe distance if he didn't plan to get serious.

He finished off his beer, set the bottle on the railing, and descended the steps. Bending down, he scooped up a few lighter pebbles from the landscape bed next to him. A light toss assured him the weight wouldn't break a window.

When he was only a few feet away from Margaret's house, Gabriel threw one stone and held his breath as the sound echoed from the glass. Damn, who knew it would be so loud?

Ten seconds later, he chucked another.

Still nothing.

With a frown, he moved closer and peeked around the side of the house. He supposed it was possible she had moved into the bathroom or living room. This time he tossed the pebble at the back window.

The blinds were raised, and Margie peered into the night. She cracked the window a few inches and put her mouth next to the screen. "Who's there?"

He hadn't taken into account that the darkened back yard would make it difficult for her to see out. "It's Gabriel."

The window was shoved higher, and she rested her crossed arms on the sill. "Come closer, I can only see your outline."

He complied and got an eyeful of cleavage as she bent to talk to him. *And good Lord, what cleavage she had!* Thank God for V-neck t-shirts.

"What are you doing?"

"I came to break you out."

"Break me out?" She snorted.

"It occurred to me you might be lonely. I figured with your kids asleep and your brother crashing on your couch, now was the perfect time for you to sneak out."

"Hmm, so the very thing I lectured my daughter about is the thing you want me to do with you?"

"Precisely."

Her genuine laughter hit him low in the gut. "Okay. Meet me at the window around the corner to your left in exactly one minute. I have to find some shoes."

"It's Florida. You don't need shoes."

"There could be anything in that grass. Fire ants, snakes, a spider or two."

"Margaret, you're as fierce as they come. Are you telling me you're afraid of a few bugs?"

"Yes."

"Fair enough. But come on, I'll carry you."

"You can't carry me. You'll break your damned back."

"Seriously, woman, you're wasting valuable time."

"I don't know if I should, now that I think about it. My mother always told me never to talk to strange men."

"You think I'm strange?" Her stalling amused him.

"No. I think you're perfect," she replied with a soft, girly sigh.

Gabriel grinned at her choked sound. Apparently, the lovely Margaret hadn't meant to say that aloud. He lowered his voice in invitation. "Come out and play with me, Margaret."

"Fine. Help me pop the screen."

When she pulled the tabs up, he wedged his fingers under the frame and helped dislodge it. He caught her in his arms as she lunged out the opening.

"You're good at this. How many damsels have you freed from their towers?" she asked, admiration in her voice.

"Enough. Now shut the window to keep mosquitoes out."

He held her as she twisted around to comply. The light musky scent of vanilla teased his nostrils, and he lowered his head to rub his nose along her throat. He chuckled when she let out a startled "meep."

"Fuck, you smell good, Margaret." He couldn't wait. He *had* to sample her lips. As he lowered his head, the outside floodlights bathed them in its bright glow.

"Oh, shit. *Run!*"

"Run?" He stood dumbly as she jumped from his arms and took off in the direction of his house.

"Run," she called over her shoulder, laughing at his bewilderment.

The sliding door behind him cracked open, and Gabriel wasted no time making tracks. He flew past Margaret and was helpless to resist delivering a sharp smack to her shapely ass encased in curve-hugging shorts. Her muffled yelp had him laughing all the way to his front porch.

JAMES HOLT CROSSED HIS ARMS AND WATCHED AS HIS SISTER RAN INTO the night with Gabriel. When Opal Sutherland's translucent form materialized at his side, he was careful to keep his voice low so the echo wouldn't carry across the distance. "I like him, and I think he'll be good for Margie."

"They do make the perfect couple, don't they? As if they were meant for each other." She sighed, but there was a sadness to the sound.

He shot her a look from the corner of his eye. "Is there something you're not telling me, Opal?"

"There's probably a lot of things I refuse to tell you, young man, but if I don't, it's because they need to play out as intended."

"That sounds ominous."

"Unfortunately, for your sister, it is."

The gloominess radiating off of Opal bothered him. When it came to his family, he'd do whatever was necessary to protect them. His temper ignited, but he had the presence of mind to keep his voice low and controlled. "What the hell is that supposed to mean? Because your nephew or not, if he hurts her, I will break him in half."

She patted his forearm, and her touch was a simple caress of wind. "Calm down, dear boy. Gabriel is well on his way to falling in love with her. And if there's one thing about my dear nephew you should know, it's that he protects his own, as you do. No, I'm afraid your sister is facing another threat. One only time, patience, and love can resolve."

"How cryptic," James snapped. "You know what I hate most about the spirits in the afterlife? Not a damned one of you can be straightforward." He pivoted to go back inside. "Do me a favor, wake me when she's ready to come back. I feel like holding her feet to the coals for sneaking out."

"WINE?" GABRIEL ASKED.

"I'm cool with beer if you have it. And maybe a blanket. I didn't realize it would be so damp out tonight."

"Would you rather hang out in my bedroom?"

"Is that the line all the cool kids are using these days?" she asked with a soft laugh.

"Think it'll work?"

"Probably not, but you can keep trying. It's flattering."

"I'll be right back."

Margie wandered the length of the porch. It wasn't very long— probably no more than twelve feet—but it was wide enough to allow for the two Adirondack chairs with their pullout footstools and a table between. They were left over from when Opal was alive. The lime-green color was beachy and bright, making her happy just to look at them. Gabriel either liked them or hadn't gotten around to changing the decor out yet. Maybe she'd tell him she'd like to buy the set if he decided to replace them. They reminded her of magical mornings when she and Opal would share a cup of coffee and discuss the meaning of life.

A wave of moodiness washed over her, and Margie raised her eyes skyward. If Opal could see down upon them, she wondered what the woman would have to say about this little development between Gabriel and her.

The breeze kicked up and caressed her cheeks before calming again. The sensation was reminiscent of the affectionate way Opal would cup her face as she imparted her wisdom.

An icy sensation traced across Margie's skin. She believed in spirits. How could she not? The past-life recollection she'd been gifted with told her the soul didn't die. It moved to another time or dimension. She'd been friends with Opal in a previous life as well. They'd met the day, a little more than a hundred years ago, when Margie, as Lucy, had gone to speak to Sebastian's mother.

The soft pad of Gabriel's soles on the concrete distracted her from her memories. His arm came around in front of her to present the beer minus the cap. With a flourish, he produced a light blanket and wrapped it around her shoulders. "Warm enough?"

"Yes. Perfect."

"Come sit with me."

He tugged her over to the chairs and held her beer while she sat down. Once she was in place, he pulled out the footrest for her to kick up her heels. Margie admired how fluidly he moved for a man his size as he settled in the other chair. He exhibited a casual grace with every movement he made.

Together, they stared out over the darkened street in companionable silence. He had Opal's easy way about him, and simply being in his calming presence chased away the constant loneliness Margie couldn't otherwise shake.

Unable not to feast on his beautiful form with her hungry eyes, she shifted sideways and drew up her legs as she studied him.

He'd changed into an old college hoodie but was still sporting the same jeans as earlier. When she trailed her gaze back to his face, he was staring, a small smirk in place.

"Like what you see?" The warm-whiskey quality to his voice sent a shot of desire coursing through her. The man oozed sex appeal. Surely he had to know it?

"What's not to like?"

He grinned and took a pull of his beer.

She followed suit, maintaining eye contact with his twinkling gray peepers. "Was this what you had in mind when you threw rocks at my window?"

"Pebbles. And I had nothing in mind except to see you again."

She caught her breath at the perfection of his response. It was a rare day when someone wasn't demanding something from her for their own gain. She should've known Gabriel would come up with the right words to make her feel wanted and like a woman instead of a broodmare or maid to her children.

"I don't know if I thanked you for all you did for us today. But I owe you a debt of gratitude."

A flash of irritation crossed his face. "I don't want your gratitude, Margaret. I didn't step in today for personal gain."

"I know that, Gabriel. But what you did... it was more than anyone's done for me in a long while. Possibly ever."

He nodded. "So are you in a serious relationship with anyone?" The change of subject was a typical Sebastian/Gabriel move.

"Would I be sitting here with you if I was?"

"Do you realize you have a tendency to answer a question with a question?"

She gave a short laugh. "Sorry. All these years of raising kids has conditioned me to try to encourage independent thinking."

"Ah. Does it work?"

"Not really. But I'm a Holt, and with the name comes a hard head. I'll keep trying until I draw my last breath."

He chuckled and raised the bottle to his lips.

"No."

Her comment had him pause in taking a drink. "No?"

"No, I am not in a serious relationship."

A smile played about his mouth. "Good to know."

"And you, is there anyone other than Tamara?"

"Nope, and my soon-to-be-ex is a non-issue."

"Good to know," she said teasingly and mimicked his action by taking a sip of beer.

"This is going to sound weird, but have we met before?"

She choked on her drink. "Why do you ask?"

A furrow developed between his dark brows. "It's more of a feeling than anything else. This seems so familiar to me, but I can't place where we might have met or why I would've forgotten."

Most people didn't remember their past lives, but Margie would be damned if she'd say that out loud. Her own family wasn't even aware of her gift. Sharing it with an outsider would likely see her ostracized or ridiculed. "We haven't met. It's one of those things. Similar to déjà vu."

"Hmm. Must be. On a different subject, how's Kaley tonight?"

"Still sporting a headache." Margie toyed with the label on her bottle. "It's extremely upsetting to think someone was in my house and hurt my child while I sat right outside the open door. I can't get rid of this sick feeling in the pit of my stomach."

Gabriel shifted to face her. "I can see where it would be, but the attack on Kaley was in no way your fault."

"That's not the conclusion we came to earlier about why someone was in my house."

"Again, being the target of another person *is not your fault.* You need to get that through your head, Margaret. There are things in this world you can't control."

She looked up sharply. "Why would you say that? About control?"

He'd known her the sum total of a day. Was she as bad as Scott had previously claimed?

"Do I seem controlling to you?" Inside, her heart hammered.

His expression softened, and a sweet smile graced his lips. "No. Not in the way you think I mean. But I noticed on more than one occasion today, you washed your hands when you were upset. If you add in the excessively organized cabinets, I suspect you feel there are a lot of situations out of your control."

Unable to meet his gaze, Margie took another sip of her beer, but for some inexplicable reason, she found it difficult to swallow.

"It wasn't a criticism, Margaret. I would never do that."

Her feelings of inadequacy worsened. But because he was watching her expectantly, she said, "I know." Mood ruined, she rose to her feet, folded the blanket, and shoved in the footrest in preparation to leave. "Thanks for the drink."

"Don't go."

"I have to. Tomorrow comes early, and the kids will want breakfast."

"Will you have dinner with me one night soon?"

How did any woman deny him? But tell him no, she must. They were worlds apart this time around. Earlier, she'd taken the time to google him and found out he was a high-end criminal attorney with no children and an easy-going, partying lifestyle. She, on the other hand, was a mother of three who'd never had a thought as to a life outside of caring for her children. There was a distinct possibility that she didn't even own a nice dress anymore.

"I'm not sure it's a good idea, Gabriel."

"Why? The attraction is mutual. Neither of us is in a relation-ship. What's stopping you from saying yes?"

"I have to defend my no?"

"If that's how you truly feel, you don't." He stood and held out a hand. "Come on, I'll see you home."

"I live fifty feet away. I think I'm safe."

"It's not a request. Someone broke into your home and attacked your daughter this morning. If you think I'm not escorting you home, you're cracked in the head."

"Well, when you put it that way," Margie muttered.

They strolled back in silence. Regret for turning him down plagued her. He'd been wonderful today—her dream man in every way. Had she met him nine years ago, she'd be jumping for joy at the thought of going on a date with him. However, at this point in her life, when she was pushing forty and couldn't spare an hour for a damned pedicure, why would she dream of complicating her life with one more person who needed her attention? She was stretched too thin as it was.

"I don't want you to think I'm ungrateful."

With a hand on her arm, he halted her. "I already said I don't want your damned gratitude. There wasn't one thing I did today that I expected anything in return. I want to take you out because you intrigue me and I find you attractive." His hot-eyed gaze dropped to her lips. "And I've wanted to kiss that lush, pouty mouth of yours since I saw you in your hammock."

Well, when he put it like that!

Her resistance dissolved, and she reached for him as he reached for her. When their lips touched, the explosion of need made her gasp. His tongue savaged her mouth and demanded a reciprocal response. Her moan echoed in the still night.

Holy hell, the man could kiss.

Her world, as she'd previously known it, was shattered. Never would she be able to kiss another man without comparing it to this moment, to Gabriel's possession.

He tangled his fingers in her wild hair, and he gently tugged her head back, only allowing enough space for the both of them to take a few deep inhales. The puffs of his rapid breath brought with them the teasing scent of beer, and Margie smiled at the one moment of realness in what must be a fantasy her mind conjured up.

Their eyes met. His were the color of molten silver, practically glowing with his desire. She'd never met anyone whose eyes changed with their moods before.

He ran the rough pad of his thumb the width of her bottom lip before plunging it inside. Her lips closed around it in a compressed O, and she sucked gently before nipping the tip with her teeth.

He groaned and closed his eyes. *"Jesus."*

"I have to go."

A heartfelt sigh was his answer. He put his hands on her shoulders and spun her around, but instead of marching her forward, he pulled her back against him.

The full length of his erection nestled against her ass, and his teeth found her earlobe. The sharp nip sent a shock wave through her system, and she instinctively pressed back into him. He moved his hand to apply pressure to her abdomen, making the contact of their bodies complete.

"Just so we're clear, I would take you where we stand." His raw, hungry voice caused her to whimper. His arms tightened a fraction, and he leaned down to growl into her ear. "Run while you can, Margaret. One day soon, this *will* happen."

But she didn't want to run. She wanted to climb onto him and cling for dear life.

Perhaps he sensed her hesitation, or her wanton desire to run away with him put off a unique vibe, because his arms tightened briefly.

She patted his forearms. Whether to encourage him to steal her away or to release her, she was clueless to know.

With a rough sigh, he let her go.

They walked the last ten steps to her window, and he reached forward to shove it open. It didn't budge. He tried twice more before giving up. "Does it automatically lock?"

"No. There's no way it should be locked at all."

"Think your brother decided to get even with you for running off?"

"That toad," she muttered.

A hand reached out of the dark and grabbed her.

She opened her mouth to scream.

Luckily, Gabriel had the fast reflexes of a superhero, and he clamped a hand over her mouth and stifled her bloodcurdling scream before it escaped.

When he released a hearty laugh, Margie elbowed him in the ribs and turned her temper on her brother. "You're a freaking jerk, Jamie! You nearly gave me a heart attack."

James's unrepentant grin earned him a punch to the upper arm. "That hurt about as much as a mosquito bite."

"You're an asshole!"

"Shhh, keep it down. Some people are actually trying to sleep around here." James's laughter lurked below the surface, indicating he was only half-serious.

Gabriel placed his lips next to her ear. "Should I stay for your brother's safety?"

"No. I don't want witnesses when I bury the body."

"Okay, remember I'm a criminal attorney if you need one." He squeezed her hip. "I'll bid you both a good night. Until next time, Margaret."

His tone was silky smooth and his meaning clear.

After he removed his large, warm hand, Margie felt desolate. He was only ten feet away when she opened her mouth to call him back.

"Come on, it's been a long day, and you need sleep." Jamie stepped in front of her. "He just moved in. He's not going anywhere."

As she followed her brother toward the front of the house, she glanced over her shoulder.

Gabriel had paused on his porch to gather up the blanket and beer bottles. With one last long look in her direction, he disappeared into his house.

Margie pressed a hand to her belly to calm the butterflies. The man was a god. There were no two ways about it. How else could he melt her resistance and obliterate her resolve with so little effort?

CHAPTER 7

APRIL 1912 -

*L*ucy Reddington-Hale was a passenger on the ship called the RMS Titanic, with the intent to travel home to America after an extended visit in England. During the first evening out at sea, the opulent dining salon had been filled to almost overflowing. Capacity stood at roughly five hundred and fifty. There had to be close to that many occupants seated, all dressed to the nines. The who's who of the upper class could be observed sipping champagne from the finest crystal. Among them, Lucy, her brand-new husband, Andrew, and her sister, Rosalie.

Conversation flowed, and Lucy rolled her eyes at the sameness of it all. She was bored. Tired of the socialites flaunting their wealth. Tired of the men displaying their wives and mistresses like arm candy. Tired of watching her sister turn the head of every male in a twenty-yard vicinity. She assured herself she wasn't jealous of Rosie or of her vivacious, charming nature. One day, she might even believe it.

If Lucy drank a little more champagne than she should've that night, who was to keep her in check? And if her smile was a little more brittle *than bright, who was to notice? She was gearing up to claim a headache and make her escape back to her stateroom, when he strolled in.*

Women's heads turned to admire the new passenger's masculine beauty, jaws agape.

The man was simply splendid. No other word could do him justice. With his dark hair slicked back, the exact color was difficult to tell, but Lucy perceived the thick mass to be brown or possibly black. The carefree air he exuded was enhanced by a pair of wicked silver-gray eyes.

A thrill electrified her insides when he was escorted to their table.

When he spoke, the deep baritone seemed to come from God Himself, and the British accent was positively swoon-worthy. Admittedly, Lucy had always admired the English accent. The deliciousness of his speech had her heart quickening and a bolt of awareness sizzling along her spine.

He introduced himself as Sebastian Harwick, and the name teased Lucy's memory. Another member of their elite crowd, no doubt, although she couldn't place him. More than once, over the short distance between his seat and hers, their eyes connected. His were knowing, as if he could delve into her deepest, darkest secrets without her ever voicing them.

As the dinner hour passed, Lucy hid her fascination behind cool indifference. His devil-may-care attitude called to the rebellious part of her soul. The part she'd always kept buried deep and that never saw the light of day. Even now, she had to fight his seductive pull. Had she been unmarried, her obsession with Sebastian might have been a tad more acceptable. As a newlywed woman, she had no right to ogle him.

Of the thirteen couples honeymooning on the maiden voyage, she and Andrew Hale were one. Although she and Andrew had yet to consummate their vows, they were bound together as man and wife, and to show interest in another while sitting next to the one whose ring she wore was inexcusable, especially if she was caught. Still, she peeked under her lashes at the gorgeous specimen across from her when she thought no one was looking.

As the night wore on, Sebastian showed a marked interest in her, too. He seemed uncaring of Andrew on her left, who glowered at every flirty topic Sebastian used to challenge her. The compliments and single-minded attention he showered on Lucy made her soul sparkle. While she'd never been an incomparable beauty, the way Rosie was, Lucy had held her own at the soirees and parties. But now, in this time and place, Sebastian's warm regard convinced her she was the most desired woman alive.

She had just lifted her glass in response to Sebastian's impromptu toast when a loud, obnoxious buzzing began, repeating over and over, directly in her ear. With nothing more than a desire to silence the noise, she flailed a hand in the direction of the sound and encountered a small square box.

Frowning her confusion, she squinted and peered around.

Margie was in her Palm Coast home, snuggled beneath her soft down comforter. The annoying buzzer happened to be her alarm clock, reminding her it was time to get up and nag her children until they consumed some semblance of a nutritious breakfast.

Sebastian.

She hadn't dreamed of him in over five months, but after the bone-melting kiss she shared with Gabriel, it was easy to see why she had. She touched her lips and grinned. Sitting up, she eased open the nightstand drawer and removed her drawing supplies. A check of the clock showed she had seven of her nine-minute snooze allotment left. Charcoal firmly in hand, she began to sketch Sebastian as she'd first seen him that night a hundred and six years ago.

He was a masterpiece of pure male beauty, and her artistic skills captured him to perfection. With a few swipes of her charcoal, she recreated the moment when he'd sipped his champagne and graced her with a look of such sizzling intensity she thought her unmentionables would melt. Goodness, she'd loved him then. She'd loved him in every incarnation they shared, and in the ones they hadn't, she pined for what she didn't know she was missing.

The gift she'd been born with in this lifetime allowed her to look back, to remember with such detail, such ease, it seemed as if her imagination got carried away.

Meeting him in the flesh had helped. From the morning in her hammock, she no longer questioned the images crowding her brain. No longer believed she was in love with a phantom who didn't exist.

After she saw her children were fed, she'd call Annie to see what she could dig up in the ancestry databases. Now Margie knew she hadn't dreamed him up, she wanted to verify Sebastian's existence.

The door opened, and Kaley lurked in the doorway, looking unsure of her welcome. In her hand was a steaming mug of coffee. Margie took an appreciative sniff and gestured her daughter to come join her.

"Good morning. Your color's back. How are you feeling today?"

"Better. Still a bit of a headache." Kaley placed the mug on the bed stand and sat on the edge of the mattress. She twisted to get a better look at what Margie was shading, not at all subtle about her curiosity. "Is that Mr. James?"

"Yes." Margie shifted the pad to allow her daughter a better look.

"Why does he look different?"

How did she answer? How did she say "because this was how he looked in a previous life"? *She didn't.* Not without sounding like she'd lost her mind.

"I'm a bit obsessed with the early nineteen hundreds. I suppose I drew him in that time period without thinking," she lied.

"He's hot. For an old guy."

A laugh escaped, and Margie gently nudged Kaley's shoulder with her own. Everyone was old when you were fourteen. "Watch it, you little brat."

"He really likes you, Mom."

"I like him, too."

"But?"

Age-old doubts flooded in, and Margie tried to blank her face before Kaley saw them. Why she felt the need to hide her vulnerability was anyone's guess. Perhaps if she was honest, they would have one more thing to connect over. "I don't know. Maybe I worry I'm too old for romance. Like my chance has passed me by."

Kaley looked thoughtful as she frowned down at the portrait and bit her lip. It startled Margie to realize the gesture was inherited from her.

"What is it, honey?"

"I think that's the first time you've answered me like I'm not a kid."

"You've turned into a beautiful young woman, and I need to remember you're not a small child to be sheltered from all the grown-up worries." She smiled softly. "It's not to say I won't continue to *try* and protect you from the ugliness of the world, but you deserve to be in the know."

They shared a moment of understanding, and she imagined she felt some of Kaley's ever-present animosity ease.

"You're not too old." Kaley shrugged. "And I like him. He'd be better for you than Dad ever was."

The bitterness in her daughter's voice wasn't anything new, but for once, Margie could see it wasn't directed at her and was completely intended for Scott.

"Kaley... your dad, he hasn't done anything to hurt you, has he?"

Shocked outrage met her question. Kaley violently shook her head then winced. "Ouch!"

"Are you okay?"

"Yeah, I'm good." Her hand went up to touch the stitches, and as quickly, she dropped it to her lap. "I'm good," she repeated.

Margie wanted to kiss the boo-boo better, but that's what one did for a toddler. Her teenage daughter would likely throat punch her for attempting to soothe the hurt. "I didn't mean to insinuate your father wasn't a good man, Kaley. He..."

Scott was a deadbeat, for sure, but if there was something more at play, Margie needed to take action.

"I know what you're trying to ask, and he's not like that, Mom. I swear. He just doesn't give a shit about us, that's all."

"Language," Margie corrected absently. In her mind, she struggled to formulate the proper words to assure Kaley Scott did care. Her mind drew a blank. Really, Scott was an ass of the highest magnitude.

"Anyway," Kaley said, drawing out the word to change the subject. "Are you going to date Mr. James? I totally think you should."

Chuckling at her daughter's waggling eyebrows, Margie kissed her cheek and was happy, for once, Kaley didn't balk at the contact. "Perhaps. We'll have to see. I doubt he realizes what he's getting into with this family."

"True."

"Enough of all that. I want to show you my gratitude for delivering unto me the nectar of the gods."

Kaley giggled.

Margie hid her smile with the rim of the mug. A sip and a sigh showed her true appreciation as the tasty coffee slid down her throat.

"God, this is good. Thank you, honey." The beaming smile she received brightened her morning. "What say we go shopping today? If you're up to it, that is. I can call Sammy—I need to apologize for yesterday—and we can see if she wants to go with us. Make it a girls' day."

"Really?"

"Sure, why not?"

The wattage of Kaley's smile doubled. "Can I call her?"

Margie bit her lip but nodded. "I'd like to talk to her after you're done, okay? I really need to set things to rights."

"She'll understand, Mom. She always does."

Yes, such was Sammy's gift. Not only was she psychic, but her ability had come with a deep sense of understanding. Margie sometimes envied her younger sister. Not because of her bubbly personality and good looks, but because of her ease with everyone around her.

"I still need to apologize. I was a total bitch, as you said."

"I'm sorry."

The tearful quality in Kaley's voice ripped Margie's fixation from Sebastian's likeness.

"Apology accepted, but only if you forgive me, too."

A tentative smile returned to her daughter's youthful face. "I can do that."

Margie set aside the sketchpad and shifted to hug Kaley. "Good.

Now get going. I need to finish my coffee and stare at this beautiful man for a bit longer."

Kaley smirked and scurried away.

The black-and-white image drew Margie's attention again. Somehow, she'd managed to recreate the ever-present twinkle in his silvery eyes. Her heart gave a hard thunk.

Shit.

She was a goner already.

CHAPTER 8

"You should have a security system installed."

Margie looked up from the soft-pink blouse she'd been contemplating purchasing and met her sister's steady blue-eyed stare. "I seriously considered it, but I'm afraid the kids or I would keep setting it off with all the coming and going."

"Still, if you set up something with security cameras..." Sammy shrugged and nodded to the shirt. "It suits you." A small smile tugged at her lips. "And it's on sale, so you won't mind if the buttons get ripped off."

Biting her lip against a laugh, Margie added the shirt to her shopping basket. The day would probably never come when any man ripped off her clothing in a passionate frenzy, but a girl could dream. Recalling the kiss from last night, Margie had the overwhelming urge to fan her warming face.

"Who is he?" Sammy tossed another top her way.

Kaley cast Margie a twinkling glance and opened her mouth to pipe up from one rack over.

"Shut it, kid!" Margie ordered, adopting her sister's slang.

"Doesn't one of your neighbors have an alarm company?" Sammy asked in an abrupt departure from teasing.

"You mean Don?" At Sammy's nod, Margie grimaced. "Yes. I feel weird asking him to install it though."

"Why?"

"He's asked me to dinner a few times, and I've turned him down. I'm afraid running to him with this is like encouragement for him to start his pursuit again."

"Ugh, yeah. I get it."

Margie figured she would. When her sister had just entered college, one of the local boys began harassing Sammy. At the time, Margie hadn't known, but it came to light a few years later at a family gathering. James had mentioned running into Rob and talked about the hostility the guy still held for her two siblings. "Sammy? All those years ago, I had no idea that guy you went to school with—Rob—was such a jerk. I'd never have encouraged you to date someone like him if I'd known."

Sammy waved a hand. "Water under the bridge. I haven't seen that asshat for years." Without warning, her body gave an odd jerk and shudder.

"What is it? You okay?"

"Yeah, I think a ghost walked over my grave."

"Did you see something?"

"No, more like a feeling. Must be a twisted Pavlovian response to Rob's name." This time Sammy gave an exaggerated shiver. "See?"

They laughed, and the mood was lighter as they moved to another circular sale rack.

Later that evening, Margie spread her haul out on the bed and smiled as she recalled the fun they'd had. Deep down, she understood where her animosity toward Sammy stemmed from, but pushing it aside to enjoy the day had been refreshing. Going forward, she'd try to be better. Past-life hurts should remain history, not bleed into the here and now. With age, came wisdom. It had taken a while for Margie to reconcile the tragic events associated surrounding the Titanic, but she was getting there.

As she carefully removed tags, she admired the new dress Kaley and Sammy had bullied her into buying. Her sister had insisted

Margie would be "sexy as hell." With a sigh, she picked up the black wrap dress and faced the mirror, holding it in front of her and twisting this way and that. After four full-term births, sexy felt like a thing of the past. It could be argued confidence was attractive and self-doubt was just a state of mind, but Margie was short on the first one and had a wealth of the second.

"Oh, fuck it." She bundled the dress and put it on a chair so she remembered to drop it off to be dry cleaned. The damned thing would probably hang in her closet until some distant special occasion that may never come. If nothing else, it could be worn to a funeral.

"Fuck what?"

Gabriel's voice startled a scream from as far down as Margie's toes. The unrepentant jerk grinned for all he was worth.

"What are you doing here?" she demanded, embarrassed to be caught talking to herself.

"I came to see you."

Seeing him relaxed with his arms crossed and one shoulder resting against the white trim molding sent Margie's heart rate into overdrive. The man was tantalizing. Like a warm, moist chocolate cake with thick, creamy frosting. And she wanted to eat him up.

"No, I mean here. In my room." Her voice broke, and she blushed like a shy virgin. Why the hell couldn't she act normal around him for two minutes?

"Kaley let me in." He cocked his head to the side and narrowed his eyes.

When he didn't say anything else, Margie crossed her arms over her chest and dropped her gaze to the floor. Yep, she definitely had insecurities.

"I can go." The words were said softly, almost as a question, and they made her stomach knot. The problem wasn't that she wanted him to go. *Hell no!* She wanted him to enter her room more fully, turn the lock, and ravish her until she forgot her own name.

He shoved away from the doorframe and shifted to leave.

"Gabriel." His name on her lips was a plea. Her utmost desire was for him to stay and chase away her personal demons. A huge part of her wished for the easy friendship she'd been missing since Opal's death, and Margie suspected only Gabriel could see past her prickly nature. But with male friendships came complications, and for some guys, the push for more. She wasn't prepared for the repercussions of a short-lived affair. At least not yet.

He glanced back over his shoulder, waiting for her to continue.

"I'm sorry if I seemed cranky. I was surprised to see you." She offered up a tentative smile. "It's not fine dining, but I was going to whip up grilled cheese sandwiches for dinner. You're welcome to join us."

His all-seeing stare made her insides writhe, and Margie had a strong compulsion to hide. She feared what he'd discover under her tough-as-nails exterior. Just when she thought she couldn't tolerate another second of his searching gaze, his focus shifted to the bunched-up dress. Had she not been watching him as closely as she was, she'd have missed the quicksilver frown. Was he weighing the aggravation of being with her against the ultimate reward?

When his eyes met hers again, he gave her a slow smile.

Her insides turned gooey.

He did nothing more than nod his agreement, but it was as if he offered her the moon and stars on a silver platter. He held out his hand, and the gesture seemed symbolic. If she took it, would she be acknowledging what they were flirting with was real?

She clasped it anyway. Helpless not to.

They entered the kitchen to find Kaley at the island, serving up dinner to her brothers. Margie had to give her daughter credit for not laughing at their joined hands. Instead, Kaley pointed with the spatula to the remaining seats. "I wanted to do something to thank you for today, Mom. Don't make a big deal, okay?"

Margie released Gabriel to give Kaley's temple a light kiss. "I wouldn't dream of it. But I wish you'd rest." Heading to the fridge, she called, "What is everyone drinking?"

"Beer," Scotty called.

"Try again."

"Fine. I'll take milk."

Margie hid her grin and removed five clear glasses from the cabinet. "Aaron? Gabriel?"

"Beer," Aaron parroted his older brother.

She gave him a narrowed-eye stare.

"Fine. I'll take milk."

"Better make mine milk, too," Gabriel said. The laughter in his voice brought a smile to her lips.

"Three milks coming up. Kaley?"

When the beverages were distributed and the sandwiches dished up, they all hung about the island, chatting and joking. Kaley sat perched on the counter, swinging her legs as she and Gabriel debated the merits of Velveeta versus real cheddar cheese.

Margie found it difficult to recall when her daughter had been so carefree. Without a doubt, Kaley had missed the influence of a constant, caring father figure in her life.

"Where's Jamie?" Margie asked when the discussion of tasty cheeses ended.

"He went with Michael to pick out Aunt Sammy's Christmas present," Aaron volunteered. "He's going to ask her to marry him."

Margie nearly choked on her bite of sandwich. *"What?"* she finally managed to ask.

"Yep. That's what he said to Uncle Jamie. I heard him."

Carefully, she wiped each of her fingers on her napkin as she chose her words. "Aaron, if that's true, you shouldn't blurt it out. Michael will want it to be a surprise until after Sammy says yes."

"But it's not a surprise. We all know she's gonna say yes," he argued with little-boy logic.

"True. However, the proposal is going to be a surprise to *her* until he asks. It's a tradition people cling to. Men buy a ring, pick a romantic moment, then ask the woman they love to marry them."

"Is that what Dad did?"

Margie could feel four sets of eyes on her, and she never wanted to get up and clean the kitchen more. Anything to avoid the avid curiosity. She should lie and say yes so she could let it go, but the truth was, Scott hadn't been romantic at all. He'd simply convinced her "getting hitched because of the baby" was the right thing to do. Even after they'd lost their first child, she remained with him, because by then, she felt stuck. A teenager with no real choice or future. God, she'd been naive.

"Not really." For the second time in as many minutes, she wiped her fingertips.

Gabriel's large hand settled over hers to still her movements. With a light squeeze, he asked, "Is it okay to take everyone for pie? Or is it too much sugar this close to bedtime?"

Because she couldn't speak past the odd lump in her throat, she nodded her agreement and smiled her thanks. She didn't know whether to be freaked out or grateful Gabriel was this in-tune with her feelings.

Gabriel helped Kaley clean up the kitchen as Margaret wrestled her sons into jackets and shoes. He hadn't failed to notice her uncomfortableness when Aaron asked about her own proposal. Clearly, her deadbeat ex hadn't bothered to give her the romance she craved.

As he handed Kaley the plates to load into the dishwasher, he asked, "Where's the best place for pie around here?"

She paused and gave him an incredulous look. "You offered to feed the animals without thinking it through, didn't you?"

His aborted laughter came out as a snort. "The animals? I assume you mean your brothers. That's kind of mean, isn't it?"

"You don't live with them."

"Valid point."

"The Cool Beans Way." She glanced at the stovetop clock. "They close in twenty minutes."

"Shit."

She giggled and shoved him toward the garage door. "Come on. This can wait. The animals can't."

They made it to the restaurant with minutes to spare. The pastry display was packed with a multitude of delightfully flavored pie slices, and for their group of five, the decision making was a challenging process. Gabriel was grateful the cafe owner didn't seem to be in a hurry. After everyone chose their favorite, they took the food to go and sat at the outside table to eat.

He was surprised by how much he enjoyed himself. The boys were inquisitive, and Kaley was a smaller, sassier, pink-haired version of her mother. Already, Gabriel adored her.

But it was Margaret who held all the fascination for him. The times she lowered her guard, she was breathtakingly beautiful. Like now, her face lit and her cheeks became rosy as she laughed at the antics of Aaron, the whipped-cream thief. Whenever his brother was distracted, her youngest would swipe a glob to add to his own pie.

Scotty eventually caught on and wasn't at all happy. "Mom! Tell Aaron to stop."

"Aaron, stop," Margaret obligingly ordered. There was no heat behind her words, and the sparkle in her eyes was nothing short of mischievous when she hooked her finger and swiped the last of Scotty's whipped cream.

"*Mom!*"

Gabriel loved it when she grinned unrepentantly, and he felt something within him go soft. He gave Margaret a severe warning look as he rose to his feet. "Don't even *think* about stealing mine."

Since his brother's pub bordered The Cool Beans Way, he strode through the doors and straight back to the kitchen area.

"Gabe. What are you doing here, man?"

"I need a large bowl of whipped cream."

Grey laughed and wiped his hands on the towel tucked into his apron. "Do I want to know why you couldn't simply go to the store and purchase a can for your nightly activities?"

"Okay, a) there are no nightly activities happening—not in the way you are suggesting. And b) you make yours from scratch. It's excellent."

All the while Gabriel spoke, Grey was adding the whipped cream into a medium-sized to-go container. "Still not sure why you drove all the way here for this."

"Margaret and her kids are outside the coffee shop next door, eating pie. I'm trying to prevent a war between the brothers."

"Ah." Grey grinned but didn't punctuate his reply with a snarky comment as expected. He slid the container across the workstation. "Enjoy."

Gabriel returned to their table to find another man crowding Margaret.

Discomfort was etched in every line of her face.

Kaley's attitude was back, firmly on display, and the two boys were in the process of shoving one another. A full-blown fight was on the horizon.

A protective instinct emerged, and not caring to dig too deeply into the reason at the moment, Gabriel stepped behind Margaret and placed his hand on her shoulder. Plopping the container on the table between her sons, he said, "Crisis averted. Leave enough for your mom and sister."

Margaret's hand came up and covered his, as if she sought comfort, and Kaley's undisguised look of relief made him feel ten-feet tall.

Finally, he faced the man.

The guy stood at least eight inches shorter than Gabriel and was about forty pounds heavier. His blond hair had a tendency toward thinning with a bald spot forming at the top of his head. Added to that unfortunate genetic blessing was the receding hairline. Still, he had a nice face. Somewhat round and ruddy, but pleasant. He was the kind of guy women found non-threatening, but Gabriel couldn't shake the impression the man wasn't as benign as he seemed.

"Gabriel, this is Don. He lives on our block."

Out of politeness, he nodded to the neighbor he had no pressing desire to meet. "Don."

Gabriel didn't miss the look of annoyance as it flashed a second before the stranger could put a jovial mask in place. He shifted to put himself between Margaret and Don then held out a hand. "Pleasure to meet you," he lied.

Don glared at his hand as if it were a poisonous serpent ready to strike. Three steady heartbeats passed before he offered a limp shake.

Gabriel resumed his seat with a challenging stare, hoping the fucker would take a hint.

Don didn't linger and hustled toward Grey's bar, looking back to glare his displeasure.

"Could he be any more of a douche flute?" Kaley muttered.

"We don't talk like that, Kaley," Margaret admonished.

"Can I help it if he's creepy?"

Gabriel gave Kaley an approving look. "Savage, but I like it."

He finally noticed a spoon-sized chunk of whipped cream was missing from his pie. He shot Margaret a narrow-eyed glare and pitched his voice low. "I leave for less than five minutes and come back to find Chester the Molester trying to make time with you. To add insult to injury, my pie is half gone. What do you have to say for yourself, Margaret?"

She reached over to take another stab at his dessert.

He held it up and away. "I draw the line at sharing my pie." He gobbled it down in three bites.

When they were finished, the kids ran ahead to the Suburban, laughing and calling half-hearted insults to one another, as Gabriel and Margaret strolled through the parking lot.

"What does a 'douche flute' even mean?" he asked quietly.

"Are you not hip to teen slang, Gabriel?" She made a tsk-tsk sound and smirked.

"Apparently not."

Margie laughed, and he reveled in the sound.

"Thanks for spending the evening with us. The kids loved it."

With his hand in hers, he drew her to a stop and twirled her like a dancer to face him, halting her with a light arm around her waist. "And you? Did you love it, Margaret?" He led her in an impromptu waltz.

Pink crept into her cheeks, and she bit her lip. A gesture he was coming to associate with her nervousness.

"I did," she admitted.

Wanting nothing more than to kiss her but knowing it wasn't the time or place, he simply said, "Good." Gabriel put his palm to her lower back and guided her toward the vehicle. Before he opened the driver-side door, he asked, "Will you come by for a nightcap tonight? After James returns?" Her obvious indecision prompted him to add, "I'll be out on the porch until ten. If you want to join me for a glass of wine, the offer stands. If you don't show up, I'll understand. No pressure."

He opened the door and assisted her inside. As he strode to his side of the vehicle, he instinctively knew she'd pull back. For someone like Margaret, Gabriel had come on too strong, too fast. He silently cursed himself for putting the ball in her court.

CHAPTER 9

Flowers, a giant stuffed bear, and a brand new iPad Pro showed up on her doorstep the next day, courtesy of the James brothers for Kaley. Her daughter's squeal echoed through the house, and Margie had to smile at the consideration the guys had shown. They must've figured Kaley would be home for a few days, bored out of her mind while her friends were at school.

Margie didn't want to contemplate the cost involved. From Opal, she knew the men were all successful in their own right. She imagined they had the money to spare. And while normally she wouldn't dream of allowing Kaley to keep such an expensive gift from a stranger, she didn't really view the James brothers as strangers anymore. Yesterday had caused a shift in Margie's and Gabriel's relationship—even if she wasn't ready to explore it.

"Mom, here's a note for you." Kaley surprised her from her musings and passed the hand-written message to her with a smirk.

I had fun last night. Have dinner with me.
Gabriel

His handwriting was as bold and beautiful as the man himself, and Margie couldn't help but smile. He'd always written her notes in the past. She distinctly remembered the one and only from their first night together on the Titanic.

APRIL 1912-

Her sister sat on the other side of Andrew, drawing the gaze of all the men with her musical laughter. All but Sebastian's. With her shining blue-black hair and laughing, electric eyes, Rosie commanded notice. Her behavior was outrageous most nights, and she had had no sense of decorum.

Ofttimes, it enraged Lucy.

That night, it didn't.

That night, she'd welcomed Rosie's flirty behavior because it distracted Andrew, who had not-so-secretly lusted after her sister for the better part of two years.

Lucy assumed, if their fathers hadn't contracted her marriage from the time the couple were in the cradle, Andrew would've acted on his feelings for Rosie long ago. But he'd been honor bound to marry Lucy, and he'd done his duty, making everyone involved deeply unhappy—minus their parents. Neither he nor Lucy could bring themselves to make their marriage a real one. Having grown up together, raised more like brother and sister, the idea of carnal relations turned them both green. Even the chaste kiss at their wedding ceremony had presented a loathsome factor neither could get past.

Andrew's preoccupation with Rosie had allowed Sebastian to slip Lucy a note across the table without being seen. It also allowed her to read the message and give a barely discernible nod in agreement to a private meeting.

Heart pounding hard enough to rock the ship, Lucy had begged everyone's pardon, utilized the headache excuse she'd planned earlier, and convinced Andrew there was no need to see her back to her room.

Sebastian jumped up with a gallant offer to escort her. "I don't intend to partake of the cigars and port this evening. I'm happy to see her safely to your stateroom."

Andrew opened his mouth to protest, but never got the chance.

With a mischievous smirk, Rosie touched his sleeve and said, "Oh, do stay and keep me company, Andrew."

Lucy met her sister's laughing eyes. A silent communication passed between the two women. Without words needing to be spoken, Rosie had agreed to distract Andrew so Lucy could have a bit of fun for a change.

A half smile tugged at Lucy's lips.

Rosie loved mischief, and if she thought she was pulling something over on "stuffy old Andrew," as she was fond of calling him, she would.

"ARE YOU GOING TO GO OUT WITH HIM?"

Startled from the past, Margie glanced up from running her fingertips over Gabriel's name. "Should I?"

"Duh, of course. For an old guy, he's cool."

Shaking her head, she laughed.

Kaley joined in, and being in complete accord was nice.

Margie glanced back down at the note in her hand and, once again, traced the elegant scrawl.

"Why don't you want to go out with him?"

Sometimes Margie hated how perceptive her daughter could be. But Kaley's question required honesty. "I feel old and frumpy. I can't imagine what he sees in me."

"Mom, you are *not* old and frumpy. Stace's mom is older than you, and she's on Tinder."

"What's Tinder?" Margie knew very well it was a dating app, but it was a helluva lot of fun to tease and pretend she was clueless.

Kaley rolled her eyes. "Seriously? Okay. I'm staging an intervention. I'm calling Aunt Sammy, and we're going to have a spa day. By the time we're done, you'll be a babe."

"All right. Will they teach me how to lose ten pounds in a week?" Kaley's giggle was wonderful to hear. "Is Stacey bringing your homework by tonight, or do I need to call the school to get your assignments?"

"Stace is popping by. Can Dalton come, too?"

"Who's Dalton?"

A long, awkward pause filled the air between them.

Margie patiently waited her out.

"He was the guy I was skipping school with two days ago."

Margie bit her tongue against a lecture. "Tell me three things you like about him," she ordered gently, wanting Kaley to truly think about all the reasons why she actually liked the boy.

"He's funny."

"Okay. What else?"

"He doesn't treat me like a freak."

Concerned she might've missed signs of bullying, Margie asked, "Why would anyone treat you like a freak, honey?"

Kaley shrugged and avoided her eyes.

Acting on impulse, Margie reached out to grab her hand and dragged her to the kitchen. "Sit."

She dug in the cabinet for two bowls, placed them on the granite countertop, and pulled out two pints of Häagen-Dazs from the freezer. Glancing between the pints, the white bowls, and Kaley, Margie went with something completely spontaneous and put the bowls back. "Let's eat from the cartons."

Kaley's gasp made her cringe. "Not a good idea? Does it gross you out?"

"No, Mom. I just never thought I'd see the day you would. Can I have the chocolate, chocolate chip?" The grin Kaley blessed her with made Margie feel as if she'd finally done something right in her daughter's eyes.

"How about we share them both?"

"Deal."

"So, about this boy, Dalton. What's the third thing you like about him?"

"He doesn't push for sex."

"*Bingo!* He can come over."

Kaley laughed around a spoonful of ice cream. "Now it's your turn."

"My turn?"

"Name three things you like about Gabriel."

Margie froze like a deer caught in a driver's high beams. She liked everything about Gabriel, but she wasn't sure she was ready to share yet.

"Come on, Mom. Fair's fair."

Margie stalled by stuffing her mouth full of cookies and cream, then reached for a scoop of the pint Kaley was hoarding.

"Not until you fess up," Kaley said and shifted the ice cream away from her reach.

"You're a rotten kid. I gave birth to you."

"How long are you going to continue to use that one?"

"How long can I get away with it?"

"You still owe me three things. Go."

"Well, the obvious one is how hot he is."

"Pfft. Really? It's all about looks? Shallow much?" Sammy's amused voice came from behind her and almost drove Margie out of her own skin.

Pressing her hand to her chest, Margie scowled. "Where the hell did you come from? You nearly gave me a heart attack!"

Kaley and Sammy wore matching grins.

"Ah, the intervention. I didn't realize we were starting so soon. When did this one have a chance to text you, and how did you get here so fast?" Margie pointed her spoon at Kaley.

"Damn, you're chatty today. First, I was on my way over to see if you needed a break from nurse duty. Second, I was in the driveway when I got the text a few minutes ago. I was ogling that sexy neighbor of yours, who just happens to be mowing the lawn as we speak."

All three of them ran for Margie's bedroom window.

"Jesus! He's shirtless!" Margie huffed out on a breath as she admired the tapered, muscled back.

From behind, she thought it was Gabriel, but when he turned, she saw it was actually Gordon. Disappointment filled her. What she wouldn't have given to see Gabriel shirtless! The little devil on her shoulder told her she could if she just went to dinner with him.

85

"That's Gordon," Kaley said.

"Not bad for mid-day eye candy." Sammy frowned. "Gordon? He isn't by chance Gordon James, the rockstar?"

"Ohmygod! Sammy, I think you're right!" Margie locked onto the tanned torso. The mouth-watering eight-pack stomach dipping into the low-slung shorts definitely belonged to Gordon James. "I recognize those abs from his album cover. I can't believe I never made the connection." She shook her head. "Opal only said that one of her nephews was a musician. Not that he was famous."

They all watched Gordon in amazed wonder, each locked in their own private thoughts, until he cut the engine and glanced their way. As one, they ducked.

"Okay, hot-guy-mowing-the-lawn break is over. Let's head back for the ice cream before it melts," Sammy suggested.

They duck-walked to the hall then ran, laughing, to the kitchen. Margie pulled a third pint from the freezer and handed it over to Sammy along with a spoon.

Her sister went still and stared at her wide-eyed.

"What?"

"Since when do you eat from a carton? And how did you know my favorite brand of gelato? And for that matter, why do you have it stocked?"

Margie offered up a mysterious smile. "People change. And I overheard you telling Annie that stuff was to die for. As for why I have it stocked. Meh."

Sammy shook her head in wonder and shoveled a spoonful into her mouth. *"Ohdeargodinheaven!"*

"That good?"

"Mmhmm."

"I'm going to need a bite of that. Everyone pass their containers to the left." Margie ordered. She took her time, packing the creamy mixture onto her spoon.

Spa day forgotten, they gorged on ice cream and gelato.

"Sammy?"

"Hmm?"

"I know I apologized, but I wanted to stress how sorry I am for being a bitch the day Kaley was hurt. Not once, but twice. There was no excuse."

"There was every excuse. Your child was attacked. Mama bear was coming out. I can't say I wouldn't have done the same if it were my own."

Margie had never wanted to hug her sister more. "Thank you," she said huskily.

"We're cool. Now shut up and eat your ice cream."

Kaley, who had remained quiet while the sisters worked to build their bond, piped up. "You owe me two more things you like about Gabriel."

"Who's Gabriel?" Sammy asked as she passed her container to Margie and grabbed Kaley's.

"A guy Mom thinks is hot."

Sammy gave her a superior look. "I don't know. Gordon's *smokin'*. You should go for him. I doubt anyone could be better looking."

"I'm telling Uncle Michael."

"Don't you dare, or I'll have to cut you."

Kaley rolled her eyes. "Like anyone fears *that* threat."

Sammy turned to Margie with a frown. "When did your kid become such a wise-ass?"

"She showed up that way one morning after she stayed the night at your house. Must've been two or three years ago now."

"I can hear you," Kaley reminded them. "I'm holding you to two more things, so they'd better be good."

Never had Margie fit in with Sammy's and Kaley's little clique, but today—at this moment—she did. She loved the easy camaraderie. "Should we call Annie and make this a party?"

Sammy grinned. "Since it's Monday afternoon and your boys will be home soon, I can ask Michael to babysit for a few hours."

"Great idea. You ask him, and I'll see what Annie's up to." Margie shot off a text.

Within a half hour, Annie had shown up with a bag of junk food and two bottles of wine. "Not a girls' night without the wine. I brought supplies."

"Pull up a seat and let's pop the cork." Sammy jumped up to hug the newest member of their group.

"Mom, when Stace comes, can she join us?"

"Sure, but no wine. Oh, and what about Dalton?"

Kaley shrugged and offered a shy smile. "I think I want to hang with you guys. Is that cool?"

"Absolutely uncool if your friends find out, but I'd love it anyway. Now where was I? The second thing about Gabriel? He's hot."

"That was number one."

"Yes, but it needs to be repeated because he kisses like—" Margie slammed her eyes shut as she realized she gave too much away. Her family wasn't going to miss that one or let it go.

Three female screams sounded in unison.

GABRIEL WAS ABOUT TO KNOCK ON MARGARET'S FRONT DOOR WHEN he heard the screams. Heart racing, he tried the handle and, finding it unlocked, barged in.

He cleared the foyer and was headed in the direction of the kitchen when he realized laughter accompanied the sound.

"Ohmygod! You kissed Gabriel? What was it like?" he heard a woman ask.

Jerking to a halt on the other side of the wall, he waited for Margaret's response.

"Fucking amazing," Margaret said on a sigh.

"Mom!" he heard Kaley scold.

"Well, it was!" Margaret defended.

"That's right, kid. A Holt always tells it like it is. Remember that," one of the women said. "Now hush while we get the details. Shoot."

A somewhat quieter female spoke up, "You're crazy about him. It's written all over your energy."

Energy?

Dismissing the comment, Gabriel focused on Margaret being crazy about him. He couldn't hold back his grin. *Good to know.*

"He showed up the night of Kaley's, uh, the night she was hurt, and he threw pebbles at my window. We snu—uh, went over to his house and sat on the porch. We just talked. Then he walked me back."

"That sounds lame."

Gabriel wanted to laugh at Kaley's disgusted tone, and he struggled not to make a sound. He'd be embarrassed as hell to be caught spying.

"I thought you said you kissed him? When did that happen?" someone asked.

"Wait, hold that thought. I have to go to the bathroom."

"*Sammy!*" It must've been Annie who groaned.

"Sorry, nature calls. Don't you dare spill until I'm back, Margie. *I mean it.*"

A chair scraped against the tile. Gabriel heard a low murmur of voices, but then absolute silence. He pushed off the wall to peek around the corner and came face to face with Margaret.

"Hey." He was *so* busted.

"Hey." She crossed her arms. "Want to tell me why you're hanging in my foyer like a stalker?"

"How did you know I was here?"

"My sister, Annie." When he would've delved deeper into her answer, she lifted a brow. "Start talking."

"You're adorable when you blush, you know that?" he teased, running the tip of his finger along her nose.

Margaret swatted his hand away. "I'm waiting."

He leaned in close. "For another *fucking amazing* kiss?"

"Gabriel James, I'm warning yo—"

He claimed her mouth. Burrowing his fingers into her thick, messy mane of dark hair, he drew her closer. In the span of a minute, he had her pressed to the wall, taking everything she had to give and more. Kissing her, over and over, between ragged inhalations.

The sound of a female frantically clearing her throat eventually penetrated his passion-drugged brain, and Gabriel pulled back to rest his brow against Margaret's. He closed his eyes and stayed there until his world righted itself.

"Yeah, it was definitely fucking amazing." He delivered one last gentle peck and turned to leave. "Oh, I came over to find out your answer about dinner, and I only barged in because I heard screaming. I'll stop back by tomorrow, Margaret." They locked eyes. "I'm hoping for a yes."

MARGIE SAGGED AGAINST THE WALL AS GABRIEL EXITED THE HOUSE.

"I think Kaley just got an education she may not have been ready for."

"Speak for yourself, Aunt Annie."

Sammy came running up. "What happened? What did I miss?"

"Mom just had another *fucking amazing* kiss."

"Kaley!" Margie scolded half-heartedly.

"Don't act like it wasn't, Mom. That guy is *so* into you."

Margie couldn't help but grin. "He does seem to be, doesn't he?" She rode a thirty-second high before she frowned. "Do you suppose something's wrong with him? Why would he want a middle-aged mother of three?"

Sammy laughed and turned her to face the hall mirror. "That's no middle-aged woman. That's one sexy bitch."

The glowing woman who returned her gaze *did* look like one hot bitch—*as long as she didn't look lower than her neck.*

Again, Gabriel had stumbled upon her sporting her normal daywear of yoga pants and a t-shirt. If he intended to keep popping in unannounced, she was going to need to spruce up her daily uniform.

"I'm pissed I missed the fireworks." Sammy gave her a sour look. "I've missed seeing the now-infamous Gabriel. How does that happen?"

"I thought he was going to swallow her tonsils," Kaley chirped. "Wait until Stace hears about this!"

A groan escaped Margie as Kaley ran to text her friend. "I'm not sure I can stand on my own."

Her sisters laughed and dragged her into the living room to plop down on the couch. They peppered her with all kinds of questions she had no answers for, only leaving her alone long enough to go pour wine and grab snacks.

As she sat in silence, Margie ran her fingertips over her swollen lips and relived their second kiss.

Gabriel was irresistible. There were no two ways about it.

To preserve her dignity and sanity, she'd need to avoid him whenever possible. But she feared he was nothing, if not persistent. Previous incarnations had proven as much.

Wasn't it thrilling though? To be his sole focus, to be the one he wanted time and again? The rush of it was enough to put stars in a woman's eyes. She pushed her ping-ponging thoughts away and decided to enjoy the family time with her sisters and daughter. This easy friendship wasn't always available to her, so she'd take it when she could. Things could change on a dime. And they always did.

CHAPTER 10

*B*ecause she wasn't prepared for a relationship—or at least she'd convinced herself she wasn't—Margie had done an admirable job of avoiding Gabriel over the next couple of weeks. She'd managed to not be home—or pretended she wasn't by not answering the door. Any texts between them, she kept impersonal and friendly.

The day avoiding Gabriel became a problem was the day her neighbor installed the new security system. Because James needed to be out of town and Kaley felt uncomfortable still, Margaret had caved from her family's nagging and called Don Acker's alarm company.

When he pulled into the drive, she went outside to greet him.

From the corner of her eye, she caught a movement on Gabriel's front porch. Of its own volition, her head whipped in his direction.

He was leaning with one shoulder against a wooden post, staring her way.

Her stomach flipped. *Magnificent*—the only word her mind could drum up in its befuddled state whenever she saw him.

The mid-morning breeze kicked up, and a chill chased along the exposed skin of Margie's neck.

"Call him over. Now."

She turned to look at Don, a question on her face. "Excuse me?"

He glanced up from the box of equipment he was removing from his company van. "I didn't say anything."

Feeling foolish, she wrapped her arms around her middle and pivoted to head back inside.

"Margaret, call Gabriel." The whispered words were unmistakable this time.

She whipped back to stare at Don. Sure enough, he was piling items into his tool bag, paying no mind to her. With a frown, she turned toward Gabriel. Across the distance, they had a stare off. He'd taken the hint, and she knew she'd need to be the one to make the next move if she wanted him to give her the time of day.

Dammit!

If a phantom voice was telling her to have him come over, she knew well enough to listen to it. There was a saying in the Holt family: you don't disregard a direct order from the ancestors. For generations, those strange warnings had saved more than one family member. Why now? Why Gabriel? And where was the threat?

He took a casual sip from his mug, his eyes never leaving hers.

She waved him over.

With an exaggerated look of surprise, he gestured to himself then to her.

She nodded her head.

Gabriel straightened to his full height and twisted to look behind him. Once more, he pointed to himself. The devil in him had come out to play. And didn't she find it amusing?

Lips twitching, she nodded her head again, vigorously this time.

With a shrug of his shoulders, he stepped off the porch.

"Margie?"

She faced Don. Without meaning to, she compared him to Gabriel and found him woefully lacking. She noted his usual soft, welcoming eyes were narrowed with irritation. Apparently, he'd been talking to her, and she missed everything he'd said.

"I'm sorry, Don. I was distracted."

Before he could repeat himself, Gabriel joined them.

Don's hurt was mixed with resentment, and he didn't bother to hide it.

Unease tickled Margie's nerve endings. The hurt, she could somewhat understand because of the number of times she'd turned him down, but what did he have to be resentful about? She scooted closer to Gabriel and drew comfort from his size. A girly move other independent females would scoff at, yes, but she wasn't beyond employing it.

Trying to appear casual and failing abysmally, Don offered Gabriel a business card. "My company installed and monitored Opal's system. If you wish to continue or upgrade, I'm your man."

"Thank you. I'll keep that in mind," Gabriel returned smoothly, pocketing the card. "Don't let us keep you. Margaret and I have things to discuss."

A muscle twitched along Don's jaw, and his gaze darted back and forth between them. The reluctant interest in their relationship was obvious, but he didn't ask. "Mind if I let myself in?"

"Not at all. We'll be right there." She smiled.

"I'll start with the front sensors."

"Thanks, Don."

Neither she nor Gabriel said a word until Don was free of earshot.

Gabriel got right to the point. "What's going on?"

"Call it a feeling, but I..." How did she explain the warning? He'd think she was losing her mind.

"Say no more." He tossed what remained in his mug onto a nearby azalea bush. "Come on. You can make me a second cup of coffee while he installs your system."

"Thank you."

He slipped his hand in hers and tugged her toward the open front door. "Don't thank me yet. When he leaves, I'm going to do my best to convince you to make out with me. Maybe even before he leaves. We can give him an eyeful."

She laughed, and the tension between them disappeared as if it had never existed.

"Am I making you late for work?"

"No, I don't work Fridays. It's reserved for pro bono or as a volunteer day for a local boys' club."

"Gag. Could you be any more perfect?"

He halted in his tracks and confronted her. "If I'm so perfect, why won't you go out with me?"

"Because you *are* perfect, and no one woman could live up to *that.*" Also, she had a major hang-up about her age, and she strongly suspected she had him by a few years.

"Would it make you feel better to know I sometimes throw my dirty socks on the floor?"

"Liar." She giggled; she couldn't help herself. The idea of the impeccable Gabriel throwing his socks on the floor—dirty or other-wise—was amusing.

"True, I don't. But I had to come up with something. Give me a little time to think about it, and I'll make you a list of my flaws."

"It had better be good."

"If worse comes to worst, I'll drag my brothers over to talk to you. They are always quick to point out how imperfect I am."

"Fair enough."

They continued their way to her kitchen. Gabriel went straight for the cabinet with the dishes while Margie prepped the coffee machine. She marveled at how easily they fell into a rhythm. As natural as breathing.

"How's Kaley? Headaches gone?"

"Yes. She's back to normal. Oddly enough, I think the incident was the best thing that could have happened to our relationship. I'm no longer the enemy."

"Will wonders never cease?"

Gabriel's dry tone elicited an amused snort from Margie. Smil-ing, she busied herself, preparing their drinks. She hadn't spent one second in his company that didn't leave her day brighter and lighter. For a second, self-doubt snuck in. Was she sabotaging her own chance at happiness? She mentally pushed aside her angst. Right now, she would live in the moment and enjoy a cuppa Joe with him. Tomorrow would take care of itself. And if it excited her to have him lean back against the counter next to her, with his muscular thigh mere inches from touching hers, well, she had to take her thrills where she could get them.

"It helps that I told her she could date Dalton after she turns fifteen in a few weeks, but he has to show up like a real man, and no sneaking out."

"Pot, meet kettle."

He smirked when she gave a cry of mock outrage.

"You know that night was all *your* fault, Gabriel James! You can't show up like some fairy-tale prince and sweep a woman out of her bedroom window then expect her not to run away with you."

His deep laughter warmed her insides, as did the way he entwined their fingers to draw her closer. "I'll remember to recycle that move for a later date."

"Better not. I don't know if I can handle the fright if Jamie catches us again."

"Pfft, you're fearless. I already know that much about you."

Don's voice broke through their conversation and intruded on their little bubble, effectively disrupting their flirtation. "May I have a glass of water?"

"Oh, yes. Sure." Margie had forgotten he was there. Odd, since her plan to use Gabriel as a buffer was the primary reason she'd called him over. "There's bottled water in the fridge, but you're more than welcome to share a cup of coffee with us."

"Don't mind if I do."

Don grinned happily, and Gabriel glared at her over the other man's head.

She was forced to bite her lip and turn her back to keep from breaking up.

Once they were seated all around the dining room table, with Gabriel taking the dominant position at the head to separate her from Don, they settled in to converse over their coffee. An uncomfortable tension filled the air, as if each man recognized the other intended to stake a claim.

While she'd never given Don any encouragement, he still managed to work up the nerve to ask her out every four weeks. As if he stuck to a schedule these last two years. The first Monday of the new month, like clockwork, he made a point to invite her to dinner.

Margie had been careful to remain kind but firm in her refusal. The sexual chemistry was nonexistent on her side. He was a decent man, but a far cry from exciting and miles away from how fascinating she found Gabriel to be.

Her focus was drawn by Gabriel—the man she'd long ago claimed as her soulmate. How many lifetimes had it been? She thanked her lucky stars to have always been chosen as the object of his affections. Should she just give in this time, too? Forget her hang-ups and all the other ridiculous reasons she used to avoid a relationship?

Don's words faded into the background, reminiscent of Charlie Brown's teacher. "Wa, wa, wa, wa. Wa, wa, wa."

The conversation was meaningless as she concentrated on Gabriel. And when he cut her a sideways glance from those dancing gray eyes, she was lost. She sat like a teenager mooning over her favorite rockstar; chin firmly cupped in the palm of her hand, eyes dewy and locked solely on him. It took an effort, but she quashed a heavy sigh when he smiled her way.

Without breaking visual contact with her, Gabriel said, "I'm sorry, Don, is it? Don, I don't mean to cut this short, but Margaret and I have a lunch date. How much longer do you think it will take to install the system?"

She could've jumped up and kissed Gabriel for the direct approach to get rid of him.

"A lunch date?" The coldness in Don's tone was enough to give a person frostbite.

The coward in her wanted to avoid what came next. As much as she hated hurting anyone's feelings, she refused to give false hope.

"Yes, Don." She smiled to ease her rejection. "Gabriel and I are heading out to lunch soon. Opal had been trying to set us up for ages. We thought we'd get together to reminisce about her. She's dearly missed." Her explanation made it appear more like two friends discussing a loved one, and she hoped it helped to soothe Don's ruffled feathers.

A tense minute passed with him saying nothing. Based on the ugly glare between the two men, Don wasn't buying it, and Gabriel didn't care if the other man did or not.

"We'll finish our coffee on the deck and let you get back to work, Don. I'm sure you have other clients after this." Margie stood up and gave a not-so-subtle tug of Gabriel's arm. It was like trying to relocate Mount Rushmore, and she grunted when he refused to budge.

Without breaking eye contact with Don, Gabriel reached for her hand and brought it to his lips, effectively staking his claim. And although Margie didn't appreciate the tactic, she was grateful it resulted in Don leaving the room.

"I don't like him."

"I think you made that fairly obvious," she returned over her shoulder as she placed the mugs on the counter. "Don't you think you were a little mean?"

"No, I don't. You should use a different company, Margaret."

"He's harmless, Gabriel. I've known him for years."

His frown deepened, and his mouth turned down at the corners. His displeased look meant a change of subject was in order.

"Are you coffee'd out, or would you care for another cup?"

"I'm good. Come swing in the hammock with me." His request had an edge of demand about it, and perhaps she should've been concerned, but she wasn't. A territorial Gabriel made her soft inner female preen.

As one, they sat with their legs dangling over the edge. Because it was a hammock and there was little to no stability, she rolled into his side. He curled an arm around her shoulders and dropped a kiss on her forehead. If they stayed this way forever, Margie couldn't say she'd mind.

"So, you basically trapped me into a date."

His laugh rumbled in her ear. "You know you want to go out with me. Our kiss was—how did you put it—*fucking amazing*. If we go out, there's more where that came from."

"Anyone ever tell you, you're an arrogant sonofabitch?" There was no heat in her words.

"All the time, love. All the time."

GABRIEL ENJOYED THE QUIET MOMENTS SPENT HOLDING MARGARET IN the hammock. Having her snuggled against his chest made everything seem right with his world. It was a stroke of luck when his pro bono client had called this morning to reschedule. Gabriel had needed the break. He'd spent every day either working, unpacking household items, or helping his brother get settled into the condo. When he wasn't doing any of the other things, he spent his time dreaming up ways to get Margaret to stop avoiding him.

Today had worked to his benefit. He almost couldn't believe it when she waved him over. Yet having met the little pissant installing her alarm system, he could understand why. As a man obsessed with Margaret, Gabriel easily recognized another. Part of her did, too, if she didn't want to be alone with the guy. Did she even understand why she'd turned to him for assistance?

Speaking of the dweeb, Don glared at them from the other side of the glass as he took an inordinate amount of time attaching a sensor to the sliding door.

The little fucker really was on Gabriel's last nerve. He wouldn't put it past the guy to rifle through Margaret's underwear drawer and take a collectible.

For a brief second, he was sidetracked by the idea of Margaret's underwear. What did she go for? Lace? Hip-huggers? Comfortable cotton? While Gabriel preferred the image of her in lace or, better yet, nothing at all, he doubted it was her clothing of choice.

"Margaret."

She sounded half asleep when she answered. "Hmm?"

"I'm curious about something."

Her dark head lifted, and she peered up at him through drowsy eyes.

He was correct; she'd been ready to doze off. A smile played about her lips, taunting him. He abandoned his intended question regarding her panties, and gave in to the urge to taste her. In one fluid motion, he rolled on top of her, careful not to capsize their little nest.

All trace of sleepiness disappeared from her wide sapphire eyes.

When she laughed up at him, breathless and a little stunned by his move, he lowered his lips to hers. Exploring her mouth was nirvana. Gabriel never wanted to stop.

"Ahem!"

Ah, yes. Don—the pain in his ass. Right on time.

"I'm done with the installation, Margie. It's time for keypad programming and instruction."

As Gabriel stared down into her face, he saw a flash of chagrin. He gently rubbed his nose against hers and helped her to her feet.

As they listened to how to arm and disarm the system, Gabriel observed Don trying to get cozy.

Anger began to simmer below Gabriel's seemingly calm exterior. He didn't care for how the other man would not-so-innocently touch her back or shoulder. Margaret's uncomfortableness came through as she tried to sidestep or shift away without being rude.

Don didn't know it, but he was about to have his arm ripped off and shoved up his ass—*sideways.*

Deciding he had no problem with rudeness, Gabriel stepped forward and placed an arm around her waist. "I think it's pretty cut and dried. Does she need to sign anything for you to go?"

Raw hatred flared to life in Don's eyes, and the ugliness shone hot and bright before he could temper his emotions.

Having dealt with criminals on a daily basis, Gabriel had a good idea who had it in them to transition into a monster or not. This seemingly ordinary, middle-aged man before him definitely fit the bill. Worry for Margaret stirred in Gabriel's gut.

When they were finally alone, he escorted her into the kitchen and urged her to sit. Forming the perfect words of warning took finesse, and he didn't want to offend her or get her defenses up. While she didn't want to date the other guy—that much was obvious—she still viewed him as a congenial neighbor. Gabriel didn't want to destroy her sense of security, but something was off with Don, in a big way.

"You don't have to say it."

Her quiet statement had him halting his pacing. "What?"

"I get you don't like Don. You felt he was cock-blocking you. But he's really very nice. I've known him for years."

"Margaret, there is something seriously not right about him. I can see it. It's like he's unable to understand you don't want to be with him. In his mind, you're his. Do you understand what I'm saying?"

"Are you accusing me of leading him on?" she demanded, furious for some reason Gabriel couldn't fathom. "I've given him no reason to believe that."

He approached her as one would a wild horse—hands up and cautiously. When he reached her, he stroked her dark hair back from her flushed face. "Love, listen to me. I'm not accusing you of anything. I'm warning you to stay away from him. He could be dangerous because he's the type who refuses to accept no."

She sighed, closed her eyes, and nodded. "I'm sorry. Past baggage. When I feel someone is ordering me around, I get testy."

"Understandable. I don't care for it either. How soon before you can be ready for lunch?"

"Ten minutes."

He grinned, back on his high because she'd agreed to the date. "Ten minutes it is. I'll go grab my wallet and keys."

As Gabriel swung open the door, Don flipped him the bird from behind the van's windshield and slammed the vehicle in reverse. Gabriel waited until he'd driven off and backtracked to Margaret, who was in the process of wiping the counter.

"Hey, do me a favor."

She lifted a dark brow in question.

"Change the code on the alarm system. Today. Before we leave. Will you do that?"

Her frown told him she thought he was being ridiculous, but she nodded all the same.

The relief he felt was profound, and he offered up a warm smile. "Okay. I'll be back in ten. Don't forget about the code."

———

DON DROVE AWAY IN A TOWERING RAGE.

Margie was his!

If Gabriel James thought he was going to come in and try to steal her away, well, Don would see him dead and buried first. With the way that overgrown dick had grabbed her hand and slobbered all over her in the hammock, Don was positive Margie had been disgusted by the overt display of testosterone. *His* woman didn't care for Neanderthals like Gabriel. It was obvious by how she'd invited him to join the two of them for coffee and how quickly she came running when he offered to show her the control panel. She didn't want to be alone with the overbearing brute.

To make it easy on her, Don would move their relationship forward. He had a few things left to set up before securing Margie's affections, and once they were in place, he would make his move. Women loved romance. He'd start with flowers and candy. Perhaps take her to a swanky place for dinner. The view from the twenty-ninth floor of the Top of Daytona would likely appeal to her. She was sure to be his before their date was over.

CHAPTER 11

"*D*o you have any preference where you want to go to lunch?"

"Nope. I'm all yours."

Gabriel fought the desire to turn the car around, head straight back to his house, and whisk her into the bedroom. "You can't throw around statements like 'I'm all yours.' You're begging for me to go all caveman, Margaret."

Her giggle pleased him. From anyone else, an actual giggle would put him off, but her light laugh had a sexy, breathy quality. He doubted he'd ever get tired of hearing it.

"How does the beach sound? Unless you were hoping for more formal?" she asked.

"Perfect. Subs or fried chicken?"

"Let's go with the chicken and some macaroni salad."

Together they strolled into Publix, grabbed one of the green shopping carts, and loaded up on supplies for their beach picnic.

Gabriel wasn't a fan of shopping, and going with Tamara had been an exercise in frustration. But debating the merits of crispy versus non-crispy with Margaret brought a happiness he'd never experienced before. Odd, but he suspected he'd never tire of trailing her around the grocery store as she chatted happily about nothing.

After Gabriel paid for the groceries, ice, and a small cooler, they walked back to his car hand in hand. They happened to run into James, who was headed inside.

"Playing hooky?" James asked with a nod.

"Something like that," Gabriel returned as he released Margaret's hand to shake her brother's.

"Want to have lunch with us, Jamie? We have more than enough," she offered.

Gabriel could've cheerfully throttled her. What was it with her inviting other men to join their little duo? The only positive was that she'd asked her brother and not another rival for her affections.

James shot him an amused look. "No, you two should go enjoy yourselves. I only have a limited time for lunch. I'm grabbing a sub before heading back to work." His grin widened as Margie ducked to put her purse in the car.

Gabriel rolled his eyes and gave a slight shake of his head. They shared the age-old silent communication of two men marveling over one woman's cluelessness.

Once they were on their way, Gabriel addressed his most pressing issue. "Care to explain to me why you keep inviting other men to join us?"

At her horrified gasp, he shot her a sideways glance.

"With such a big family, we are always doing things like that," she said.

The apology was heavy in her voice, and tension eased from Gabriel's shoulders. A distinct relief filled him because it seemed her actions were ingrained and not any desire to avoid time alone with him. "Do you go on James's dates?"

"*God, no!* I wouldn't dream of—oh, I see what you mean." She smothered a laugh. "I'm sorry."

"For the record, if I was interested in taking out a group of people, I'd invite them. But right now, I'm only interested in spending time with you."

The cute way she bit her lip and peered at him from beneath her lashes turned him on. What the hell was it about her? The most innocent gestures made him mad with desire. In his need to touch her, he shifted to his right and reached for her hand.

Once they reached the beach, they laid out the blanket, and Gabriel positioned the cooler to secure it. After the food was spread out, they took their time sampling the assortment of dishes.

"I think I like the macaroni salad the best."

"Mmm, no. It's the chicken, hands down."

She laughed and dug a fork into the container. "Spoken like a true protein-obsessed male."

Before long, their meal was complete, and bellies full, they sprawled side by side. The salty sea air and repetitive crash of the waves lulled them, dispersing any remaining tension.

Gabriel rested on his right side, his head in his hand, and gazed down at Margaret's flushed face. He could spend every day this way. "True confession time."

"Oh? What exactly does that entail?" she asked, a slight, curious smile in place.

"I want to know why you were avoiding me."

Her smile turned to a grimace. "Truthfully? I don't know if I want the complication of dating you."

"Why does it have to be complicated?"

In an abrupt, jerky movement, she sat up. Gabriel stayed in place, although his casual air was all a ruse. Inside, his heart had kicked up its pace. He hoped "complicated" wasn't as dire as it sounded.

"Are you even looking for a relationship, Gabriel?"

Trust her to dig right to the meat of the matter.

"I don't know. I only know I like you and want to spend time with you."

"And sex?"

"*Hell yes!* That, too. But I won't pressure you if it's not what you want."

She nodded as if she already suspected his answer.

"Is that a bad thing, Margaret?"

"It's not."

She stared out over the horizon, and Gabriel gave her time to formulate what she wanted to say.

"You aren't getting a spring chicken. I'm close to forty, with a ton of scars and stretch marks. I can't compete with the beautiful women you must attract." The worried look she gave him was bothersome. "And I've got children."

"Margaret, listen to me. I like your kids. And I couldn't give two shits if you were forty or fifty, because you're beautiful. Sexy as hell to boot. Who I do or don't attract has no bearing on you and me. What matters is, while we're exploring whatever this is between us, I'm not receptive to any other woman."

Her troubled expression didn't ease. "We are from two different worlds. You're a high-powered attorney, and I suspect a brilliant one at that. I'm an ex-housewife and single mom with nothing beyond a high school diploma and a box of paintbrushes."

"It doesn't bother me."

"It bothers *me*. I'd be an embarrassment to you in your social circles."

"We're getting ahead of ourselves. First and foremost, let's take the time to get to know one another. After that, we can explore this off-the-charts sexual chemistry between us. Anything else, we can take from there."

"I don't think this is a good idea." She turned regretful blue eyes upon him.

He sat up and bracketed her between his raised legs. "Then don't think. *Feel.*" He kissed her. She tasted of spices mixed with pure Margaret. A heady combination. And although he had the hardest time remembering they were in a public place, he halted their necking at a PG-rating. "I don't know what it is about you, but I've never been so obsessed so quickly."

A frown tugged at her brow. "Do you become obsessed often?"

"No. Poor choice of words. I should've said, I've never been obsessed in my life. *Not until you.* You're all I've thought about since the first moment I saw you."

She traced the outline of his upper lip, and he felt it down to his groin. He wanted nothing more than to tumble her onto the blanket for a make-out session, but the curious glances from the other beach-goers were becoming more frequent due to their close proximity.

Gabriel eased back and busied himself with putting the food in the cooler. Once he was done and his erection was down to a more manageable, less embarrassing state, he stood and offered a hand. "Shall we take a walk?"

"I'd love that." Margaret rose gracefully to her feet.

Hand in hand, they strolled along the water's edge. Periodically, she would stop and pick up a shell to admire before putting it back.

"Why don't you keep them?"

"Because they are beautiful right here, where they belong. They'd lose their appeal if they were cluttering up my house and I had to dust around them all the time."

"You have a unique way of looking at life." Gabriel raised their joined hands and kissed her knuckles. Looking out over the water, he saw a fin, and an idea formed. He knew the perfect way to extend their date. Something that would appeal directly to Margaret. "What time do I have to have you home?"

"Why? Are you planning to abduct me?" she teased.

"You are playing with fire, Margaret. I'm barely containing myself."

Her deep, throaty laugh hit him swift and hard. "I bet you say that to all the girls."

"Only to dark-haired beauties with large, sparkling blue eyes and a curvy body designed to make a man weep."

"Ah, so you have a type."

"Nope. That was strictly directed at you." He steered her back the way they'd come. "So? Do you have the afternoon free?"

"I could call my mother to see if she'd pick up the boys. Kaley has soccer practice after school."

"Is that a yes?"

"Yes."

Satisfaction curled within him. "Good."

"Do I get to know what you have planned?"

"Nope. Not until we get there."

"Now you're making me nervous, Gabriel."

"Come on. Last one back to the blanket has to pay a forfeit."

Margaret stunned him when she hooked a leg behind his and shoved him down in the sand. As he regained his feet, he judged the distance he needed to make up. With a grin, he charged full-steam ahead. Just before she reached the blanket, he cut her off, scooped her over his shoulder, and headed for the water.

"Gabriel James, if you throw me in the water, I'll never speak to you again!" She pounded his back to emphasize her point.

"Now I see where Kaley gets her temper."

"Bite me!"

He let loose a low growl. "Margaret, I thought we talked about you throwing out statements that challenge me to take you up on your offer." He turned his head enough to nip her left butt cheek.

Her screech almost deafened him as her hands flew to her bottom. They were a foot away from the water, and he shifted to cradle her in his arms. "To dump you or not to dump you, that is the question."

"Don't even think about it."

"Hmm, I'm thinking we need to cool off that temper of yours."

"Gabriel, I'm—"

He silenced her with a bold kiss. When they parted, her eyes were soft and dewy.

"Now there are other things to cool off," he told her.

She giggled and wound her arms around his neck. "You weren't really going to throw me in, were you?"

"I did think about it."

"And?"

"I didn't want to ruin any chance of getting lucky later."

"Who said you were going to get lucky?"

"In that case..." He pretended he was going to toss her in.

She laughed and clung to him. "Okay! Okay! You can get lucky."

He chuckled as he carried her back to the blanket. "I was hoping you'd say that."

"But not today."

With an abrupt about-face, Gabriel headed toward the water.

"*Okay!* A *little* lucky today."

"I'm not sure what a little lucky is, but I'll take it."

MARGIE HAD NEVER HAD A MORE ENJOYABLE DAY. AFTER THEIR BEACH picnic, Gabriel took her to Marineland, where his friend Paul happened to be on staff. She got an up-close view of what went on behind the scenes and how the employees and volunteers worked tirelessly to care for injured sea creatures.

"A baby dolphin!" Her insides went to mush when she saw the little one in the pool behind the main headquarters. "Why is it back here without its mama?"

"We found her stranded on the beach. She'd ingested plastic." Paul dipped an arm in the water and caressed the calf as she bumped her rostrum into his hand. "We've been able to remove it, but now it's a matter of tube-feeding her, providing antibiotics, and getting her stronger with the proper nutrients."

Her heart ached for the missing mother of the dolphin. What must it be like for your sweet baby to disappear? She wanted to gather the calf up to care for her until the poor thing was stronger and ready to swim away. "Will she be able to be released back in the wild?"

"She's too young to be on her own. Without knowing where her pod is, it's doubtful."

"Does this happen a lot?"

"Enough," Paul confirmed. "People insist on plastic everything: bags, bottles, Mylar balloons." He shrugged off his apparent anger. Giving one last rub to the calf's pectoral fin, he nodded to a large pool by the fence. "We're rehabbing a sea turtle if you want to see it."

Margie couldn't believe its size. "It's huge!"

Gabriel laughed as Paul concurred.

"Would you like to see the reptile building?"

She shuddered. The idea of snakes didn't appeal to her in any way, shape, or form. "Nope."

Gabriel sidled close and stirred the hairs on her neck when he murmured, "Chicken."

"I'm not ashamed to admit it."

"I'll protect you," he promised with a grin.

"Nope. Still going to be a hard pass."

He laughed and shifted to converse with Paul as Margie crossed to the pool with the baby dolphin. As the calf grinned and clicked in greeting, she smiled. She'd have to ask Paul what the minimum age requirement was for their volunteer program. Without a doubt, her children would love interacting with the sea creatures. Gabriel had given her a beautiful gift today, and he probably had no idea he'd done it.

A short while later, Gabriel and Margie were back in his Lexus and headed south on A1A.

"That was a nice surprise. I appreciate it."

"My pleasure, Margaret."

He reached across the console to clasp her hand.

Margie found it tough to recall a more perfect moment. She studied his profile as he drove, and he cast her a curious, smiling glance. There was a rightness to being here with him. Gabriel had an easygoing way about him that fit with her desire to be drama free. He didn't argue or make her feel uncomfortable. He just was.

"You're a nice man."

"Uh-oh. That sounds like you're ready to shove me in the friend zone."

She released a soft laugh. That was the beauty of being in his presence; he made her feel light and happy. He always had. "I can't imagine us not being friends. But I meant, I like you. You're easy to be with."

"I like you, too, Margaret." He grinned, and it lit something within her.

"In the spirit of honesty, it's been a long time since I've been with anyone."

"Dating or sex?"

"Both."

He nodded, not taking his eyes from the road, but his fingers tightened around hers. "We can take it as fast or as slow as you wish. And although I'm finding myself worse than a horny teenager around you, I'm not going to ask for more than you're willing to give."

"Are you real?"

His deep chuckle reached in and stroked her lady bits. Once again, she wondered if she was being ridiculous to apply the brakes on their romance. The rest of the way home, they made small talk. Each asked questions about the other, and Margie thoroughly enjoyed this getting-to-know-you stage.

Gabriel stopped his car a few feet from her place. "Do you still have time before the kids are home?"

"I do."

"Good."

He whipped into his driveway and pulled into his garage. Inside the house, he gave her the grand tour.

She shook her head as she looked around. "It's hard to believe this was once Opal's house. Everything is so drastically different with a little paint and new furniture."

"Yes."

The sadness in his voice was something she understood. "She was like a mother to you, wasn't she?"

"She was."

Not surprising. In their previous incarnations, Opal actually *had* been his mother.

"She loved you. All she could talk about was Gabriel this or

Greyson and Gordon that. She was so proud of all you boys. That's how she referred to you, as boys."

"Thank you. Sometimes it's hard to believe she's gone. She was larger than life." He smiled even as he cleared his throat.

"I know. I completely adored her." Margaret followed him to the kitchen where he removed two wineglasses and a chilled bottle of vino. "She and I would sit on her front porch nearly every morning, enjoying a cup of coffee while we waited for the kids to catch the bus. It was the best part of my day."

"That's a great memory."

"I miss her."

"Me, too." He raised his glass in a toast. "To Opal. May she terrorize the angels in the afterlife."

Margie could imagine her doing exactly that. She sipped her wine around a soft smile.

"She was a character." Gabriel continued. He was about to take another sip when he remembered something. "Wait! You were serious when you told Don she'd been trying to set us up. You're the neighbor she talked so much about."

"Yep. I can't tell you how many times she tried."

"I wonder why it never worked."

A single glance showed he was serious. "Would you have *wanted* to be set up?"

"If I'd have known it was you? Most definitely."

Unable to withstand the heat in his gaze without doing something drastically out of character, Margie took stock of her surroundings. When her eyes fell on the wall clock, she gasped. "Crap! I have to go. Kaley will be home any minute."

"She's a big girl, Margaret."

"I know. But since the incident, she's a little freaked to be home alone. Plus the new alarm, remember?"

"Right. How about I walk you back, and we can both be there to greet her?"

"I..." How could she tell him she needed time to process the emotions he stirred in her?

"Unless you've had enough of me for one day."

Margie detected a vulnerability he failed to hide. What would a man who looked like an Adonis have to be insecure about? Any woman, her included, would trade their soul for a chance to have someone as gorgeous, generous, and caring as Gabriel interested in them. Again, she wondered why she was fighting against their attraction this time around when all she wanted to do was dive into his embrace and take all he had to offer.

"No, I haven't had enough." The breathiness in her voice betrayed her thoughts.

His smile started slowly and spread until his whole face was lit with wicked delight and a promise of passion. "That's precisely what I was hoping you'd say."

Before she could blink, he'd removed the glass from her hand and set it on the granite counter. One muscled forearm wrapped around her lower back and urged her closer. He toyed with the dark wisps of hair curling across her cheek and tucked a strand behind her ear. His fingers were as light as air as he traced the outer shell. When he skimmed his fingertips along her jaw, Margie was a goner.

All light was blocked by his large frame as he leaned in. The subtle taste of red wine on his tongue was like an aphrodisiac, and Margie moaned when he deepened the kiss. One second she was standing, his arms wrapped around her, full chest to chest, and the next she was sitting on his counter with him nestled between her thighs. Their contact had become groin on groin, and his erection could be felt along the most sensitive area of her body. Without thinking about her actions, she shifted her hips to rub against him. His deep groan made her deep-down happy. She, middle-aged Margie Holt, evoked such an ardent response from a man who was off-the-charts sexy, and it tickled the hell out of her.

"Gabriel." With great reluctance, she whispered, "I have to go."

He rested his forehead against hers and struggled to regulate his breathing. "Yeah, I know. But before we leave this kitchen, I need to know when I can see you again."

"You aren't going to want to hear this, but I have to check the family calendar."

His second groan was pure frustration.

"The pitfalls of hooking up with a single mom," she teased. And while she would never wish her children away, she did wish she had more freedom to be carefree and spontaneous.

"I'll take what I can get and be happy for it," he assured her. "Come on. I'll walk you home."

CHAPTER 12

The next weeks, Margie and Gabriel stole moments when they could. Between his heavy caseload and Margie's kids' after-school activities, their meetings were few and far between. Each time they were together, they left each other more frustrated than the last.

Still, she hadn't told anyone about their relationship, preferring to savor the newness and the clandestine feel of it all for a while longer. Wasn't it exciting to have a secret this scrumptious?

October morphed into November, with the Thanksgiving holiday less than a week away and fast approaching. The two of them chiseled out coffee time every Friday morning before Gabriel left to spend his time at the Big Brother program or with a pro bono client.

Margie strongly suspected he wanted to provide a new morning memory for her to look forward to since he understood how much her mornings with Opal had meant to her.

"What are your plans for Thanksgiving?" She returned Kaley's wave, feeling a little melancholy to see her daughter climb into the truck, beside her boyfriend, Dalton. But Margie recognized her need for some freedom.

"Grey, Gordie, and I used to spend it with Opal. We don't have any plans this year other than to get together to watch the game."

"I never asked, but are they in relationships?"

"No. I think we were all tainted by the same dysfunctional-family brush when we were growing up."

Because she knew a little of his backstory from Opal, she'd never pushed Gabriel for information about his childhood. Margie sipped her coffee and wondered how to question him without seeming to pry.

Gabriel rose and perched a hip against the porch railing. "You should just ask, Margaret."

Whenever he said her full name in that warm, resonating way, she felt it down to her toes. She sighed and lassoed her courage. "Have all of you sworn off marriage?"

He frowned down into his coffee. "Not intentionally, I don't suppose. But it's possible Grey and Gordie have a subconscious wish to avoid commitment. Perhaps I do, too, after Tamara." His troubled eyes watched her carefully. "Is that a deal breaker?"

"We'd have to have a deal to break."

Margie hadn't meant to sound snarky, but he laughed all the same.

"When are you going to put me out of my misery and sleep with me, Margaret?"

She wanted to jump up and drag him to the bedroom when he employed his raspy growl. Instead, she shrugged and finished her drink. She handed him the mug and dropped a kiss on his cheek.

"Thanks for the coffee, Gabriel."

"Is that all I get by way of a morning kiss?"

"The neighbors are watching," she chided.

He snorted and tossed the remains of his cup into the bushes. Once he placed both mugs on the rail, he tugged her between his outstretched legs. Drawn to the way he played with her hands and placed his large palm flat against hers, she didn't pull away when he intertwined his fingers with hers. After a short pause, he said, "Like I care."

"You don't, but maybe I do."

Ever so gently, he twisted her arms to rest behind her back, their hands still connected. The gesture pushed out her chest and gained his undivided attention. She bit her lip to contain a laugh when he heaved an appreciative sigh and lifted his scintillating gaze from her girls. "One day soon, Margaret, you're going to have to put out. You can't keep teasing me."

She did laugh then. "You tease yourself, Gabriel." Shifting closer, she nudged his jaw with the tip of her nose.

"True," he agreed. "Now kiss me like you mean it."

Margie raised up on tiptoes and fastened her mouth to his. After three long, mind-drugging kisses that left them feverish and bothered, she drew away. "You have to go do your pro bono work."

"I could blow it off today if you'll swear to be my sexual plaything."

"Not going to happen. I have goods to whip up for the bake sale this weekend."

"I could come sample your goods."

The dirty connotation had her woman parts heating up and her longing to say yes. Margie wanted nothing more than to make love with Gabriel. Her only hang-up? Her mom bod. After children, her stomach and hips boasted extra weight along with some loose skin no amount of crunches could tighten.

"You've sampled all the goods you're going to get today." She drew back.

"For the record, I've got the worst case of blue balls in the history of mankind."

"Should I feel sorry for you and give in?"

"Hell, yes! How about right now?"

Before she could say yay or nay, he straightened and grabbed her hand, dragging her toward the front door.

"Mom! Mom!"

Gabriel sighed heavily. "Don't take this the wrong way, but sometimes I despise your children."

"No offense taken." She giggled and lightly squeezed his fingers.

Margie jogged down the steps to where her sons waited on the sidewalk. Pausing midway, she glanced back over her shoulder and flushed to see Gabriel's eyes zeroed in on her ass. Her hands dropped down to hide her butt from his view, and she twisted to walk backwards.

His sinful grin flashed, and she was sure her skin darkened three shades.

"Let me know if you and your brothers want to join the family for Thanksgiving dinner at my parents'. Mom would love it if you showed."

Without saying a word, he rested a shoulder against the pillar of his porch and crossed his arms over his chest. His eyes dropped pointedly to her mouth. When she thought he wouldn't respond, he called out, "Will you bake me a pie, Margaret? My favorite is cherry."

"For you, Gabriel James, I'd bake five pies."

"Ah, you do know how to tease a man, love."

GABRIEL WATCHED MARGARET HERD HER BOYS TOWARD THE BUS STOP. On the way, she checked their breath and their backpacks. Her morning routine was always the same, and the sight made him smile.

He'd never fully cop to it, but he enjoyed their little mating dance. He'd be lying if he said he hadn't hoped to be in her bed by now, but he also understood her issues. She'd stated her objections the first day they went out to lunch, and he suspected they hadn't lessened any, if at all. As he'd promised her then, he wouldn't push. Okay, he wouldn't push *much*. But teasing her was fun as hell.

She'd told him she'd be baking today, and he imagined her in nothing but an apron as she danced about her kitchen. All her woman parts would jiggle in time to her movements. If he were there with her, he'd eat small brownie bites off her stomach while he worked his way up to taste her delicious breasts. His mouth watered at his own fantasy.

With a hard shake of his head, he glanced around. She was already gone, and he grinned at how easily he added to his sexual frustration. What would she do if he showed up in only an apron of his own to help her? He snorted. She'd probably claim he was being unsanitary. A deep sigh of regret escaped him, and he went inside.

As he was cleaning the morning dishes, his phone dinged. The image on the screen brought a wide smile to his mouth. Margie had a bowl of brownie batter on the counter in front of her while she stood with her index finger between her lips as if to sample the batter—or something else.

The little tease.

He typed his reply.

"I've got a better idea for that mouth than the batter! I'll be over in two minutes."

She returned a laughing emoji and the words, *"go to work."*

"Fine, but you'd better bake me my promised pie."

Her reply was immediate.

"Done. Come collect for dinner tonight."

What did she mean by the invite? Was it to be just the two of them? God, he hoped so.

"What time? And should I be wearing pants?"

Again, she sent a laughing emoji, but this time with tears streaming from its eyes.

"Six-thirty. Yes to pants unless you want to shock my children and take the chance of being reported to child services."

Gabriel found himself laughing at the silliness of their conversation. With no one else would he ever be so frivolous and unguarded. Yet with Margaret, he was able to shed the carefully constructed persona he presented the outside world and become his true self.

DON ACKER WATCHED AS MARGIE LAUGHED AND TEXTED. WATCHED as she struck a sexy pose with the batter on her finger. Watched as she blushed and went about her morning, preparing to bake. He also divided his time with another monitor. The one where Gabriel James laughed and texted Margie in return as he prepared for his day.

Fury exploded like a grenade inside his brain. Don reached for the only thing capable of calming him—the bra he'd pocketed from Margie's hamper the month before. He'd been careful not to touch it too much because he didn't wish to ruin the scent. The hints of vanilla and citrus were all Margie. But today, he buried his face in the V of the material and pretended it was the valley of her D-cup breasts. Imagined he ran his fingers over their dusky red tips and pinched her nipples until they grew hard for him and him alone.

Tomorrow, she would leave to take her little brats to the school bake sale. He had no doubt Margie's troublemaker daughter would disappear with her boyfriend for the day. That would leave plenty of time for Don to go through Margie's room. Time for him to touch her things and take pictures. He needed to have everything perfect for her, and he couldn't be caught unaware again. He'd narrowly escaped the day Kaley was supposed to be at her father's.

Gingerly replacing the bra on its satin pillow, Don turned to watch the monitors again. Gabriel was backing out of the garage, so he paid him no mind, choosing to focus on Margie.

While she measured ingredients, Don rewound the video of her morning meeting with Gabriel. He noted the way the other man attempted to pull her close. Studied how she laughingly resisted at first but then gave in. Don practiced the move until he was sure he had it correct. With a few clicks of his mouse, he cropped that particular section of video and added it to the movie loop he was in the process of creating. When the time was right, he would show her exactly how skilled he was at seduction. She'd never look at Gabriel again.

CHAPTER 13

"Hey, neighbor. I've come for some sugar." Gabriel's voice called through her screen enclosure.

Margie let out a gasp of fright. She'd been lost in the past, not expecting to see him tonight.

With one hand in his pocket and the other holding up an empty measuring cup, he seemed genuine. Yet even in the darkness, she could see the gleam of mischievous intent lighting his eyes.

"What the hell are you doing here so late?"

He shrugged. "I saw your pool light on and thought I'd take a chance."

"Hmm, and what if I don't happen to have any sugar to spare?" Margie set down her glass of wine and meandered to the screen door.

"Ah, Margaret. Would you deny a man sustenance?"

"Sugar isn't sustenance, nor is it a necessity, Gabriel. You're trying to find any excuse to make out."

"And is it working?" His grin brightened the night sky.

Boy, was it ever!

After she unlatched the lock, she went straight to the cabinet containing the sugar. She spun back to ask him how much he needed, but he was already on her heels and crowded her against the counter. Both of his arms bracketed her to lock her in place.

"Did you really think I wouldn't make a trip to the store if I needed something?" He nibbled the sensitive place behind her ear.

"I *knew* it was all a ruse," she said with a breathless laugh.

"I've decided to give you one last chance to cave before I steal you away and hold you hostage."

"Hostage?" His idea had merit, and Margie was all for a getaway with just the two of them. She'd already decided it was past time for her to get over her objections.

"Yes, I'll make love to you night and day."

Gabriel's lips trailed the column of her throat to the V of her neckline, and his fingers toyed with the mother-of-pearl button at the top of her sweater.

Getting into their game, she felt under his sweatshirt and traced the hard ridges of his abs. "Mmm, for how long?"

"At least a month. I'm sure it would take me that long to satisfy my voracious appetite."

She narrowed her eyes and pressed a hand to his chest. "Only a month?"

"Okay, two months. But I need to sleep every third or fourth day for a few hours."

Margie pretended to think about it before she leaned forward and gave him a love bite on his chin. "Deal."

It was Gabriel's turn to pause their game. "Did you just agree to have sex with me?"

"I agreed to be abducted by you. You'll have to make sure you have a babysitter lined up for the kids."

He gripped her hips and hauled her close. "Not a problem. My brothers owe me." The second he registered the lack of noise in the house, he reared up from kissing her. "Wait a minute! Where is everyone? Are we going to be interrupted by Kaley or the boys at any second?"

"The boys are at their friends' houses, and Kaley is staying at my mother's. She's going to help with early prep for the Thanksgiving feast."

"Are you saying we're all alone? Please tell me we are."

"We are."

"Oh, thank God!"

At that precise moment, the house telephone rang.

"Don't answer it," he whispered, nuzzling her earlobe. "They'll leave a message."

"You're a terrible influence," she admonished with a throaty laugh. She'd half a mind to listen to him, but motherhood came with constant interruptions. "But I should get it. What if it's one of the children?"

The ringing stopped, and the answering machine kicked on. "Margie, it's Mom. Pick up!"

Gabriel and Margie froze as the panic in her mother's voice came through the line.

"Margie? Are you there? I need you to pick up."

She ran for the receiver. "Mom? What's going on?"

"Turn on the news."

"What channel?"

"It doesn't matter."

"You're scaring me, Mom. What's going on?"

"I think... Michael's plane..."

When Violet started to cry, Margie rushed to the family room and hit the remote. The video was from a news helicopter's perspective. A plane was three quarters of the way submerged in the ocean. Searchlights veered left and right. Front to back.

"Fire rages out of control as Coast Guard workers and divers struggle to locate any survivors. The cause of the crash has been undetermined. Search and rescue is on scene..."

Margie sat on the edge of the sofa and cried, *"Ohmygod!* Mom, was that Michael's? Ohmygod!"

Gabriel removed the phone from her death grip. From a great distance, she heard him ask, "Violet? Is there another adult there with you?" Her mother must have responded in the affirmative because his next questions were about Sammy's welfare. Margie half listened as she stared at the carnage on the television.

Shock held her immobile. Michael had been a major part of their lives for the last ten years. She couldn't imagine a world without him in it. Kaley, Scotty, and Aaron all adored him, and she knew how devastated they would be if Michael had truly been on that plane.

She belatedly noted Gabriel had hung up the phone and sat next to her, one hand on her back, watching her with concern. Shakily, she rose to her feet. "My boys. I have to pick up Scotty and Aaron from their friends' houses. I want them close until we know for certain."

"You're in no condition to drive, love. I'll take you."

Tears blurred her vision and raced down her cheeks. "Oh, Gabriel. He was supposed to fly home tonight. I don't know what Sammy is going to do without him if..." She sucked in a deep breath in an attempt to control her hysteria. "Michael's her rock. Her everything," she whispered.

Gabriel rose and gathered her close, tucking her against his heart. "It's going to be all right. Anything could've happened. Maybe he missed his flight. Your mom might have the wrong information. *Anything.* You have to wait until your sister can confirm it either way."

With a shake of her head, she said, "No. Mom told me Sammy was having nightmares. They're like the family's early warning system when something bad is going to happen."

"Let's go get the boys and wait for more news. You lock the back door and set the alarm. Don't forget your cell phone so we can call ahead. I'm sure their friends' parents don't need the fright of a late-night visit. I'll go get the Suburban started."

He had almost reached the door to the garage when she called out. "Gabriel!" He turned, and her heart stuttered to see him so solemn and concerned for her welfare. "Thank you."

His soft smile, full of warmth and caring, melted the last of her resistance. She flew into his embrace and clung to him for all she was worth. The corded muscles of his arms held her tightly to his solid frame as she sought solace, knowing there was nowhere else on earth she'd rather be at that moment. She loved him, and she was tired of fighting it. She'd always loved him and most likely always would.

"Come on. Let's go get Scotty and Aaron," he urged.

ALONG THE WAY, MARGARET RECEIVED CONFIRMATION THE FLIGHT was indeed the one Michael had booked. Gabriel pulled her vehicle off the road to give her time to compose herself before she had to face her children. Moving to her side of the Suburban, he cradled her as she wept for their lost family member.

When they arrived at the first house, he listened as she gently explained to Scotty why she'd come. The boy resembled his mother a great deal. The chin went up, and although Scotty's eyes were brimming with unshed tears, he put on a brave face. More than once, Gabriel had seen Margaret react with the same defiant tilt of her chin. Even hurting, this family would take on the world.

Next, they retrieved Aaron. His reaction was similar to Scotty's, but his voice wobbled as he struggled to make sense of what they tried to tell him. "Uncle Michael?"

Margaret squatted in front of him and straightened the line of his little shirt. "Yes, baby. We believe Uncle Michael was in an accident."

Gabriel's heart shifted in his chest at seeing her love for her son. For himself, he didn't remember much about his mother. She'd died shortly after Grey was born. As for his father, there had been no affection there. Only rules and beatings. Opal had been the one bright spot in the lives of his brothers and him.

From the corner of his eye, Gabriel saw Scotty had inched closer to his side, and the thought flitted through his mind that perhaps the boy needed contact. He placed his arm around Scotty's thin shoulders and gave a light squeeze. Once again, the boy's chin came up as he struggled to remain strong. Gabriel had been there himself once upon a time—the older sibling trying to be the man of the family.

"Come on, son. Let's head outside."

Scotty's reaction was immediate and fierce. "I'm not your son! *And you're not my dad!*"

"*Scotty!*" Margaret's sharp voice whipped out. "Apologize to Gabriel at once."

"No." Gabriel held up his hand with a severe look at her. Scotty's reaction was understandable, and he shouldn't be reprimanded for being honest. "There's no need. Emotions are high right now."

But she glared at her son, and the boy caved. "I'm sorry, sir."

"I appreciate the apology, Scott. No harm done. Let's get you all home, okay?"

The boys piled into the vehicle as Margaret made her apologies to the parents of Aaron's friend. When she joined them, Gabriel asked, "Your house or your mother's?"

"I don't want to take any more of your time tonight. I..."

He patiently waited for her to continue, but she'd run out of steam. "Margaret, look at me." She raised tear-filled eyes. "I'm not going anywhere. Not until you're okay to be alone. And even then, it goes against my better nature."

One solitary teardrop fell, directly at odds with the smile she sent him. He'd never seen a more tragically beautiful sight. He cupped her face and brushed a thumb across her cheek.

I love her.

Feeling pole-axed by the thought, he gave a small shake of his head. Their mutual attraction had been there from the start, but at some point in the last weeks, his simple want had morphed into full-blown love. Without question, he wanted to spend the rest of his life with this woman.

"Will you take us home, Gabriel?"

A nod was all he could muster as the waves of realization tried to paralyze him.

When they arrived at the house, they answered questions from her sons as best they could, but there were no answers to be had at the moment. Emotionally wrung out and exhausted, Margaret shuffled her boys off to bed.

Gabriel hovered in the doorway as she tucked each one in. With great care, she folded the coverlet over, approximately eight inches from the top. Next came the sheet, over the covers. He smiled at the quirky ways her compulsive disorder became apparent.

As Margaret closed their bedroom door, she asked, "Would you like some coffee?"

The dark circles under her eyes highlighted her fatigue. "No. Come on, Margaret. It's time for you to be in bed, too."

"I won't be able to sleep."

"Then I'll hold you, and you can talk if you need to or simply take any comfort you can. Come."

He led her to her pristine bedroom and watched her strip down. She didn't try to hide herself or turn her back to change, and he realized, for once, she wasn't self-conscious about her body. Dressed in an over-large t-shirt and undies, she climbed beneath the covers.

As Gabriel kicked off his shoes and prepared to join her, Margaret gestured to his body. "You don't have to keep them on. I know it can't be comfortable to try to sleep fully clothed."

His heart nearly stopped. "You're okay with me staying the night?"

She folded back the corner of the blanket. An open invitation.

Gabriel lifted his sweatshirt over his head and shucked his jeans before climbing in beside her. When her bare leg settled between his thighs, he prayed for control. Tonight was *not* the night to put the moves on her. To keep his mind occupied and away from all things carnal in nature, he thought about old case files.

She rested her head on his chest and began to explore his exposed skin.

His muscles contracted under her swirling fingers.

Christ!

Was she even aware of the havoc she caused?

He forced himself to stop her hand from dipping lower.

"Margaret." His voice held a warning.

"I thought you wanted to."

"Believe me, I really do. That's not a banana pressing against your hip, love. But making decisions like this in an emotional state isn't wise."

She rose up on her knees and whipped her shirt over her head. With a mere flick of her wrist, she tossed it to the floor.

He held his breath, afraid to move for fear he'd fallen asleep and was now in the best dream of his life.

"I made the decision earlier when I first saw you at the screen door." She ran a hand along his chest and smiled sadly. "Tonight's taught me one thing—life is unpredictable and shorter than we know. I don't want to waste a minute of it." She worried her lip as she lifted her gaze to his. "If you want me, I'm yours."

Gabriel wasted no time in pulling her down atop him. "You have no idea how long I've waited to hear you say that," he growled and claimed her lips. Drawing back, he gazed into her wide blue eyes and looked for any hesitancy. Finding none, he kissed her again. She tasted like heaven. Or maybe his love for her made everything sweeter.

Her hand wandered the length of his back and slid under the waistband of his boxer-briefs. She explored the contour of his ass, and he silently congratulated himself for his dedication to squats when she sighed her pleasure. Continuing her journey, she caressed his hips, stroking the skin as if to memorize the texture. When she got to the front and gripped his dick, her eyes flew wide. She distanced herself slightly to look down between them.

"It's a good thing I've had children, or that thing would never fit."

Gabriel couldn't prevent his laughter. He couldn't recall a single time when he'd felt the desire to laugh as strongly as his urge to fuck. He simply stared down at her with all the tenderness he felt, laced with a heavy dose of amusement.

"Why did you stop, Gabriel?"

"I'm memorizing this moment in all its perfection."

A soft light entered her eyes, and she reached a hand to caress his jaw. "I'm all for taking time to smell the roses, but we've waited long enough. Also, we've a horrible tendency of getting interrupted."

Although he knew, he still asked, "What are you saying, Margaret?"

"I'm saying let's get this damned show on the road before all the entities who like to conspire against us catch on to what we're doing."

"I'm on it."

"You most certainly are."

Again, he laughed.

Sitting back on his heels, he looked his fill.

"If you're going to stare at me like that, I'm turning off the lights and lighting a candle."

"Now that would be a damned shame."

"No, I promise the soft light is more flattering."

If the words hadn't alerted him to her self-consciousness, the trepidation in her voice would've. Grasping her elbows, he helped her shift to a kneeling position so they faced each other. "I understand your reservations. I have from the beginning. But when a man is crazy about a woman, he doesn't see all the things you've built up in your mind, Margaret. He simply sees the person he wants to make love to." Wrapping one arm loosely around her waist, he trailed his fingertips along her jawline and down her neck until he reached her breast. Cupping its fullness, he smiled. "The person whose skin he wants to touch and whose nipples he's dying to latch onto." His hand trailed lower. "And whose pus—"

She clamped a hand over his mouth. "I get it."

His grin came unbidden. She sounded so prim and proper, he couldn't help himself. Teasing Margaret had become his favorite pastime.

· · ·

MARGIE WASN'T AS UPTIGHT AS GABRIEL LIKED TO BELIEVE. SHE'D already envisioned this moment. Hell, she'd done more than fantasize in the privacy of her bedroom. It warmed her to know he cared enough to reassure her, but it was difficult not to feel unworthy in the presence of a man so freaking spectacular.

Speaking of gorgeous...

Her eyes devoured his beautifully sculpted chest, and she let her hands wander over his golden skin.

"Focus, Margaret." Laughter was evident just beneath the surface.

She exhaled a sigh of regret. "Sorry. Other than your brother's, this is the first playgirl-worthy chest I've seen in a long while."

A black scowl hijacked his features, and he halted her exploration. *"My brother's?"*

Surprised and more than a little thrilled by his jealous reaction, she giggled. "Not in the way you think. Gordie was mowing your lawn one day. Sammy and I—were sneaking a peek. In my defense, I thought it was you at first. The two of you look a lot alike from a distance."

Mollified, he replaced her palms flat against his pecs. "You're forgiven. Carry on."

Margie smiled and patted his chest. "You're so magnanimous."

"Indeed."

That one word, spoken with the arrogance of a man who knew just how damned sexy he was, reminded her of his previous incarnations. Once, a few centuries ago, he'd been a poor farmer with only a small plot of rented land. Yet, even then, he'd been proud and displayed all the arrogance of the local land barons.

Leaning in, she licked the tight bud of his nipple. His hands came up, and he threaded his fingers through her hair, holding her in place. Another lick elicited his soft sigh. Latching on, as he'd claimed he wanted to do to her breast, she suckled his nipple.

"Mmm."

She grinned and rained light, clinging kisses along the plane of his abdomen, enjoying her effect on him. Although his fingers tightened in her hair, he didn't direct her lower. No, she went there all on her own. His hiss of pleasure was empowering, and she wrapped both hands around his engorged staff as she worked him with her mouth.

His breathing altered, telling her he was getting close. She didn't mind finishing him this way, but he had other ideas and eased her away.

"No, love. Not for our first time."

Their eyes met and held.

She wondered what hers said, because the fierce longing in his was her undoing. Cradling his face in her palms, she brought his head down to hers, kissing him like there was no tomorrow. As if this moment was all they'd ever have. Making love with Gabriel was the perfect affirmation of life when she needed it the most. And picking up on her need, he returned her passion with an urgency of his own.

His lips and hands seemed to be everywhere at once, but nothing felt rushed. He caressed her as if he'd done it a thousand times, finding all her erogenous zones without fail. Stimulating her and driving her into a frenzy over and over again.

"Now, Gabriel," she demanded. "I want you inside me, right now."

She felt his smile against her inner thigh. "I don't feel two orgasms are enough for you, love," he murmured right before he ran his tongue along her opening. He lifted his head to look at her, and the wickedness of his expression turned her insides to molten lava.

"Okay. But only one more then I'm going to—ah!" His mouth latched onto her again, and she came without delay. He crawled up her body, kissing and tasting as he went.

"You were saying?"

"I was?"

His sinful chuckle triggered a delicious full-body tremble.

"Oh, right. I was." She wrapped her hand around his hard length and glided the tip of his penis along her swollen, wet flesh. "I need you. Right now."

He stole her breath with his first thrust, and she expelled an unladylike grunt.

"Is that 'right now' enough for you?"

"Yep."

She had to give him credit for trying to hide his laughter at her chirped response, but he could've saved himself the effort. Gripping his hair, she turned her head slightly to whisper into the shell of his ear. "Fuck me like you mean it, Gabriel James."

All amusement vanished, and his body went tense at her command. He inched his head up, and the burning desire in his smoldering gaze made her wonder what she'd unleashed. Never breaking eye contact, he eased out only to thrust back, time and time again, with renewed vigor. His name danced upon her lips between cries and pants. And when she came for the final time, she buried her mouth against the hollow of his throat to deaden her scream. His muffled cry of release followed on the heels of hers.

Rolling to the side, he pulled her against him.

As Margie's breathing regulated, she listened to his heartbeat slowing. The calming sound made her happy in a way she never had been, and she had to admit her decision to make love with Gabriel had been a fantastic one. "I'm an idiot."

The hand stroking her hair stopped. "Why do you say that?"

"Because I held out so long."

His chuckle was deep and delicious. "The wait was worth it, love."

She sighed her contentment and snuggled closer.

CHAPTER 14

APRIL 1912 -

*L*ucy had her hand on the doorknob when a familiar girly giggle resounded from the other side of the door. Her heart plummeted to somewhere below her kneecaps. Shoving the door open, she was greeted by her sister lounging across Andrew's lap.

Shocked senseless, Lucy forgot her standard decorum. "What the hell is going on here?"

Rosie jumped up and yanked her gown up to cover her breasts. Andrew followed suit with his own clothing, with the added bonus of whipping a frilly pillow in front of his man parts.

Too late. Lucy had already caught a glimpse of the epic erection he was sporting. It wasn't a sight she cared to see. "Rosie, how coul—"

The ship pitched, sending her sailing across the room.

Her hip impacted with a dressing table and knocked her to the ground.

Rosalie and Andrew fared no better.

The flickering lights gave Lucy another fearful jolt.

When they were all back on their feet, they shared a concerned look.

The very real fear Sebastian might be lost in the bowels of the ship when the darkness descended, sent Lucy's panic spiraling out of control.

"The ship is sinking, and you two have been in here? Doing this?" she asked, clear censure in her tone.

Their half-hearted protests died on their lips as, once again, the ship rocked, bringing with it a loud groan.

The building terror tried its best to paralyze her, but Lucy wrestled it down to take charge of the situation. "Rosie, you must put on a vest and find a lifeboat. Grab your warmest coat and go. Now! Andrew, come with me."

She spun on her heel, ready to head back the way she had come—her urgency to find Sebastian and stop his needless search, utmost in her mind.

Andrew lunged forward and caught her arm in a tight hold. "Where do you think you are going?"

"I have to find Sebastian. He is still looking for Rosie. We thought... we..." The horror of the night sunk in, and the strength was sapped right out of her. "He went down to third class to look for her when we couldn't find her anywhere else. Andrew, you have to help me find him."

Andrew, gazing into her distraught face, looked pained but nodded. "I'll find him. In the meantime, you will accompany Rosalie to safety."

"But—"

"No argument, Lucy." Andrew's hard tone left no room for debate. "I will find him. But you must promise me you'll look after your own welfare and that of Rosie. I cannot be distracted by my worry for you both, and time is of the essence. Do you understand?"

"You'll find him?"

"You have my word," he assured her, expression solemn.

The firm resolve she saw in his face convinced her, and Lucy latched onto Rosalie's wrist to drag her from the room.

When the ship pitched for the third time, Andrew caught both women close to steady them. He bussed a kiss on Lucy's forehead and turned to gaze down into Rosie's frightened blue eyes. The brief thought struck Lucy that this was the only time she'd seen her sister without her usual laughing glow.

Andrew, obviously not caring his wife of less than a week bore witness to their passion, kissed Rosie for all he was worth. As if, knowing this might be the last time he saw her, he wanted to imprint on her memory.

Heat rose in Lucy's face, and she was certain a permanent blush would stain her cheeks.

He pulled back and trailed his thumb across Rosie's pouting lips. "I love you, my darling Rosie. Promise you'll do as your sister says."

Rosalie pulled him close for one last fierce hug. "I love you, Andrew."

He offered her a rakish grin as he took the life vest Lucy offered and buckled Rosie up. "I'll see you on the other side, darling."

THE CELLPHONE BESIDE MARGIE'S BED BUZZED, CHASING AWAY HER dream of the past. A glance at the clock showed five a.m., and she suppressed a groan. It seemed as if she'd just gotten to sleep.

In order not to disturb Gabriel, she rolled to her side and tried to shield the light from the screen as she conversed with Annie via text.

"Is Mom with her now?"

"No, Sammy insisted on being alone last night."

"Has anyone called Jamie? If anyone can reach her, it's him."

"I left him a message but haven't heard back yet."

"I'll get a shower now. I'll see if Gabriel can watch the boys."

"Mom will run Kaley over and pick you up."

"Thanks."

As quietly as she could, Margie eased back the comforter and climbed from the bed. She shut herself in the bathroom and flipped the light switch. Once she'd dialed the water temperature to scorching, she stepped underneath the spray and allowed the heat to soothe her aching muscles. The water poured over her and mingled with the tears of grief she could no longer hold back.

Michael.

Last night, Gabriel had been a perfect distraction.

Today, she was struck with the reality of their lost family member.

Michael had been like a brother to her. The one calm in their world. When the Holts' tempers were erupting, he played peacemaker, using a calm logic to soothe ruffled feathers. Now he was gone, and Margie didn't know how to handle the excess of emotion. Because she not only remembered past tragedies and all the feelings associated with them, but she had this one to contend with, too. This was another lifetime Michael and Sammy were destined for heartache.

The bathroom door closed, and Margie jerked her head up as Gabriel opened the glass enclosure to join her. He took one look at her tear-ravaged face and opened his arms.

Lost in his embrace, it seemed an eternity before her tears dried up. "It feels like I'm always thanking you." She placed a butterfly-soft kiss on his chest.

"No need." He touched his nose to hers before he kissed her temple. He tried to mask the concern in his gaze with teasing light. "You suck at stealth mode."

The words were meant to be playful and distracting, but all she could manage was a wobbly smile. Laughter would definitely be in short supply in the coming weeks now that Michael was gone. She shut off the water and grabbed a towel for each of them.

"I have a favor to ask."

"Is your favor to have me slip out the back so no one knows I was here?"

She couldn't fail to note the ire in his tone. Seemed like he, too, was feeling the strain of the situation. "No, Gabriel. I would never do that to you. Granted, I don't want to confuse the children until we decide where this is going, but I don't care if the whole world knows you stayed last night." She patted his chest. "My favor is to ask if you could keep an eye on Kaley and the boys for a while. We're going to head over to Sammy's this morning."

"Of course. Any special diets, medication, or such that I should be aware of?"

"No. Today they can eat what they want. But don't let them run you ragged. I'll be home or send someone to relieve you as soon as possible."

GABRIEL SURFED THE INTERNET FOR NEWS WHILE KALEY SAT GLUED TO the television. He hoped like hell he was doing the right thing by allowing her to continue to watch for updates on the wreckage.

Grey had come over a few hours before, at Gabriel's urging, and was helping entertain Scotty and Aaron.

When Margaret returned, her upset was immediately obvious though she attempted to hide it for her children's benefit.

Gabriel hung back as she hugged each tightly in turn.

Her clinginess was easy to understand. Losing a family member made you hold tighter to those left behind.

He led her into the kitchen, out of sight of the children, and gathered her close. "How's your sister?"

"Not good. She's refusing to acknowledge he's gone. Insisted he wasn't on the plane and we'd see when he came home. She's so angry, Gabriel, and I don't blame her."

"Do you think she could be right? Maybe Michael wasn't on the plane?"

"Anything is possible, I suppose."

Margie looked so worn out his heart ached for her.

"Why don't you have a seat and tell me what happened?" He began the preparations for her favorite mint tea.

"Sammy told Mom about a dream she had a few days back. One of Michael boarding his flight and the plane going down." She compressed her lips and shook her head. When she could speak again, she said, "The second half of the dream was one of Michael missing his flight due to a mugger and chasing him into traffic. Like an alternative version of the same nightmare." Margie accepted the mug he offered with a grateful smile. "Thanks."

"No need to thank me, love." He smoothed back an unruly strand of her hair. "Go on."

"I don't get it, Gabriel. If any of this is true, the outcome is bleak. Dying in a plane crash or being hit by a car. Pick your poison." She hiccuped a sob. "But if he's alive, as Sammy insists she feels, why hasn't he called? He has to have seen the news, right?"

Gabriel had no answers. He'd never dealt with psychics or visions or woo-woo things that went bump in the night. "You can only be there to support her, Margaret. Try to be patient."

"God, you must think this family is a disaster."

"No. I think this family has had its share of hard times."

"Will you stay today and again tonight?"

He didn't want to reject her request, but she was dead on her feet. "I think you need rest."

She released a weary sigh. "I like the way you think, but I was only asking if you'd stay. I don't have the energy for anything else."

"I'm happy to be here for whatever you need." He glanced toward the living room. Now didn't seem like a good time, but he had to ask. "Do you want to inform the kids we're starting a relationship here, or do you want me to go and come back after they're asleep?"

He remained quiet as she gave serious consideration to his question.

Lifting his hand, she placed his palm against her cheek. Although thoroughly wrecked and exhausted, she looked lovely in the mid-morning light. Even packed with tragedy, the poignant scene made him want to freeze this moment with her forever.

"They like you, Gabriel, and you're good to my family. I'm cool with letting them know if you are. I don't want a deep discussion right now, but I don't want you to leave and come back either." She made a face. "If you're uncomfortable, you can head out in the morning before everyone gets up."

"We don't have to tell them anything until they ask." He pressed a tender kiss to her brow. "Go sit with them. Have you had anything to eat? I can whip something up."

"No. I'm not sure I can."

"Try, okay?"

She nodded and stretched to kiss him. The contact was lacking passion, but not warmth. It occurred to him that this was how a good marriage must feel. Comfortable. Loving. Not the toxic mess he'd been involved in.

His concerned gaze followed her from the room, and he lounged in the doorway as she settled between her boys.

The family grieved together, one solid unit. Yes, sadness hung in the air, but it didn't make their bond any weaker. The opposite was true. Their pain reinforced their relationship.

He'd never wanted to be part of a family more than right that second.

"You okay, bro? You look a bit shell-shocked yourself."

Gabriel hadn't heard Grey enter the kitchen and jumped in reaction. He turned so his back was to the living room and noted the worry on his brother's face. Grey's concern was well-founded. Gabriel's relationship with Margaret had been a whirlwind romance, and as it stood now, he was fully emerged in her family's problems.

"I think maybe I am. For multiple reasons."

Grey nodded grimly and squeezed his shoulder. "Whatever you need, I'm here for you."

"Thanks." Gabriel's mind shifted gears, and he cast a glance back at Margaret. "I somehow doubt the Holts are going to be up for a Thanksgiving celebration this year. If you and Gordie are willing, we can do a small get-together."

"The restaurant is open for the holiday, so we can eat there. We'll use the private dining room for just us. I'm happy to extend the invite to the Holts, but I don't want to be insensitive."

"I'll bring it up to Margaret later tonight. In the meantime, I need to run home to grab a change of clothes. Feel like hanging here for a few?"

"Sure. Go ahead."

"If she asks, tell her I'll make soup and sandwiches when I get back."

"I'll start them now. Go out through the garage. I doubt she'll miss you for the five minutes you're gone."

Gabriel cast one last long look into the living room.

Kaley was on the floor with her head on her mother's knee. Margaret watched him across the distance. Her drawn expression slayed him. Gazes locked, he kissed the tips of his fingers and placed them over his heart. Her lips moved in a semblance of a smile, but he hadn't chased the grief away. He didn't expect to.

Aaron demanded her attention, providing the perfect timing for Gabriel to slip away.

As he added items to a duffle bag, he wondered if he was pushing too hard, too fast. Was he being more of a nuisance than a help? Margaret was in no condition to deal with a new boyfriend on top of everything else.

Old demons woke to taunt him.

Twice he took his phone out to text he intended to stay home.

Twice he deleted the unsent message.

He scrubbed his face with his hands, unsure what to do.

He tried to tell himself she wouldn't have asked him to stay if she didn't want him there.

After all this time, he should've gotten over the fact his father hated him. Over the feeling he was unloveable. Over the fear no woman could truly care about him.

But he couldn't.

Yes, he exuded confidence in his everyday life—he refused to show anything less—but on occasion, the scared little boy residing inside him reared his head.

His phone buzzed with a text.

"Where you at, bro? That's the longest five minutes I've ever seen. Dinner's ready, and we have unexpected company."

Fuck it. He'd be there for Margaret come hell or high water, as long as she needed or wanted him. All other worries and fears could go hang.

Gabriel shot off a reply and grabbed his bag.

As he entered through the garage, the first thing he saw was Don attempting to hug a reluctant Margaret. Grey didn't look pleased, but he tended to be a little more diplomatic than Gabriel.

He dropped his bag with a loud thud, and all eyes turned to him. Don paled then flushed. The glare the other man shot Gabriel verged on loathing, and he'd been careful to turn away from Margaret so she didn't see.

But Gabriel did, and the ugliness inside Don was easily recognizable. His father had sported the same expression often enough— right before a fist found its way into his, Grey's, or Gordie's gut.

Margaret's relief was palpable as she rushed to his side. "You're back. Just in time for dinner." The brightness in her tone was patently false. Gabriel doubted she fooled anyone. "Don, thanks for stopping by. I'm not even sure how you heard about the news, but if you don't mind, the family needs private time."

Had Gabriel not been watching the guy closely, he'd have missed the micro expression on the other man's face before he hid his response to her rejection.

"Of course, Margie." Don crossed to her and grabbed her hand, lifting it to his lips. "If you need anything, anything at all, you have my number, my dear."

The jealous, territorial beast rose up inside Gabriel, and he growled low in his throat like the veriest of wild animals.

Margaret snatched her hand from Don and hid it behind her back. "I do. Thanks, Don."

After Don left, Gabriel grasped her elbow and led her down the hall. Over his shoulder, he told the others to start the meal without them. Once he had her alone, he spun her to face him, grabbing her by her upper arms.

"He's dangerous, Margaret. Any kindness on your part, and you'll never be rid of him."

"Gabriel, *stop*. He was only offering condolences."

She attempted to jerk away, but he held tight.

"You're wrong, love." He gentled his tone. "I know the type. You have to be firm and tell him to get lost, or he'll keep coming back. Each time he'll be more aggressive. He thinks your lack of *discouragement* is actually *encouragement*."

"I don't want to talk about this now. He's gone. All I want is to wash up and eat."

One by one, he loosened his fingers to release her. His spidey senses were screaming the situation was off, but she refused to listen. "I'm sorry. I only wanted to stress the danger."

She avoided his eyes as she slipped into the master bathroom. From his vantage point, he could see her scrubbing her hands, in between each finger and under each nail, three times. A sure sign of her agitation.

"Margaret, if you want me to go…" It killed him to bring it up, but he wouldn't stay where he wasn't wanted.

She frowned. "Why would I want you to leave?"

Her confusion fed his hope.

Throat as dry as desert sand, he said, "I thought maybe I upset you."

"Gabriel, I'll never be upset by your concern. It's nice to think someone cares enough to look out for my best interests." She stepped up to him and flattened her hand over his heart. "Thank you."

His shoulders sagged in relief. "We should go eat. As it is, Grey will lose his mind if the food gets cold."

She smiled. "Well, we wouldn't want to send Grey over the edge."

Later in the evening, after everyone had gone to bed, Gabriel reclined with his back against the headboard and held Margaret as she talked about Michael. A small part of him was jealous the other man had been such a large part of her life, even if it was platonic.

"He sounds like quite a guy."

"He is… was…" She wiped a stray tear.

"About Thanksgiving…"

She rose up and twisted to face him. "Oh, Gabriel. I completely forgot. I don't know if it's a good—"

He cut her off with a soft brush of his lips on hers. "I know. I've already spoken to Grey. My brothers and I will eat at the restaurant. But I wanted to let you know, if you or your family care to join us, the invitation is open. That way, no one has to cook, and your family has one less thing to worry about."

"I appreciate it. I imagine Mom will still want to make something. It's what we do. If we're stressed, we cook and eat."

"Fair enough. Keep it in the back of your mind. Grey can always prep any extra dishes if need be."

She shifted to her knees, straddled him, and cupped his face in her hands. "I'm not sure what I did to deserve someone as incredible as you or how you can be interested in someone as plain as me, but I'm thankful."

"There's nothing plain about you, lady. You're bright and beautiful in every way."

His words were nothing less than the truth. And he was crazy about her.

CHAPTER 15

"My sister needs help, Gabriel."

Sammy had hit an emotional low and couldn't seem to recover. When she wasn't sad and depressed, she was angry and confrontational. Such had been the case during the church service this past week; an altercation had occurred between Sammy and the pastor. The local news cameraman hadn't fared well either. As it stood, Sammy faced serious legal issues.

"She needs help," Margie repeated.

Gabriel placed his sandwich back on the plate and dusted off his hands. "I assumed as much when I saw her strike Simms. I didn't figure he'd let it go."

"Do you know him? Can he be reasoned with?"

"His wife is good friends with the D.A.'s wife. And no, he's a complete ass from what I've gathered."

"She has a little money, but not a lot. It will take a while for the life insurance company to pay out, but I'll make sure you're paid if you're willing to take her case." In her nervousness, she fluttered about the kitchen, wiping counters and cabinets, only stopping when Gabriel wrapped an arm around her waist. "I hate asking, and

I don't mean to put pressure on you. If it's not something you would normally do—"

"Margaret." He said her name in a soft, commanding way. When she drummed up the courage to meet his eyes, warmth and understanding shone brightly. "I'll help her, love."

"You will?"

"I'll do everything in my power to make this go away."

Margie placed her palms on either side of his face and touched her brow to his. "Thank you, Gabriel."

"And I won't take any money from her, but it's going to cost *you*." His lowered voice and the intimate suggestion made her tingle.

"Mmm. Why do I have the feeling you're going to require something completely naughty and inappropriate?"

"Because I totally am," he assured her with a wolfish grin.

Inside her belly, it felt like a thousand jumping beans pinged off the walls of her stomach. With one hot glance, one suggestive remark, or one low-voiced comment, he had the ability to turn her insides gooey.

Gabriel tugged her onto his lap, kissing her with a mind-numbing passion that made her forget her own name.

When she could gather her wits again, she touched her mouth in wonder. "Damn, you're good at that," she said on a pant.

"I'm good at a lot of things, or do I need to prove myself some more?"

"Oh, you're definitely going to have to prove yourself more." Laughing, she wiggled, brushing his stirring erection. "You're going to ha—"

"Mom! We're home!"

"Goddammit!" she muttered as she scrambled to her feet.

Gabriel, the toad, almost busted a gut laughing.

"It's not funny. Fucking Scott was supposed to have the boys until tomorrow."

"Fucking Scott is a prick, and I don't know why you ever married him," Gabriel returned in a hushed voice, dropping a quick kiss on her lips right before her sons rounded the corner to the kitchen.

"Me either." She bent to give Aaron a hug. "Hi, sweetheart. What are you guys doing home today?"

Scott strutted around the corner to join them, walking in a cocksure manner as if he owned the place. Margie had to make a conscious effort to unclench her jaw.

The expression on Scott's face soured when he saw Gabriel sitting at the counter. "You'd think you couldn't afford a decent meal, the way you're always hanging around here, eating. Lexus payment too high?"

"*Scott!*" Margie was horrified and furious at once. She would've reamed him a new asshole if Gabriel hadn't chuckled.

He picked up a potato chip, and after he examined it, he popped it into his mouth, crunching down with a wide, toothy grin. His cheekiness knew no bounds, and Margie bit her lip to keep her laughter contained.

Based on the daggers her ex was shooting Gabriel, he'd succeeded in getting under Scott's skin.

"Yeah, whatever." He dismissed him with a wave of his hand. "Something came up, and I had to return the kids earlier than expected."

"Crystal couldn't handle them while you went out drinking with your friends again?" Margie's voice dripped with false sympathy.

His deep flush indicated she'd struck a nerve.

Margie shook her head.

If Scott continued with his selfish ways, he risked losing his latest girlfriend. She'd go by way of all the others and leave him choking on her dust when she fled as fast as her stick-thin legs could carry her.

"She called us 'little bastards,'" Aaron volunteered.

A single glance at Scotty confirmed what his brother had said.

Margie saw red.

"Scotty, take Aaron into the other room. *Now.*" Her tone was low and dangerous, making her eldest son usher his brother out of the kitchen as if their little butts were afire.

With a hard poke to Scott's chest, she let out a growl. "That twat-sicle better never..." Jab. "... I mean *never* call my children 'little bastards' again. Do you understand me?" Jab. Jab. "As a matter of fact, they won't be visiting you any time she's around." Jab. Margie's finger was hurting from the continued assault, but she'd be damned if she showed discomfort. She was receiving too much satisfaction from watching the color drain from Scott's face. "If I find out she's anywhere in their general vicinity, there will be fucking hell to pay. Do I make myself clear?" Jab.

"Margie, babe—"

Gabriel rose with such force, the stool flew backwards and scraped along the tiled floor with a harsh, discordant sound. "She's not your *babe*. Unless I'm sorely mistaken, you forfeited that right years ago."

His tone was lethal, and Margie derived even more satisfaction when Scott's complexion turned a distinct shade of green. Gabriel had to be an imposing figure as he stood behind her, all bowed up to his full height and giving off an aggressive vibe. Never had she been happier to have someone on her side.

Somehow, Scott drudged up the courage to mouth off. "If Crystal can't be around my kids, then neither can he."

"The difference is Gabriel is a positive influence on the children. They happen to like *him*. Maybe because he's not verbally abusive." She stepped into Scott's space. She lowered her voice because she hadn't missed the young, curious faces turned their way. "Don't even think of pushing me on this, Scott. You won't like the result."

"I'm outta here." He glared once more at Gabriel before he hustled out the front door.

Gabriel's muscled arm hugged her across her upper chest and pulled her back against him. "I'm sorry," he whispered.

"You have nothing to be sorry for. *I'm* sorry my boys have such a deadbeat for a dad."

"How about I take you all to the beach?"

She tilted her head back to gaze up at him. "You don't have to try to make up for him being a shitty parent, Gabriel."

"I'm not trying to. You and I had planned to spend the day together anyway. Why not make it a family day?"

Why couldn't she have met him sooner? She smiled despite her desire to cry.

"Is that a yes, Margaret?"

"That's a yes, as long as Aaron and Scotty are game."

Since the boys had moved into the living room to play video games, Gabriel had to raise his voice to be heard over the noise. "Either of you know how to surf?"

Both boys stared at him in wide-eyed surprise. Aaron's expression was tinged with hero worship.

"*You're* going to teach us?" Scotty asked. A hint of attitude was present, but Gabriel either missed the snark or chose to ignore it altogether.

"If you want to learn."

Aaron whooped as his older brother neatly put away the controllers and turned off the television. Margie had to admit, it was a first. Scotty must be more excited by the prospect of surfing than he let on if he was going so far as to clean up his mess.

Casting Gabriel a laughing glance, she asked, "Is now the wrong time to tell you they already know how to surf?" His dark brows shot up in surprise. "They've been surfing from the time they could stand."

He grinned as the boys ran to their rooms. "I should've known, considering we live so close to the beach."

"We leave our boards in Sammy's garage."

Her mind flashed back to all the times Michael had joined her and her siblings to surf. Whenever the waves were high, they could all be found trying to outdo each other in a friendly competition. Ten years. Michael had been part of their world so long, the loss now felt like a missing limb.

．　．　．

THE QUICKSILVER CHANGE IN HER MOOD TOLD GABRIEL WHERE HER mind had gone. Drawing her into his embrace, he kissed her temple and rubbed her back. "I have extras in case you don't want to disturb her."

"No, it's okay. We have the garage code. I just..."

"You don't need to explain, love. I get it."

And he did. The recent loss of Opal hit him harder than he let on. There were times when he became downright moody and morose, knowing he'd never be able to speak to her again.

"I have a friend who is a psychiatrist. I can call him if you or your family need someone to help with grief counseling."

Her arms tightened around him. "I'll let you know."

They stood locked together as if the rest of the world didn't exist, and Gabriel savored simply holding her.

"I don't think I've ever met anyone as incredible as you." She spoke so softly, he almost missed it.

"I'm not anything special, Margaret."

"Yes, you are. You just don't know it."

"I'm glad *you* think so," he said dryly, knowing she was giving more credit than was his due. "Go get changed. Unless you need help. In that case, I'm all yours."

She laughed, and it made his heart lighter, knowing she was past the momentary grief.

As she started to separate from him, he drew her back for a gentle kiss. "I forgot to ask. Do you surf, Margaret?" Her wicked grin nearly brought him to his knees. "I take it by that look, you do. What don't I know?"

"Mom was gonna go pro before she married Dad," Scotty said from behind him. There was a wealth of arrogance and hostility in his tone.

Gabriel chose to ignore it for the second time. "Seriously?" Surfing was one of his favorite pastimes. "How am I only learning this about you now?"

"Because my son is a big mouth." She shot a wide grin at Scotty. "I had intended to show Gabriel up in the water today."

"Ah, Margaret, you have hidden talents." Gabriel leaned in to whisper, "And I'm excited to discover more."

"Scotty, keep Gabriel company while I change, won't you?"

He watched her sashay down the hallway toward her room. "I'm crazy about your mom, Scott. If you have a problem with it, perhaps we should talk man to man."

"She's been hurt enough by my asshole dad."

Gabriel looked down at the boy. Pain was reflected in the child's eyes, and so was the challenge. "It's not my intent, son. She doesn't deserve the treatment she gets from your father. And she sure as hell won't receive anything like it from me."

He tried to appear as open and straightforward as possible to show his true intentions.

The resentfulness dissolved in slow increments, and Scotty nodded. "Okay."

A strong wind could've knocked him over when Margie's son held out his hand. Gabriel gave him a manly shake. "Are we good?"

"Yeah. Thanks for offering to take us."

Gabriel wanted to smile at his serious tone. "My pleasure. Want to see what's taking your brother so long?"

"He's outgrown his wetsuit but is still trying to squeeze into it. I offered him one of mine." Scotty shrugged as if to say, "Kids these days."

Gabriel pursed his lips to stem his desire to laugh. When he could manage speech, he said, "Tell Aaron we'll pick him up another wetsuit in town, okay?"

As Scotty hurried away, Gabriel allowed his smile. The boy was a lot like his mother. He appeared all bristly and ready to fight, but deep down, the kid was a softy.

"What's amusing you?" Margaret asked.

He turned and nearly swallowed his tongue. She'd changed into a one-piece suit with a white sheer wrap around her waist. The sarong accented the curve of her hips and length of her shapely legs. At five-feet-six, she wasn't overly tall, but she had legs that went on for days.

"Gabriel?"

"Yeah, sorry. You're going to have to wear a muumuu, Margaret. Other men can't be allowed to see you that way."

Her light laugh was music to the soul, and he grinned his appreciation. Before he could say anything further, her sons joined them.

"Should we call Grandma and see if Kaley wants to go?" Aaron asked.

"She's actually with Annie over at Sammy's place. But why don't you text her and ask if she wants us to pick her up when we get the boards?" Margaret smoothed back the hair from Aaron's forehead just before she bent and kissed him. A motherly habit Gabriel felt cheated of in growing up without his mom. Her son gazed back at her adoringly, and Gabriel felt a deep kinship with the boy.

CHAPTER 16

*L*ater that night, Margie stepped into her walk-in closet, looking for a change of clothes. The first thing her brain registered was a pair of shoes lying sideways. Bending down, she put them back in place, careful to space them an equal distance between the neighboring pairs. It wasn't until she opened the dresser drawer to retrieve undies that she registered the anomaly. She froze. Her heart gave an extra heavy thud or two. The disarray was impossible to miss or write off as her out-of-place shoes had been.

Careful not to touch anything, she gave the closet another cursory glance then hurried to the kitchen where Aaron and Scotty were gobbling down the tacos Gabriel bought them.

"Boys, did either of you go into my closet when we got home from the beach today?"

They shook their heads and went back to cramming food in their pie holes.

She met Gabriel's curious gaze across the island.

"What's going on, Margaret?"

"I'm sure it's nothing." She didn't want to express concern in front of her sons, and she gave a slight tilt of her head toward the bedroom.

"Be right back, fellas. Save some for your mother, okay?" Once the door of her bedroom was shut, he asked, "What's wrong?"

"I think someone was in my room."

They stared at each other for a long moment. Her, with a deep-seated knowledge her things had been disturbed, and him, with concern for her sanity. Okay, maybe the last little bit was her own personal fear he'd had enough and would run for the hills.

"I'm not crazy, Gabriel. You know how I am about my things." She grabbed his hand and tugged him into the closet. "Those shoes. When I came in, they were like this." Margie placed them in the position she'd originally found them. "And my underwear..." She opened the drawer.

His frown deepened, his expression growing stormy. The shoes he might have dismissed. The unfolded panties, he couldn't. Hell, anyone who knew her would realize this was out of character.

"I think we need to get the kids and get out of here."

She looked up from counting her clothing. "I don't understand."

"Margaret, you set your alarm when we left." He let it sink in, and when she reached the same conclusion, her heart began a hard hammering.

"Someone knows my code. It's the only way they didn't set off the alarm."

"Exactly." His troubled eyes drifted to the drawer then snapped back to her. "The day the alarm was installed. Did you change the code?"

"Yes."

"Did you give it to anyone outside your family?"

"No."

"Would your kids?"

"Perhaps to Scott? But he wouldn't do this. He'd have no reason."

"Wouldn't he?"

Sweat beaded on her upper lip, and her hands grew clammy. Could she have misjudged Scott all these years? Yes, he had been a cheating sonofabitch, but spiteful to the point of trying to terrorize her?

"I don't think so, Gabriel." She shook her head when he would've argued. "I know he's an ass and a bit of a bully, but he would draw the line at trying to scare me."

"What if he thought it was the only way you'd allow him to see the children? Especially after you humiliated him today over his girlfriend?"

Margie worried her lip as her gaze fell back to the open drawer, and she did a quick tally. "There is a pair of panties missing."

"Are you sure?"

"All the laundry was folded and put away last night."

"All right. Let's call your alarm company and see if any of the outside cameras picked up anything."

"I'm scared, Gabriel."

"We'll get to the bottom of this. I promise."

She nodded but remained unconvinced. She wiped her damp hands down her sides and shook her head. Whatever was happening here, he didn't need to chase her boogeyman away. "You aren't responsible for us. I..." What could she say? That she was beginning to realize a larger problem existed? Someone had her in their sights and decided to fuck with her. Today's incident made discovering who and why paramount. Sick mind, sick game, or both?

"Margaret. Look at me."

Her eyes flew to his.

"I won't let anything happen to you or your family. *Ever.*"

The hair on the back of her neck lifted. "You can't promise that, Gabriel. You shouldn't."

"Yes, I can, and I will."

Dread settled in the pit of her stomach, and she knew, by stating what he had, he'd challenged fate to do its worst.

"Call your neighbor, Margaret. You should find out what time the alarm was deactivated and reset. I think it would be wise to file a police report, too."

"It won't do any good. What am I going to say? My shoes were moved and a pair of undies happen to be missing?"

"Have you checked jewelry or the other rooms?"

"Well, no. Not yet."

"Let's do it now."

Because of her hyper-organizational skills, it was a simple matter to determine all her things were in their proper place. The exception was a bottle of her favorite fragrance, which appeared to be missing.

"So, our pervert has taken your underwear and perfume. No doubt about what he intends to do with those."

The clear picture made her ill, and she didn't object when Gabriel gathered her close.

"I'm sorry. I shouldn't have said that."

"It doesn't mean you're wrong," she said quietly. "I don't understand why anyone would target me."

"Then you're blind, love. There's much to admire about you."

She hugged him tighter. If she could climb inside his skin to merge with him more completely, she would. Gabriel was all things desirable, and he always managed to say what she needed to hear. "Thank you."

"For being bright enough to recognize an incredible woman when I find one?"

With a snort, Margie said, "We'll go with that."

As Don watched his monitor, Margie snuggled into Gabriel's embrace. Don clenched his fists around the panties in his hand. Somewhere along the way, she'd fallen victim to Gabriel's charms and foiled Don's planned seduction before he'd had a chance to implement it. The need to find a way to break up their romance rode him hard, and he knew he'd have to transition to Plan B.

Making a split-second decision, he rewound the video until the moment Margie and her family left the house to go to the beach with her neighbor. He spliced it with blacked-out footage then spliced it back in to about thirty-minutes before they came home.

Over and over, Don replayed the video, making sure there were no obvious glitches. Once he was satisfied it looked as if someone had interrupted the video feed, he pulled up the entry log for Margie's home. A quick copy and paste to a word document, with a simple modification of times, and he was set to print it out for his needs. He saved the footage to an external drive and collected his van keys.

———

JUST AS MARGARET WAS PICKING UP THE PHONE TO DIAL THE ALARM company, the doorbell rang. Gabriel glanced at his watch and went to confront their visitor. Instinct told him it would be her creepy-ass neighbor. The guy had been popping by more and more, as if hoping to catch Margaret home late at night by herself.

"Don," Gabriel said flatly as he swung the door open. "Who would've guessed?"

The little weasel glared his disdain, his body practically bristling with anger at finding Gabriel present. "Is Margie home? I need to speak with her."

"She was about to phone your call center. Seems she had a break-in. I don't suppose you'd know anything about that, would you?"

"What are you implying?" Don snapped.

"I'm not *implying* a damned thing. I'm asking outright what you know."

The other man tried to muscle by him, but Gabriel stood firm and put up a hand to push him back. "You should know, I don't trust you, you fucker. I've dealt with many men like you my entire career." He refused to provide a hint of his childhood trauma. "You're a sneaky little liar, and the first time I catch you being untruthful, your connection with Margaret will be severed. You got me?"

"Gabriel!"

He spun around to stare down into Margaret's shocked face. The words explaining his actions wouldn't come, which was odd because he made his living concocting the perfect phrase to defend people. How did he tell her his behavior was all for her? For sure, she'd view this confrontation as jealousy, but it went much deeper.

"Don, come inside." She gave Gabriel a severe side look.

Because his body was blocking the swine, Margaret missed Don's smug satisfaction. Gabriel didn't. He growled, causing the other man to skitter sideways.

Margaret bit her lip and dropped her eyes to the floor. Either she was super pissed, or she was struggling not to laugh. Gabriel suspected the latter. Her hand brushed his, and they entwined fingers. All was forgiven, and he understood her show of shock wasn't real.

Together, they followed Don into the living room.

When the shorter man turned back around, his gaze zeroed in on their joined hands, and white lines formed around his compressed mouth.

Gabriel fought like hell to prevent his mocking smile. He failed. Okay, so maybe he didn't try all that hard.

"Margie, I was notified by one of my employees that—"

"Which employee?" Gabriel demanded.

"What?"

"Which employee notified you there was a problem?"

Don's mouth opened and closed as his mind worked to come up with an answer.

No employee found the problem. The man standing before them had. Why he needed to lie about it was anyone's guess. In all likelihood, Don watched her account closely for the very reason he was here now—he wanted to appear important in her eyes by responding so quickly.

Since Gabriel had no way of proving any of the things he suspected, he let it go.

Ripping his hostile stare from Gabriel, Don waved a USB memory stick in the air. From his back pocket, he pulled a folded sheet of paper. "At eleven-forty-three a.m., it shows the system was armed. Twenty minutes later, it was disarmed and not armed again until two hours later. At four-fifteen p.m., the alarm was shut off a second time."

"That's when we arrived home. So between noon and two, someone else was definitely in my home. What about the exterior cameras? Do they show an intruder?" The furrow between Margaret's brows deepened.

"I'm afraid not." Don handed her the stick, holding onto it a little longer than necessary. He stroked the back of her hand once before she jerked away. "They must've had a scrambler to disrupt the signal. The video is blank between the times I told you." He looked between them. "I'm happy to contact the police for you."

"You've done enough." Gabriel stepped forward to create a buffer between Margaret and Don. "Thanks for the memory stick. We'll turn it over to the proper authorities."

Don glared at him a moment before his look turned calculating. Without taking his eyes from Gabriel, he leaned sideways and spoke to Margaret. "You should know, dear, the panel was accessed by someone with your code. Whoever came through your door, knew your schedule."

Fury fueled every cell in Gabriel's body when the smarmy weasel used an endearment. "First, she's not your 'dear,' and second—"

Margaret's hand on his forearm calmed him—marginally. "Thank you, Don. We'll take it from here. In the future, you can just call with this information or email it to me. We don't want to take you away from your business any more than you need to be."

"I don't mind. *For you.*" Don's gaze was worshipful.

Unease snaked along Gabriel's spine. Something was seriously off with this little toadstool, and he intended to discover exactly what.

"Good night, Don," Margaret stated firmly. Her mom voice caused him to jump into action and scurry toward the exit.

Gabriel laughed aloud after the door closed. "Impressive. Now, let's phone the police to get a report on record."

CHAPTER 17

*T*he holidays swept past in a blur, and Margie saw Gabriel when they could carve out time from their schedules. Mostly, in connection to Sammy's legal troubles, since Scott and Crystal were still an item, and he refused to make time for the children.

Gabriel was only able to get Sammy's sentence reduced to a ninety-day stay in a local mental health care facility. Brookhaven was upscale, and his friend Stephen had agreed to treat her.

But Christmas without Sammy and Michael had been a somber affair.

Earlier in the week, Gabriel invited Margie to a New Year's celebration, but she'd declined. Once again, she had to care for the kids. Sure, she could've asked her mom to watch them, but because they were all still feeling Michael's loss, Margie wanted to stay home.

Tonight, she was well into a steamy romance by her favorite historical author, Kate Bateman, when she heard the distinctive clink of a pebble against her window. A glance at her clock showed eleven-fifty-two. A second pebble collided with the glass, and she grinned.

Gabriel.

It thrilled her to think he'd left his party early to see her. Utilizing her phone app, she shut off the alarm. Butterflies danced in her belly, and she did a girly little dance right before she parted the curtains and tugged the cord for the blinds. A flick of her wrist unlocked the window, and she shoved it open. "Gabriel?"

"Margie."

Not Gabriel.

Puzzled and more than a little weirded out, she inched the window back down. "Who's there?"

"Margie, it's me. Don."

Her stomach twisted, and not in a good way. Why the hell was he outside her house, copying Gabriel's break-Margaret-out-of-her-tower game?

"What are you doing, Don?"

"I thought you could come out to play."

This guy was seriously becoming creepy as fuck!

"Sorry, I was just about to go to bed. I—"

Pitching his voice to mimic Gabriel's warm, seductive tone, Don said, "I could come in and keep you company."

Her flesh crawled, and she wasn't sure she hadn't thrown up a little in her mouth.

"Look, Don. I don't know how many times I can tell you. *Gabriel and I are in a relationship*, and I really need you to understand I'm not interested in you that way. *Don't* come here again." She didn't give him time to comment, and she slammed the window closed, drawing the blinds and curtains for good measure. As quickly as her trembling fingers would work, she opened the app and keyed the code. She made a dash for the light and flipped the switch, throwing the room into darkness. Tiptoeing back to the window, she held her breath and listened.

What to do? Did she call the police? Gabriel? No, not Gabriel. He was at a party, and dragging him back here to ease her fears only to have him tell her "I told you so" didn't sit well.

Searching through her contacts, she found Jamie's number and pressed send. She swore under her breath when her call went to voicemail.

"Hey, Jamie. It's Margie. I'm sorry I'm ringing so late, but can you call me back?"

From inside, she heard Don jiggle the handle for the screen door. Fingertips smashing her lips to stem the instinctive scream, she eased back the blinds and peered out.

Don's silhouette was visible by the glow of the pool light. Thankfully, she'd locked up earlier, but the very fact he went so far as to try to open the screen door after she specifically ordered him to leave dismayed her. What if he took it into his head to rip the screen and jimmy the lock on the slider?

She dialed Gabriel.

He picked up immediately. "Margaret! Did you change—"

"Gabriel, I'm sorry to bother you, but Jamie isn't picking up and—"

"I'm on my way, and I'm contacting Gordie. He's crashing at my place."

"Wait! You don't even know—"

"You sound scared, and you're calling me in the middle of the night. I'm on my way." She heard the slamming of a vehicle door and an engine hum to life. "All that remains is for you to tell me if I need to call the police."

"No. I don't think so."

"What's going on?"

"Don showed up. Gabriel, it was super strange, and he gave me the willies."

"That peckerhead! How long ago?"

"A few minutes maybe?" She relayed the events of her conversation with Don, desperately trying to keep the tremble from her voice.

"Margaret, how sure are you that this guy is mentally all there? Is it possible he can access your alarm to get in the house?"

"You're scaring me, Gabriel."

"You *should* be scared. I don't trust him. He hasn't gotten it through his head that you and I are a couple."

Her heart turned over in her chest. She hadn't dared call them anything more than occasional lovers, but Gabriel had just laid the truth bare. "Should I call the police?"

"If you are feeling threatened or worried he'll break in, then abso-fucking-lutely. I'm still eight minutes out." He paused a second. "Gordie's at the back of your house now."

"Don't text and drive," she ordered absently.

Easing back the curtain, she peered between the slats of the blind. The back yard was almost pitch black, so she hurried to the living room and flipped on the floodlights. Gordon James was visible, and Don was nowhere to be seen.

Next, she checked the locks on the doors. The main panel for the alarm showed it to be armed, and she breathed a sigh of relief. She peeked in on the boys, then Kaley, satisfied they were safe and still asleep.

"Margaret? You're awfully quiet. Are you okay? Talk to me."

"I was just double-checking everything is locked up tight."

"Fuck!"

"What?"

"There's a goddamn checkpoint ahead."

"Have you been drinking?"

"Nursing a single scotch over the last half hour. Nothing before that one."

"Just be careful, Gabriel. Please."

"Stay on the line with me, okay?"

"Okay. Should I invite your brother in? He shouldn't have to wait outside until you get here."

"He's at the front door."

Margie disengaged the alarm and swung open the door. She grabbed Gordon by the front of the shirt and hauled him inside, causing him to laugh at her manhandling.

"If this is the type of reception a man gets, coming to your house, I can see why you have an overabundance of admirers," he quipped.

"Shut it." She shot him a half smile to take away the sting, and secured the door. "I'm sorry you had to come out tonight."

"No harm. I was vegging on the couch, watching a movie. So, tell me. What's going on? Gabe said an unwanted visitor."

She gave him the same explanation she'd given Gabriel, watching as Gordon's scowl darkened with each word she spoke.

"I'm assuming that's my brother?"

Margie handed Gordon the phone.

"Gabe? Yeah, man. No. Right." He checked his watch. "No, we're good. He seems to be gone."

Although she could hear the deep tones of Gabriel's voice coming through the line, Margie had a hard time understanding the words. He seemed to have a lot to say on the subject of Don, and none of it was good, based on Gordon's raised brows and smirking lips.

His blue-gray eyes met hers, and he gestured to the phone in his hand. "Seems your boyfriend doesn't like your stalker much."

"Don isn't a stalker. He—"

Gordon winced and distanced the phone from his ear. "Aannnd, you just set him off."

Margie retrieved her cell and listened to Gabriel for a second before she disconnected.

"Did you just hang up on my brother?" Gordon's eyes were rounded with shock and something akin to awe.

"He had a few choice things to say about my sanity. I didn't care to hear it," she stated primly.

He laughed and gave her a one-armed hug around the neck. "You're perfect for him. You know that, right?"

Her phone lit up, and when she answered, the long stream of swearwords prompted her to disconnect again.

"He's going to stroke out if you keep doing that," Gordon warned on a laugh.

"When he can talk with some modicum of respect, then I'll listen."

"I can't wait for the show to unfold when he gets here."

Her phone lit up again, but this time, it was a sleepy Jamie on the other end. "What's going on, sis?"

"Nothing. I'm sorry I woke you, Jamie. I thought I heard something outside. I—"

Gordon practically ripped the phone from her hand and explained to her brother what had happened. He ended with, "No, man. Gabriel's on his way. We have it covered for now. Yeah, of course." He pulled out his phone and programmed in Jamie's number. "Got it. Right. Here she is." He mouthed "sorry" as he returned her cell.

"Margie, why the hell didn't you call the police right away?"

"My first instinct was to call Gabriel, but he wasn't home, so I called you. I figured Don would leave if you showed up. But then you didn't answer, and I..." The stress of the night caught up with her, and tears cut off her babbling explanation.

"Don't cry!" Jamie sounded pained. "I'm on my way."

"No. No n-need. Gordon's h-here." With a shaky hand, she swiped at the moisture on her cheeks. Gordon stepped away to allow her a minute to control her emotions. "Seriously, Jamie, I'm okay for now. I think the adrenaline is wearing off."

"I'm going to beat that fucking asshole to within an inch of his life."

"No, you aren't. I intend to have a serious conversation with him one day very soon."

"Not without Gabe or myself present, you aren't."

"I'll admit, I'd feel better if one of you were." The squeal of tires in her driveway made her wince. "I think Gabriel just arrived."

Gordon checked the peephole and nodded, so Margie disengaged the alarm to admit his brother.

The storm cloud on Gabriel's face said she was in for a stern lecture. "Gotta go, Jamie. Thanks for checking on me."

. . .

GABRIEL DIDN'T KNOW WHETHER TO HUG MARGARET OR SHAKE SENSE into her. The tears on her face triggered his compassion, and he went for the hug. "Come here, love."

She flew into his open arms, and he rested a cheek on the top of her silky hair, happy to confirm she was safe.

"Don't you ever hang up on me again. Not when it's this important."

Pulling back, she glared up at him. "You don't get to yell at me."

"I wasn't yelling."

"You were yelling," Margaret and Gordon said in unison.

"Fine, maybe I was yelling a little bit. But goddammit, I was scared, okay?"

And he had been. Completely terrified that Don would take it into his head to hurt her and the kids. Until now, Margaret had labeled her pain-in-the-ass neighbor as harmless. The man was anything but. Time and again, Gabriel had seen men like Don get away with hurting women with nothing more than a slap on the wrist. Their justice system wasn't designed to be fair to women.

"You need to file a police report," he told her.

"What can they do? He basically tapped on my window and asked me to 'come out and play.' They'll say he didn't break in or hurt me in any way."

Gabriel knew she was correct. Law enforcement would see this as tame, and on a busy New Year's Eve, they'd more likely be irritated to be called out to Margaret's home than anything. But it went against his nature to do nothing. "I think we should still get a report on record. I'm almost positive he's the one who came in here and took your things."

Margaret paled and shot an uneasy look toward her bedroom door. Apparently, she hadn't drawn the same conclusions he had.

"I should change my alarm provider," she said softly. "And get a restraining order."

"Honestly, they rarely do anything to encourage a stalker to leave you alone, but it's not a terrible idea to have one on record."

Gordon nodded his agreement with Gabriel's assessment. "Truth. In my industry, musicians deal with this constantly."

"So what do I do?"

Gabriel didn't like the shaky quality to Margaret's voice and met his brother's eyes over her head. With a grimace, he admitted, "I don't know. Pray he takes a hint after we talk to him."

CHAPTER 18

The moaning woke him. Easing up on one elbow, Gabriel watched Margaret as she slept.

Her face was slack with passion, and he turned more fully onto his side. Her hands clenched the folds of the comforter, and a pleasure-filled gasp escaped her lips. Clearly, she was having an erotic dream.

He grinned at the familiar sight of her desire.

She murmured something in her sleep, and he leaned closer to hear.

"Sebastian! Please, yes!"

Cold washed over Gabriel, and he couldn't seem to recover his breath from the shock. Although they'd never spoken of love, he had believed they were on the same page. Knowing she dreamed of another man and hearing her call his name flayed Gabriel's insides. How was he expected to push past the pain of her calling for someone else?

"Sebastian," Margaret sighed again.

He needed to leave. *Immediately.* If he didn't, he wasn't sure what he'd do. Gently, so as not to wake her, he disentangled himself from the sheets and pulled on his jeans.

He was done being a sucker for love. While he'd never truly loved Tamara to the depth or with the ferocity he loved Margaret, he had cared for her. She'd used him, though, and he couldn't fight the feeling it was happening a second time.

As he stalked toward the door, Margaret's sleepy, questioning voice halted him in his tracks.

"Sebas... uh, Gabriel? Where are you going?"

The embarrassment-saving exit he'd haphazardly planned was ruined as he stomped back to the bed.

"Who's Sebastian?" he demanded.

"You are." Her sexy, sleepy grin punched him in the gut.

Concern quickly replaced his hurt. He squatted in front of her and cupped her face in his hands. Carefully, he turned her head from side to side to get a clear look at her eyes.

"Sweetheart, I'm worried about you."

"Why?"

"Do you know my name, Margaret? My real name?"

She wrestled the covers to sit up, her brows knitting together and deepening her frown. "Of course. You're Gabriel."

Kneeling, he rested a hand on either side of her thighs. "Then who's Sebastian, love?"

"You are."

Exasperation set in. This conversation had him lost, and her next statement did nothing to clarify it.

"You are Gabriel, and you are also Sebastian. You've also been Marcus, Hugh, and a whole list of other people in the past. You can't remember, but I do."

"I don't know what the hell you're talking about."

She trailed her fingers along his jaw. Her wide, imploring eyes begged him to understand. "It means we've been together in previous lives."

"I don't believe in past lives, Margaret."

"Wait." She rifled around in the nightstand then handed him a sketch of himself. Only it didn't quite look like him. It was more like a historical rendering of what he would've looked like had he indeed lived in the past.

A crystalline image of himself dressed exactly like this, straightening his tie in a looking glass, flashed through his mind. Déjà vu struck, and the sensation was dizzying. What was she doing to him?

Making him crazy is what!

This was not a topic he felt comfortable discussing when her children were about to wake and start their day. "Look, it's getting late, and the kids will be up soon. It's better they don't find me here too often until we decide one hundred percent where this is going and what to tell them."

As Gabriel cut across the lawn to his house, he half-laughed, half-snorted at the memory of Margaret's floored expression. She'd looked like a landed trout, huffing and puffing, her mouth opening and closing.

Although he loved her, he wasn't ready for the paranormal claptrap she seemed to cling to. First Sammy with the "premonitions," James with his "channeling" spirits, and Annie with her "energy" receptors, now *this?* Yeah, it was a hard pass from him. Gabriel preferred to deal with cold, hard facts, and not "feelings" or "visions."

After stepping through the door to his house, he tossed the sketch he'd forgotten he was carrying onto the counter and headed straight for the espresso machine. He toyed with the idea of lacing his coffee with Bailey's or maybe something stronger. *God, he needed something stronger!*

He'd spent a long, rough night, tossing and turning as he stressed about the upcoming confrontation with Don. Other than in the courtroom, Gabriel wasn't argumentative by nature. He subscribed to the do-unto-others way of life. If you treated people with kindness, you received it in return. Only the Dons and the Scotts of the world brought out his inner asshat. Or maybe it was his need to make life easier for Margaret that had caused him to be more aggressive than normal.

Gabriel ran a shaky hand through his hair and began to pace.

Thinking back, he could see he'd been a borderline Neanderthal a time or two when dealing with the other men. In the case of her ex, he could admit to a bit of jealousy that Scott had met and married Margaret first. Had fathered her beautiful children. But Scott had also created hardships for her with his carelessness, and Gabriel couldn't forgive him for that.

And as for Don, well, the guy was majorly off. No one with innocent intentions showed up in the middle of the night and threw rocks at a window. He stopped short. Well, no one but him anyway. And Gabriel wasn't so sure his own intentions had been innocent at the time. Regardless, he wasn't going to let Don get close enough to hurt a hair on her head if he could help it.

The beep of his coffee maker signaled a completed brew cycle. As he sipped his drink, he calmed down and allowed his mind to go back to his conversation with Margaret. As for her past-life declaration, he didn't know what to believe. Didn't know if he wanted to. His eyes drifted to the sketch lying face up on his granite countertop.

Yes, he'd been attracted to her from the moment they met. Yes, he felt as if he'd known her forever. Yes, she held his heart in the palm of her hand. Had from day one. If she wanted him to jump through hoops for her, that's what he'd do. *But not without some grumbling.* And dealing with this type of hokey belief deserved some serious grumbling.

A tap on the glass slider dragged his focus away from the sketch. *Margaret.*

There she stood, beautiful and contrite.

When he opened the door, she said, "I'm sorry."

He could no more resist her than the oxygen his body needed to breathe, the food he needed to fuel his body, or the water he needed to drink for hydration. All were necessary to his existence. *Especially her.* But he didn't have to like it.

Moments passed while the two of them stared. Each waiting for the other to speak. As he watched, the light of hope started to fade from her eyes. It felt like he'd told a small child there was no Santa.

As she gave a resigned sigh and turned to leave, Gabriel reached for her. "Don't go."

Her face lit with her relief, and desire grabbed him by the 'nads. Would he ever not want this woman? All she had to do was crook her little finger and he came running.

He bent his head to hers. "No more talk of past lives. It freaks me the fuck out."

After two heartbeats, she agreed. "Done."

"Seriously? You're giving in just like that? You?" He nipped her lower lip.

"If it's going to get me in your bed again tonight." She grinned and reached up to pull his head down to hers for a deep, drugging kiss.

When he could gather his scattered wits, he said, "Margaret, there isn't anything you could do or say that would keep you from my bed." He felt her appreciative tremor and grinned. Yeah, they had it bad for each other.

"I love you, Gabriel."

His heart rate kicked up a few notches, and placing fingers on the underside of her jaw, he gently tilted her chin up.

"I do. I love you." She met his stunned gaze head-on.

He anchored both arms under her ass and lifted her until they were eye level.

"Say it again," he ordered before she could yelp her surprise.

A giggle erupted from her pink, kiss-swollen lips. "I love you, Gabriel."

"Again."

"I love you, Gabriel."

He lowered his mouth to her neck, nipping lightly. *"Again."*

She gasped and complied.

"Again." His mouth moved to pay tribute to her jawline.

"Mmm. I love you, Gabriel." Each time she said it, her voice became huskier, thicker with emotion, and his heart became lighter.

"I will never tire of hearing that. I'm going to make you say it all day, every day," he promised.

LATER IN THE EVENING, AFTER MARGARET'S CHILDREN HAD BEEN bundled off to their father's, she invited Gabriel back over. He'd had the bulk of the day to think about the sketch she'd created. The longer he studied it, the more he felt the rightness of her claim.

As he approached the screened deck, he noticed the small table for two. In the center, atop a white linen tablecloth, was a hurricane lantern set to low. White china dishes, gleaming silverware, and crystal champagne flutes completed the setup. Floating candles peppered the pool, and it backlit Margaret.

She was dressed in a mouthwatering side-wrap dress, and the way it hugged every curve of her body made his mouth dryer than dust.

"What's all this?"

"Our New Year's celebration." She sounded tentative and slightly breathless. In other words, completely adorable and sexy as hell.

As he opened his mouth to comment, Grey walked out, dressed like a server for a Michelin-starred restaurant, with a bottle of wine in one hand and a white towel folded over his arm. He ruined the look with a wide-ass, mocking grin. "Hello, sir. If you care to take a seat, I'll bring out the first course."

Bending slightly at the waist, Grey poured the wine into the glasses and placed the open bottle on the table. He pulled out a chair for Margaret to sit down, gesturing to the other for Gabriel. "Do you need assistance, sir?"

"Bite me," Gabriel said, good-naturedly. He wedged himself between his brother and Margaret to steal a kiss from her smiling mouth. "Hello, love."

"Do you like our surprise?"

Her hopeful expression played havoc with his heart. His Margaret only ever wanted to please people, and right now, him most of all.

"Yes, I do. Very much. Thank you." Her relieved grin filled his heart to bursting.

"It was Grey's idea. I was going to order a simple meal for us. He's the one who convinced me this setup and the catering of it would be fun."

Gabriel straightened and cuffed Grey on the shoulder. "Thank you." It meant more to him than he could say to have his brother go to these lengths for Margaret and him.

"My pleasure, bro. Now sit down, or you're going to kill the timing and ruin all my hard work."

"Pushy much?" he teased.

"Timing is everything if you don't want dry salmon."

"A true crime." Gabriel laughed as his brother disappeared into the house. "You should've chosen someone a little more chill to cater your meal, love. My brother will be removing our plates for the next course before we finish the first."

Margaret laughed. "It's all good fun."

"It is at that." He glanced around. "This is really great."

The mood was light, and their conversation flowed throughout their dinner. As their meal came to a close, Grey placed a cherry pie slice in front of each of them. "This is from Chez Margaret," he stated with a hideous French accent. After scooping out a dollop of whipped cream for the top of each slice, he smiled. "Everything is cleaned up and put away inside. Enjoy what's left of your night."

Margaret clasped Grey's hand between both of hers. "Thank you. This means the world to me."

His brother's expression softened as he stared down into Margaret's lovely face, and Gabriel had a small flare of envy that her bright, happy smile wasn't focused on him.

"It's entirely my pleasure, Margie. We all owe you for being so wonderful to our aunt while she was alive."

"Opal was an easy woman to love."

Both Gabriel and Grey scoffed their disbelief.

"What? She was!" Margaret insisted.

"We loved her, too, but let's be real. She was a cranky busybody," Gabriel corrected.

"As much as it pains me to agree with Gabe, he's right," Grey

175

said. "And on that note, I'm off. 'Night. I'll be sure to lock the front door on my way out."

They ate their pie in relative silence with Gabriel's deep moan of appreciation filling the quiet night air. When he finished, he sat back and sipped his wine, watching as the lantern's flame accentuated the soft planes of Margaret's face. Another wave of déjà vu hit. Perhaps her theory of past lives wasn't far-fetched. This was their first semi-formal dinner date, and yet, he would swear this was familiar to him, as if they'd done it multiple times before.

"Okay, I know I said I didn't want to hear it, but could you explain the past-life thing? How does it all work?"

She watched him, not answering right away. Probably worried he'd ridicule her. Coming to some sort of internal decision, she said, "I'm not sure of the science behind it. Or the religious ramifications, for that matter. I just know I have memories of us throughout history. Sometimes my family is the same, sometimes they aren't related at all. But we all rotate around one another throughout time. Family, friends, business associates. In our case, lovers."

The hairs on the back of his neck lifted after she gripped his hand and explained why she'd called him Sebastian. He felt what could only be called a transference of energy, a surge of electrical heat between them, and he could see the past as clearly as if he were currently living it. Their instant attraction, the pursuit of a relationship, making love for the first time. Then profound sadness.

"What happened? I get the impression we were on a ship."

"Titanic," she said softly.

When he was a small child, Gabriel had had an unreasonable fear of water. If a single drop touched his face, he'd experience the sensation of drowning. His father had believed it was a brilliant idea to help him conquer his phobia by throwing him into the ocean and shouting, "Swim or drown, boy." Adulthood and counseling sessions eventually helped him get beyond his aversion. After a time, he learned to enjoy the water. Now, he suspected he knew where the fear had originated.

"I died," he said flatly.

"You did."

He ran a hand over his mouth and shook his head. "I find this difficult to believe."

"I know." Margaret rose to her feet, grabbed her plate, and blew out the lantern. "Come with me. I want to show you something."

Gabriel gathered the few remaining things from the table—because Florida and ants went hand in hand—and followed her at a slower pace. Each footstep felt like a lead weight as he walked to the kitchen. He wasn't entirely certain he wanted to see what she had to show him. If she offered proof, he'd be forced to believe in other-worldly things.

She'd already placed her dishes in the sink and had moved to the island. At the center of the granite top was a file.

The sight of the Manila folder sent a chill down his spine. "I'm not sure I want to see this."

"You don't have to."

Because he'd never been a coward, and because truth was always better, he rolled his shoulders, shook out his arms, and flipped open the file. A picture of himself, similar to the one Margaret had sketched, greeted him. Gabriel sucked in his breath, gobsmacked.

"Meet Sebastian Harwick. Born December fourteenth, eighteen seventy-four."

He gave a small, disbelieving shake of his head. "Is this for real? You and Grey aren't pranking me, are you?"

"I wouldn't do that, Gabriel. This is information Annie recently dug up at my request." She shot him a fleeting smile. "It helps to have a genealogist in the family." She shrugged. "Until I met you, I thought Sebastian was a figment of my imagination. A phantom who haunted my thoughts. Who lingered between Scott and me throughout our entire marriage."

He glanced up sharply. "What's that supposed to mean?"

"I loved a fantasy man. Any commitment to Scott was difficult to maintain when all I wanted was someone I didn't believe existed."

"Jesus, Margaret."

Her eyes dropped to the file in his hand, and Gabriel followed her line of sight. He still found it difficult to comprehend, but the proof was right in front of him. Wrapping his head around reincarnation wouldn't be easy. He flipped through the paperwork and jerked at what he saw.

Sebastian Harwick was Opal's grand-uncle.

"Margaret, did you check out the tree? Is it possible you saw a picture of him at Opal's one day and dreamed all this up?"

Anger tightened her features, and she yanked the folder from his hands. "Look, if you don't want to believe it, don't. But I know I've never seen anything concrete on Sebastian before this week." She whirled around, preparing to storm away. But Gabriel blocked her path, stealing the file back.

Her furious glare almost made him laugh. Sweet, darling Margaret was about to skewer him alive, and she was cute as hell when she was spitting mad.

"I've dreamed of Sebastian since I was a child, Gabriel. *A child.*" She poked his chest. "Let that sink in. Long before I knew the history of the Titanic. Long before I met Opal."

"Okay."

"Okay, what?"

"Okay, I believe you."

She frowned her suspicion. "Why are you giving in so easily? It's not like you."

"When you first showed me the sketch, I may have had a vision of us. *Before.*"

"An image like what?"

He felt decidedly uncomfortable discussing this, but he soldiered on. "Me. Back then. Straightening my tie in the mirror. With you sitting on the bed, covers pulled up to your chest. Your hair was longer. Curlier." He trailed a finger down to just below her breast. "It came to right about here."

"I've seen that same thing, in my dreams. Last night, as a matter of fact."

"And I had a sense of familiarity when we first met. As if everything clicked into place, and the world was finally as it should be," he said softly.

Her eyes lost their wary look, and love shone bright and bold for him alone. "So you truly believe me?"

"I do." And he did. If there was such a thing as a past life, he'd have killed to find her. To find this. Despite his desire to avoid entanglements, he couldn't. Not with her. Not anymore.

Gabriel tossed the file onto the counter without caring where it landed. A light tug pulled her close, and he smoothed back the hair from her flushed face. "This thing between us? Yeah, I would've always searched for it, in every lifetime. So I believe you."

CHAPTER 19

*S*unlight streamed through the blinds, torturing a sleep-deprived Margie. Rolling onto her belly, she burrowed deeper and used the pillow to block the light.

The covers were unceremoniously yanked from her body, and the smack to her ass brought her off the bed, ready to do battle. She would've taken a page from Sammy's book and broken Gabriel's nose if he hadn't appeared so blindingly beautiful standing there, a wide, loving grin gracing his face.

"Good morning, my love. I have coffee waiting for you." The husky sound of his voice curled around her, and she lunged forward to hug him. It might've been the "my love" or possibly the mention of coffee, but either way, she was compelled to throw herself into his arms. How could she not? Especially when it placed her naked breasts in direct contact with his warm skin.

"Come on. You can down one cup before your walk of shame."

"What time is it?"

"Nine. James called to say he's already sent Scott a text to meet him at your place with the boys. Said he's picking them up at ten to take them to the beach and keeping them for a sleepover."

"He did?"

"Yeah. He mentioned something about us needing a day to ourselves." Gabriel placed a full mug in her hand. "Say what you will, but I'm really starting to like your brother."

"He has his good moments." Margie smiled and sipped her drink. "Dear God, this is the best coffee I've ever tasted! I need the brand."

"Grey said it came from the Cool Beans Way."

"Ah, I should have known. I'm sure Skye has a pact with the devil. How else can her coffee be this delicious?"

"I'd offer to review her contract with him if I thought it would keep me in a constant supply." He leaned in and kissed the column of her throat.

Tilting her head, she allowed him better access. For a few tingling moments, he nibbled his way along her skin to the lobe of her ear. He spoiled her delicious haze with a sharp bite.

"We need to have a quick chat before your beasts come home."

"Did you just call my children beasts?" she asked, incredulous.

"Don't act like you're all offended. You know the truth."

She laughed at his harried expression. Her boys *were* a little much. They'd latched onto Gabriel like a drowning man to a life preserver. Every chance they got, they followed him around, slamming him with questions about everything their young, inquisitive brains could think to ask. Quite possibly, they viewed him as a replacement for Michael, who had been gone for five months now. She shook off the sadness that came with her thoughts of him.

"You know you adore them." A swat on Gabriel's bicep emphasized her words.

"Possibly. Or maybe I like making love with their mother." He flared his eyes wide and waggled his brows.

"So sad for you, we're a package deal," she returned.

"Don't I know it."

"Oh, shut it!" She should've known she couldn't win at wordplay with a lawyer.

Taking the coffee from her hand, Gabriel sipped it and set the mug on the nightstand. His expression turned somber.

An odd fluttering started low in Margie's stomach. "What is it?"

"Your sister Sammy. James told me she isn't doing well in Brookhaven. I've been trying to get her sentence suspended, but the D.A. doesn't want to budge on our initial agreement of ninety days. In addition, she has to show improvement, or they won't release her."

"She's worse? What does Stephen say?"

"He can't break the patient/doctor confidence. Violet is Sammy's medical contact. He'll only discuss the case with her."

"I need to go see Sammy. *Today.*"

"James thought you'd react exactly that way." Gabriel sighed and rubbed a hand through his already mussed hair. "She's not responding to anyone, love. She just sits and stares since her miscarriage."

Their mom had initially kept Sammy's attack and the subsequent loss of her baby secret. When Margie first discovered the lie, she blew a gasket. Only feeling marginally better knowing Annie and James had been left in the dark along with her.

"She's my little sister, and I've been a horrible shit to her. Now she's going through this, and none of us can help? How is it fair, Gabriel?" It made her ill to learn her vivacious sister was a shell of her former self.

He gathered her close. "It isn't."

The continued strum of his fingers through her hair calmed and helped center her. "I'm okay. Really," she said when she saw his look of disbelief. "But I should get going."

"We have time to shower here. Together." The pitch of his voice was husky and filled with seductive intent.

"You know we are never that quick, and it would be the one day Scott is on time for a change." Regret hung heavily on her rejection, but she had to get home.

"Why don't we simply tell everyone we're dating and be done with it. It isn't as if I haven't spent time at your house. The kids know, Margaret. They aren't oblivious."

She couldn't explain her reticence. Perhaps her reluctance stemmed from her insecurities. Gabriel was six years younger than she was. He was educated, highly intelligent, and unencumbered by children. What if in another month he grew tired of playing house? How would her kids feel? Hell, how would *she* feel? She'd never live through the heartbreak of losing him in this lifetime as she had in the past. Better her children continued to think he was the fun neighbor who sometimes hung out at their place for dinner.

As THE WATER CASCADED OVER HER BODY, MARGIE'S MIND FLITTED TO the past. She wasn't sure why these old memories were stirring—maybe her fear?—but she couldn't seem to separate herself from them.

APRIL 1912 -

From the second he passed her the note, Sebastian swept Lucy into a whirl-wind romance. Whenever they had an opportunity, they snuck away. A stroll around the deck, the ship's entertainment, kisses in the shadows—they enjoyed it all.

Tonight, Lucy tried not to squirm as she waited for Sebastian to join her.

Well past the appointed time to eat, he arrived, accompanied by Rosalie.

A deep sense of dread wedged itself in Lucy's diaphragm and refused to budge. No one could fail to see the laughing sparkle in Rosie's eyes or her puffy lips. A telltale sign of kissing if ever Lucy saw one.

Her eyes traveled over Sebastian.

He was looking less than pristine, and she had little doubt who Rosie's kissing companion had been.

Pain nearly doubled her over, and the effort to keep a pleasant expression was mighty. Fixated on her meal, she took one dainty bite then a second. On and on, it went, and of course the food tasted like sawdust but turned to lead once it hit her stomach. Between each mouthful, she sipped her wine to wash down what fought to stick in the back of her throat.

Lucy ignored all of Sebastian's attempts at conversation, reserving her attention for the passenger in the neighboring seat.

Molly Brown. The woman was quite the character, with the eyes of a hawk. And when Molly leaned toward her, Lucy half expected a juicy bit of gossip. Not that she cared when her own world was spinning out of control, but pretenses had to be maintained.

"Everything will work out, dear. I'm sorry to say, this isn't the only heartache you'll face in life." Molly radiated understanding and sympathy.

Blinking rapidly, Lucy nodded and cleared her throat, wanting nothing more than to fall into the older woman's arms and sob. But pride kept her spine stiff, and she prayed Sebastian and Rosie didn't see the hurt they'd dealt her with their careless actions.

Lucy snuck a glance his way. Their gazes collided, and she felt the jolt to her toes. His solemn-eyed stare was hard to meet. Lucy ducked her head and developed an interest in her dessert. What had she expected? By involving herself with a man like him, with his Lothario personality, she'd set herself up for heartache. Lesson learned. Rosie, however, should've known better. When next they were alone, Lucy would set her straight.

After the gentlemen left for after-dinner entertainments, Rosie shifted to sit next to her. "What is the matter with you, Lucy? Sebastian has been trying to get your attention all night."

"I do not wish to discuss this with you, Rosalie."

"I do not understand you, sissy. The man is mad for you."

Lucy flung off the hand Rosie had placed on her knee. "Oh, and should I ignore the fact that he is mad for you as well. Or that you both show up together, looking disheveled? Do you think I'm blind to not see your mouth swollen from his kisses? Or your lip rouge on his collar?"

"Lucy, it is not what you think."

"Is it not?"

"No. And if you refuse to be reasonable, I shan't tell you the truth of it."

"I know the truth of it, Rosie," Lucy snarled, careful to keep her voice low to avoid being overheard. "You are nothing but a harlot."

"I see." Rosie dabbed her lips with a napkin, the picture of haughty arrogance, although her tear-bright eyes gave her away. "I'll remove my harlot self from your proximity. We cannot have you tainted, St. Lucy."

As Rosy exited the dining salon, head held high, regret settled in Lucy's chest. Her sister was no more than a girl, and really, wasn't she the foolish one here? Lucy had allowed herself to be seduced by another man when she hadn't even consummated her marriage to the first. How could she expect Rosie, a girl fresh from the schoolroom, to behave when men flung themselves at her feet?

With great care, Lucy placed the crumpled napkin by her plate. None of this was hers or Rosie's making. How could she blame her sister for having her head turned by a man like Sebastian when she, the elder and wiser, had fallen for his brand of charm so easily? Tomorrow, they would talk and clear the air between them.

Turning to Molly, Lucy caught the disapproval in her expression. Not wanting to feel she'd disappointed her new friend, she popped up and rushed for the door. She was only ten steps outside the dining room when Sebastian stepped from the shadows.

"Lucy, what have I done to upset you? Tell me, so that I might make it right." His voice, so warm and caring, broke what was left of her heart.

Pressing her hand to her breast, she tried to regulate the beat with a calming breath. "Mr. Harwick, I b-believe it best we not s-see each other again." Firming her resolve, she dropped her arms and lifted her chin. "I would also thank you to stay away from my sister."

He reacted as if she had taken off her shoe and beat him about the head with it. Mouth agape, he shook his head as if to clear it. As she started to go around him, he grabbed her arm, whipping her back around. "Your sister flew by me in tears just now. Does this have something to do with the two of us coming in to dinner together?"

"No, but it has everything to do with the two of you coming in, looking as if you'd just made love," she snapped.

"You cannot possibly believe I'm interested in your sister."

Seeing the raw sincerity in his eyes, she felt a swift rush of uncertainty. Could she be wrong? She shook her head, telling herself not to be naive. Some men made a game out of conning and seducing women. "Explain to me why her lip rouge was on your collar."

He sighed as if disappointed by her accusation.

"It appears your sister is a magnet for unsavory men. I stumbled upon

one of the crewmen taking liberties. When I stepped in and assisted Rosalie, she hugged me." His eyes softened and his smile matched. "It was nothing more, love. I swear it on my life. If you feel the need to verify this, check with the captain. The crewman is being detained as we speak."

He paused to pull her into the shadows and pressed his forehead to hers. "As of three days ago, I have not entertained the thought of another woman. How could I? Since meeting you..." With a shrug, he trailed a finger along her jaw. "There could never be another woman for me now, Lucy. Never."

His words held the ring of truth, and Lucy silently cursed herself for jumping to the wrong conclusion. She'd hurt Rosie for nothing.

"Oh, Sebastian. I'm sorry for being a jealous fool."

"You aren't feeling anything I haven't felt, knowing you return to Andrew each night," he growled against her lips.

Although he had to know she'd not been intimate with Andrew, Sebastian's jealousy delighted her.

He kissed her roughly once, twice, then a third time before pulling away. "Come, let us find Rosalie. I fear for that girl on her own."

"What about Andrew? He could come looking for me."

"When I abandoned the men to their evening pursuits, he was safely ensconced in the gaming room with the other gentlemen."

Hours passed, and still, they found no sign of Rosie. Beyond panicked, Lucy engaged the services of the crew to assist in their search. At one point, convinced she couldn't take another step, Lucy slumped against the closest wall.

"Why don't I return you to your cabin? I can continue on my own."

"I'll never be able to sleep until she is found. I want to go with you, Sebastian."

"You're exhausted, love."

"She's my sister, and I was horrible to her."

He seemed to understand what she couldn't say, and reluctantly, he agreed to let her stay.

"All right. Rest for a minute longer, then we'll head down to the third-class decks. It is the only place left to search."

MARGIE SHUT OFF THE WATER AND BURIED HER FACE IN THE FLUFFY towel. The bedroom door opened and closed, startling her from her memories. She glanced at the clock on the bathroom vanity and frowned. The kids weren't due home for another twenty minutes, and even if they had arrived home early, they knew better than to enter her personal space without knocking. If it was Gabriel, he'd have called out by now.

Standing stock-still, breath halted in her chest, she strained to hear. After what seemed like an hour, but was a minute at most, she tucked the ends of the towel over her breasts and tiptoed toward the door. Heart in her throat, she peeked around the opening. Her room was empty.

Just as she was about to laugh at her foolishness, the air became charged, and the fine hairs on her arms lifted straight up as goose bumps dotted her flesh.

Danger.

The same instinct that had insisted she call Gabriel over the day Don installed the alarm, was once again screaming a warning.

The closet door drew her notice, and her sixth sense told her the scene was wrong. Margie didn't remember leaving the door ajar, but she might've. Did she imagine the heavy breathing, or was that her own breath laboring past the fear lodged in her throat?

Her phone rested on the charger across the room, and Margie doubted she'd make it before she called attention to herself. Was it better to lock herself in the bathroom? Maybe try to wiggle her ass out the tiny window or signal Gabriel for help.

Frozen with indecision, she couldn't stop her shaking enough to make a move. What if the kids came home to an intruder? What then? A replay of what happened to Kaley? She'd for sure fuck someone up if they hurt her children. Her protective instincts propelled her into action. Racing across the room, she dove for the phone and rolled across the bed.

A masked figure lunged from inside the closet, and Margie knew true terror. Trying to make herself as small as possible, she wedged herself under the bed and, with trembling fingers, managed to tap the button on the side of the iPhone the required five times to contact emergency services. Just as a dispatcher's voice came through the receiver, a heavy hand wrapped around her ankle, and panic clawed at her throat. She kicked out and hollered for all she was worth. After her foot connected with her attacker's shoulder, she scrambled for the opposite side of the bed.

"Help! Help me!" she screamed.

The attacker beat on the bed frame and bellowed. In a fit of rage, he threw the mattress into the wall. The only thing between them was the box spring, and Margie's chance of survival was quickly diminishing. Whoever this man was, he sought to hurt her.

Huffing out her address and praying the dispatcher heard, she dropped the phone and latched onto the underside of the box spring. In an attempt to retain the last barrier of protection, Margie clawed through the material covering the frame and gripped the wooden slats. He tugged, but she wrapped an arm around the thin beam, desperately hoping her body weight would make it harder for him to get to her.

Sirens sounded in the distance, and the intruder stopped struggling long enough to listen. With a curse, he ran for the door.

When she was sure he'd left the room, Margie untangled herself from the underside of the wooden frame and retrieved her phone. She gushed her gratitude as the dispatcher assured her the patrolman was pulling into the driveway and less than thirty seconds away. With a prayer thanking whatever entity existed, Margie curled into herself and began to tremble. If a deputy hadn't happened to be in the general area when the call went through, and had the sirens not scared off the masked man, she'd be toast.

"Ma'am? Our officers are on the scene and in the house."

Her breath hiccuped in her chest, and she couldn't seem to drag enough air into her lungs to take a fortifying breath. The chattering of her teeth telegraphed through the phone line like freaking Morse code.

"I'm in the m-main bedroom on the r-right, at the end-d of the h-hall," she managed through a shaky exhale. "T-tell them to p-please be careful. I don't know where he is."

Her phone vibrated, and Gabriel's number popped up on the screen. As much as she wanted to take the call, to have him here and feel the comfort of his arms around her, she wasn't foolish enough to answer. She needed to stay on the line with the dispatcher until she made contact with a deputy and got the all clear.

The boots of the two uniformed officers came into view at the far end of the hall. One by one, they checked the rooms, calling the all clear to the other. The entire time, Margie maintained a quiet conversation with the dispatcher.

"Ms. Holt? Our officers are approaching your room. They need to know where you are."

"Under the bed. I'm under the bed." Prior to that moment, she hadn't thought about the loss of her towel. Now, deep embarrassment heated her skin. "Um, I don't have clothes on. I lost my towel in the struggle."

A female officer spoke in a no-nonsense tone. "The closet is clear."

"Bathroom clear," came her male counterpart. "I'll check the grounds."

The moment he left, the female officer encouraged her to come out as the dispatcher ended the call.

Shaking, Margie crawled from her hiding spot. She held it together as she met the compassionate eyes of the officer. She even managed to drag on a thick robe and belt it, but the second she heard Gabriel yelling her name, she lost her shit.

CHAPTER 20

*W*hen the two police cruisers turned onto his street, Gabriel felt his first stirrings of unease. As the sirens grew louder, his stomach knotted. He'd just dialed Margie's number and was stepping off his porch when a masked figure shot out the rear door of Margaret's house, headed for the wooded area at the back of her property.

Convinced something unspeakable had happened, Gabriel flew around the house and through the back door, screaming Margaret's name. In the blink of an eye, he was facing down the business end of a gun barrel.

"Don't move!"

He couldn't if he tried.

"On your knees! *Get on your knees!*"

He complied, but apparently not fast enough for the officer, because the other man shoved him down on the tile. The impact to his hip and shoulder was jarring, and he hissed his discomfort.

"It's all r-right. I know him."

Gabriel shifted his head a fraction and sought Margaret. The relief he felt was so profound, he closed his eyes and thanked a god he never gave much thought to.

"Ease up. Slowly."

The male officer never removed his hard stare from him, and Gabriel tried to be as unthreatening as possible. "I need to know she's okay," he croaked.

Part of the tension eased from the officer as he holstered his weapon and rolled his neck. When the guy nodded and stepped back, Gabriel sprinted to Margaret.

"Tell me you weren't hurt." With great care, he grasped her face between his hands.

"I'm okay, Gabriel. I promise."

His heart only resumed beating when she lifted tearful sapphire eyes to meet his searching gaze and gave him a watery smile. Crushing her close, he looked over his shoulder. "I'm sorry, I should have said this before, but I saw a masked man running out the back. My first concern was for Margaret, or I would've given chase."

The male deputy jumped to call dispatch, and the female rapid-fired questions at Gabriel. He described the man as best he could, but camouflage was plentiful in these parts, as was the man's heavyset body type. With the hood, there was no way to detail anything more about him.

"It was Don," Margaret said.

Gabriel separated from her and gently lifted her chin. "Are you sure?"

The uncertainty and torment in her eyes gouged his insides. After a long minute, she shook her head. "Something about the eyes, but no, I can't one-hundred percent identify him as the intruder."

"Who's Don?" The female officer pulled out a pen and pad.

"He's our neighbor," Gabriel answered for Margaret. "He started harassing her about the time I moved in next door in October. If you check your records, you'll see Margaret filed for a restraining order against him after he showed up on New Year's Eve."

The two deputies shared a grimace. They, too, knew the legal document wasn't worth the paper it was written on if the harasser had it in their head to ignore it.

"Has he bothered you since then, ma'am?"

"I can't say he has except for a phone call or two, asking me why I was doing all this to him."

Gabriel's head whipped around so fast his neck cracked. He stared in open-mouthed shock.

Color rose in Margaret's cheeks, and she dropped her eyes to the floor. "I didn't tell you, because I knew how you'd react. You and Jamie spoke to him, and I thought he got the hint after we canceled the alarm contract and filed the restraining order."

Seething inside and attempting to get a grip on his churning emotions, Gabriel nodded without answering.

"How often does he call you, ma'am?"

"He only called the two times. Once after he was served the paperwork, and then again a few days ago."

Sure his teeth were going to be ground to dust, Gabriel made a conscious effort to unclench his jaw. An image of a guilty-looking Margaret hanging up the phone flashed through his mind. She'd lied to him as little as three days ago.

Margaret went on to explain the entire situation, from Kaley's injury to today's event.

"Were either of the recent phone calls threatening, or did they give you a bad feeling?" The question came from the other woman, and Gabriel's gaze snapped to her. The sympathy stamped on her face made him wonder if she hadn't been harassed herself once or twice. It wasn't a jump to imagine her shapely body and pleasing features had attracted more than one unsavory character in her lifetime.

"Not threatening, but definitely a bad vibe," Margaret confessed.

Gabriel kept one arm around her as he rubbed the spot between his brows. Now his adrenaline was wearing off, he struggled to contain his temper over her secrecy. Why hadn't she trusted him with the information? How the hell was he supposed to protect her if she wasn't honest with him?

Protect.

His instinctive response every time he was around her. Yeah, he'd fallen for her so damned fast, and all he wanted to do was bundle her and her family up to take them far away. Somewhere the sleazy Dons of the world couldn't get to them.

"I'm sorry, Gabriel." Her soft voice dragged his mind from the violence he wanted to inflict on her stalker. Regret and apology hung heavily in the air between them. And maybe a little hurt on his part.

He tried to tell himself he had no right to be salty, but he couldn't.

"You have nothing to be sorry for, Margaret. Don is a predator. You're a victim. But I wish you would've told me." He attempted to smile, but it fell flat. "He's dangerous, and I don't understand why you can't understand that."

"I do now."

The male officer had been writing an incident report the entire time and finished it as another policeman walked through the door. The newcomer looked familiar, but Gabriel couldn't place him until Margaret gave the man a welcome smile.

"Eric!"

The memory clicked into place. They'd met in his office after Margaret's sister Sammy had punched Gabriel in the face at their first official meeting to discuss her legal issues. Deputy Eric Daniels had been the first officer to respond.

"I'd ask how you are, but…" Daniels cast a curious look around. "How's your sister Sammy?"

Tears welled in Margaret's eyes, and Gabriel could have cheerfully maimed the guy. The issue with Sammy was the *least* of their troubles.

Daniels picked up on her grief. "Right. I'm sorry." Turning to his coworkers, he said, "I've got a team searching the woods and surrounding area, but nothing so far."

"Gabriel, right?" The female deputy paused to listen to her radio. "Did you see which direction he went?"

"He ran into the woods. There's a trail behind the house."

"The boys play in there," Margaret clarified. "The underbrush isn't as thick."

At some point during the police interview, Scott brought the children home. After he discovered she was okay, he gave her a sharp, meaningful look. "I need a phone call when you're through, Margie."

The terseness and demand in Scott's comment grated on Gabriel's last nerve. "Was he always such an ass, or has he grown nastier with time?"

"I'm not sure. But he really *is* an ass, isn't he?" Margaret sighed.

James showed up a minute or two after the dickweed left, and Gabriel was profoundly grateful her brother had the good sense to usher the children out of the house. Something Scott should've done.

Fifteen minutes later, the house was silent as a tomb.

"Don't be mad at me."

Gabriel looked up from preparing their coffee.

Margaret was freshly dressed, standing at the island.

The fragility surrounding her made him wish he'd have given chase to her attacker and finished this mess for good. Because he didn't want to show his frustration, he finished fixing their drinks. "I'm not."

"You're frowning and awfully quiet."

"It's been a crazy morning. I tend to retreat into myself to process information. Or so I've been told by my family and office staff." He gave her a half-hearted grin. When she didn't smile in return, he set down the spoon and moved to stand in front of her. "I'm not mad. I'm confused why you felt you couldn't confide in me about Don's phone calls."

"I don't know. Maybe I feared you'd pay him a visit and end up in jail."

He grinned, this time with real humor. "I'm not uncivilized, Margaret. Or not completely anyway. Besides, I have a good friend or two who would post bail and get the charges dismissed."

Her relieved expression morphed into annoyance, and she crossed to look out the back window. "I suppose I need to call Scott. I already know what he's going to say."

"No need to call right away. Let him stew a bit." Gabriel approached her and tucked his head next to hers.

"Good idea." She smiled and leaned back in the circle of his arms.

He took pleasure in holding her. This simple touch reassured him she was safe and unharmed like nothing else could.

"When I saw the cars… I was terrified," he confessed.

"Probably not as much as I was when that fucker lunged at me."

A shudder wracked her body, and Gabriel hugged her tighter, unable to speak through the thickness of his emotions.

They remained locked together until a knock on the window interrupted them. Seconds later, Margaret's children tore into the kitchen and went straight for their mom.

Gabriel fielded questions as best he could, trying to appear calm and convincing when Aaron asked if the "bad guy" might come back. How did he answer? He had every doubt they'd seen the last of Don.

The boys refused to be corralled by James, insisting they needed to be with their mom.

"It's okay, Jamie. They can stay with us."

GABRIEL STUCK TO HER SIDE, SOLICITOUS AND PROTECTIVE, REFUSING to leave her alone.

Margie couldn't deny she was grateful for his care and attentiveness.

James decided to linger and entertained Scotty and Aaron with a challenging race-car game. Her brother's presence allowed her to take a much-needed second shower. Scrubbing away the sensation of the intruder's clawing hands was paramount, and she wouldn't be satisfied until the ickiness was gone.

When she stepped from the glass enclosure, Gabriel was waiting with a clean, fluffy towel. No agenda but to lovingly dry her off and cuddle her close. His hands were everywhere at once—smoothing her hair, caressing her jaw, stroking her shoulder—all in an effort to reassure her. Or maybe to reassure himself.

They climbed on the freshly made bed, and she snuggled into him, savoring the heat radiating from his large frame.

"What is this between us, Gabriel?"

He paused mid-stroke of her hip and contorted to see her expression. "What do you mean?"

"This." She gestured between them. "This emotion."

Why the sudden need to have things defined, was a mystery to her. Perhaps in her mind's effort to compartmentalize what had happened, she required clarification in every aspect of her life.

"What do you think it is, Margaret?" When she clammed up, he snorted. "I think it's pretty clear, don't you? *Love.* Undeniable, unbreakable."

Yeah, she felt it, too.

"Gabriel?"

"Hmm?"

"Do you think it was Don?" She held her breath, waiting for his answer but expecting an explosion.

He surprised her with a simple sigh. "I guess the more important question is, do you?"

A shiver ran the length of her body, and she burrowed closer. "I think maybe it was, but I couldn't swear it in a court of law."

"If it was him, and I'm not saying it wasn't, things will escalate. It's also a clear indication he's unhinged, Margaret."

She couldn't ignore the warning note, nor could she find a reason to defend Don this time. Hell, she didn't want to. He'd terrified her today. The evil intent that had emanated from him made her jittery still.

"I'm scared, Gabriel." Admitting the current situation frightened her wasn't easy. For too long, she'd had to be the strong one. A single parent—and a mother to boot—couldn't let on she was scared. Margie had learned long ago to stuff her insecurities and uncertainties down to the point they never saw the light of day. She asked what had been taunting her for the duration of her second shower. "What if he was the one who hurt Kaley last October? What kind of person attacks and terrifies a family this way?"

"A sick one." His arms tightened. "I'm scared, too."

"Because you can't predict what he'll do?"

"Mostly. And because he pops up every time we let our guard down. How do we protect against that?"

She'd wondered the same thing. "I still want to see Sammy today."

"Do you really want the additional stress?"

"If it is Don, I'm not letting him stop me from living my life, Gabriel. I can't. It would be too easy to hide out here. It's no way to live. Besides, he's already proven he can get to me here."

"Okay. You get dressed, and I'll let James know where we're going. Give me fifteen minutes, and I'll drive you."

"You don't have to."

"Yes, I do. For my own peace of mind. We're also going to talk about heightening security around here. Gordie's guy will have someone he can recommend, I'm sure."

"Are you talking about a bodyguard?" she asked, never having seriously considered hiring protection and unsure if her situation qualified for one. "I can't afford it."

"You let me worry about the particulars." He placed a hard kiss on her mouth and rose from the bed. After he double-checked the locks on her windows, he said, "See you in fifteen."

CHAPTER 21

$\mathcal{M}$argie hadn't know what to expect when she saw Sammy, but an inanimate shell of her former self wasn't it. Gabriel stood on the far side of the rec room, discussing God knew what with Dr. Montgomery, while Margie tried to draw forth some form of response from her baby sister. As she was ready to give up, Sammy grabbed her arm in a vice-like hold.

Gabriel straightened from his casual stance against the wall, drawing Stephen's attention to the two of them.

Margie gave a small wave of her hand to keep them away.

"You can't stop it, sissy."

Sweat broke out on Margie's brow, and her breath came in shallow pants. She was afraid she knew exactly what Sammy referred to, but still, she croaked, "Stop what?"

Dull eyes lifted to meet her searching gaze. For a second, recognition was present along with another unidentifiable emotion. Sammy shoved to her feet. "Don't believe him. He's lying to you."

"Who, Sammy? Who's lying?" Margie took a deep breath in her effort to calm down. "God, Sammy. Tell me how to help you." If the sound of a heart breaking could be heard, Margie was sure hers would've resounded around the cavernous recreational area.

"Tell them. Convince them. I'd know if he were dead, sissy."

"Michael?"

The momentary hope on Sammy's face faded, and she turned her head away. Maybe she recognized the anguish and pity Margie was feeling for her. But what little life she had, left her, and she stared at Margie as if she were a stranger.

"Michael's not dead," Sammy rasped. She shuffled down the hall with Stephen right on her heels.

Hot tears burned their way down Margie's cheeks, and she used the sleeve of her thin cardigan to soak up the moisture. Her little sister was seriously ill, and there was no immediate solution to ease her suffering.

"Are you all right?" Gabriel watched her closely.

"No," she confessed. "I guess I thought she..." What? Would take one look at Margie, grab onto their old animosity, and stiffen her spine? At least if Sammy could drum up a bit of fighting spirit, she might stand a chance, but this ghost of her former sister didn't.

"She seemed intense there for a bit. What did she say?"

"Gibberish. Michael was alive and someone was lying to me."

Gabriel frowned and cast a troubled glance after Sammy and Stephen. With a deep sigh, he ran a hand through his hair. "I don't know what to make of her words, but it certainly doesn't sound good."

"I know."

"Do you want to try speaking to her again?"

Margie wrapped her arm through his and rested her head on his shoulder. "I don't see the point. Not today."

"Feel like lunch? We can grab something and take it back for James and the boys."

A glance at her watch showed it was indeed lunchtime. "I'm sure he's ordered pizza for Scotty and Aaron by now. It's what they do on video-game days."

"Fair enough. Grey's place isn't far from here if you'd like to get a bite. Or I can bring you straight home."

"Lunch at your brother's restaurant sounds good."

Their conversation during the meal was practically non-existent, but Gabriel seemed comfortable with her silence, and Margie didn't feel the need to open up. Perhaps he was lost in his own thoughts regarding Sammy's issues, or maybe he had altogether different things running through his mind.

Grey joined them at Gabriel's invitation.

"I wanted to confirm everything's set for the office party next Friday, Grey. Is there anything else I need to approve?"

"Nope. Got it all covered."

Margie frowned. Gabriel hadn't mentioned he was having an office party. "Is it strictly for your employees?" she asked.

"No. Their spouses and significant others as well." He gave her a wide grin. "Do you want to be my significant other, Margaret?"

She smiled her agreement, but she couldn't help the small, niggling thought: *Why hadn't he thought to invite her before now?* Was he embarrassed to have a single mom with only a high school diploma as his date in a roomful of his degreed peers?

After a few minutes, Grey jumped up to handle a kitchen emergency, leaving the two of them alone.

"What is it, Margaret?"

She glanced up from attacking her salad. "What do you mean?"

"Ever since I mentioned the party, you became noticeably withdrawn. What's wrong?"

"Nothing." She hoped like hell the heat building in her cheeks didn't mark her for the liar she was, but his raised brow and compressed lips told her it did.

"Try again."

"Why didn't you tell me about the party sooner?"

He seemed taken aback by the question. "I thought maybe you wouldn't want to go if we're being honest. You turned me down when I invited you to the New Year's party, and—"

She cut him off with a wave of her hand. "I would still have liked to be asked. I thought we were... were..."

"Were what, Margaret? More than the 'occasional lovers' title you seem to fancy?"

The hard edge in his voice startled her, and she was at a loss to understand why he was upset.

"Sorry." He shook his head and rubbed his neck. "I don't know why I'm being pissy suddenly."

"It's been a stressful day," she replied.

"I had every intention of cajoling you into going, love," he said in a softer, more moderate tone. "I simply forgot to ask with everything happening lately. It popped up in my reminders today, so I wanted to cement the menu with Grey."

"It's okay."

"Margaret, look at me." His soft, compelling voice wrapped around her like a warm blanket, swaddling her in a wealth of confusing feelings. How he managed to melt her anger or soothe her reservations every time was a mystery. He reached for her hand and waited patiently until she placed hers in his. "I would be honored if you'd be my date for the office party. Please, say you'll go with me."

It was impossible to say no to him or be hurt for more than a millisecond when those seductive silvery eyes and his full, smiling mouth made mush of her insides. She sipped her water to hydrate her parched throat. "Yes, but you'll have to help me decide what to wear. I don't want to embarrass you with my meager wardrobe."

"You couldn't embarrass me even if you were wearing a sack, but I'm happy to help. It gives me a chance to poke through your unmentionables."

She laughed at his exaggerated leer. "I need help with the dress, you perv, not the underwear. I won't be wearing any."

He straightened in his chair and sent her a searing look. "Don't tease me, Margaret. I'll drag you into Grey's office faster than you can blink."

"Promises, promises." Her voice hitched from the thrilling idea of them doing the deed in such a public place.

"Let's go." He shoved his chair back with a speed that left her gaping, and reached for her hand.

"Are we really doing this?" Margie found herself giggling all the way down the corridor to the office.

"You can't challenge a man with 'promises, promises' and not have him take action."

A surge of excitement raced through her veins, sparking a fire within. Other than in Gabriel's office a time or two, they'd had to keep their sexual encounters confined to her bedroom or his home because of the children. But Margie loved that he was always ready and wanted her whenever or wherever they were.

Looking back, Scott had never been the adventurous type, and everything sexual in nature had been after the kids were asleep. The only exception was a little make-out session on the couch in the early days of their marriage.

When Grey passed them in the hall, he gave them a curious look but didn't say a word when Gabriel told him he needed privacy for a few minutes.

"He totally knows what we're going to do," Margie said with a snorting laugh.

"Most likely."

Gabriel locked the door behind them and pressed her against the wood panel. When his lips were a mere inch from hers, he said, "Let's make good on that promise."

DON WAS A MASTER HACKER. HE'D NEEDED TO BE, IN ORDER TO COVER his tracks up for past incidents. Currently, his eyes were fixed on the monitor as Gabriel James hammered into Margie against the office door of his brother's restaurant.

As Don watched them, his emotions went beyond fury to a strange, icy calm. His face felt numb, and he became clinical in his observations. Zooming in, he took special note of Margie's face. Her flushed cheeks and fevered eyes spoke of intense pleasure. Don couldn't help but be turned on, watching as she panted little mewling sounds of enjoyment.

Soon enough, *he'd* bring her to that level of excitement. For months now, he'd studied Gabriel's techniques, and he was an apt pupil. All that remained was to show Margie what he could do for her. *To her.*

The space he'd fixed for her was ready. He'd arranged everything down to the last pillow and even replicated her vanity with the makeup and perfume she favored. When she saw what he'd done to make her happy, she'd shower him with all her love.

Admittedly, he'd screwed up today. He'd thought she'd spend the morning with Gabriel and give him time to savor being alone in her room, surrounded by her things. Still, he'd have taken advantage of her return had the police not been in the immediate vicinity. He made a mental note to download a police scanner app if one was available.

Gabriel's hips pumped faster, and Margaret's head dropped back, her mouth open in pleasured wonder even as her eyes closed in bliss. Don knew the moment the orgasm hit her, because her body shuddered and she bit Gabriel's shoulder through the material of his shirt to temper her cry.

Don wished she'd have taken longer to come because now he was left to fantasize about the two of them together and finish his masturbating alone. Staring down at his hard dick, he stroked faster, imagining Margie's long, graceful fingers wrapped around him. Her mouth encircling his cock as he thrust so deeply she gagged and teared up from his forcefulness.

Soon.

CHAPTER 22

The party was in full swing, and Margie wished she hadn't come. She'd suspected she'd feel like an idiot, surrounded by Harvard Law School grads and the like. Being right sucked.

A heavy dose of social anxiety laced with self-doubt made her wonder what the hell Gabriel saw in her. For God's sake, she was a part-time cartoonist who drew caricatures of her children for a practically obsolete newspaper. With circulation down due to online articles, she was hanging on to her job by a thread.

She'd been cornered by a handsy, elderly client of Gabriel's, and she had no idea how to extract herself from her current situation without major insult. The man's pinching prowess would give a lobster envy.

Across the room, his wife—a tall, anorexic-looking redhead with gravity-defying breasts—flirted with Gabriel, touching him at every turn. If ever two people were made for each other, it was the pinching wonder and his Jessica Rabbit bride.

Perhaps she should talk to Gabriel about finding a better class of clientele?

Speak of the devil.

Gabriel caught Margie's eye and winked. Seemed they were on

the same wavelength. His soft smile turned to a dark frown as Handsy McHandserson not so subtly pinched her ass. If he weren't an important client, she'd have dumped her drink over his head and cooled off his needle dick.

Gordie appeared from nowhere and ushered Margie to safety. "Sorry about that, babe. Gabe should've never left you alone with that fucking pervert." The edge of anger in his voice made her feel marginally better.

As Gordie escorted her to the spread of hors d'oeuvres, she lost sight of Gabriel and Red. Margie picked at a few things here or there to curb her gnawing hunger, but because most everyone was guzzling booze and ignoring the food, she felt gauche by shoving the mini-quiches in her face.

"Eat up. Gabriel paid enough for this shindig," Grey said from beside her. "Besides, I'm starting to get a complex."

She tried some type of smoked salmon delight.

"*Goodgodthisisgood!*" she mumbled around the mouthful of deliciousness, returning his happy grin.

Grey kissed her temple as Gordie laughed. "Thank you, Margie. You're one-hundred percent authentic, and we adore you."

Uncomfortable with the praise, she avoided looking at him and cast a glance around the room.

Gabriel was nowhere to be seen.

A feeling of dread struck her right in the solar plexus when she realized Red was missing, too. And hadn't she been in this situation before with Scott on more than one occasion?

"I'll go find them," Gordie said, apparently able to read her mind. "I'm sure Gabe is dealing with a crisis, and the perv's drunk-ass wife has fallen asleep in an office somewhere."

"I trust Gabriel," Margie assured him. "You don't have to bother him if he's busy."

"Dance with me?" Grey held out a hand as the music kicked up and a fun, fast-paced song came on.

Margie drained her champagne glass and gave it to Gordie. She flared her eyes wide. "Why not?"

"That's the spirit." Gordie grinned and gave her a gentle shove toward Grey.

Twenty minutes later, after three more dance partners, Gabriel showed up. He'd discarded his tie and jacket, and a whole lot of tension if his beaming countenance was a clue.

"Sorry, Bert. The lady promised this dance to me," he said, cutting off a toupée-wearing, octogenarian whose dentures were too big for his mouth.

Margie didn't want to deny him, but she didn't think she had another butt wiggle in her. "My feet—oh!"

He pulled her close and nipped her earlobe. "Wait for it."

The music shifted to a sultry, soulful tune. The singer's raspy-voice wrapped around Margie, and the lyrics spoke straight to her soul. Lost in the music, she wanted to melt into Gabriel. To soak up every ounce of the magic of the moment.

As he spun her in a slow circle, she caught a glimpse of Gordie on a stool in the corner of the room. He was crooning into the mic, his eyes closed as he strummed an acoustic guitar.

She turned stunned eyes up to Gabriel, who laughed at her dumbfounded expression.

"Yeah, it's one he wrote. Gordie's more than a rockstar. He's a fucking artist."

"I'll say," she breathed.

Gordon sang of love and missed chances. His haunting words reached in and squeezed Margie's heart.

"It's beautiful." She did nothing to disguise her awe.

"He doesn't show this side of himself often." Gabriel's arms tightened, and he leaned down to kiss her. A semi-tame kiss, bordering on passionate with a promise of more when they were alone. "I think he's showing off for you. I may have to kick his ass later."

Margie laughed, but the joy of the moment was lost the second Red staggered up to them. Her dress was askew, and her hair was falling out of the carefully crafted creation she'd sported when she arrived tonight. Scarlet lipstick was mostly worn off, but what remained had bled above and below her puffy lips. Filler injections or kissing, it was difficult to tell which created the pouty look. Once, she would've been a stunning woman, but excess and hard living seemed to have taken their toll. When she smiled seductively at Gabriel, her face was grotesque and reminiscent of the Joker.

"Dance with me, baby. You owe me for before."

His face hardened, and Margie could feel the stiffness in his shoulders underneath her palms.

"I'm dancing with my girlfriend," he informed Red coldly.

"Girlfriend?" Red let loose a bawdy laugh resembling a braying jackass. "You couldn't remember her name in your office ten minutes ago."

Every cell in Margie's body seized, and as her arms fell from Gabriel's neck, she noticed a scarlet lipstick smudge on his collar. Her brain blanked then shot into overdrive, connecting all the dots. *That's* what had been bothering her about Red's appearance. She looked like she'd been royally fucked. The smell of sex wafted off her, creating a nauseating stench when combined with the overpowering, rose-heavy fragrance of her perfume.

Margie's gaze ping-ponged between them.

Red was insinuating she and Gabriel had been intimate in his office, and Margie couldn't keep out the doubts banging on the door to her mind. The evidence on his shirt was incriminating, and it was no secret he liked to get off in office settings. Hell, he'd bent her over his desk a time or two, not to mention the quickie at Grey's restaurant last week.

"I'll let you clear this up. I need another drink." Stomach like lead, she backed away.

He shot her a sharp look. "Margaret."

"I know she's McHandserson's wife." With a tight smile, she held up a hand. "Do what you need to."

"McHandserson?" The light of laughter entered his eyes.

But Margie didn't feel like sharing the joke. She pivoted on her heel and headed to where Grey's bartender had set up shop. The smoked salmon and mini-quiche were threatening a return trip up her esophagus.

"Are you going to talk to me, or are you going to stew the rest of the ride home?"

"I'm tired, Gabriel."

Margaret was lying. Her whole energy was wrong, and Gabriel could practically feel the anger thrumming through her veins.

A disbelieving snort worked its way up and out of him.

When Margaret didn't turn at the sound, he knew she was well and truly pissed. It didn't take a rocket scientist to figure out the formula on exactly why either—Sylvia Slater, the busty redhead with the morals of an alley cat.

Her husband, Bob, had set him up, and when Gabriel went into his office to retrieve the file his client insisted he had to have right then, Sylvia had followed. The fact the husband and wife were swingers was no surprise to anyone who'd met them, but Gabriel didn't realize they'd take it as far as to sexually assault him at his own party.

"Whatever Sylvia implied, it didn't happen."

This time Margaret's disbelieving snort echoed in the quiet car interior.

"You don't believe me," he stated flatly.

She shifted in her seat and glared. "No, Gabriel, I don't."

His throat dried up, but he kept his expression bland in the face of her attack.

"You both disappeared for well over twenty minutes, and when you returned, it was sans a coat and tie. She looked like she was rode hard and put up wet." She flicked his shirt opening. "Oh, and by the way, you have a scarlet lipstick smear on your collar. So there is *that*."

He didn't need to look at her to see the accusation radiating from her furious sapphire eyes. He could feel the burning intensity from his side of the vehicle.

"Circumstantial evidence, Margaret."

"And your preference for doing it on every surface of your office?"

"*Only with you.*"

"You're telling me you've never had sex with any other woman in there?"

A telling flush started in his chest, crawled up his neck, and took up residence on his cheeks.

"Yeah, I thought so." She faced the passenger window again.

"It doesn't mean I had sex with Sylvia tonight because I've done it in my office *prior* to my relationship with you."

She remained eerily still and silent until he pulled into his driveway. When she would've opened the door, he hit the lock to keep her in place.

"Open the door, Gabriel," she gritted out.

"I want to talk this out."

"Open the door!"

"Margaret, please listen to me."

"*If you don't open this fucking door right now, I swear to God—*"

Gabriel released the locks with a heavy sigh and a matching heavy heart.

Like a racehorse out of the gate, Margaret bolted from the car and across the lawn to her house. He watched until she was safely inside. He knew James would be there to greet her, but *he* wanted to be the one to make sure her home was secure and there were no unwanted visitors lurking in her closet, for his own peace of mind.

Gabriel closed his eyes and rested his head back on the seat. Perhaps he was destined to have rocky relationships. Yes, he knew he was attractive, but with a handsome face came unwanted advances. Because he was a man, women seemed to think he had no moral compass. And though he'd never given any of the previous women in his life cause for suspicion, it had always been present in every affair.

Always before, he'd bailed when things turned ugly. This time, he didn't want to. *This* time, he needed Margaret to see her false accusations for what they were.

He wasn't sure how long he sat there, wallowing in woes, but a ding indicated an incoming text.

James.

"What the hell did you do to my sister? She's spitting nails."

Did he bother trying to explain by text?

"Come for a beer, and I'll tell you."

He chuckled at James's response.

"Yeah, give me five. I have to sneak out of the house because if my sister knows I'm consorting with the enemy, I'm toast."

As he opened the door to step out, the overhead light caught a sequin on Margaret's forgotten shoes. The sight of the heels pissed him off. He'd fully intended to have her wear them when they made love tonight. Seeing her in them and nothing else had been a fantasy since she stepped out her door, looking like a wet dream, earlier.

Goddammit!

He scooped them up and headed toward his porch. He'd give her one hour to calm down, but then they were going to have it out. Just as he'd made his decision, a figure sped around the side of Margaret's house and across the divide of lawn. The size told him it was James.

"How stealthy of you," Gabriel said dryly.

"Look, man, you've never seen my sister in a full rage. I don't want none of that. Not sure what you did, but you screwed the pooch, dude. *Big* time."

"I didn't do a fucking thing, all right," he snapped.

James's dark brows shot skyward.

"Your sister thinks I did the no-pants dance with a client's wife in my office tonight."

Margaret's brother fell back against the railing in shocked wonder. *"Jesus!"*

"Yeah." Gabriel tugged at his collar. "Slater's wife jumped me when I went to get a file. Violated my tonsils and my limp, cowering penis with her hand, then proceeded to tell me all the detestable things she wanted to do to me." He shuddered at the memory of her sloppy groping.

"I can tell by the sickly look on your face, you're telling the truth."

"It's always been a well-known fact she and her husband were swingers, but I swear to God, it isn't my thing." He lifted his phone, scrolled to the message he intended to show Margaret later, and handed the device to James.

"You fired your client? Wow!"

"Yes, right after they set me up."

"Let me guess. Margie didn't wait around long enough for you to show her this?"

"Right in one."

"You do know Scott snuck around on her, right? And not just once." James handed the smartphone back with a hard look. "Bastard did a number on her, and she's had control issues ever since."

"The OCD."

"Yes. She's never been officially diagnosed, but we've all seen it." James shrugged. "Partly, I think it's genetic because both Sammy and Annie have manifested similar tendencies, but Margie's tends to be over the top with locks, schedules, hand washing... the whole bit."

"I've noticed." Gabriel frowned in the direction of Margaret's home. "Why has she never sought therapy?"

"She did early on. She drew the short straw and ended up with a quack."

"Once was enough for her, and she never went back?"

"Exactly."

Gabriel watched the shadow pace on the other side of the curtain. "I should go talk to her."

"Nope. Let's have that beer first."

"She's going to make herself sick over this."

"If you want to kiss your relationship goodbye, head over now. Otherwise, I'd let her cool down so she doesn't cut off your head and spit down your windpipe."

Gabriel gave a half-hearted chuckle but decided to take James's well-intended advice. "Let's get that beer."

MARGIE OPENED HER LAPTOP, INTENT ON DISTRACTING HERSELF FROM the clear recall of Sylvia's smug smile from earlier tonight. Never had she wanted to hurt a person more. Gabriel's reaction to the woman was what nagged at Margie's consciousness though. When the redhead had staggered up to them, he'd seemed repulsed. *Not the action of a lover.*

A box popped up on her screen, and she didn't have time to freak out about being hacked, because the video started playing. The location was unfamiliar, but the tall man with his shirt off and his back to the camera looked exactly like Gabriel from behind.

Her hand flew to her mouth to hold back a shocked cry.

Dry-eyed and disillusioned, Margie watched him receive oral pleasure from some, as yet, unknown woman. All she was able to make out from the grainy video was the large breasts and long red hair. *The same shade as Sylvia Slater.*

Margie rushed to the bathroom and splashed water on her hot face. The sounds of the video increased in volume until she was forced to run back and close the laptop. Dropping to her knees, she let the sobs come.

CHAPTER 23

"You're getting ready to draw a line in the sand here, Margaret. Think hard before you do it. You're throwing away something exceptionally beautiful," Gabriel warned.

"I can't trust you." Her tone was beyond icy, to the point of being void of emotion.

Disbelief clashed with his outrage.

For the better part of three days, he'd tried to defend himself. But whatever her issues and her distrust, they went deeper than the party. She was hell-bent on blowing up their relationship, uncaring of the collateral damage.

When he could trust himself to speak, it was in a low tone so as not to embarrass himself by showing the crushing weight of his disappointment and pain. "That's it then?"

She nodded her agreement.

"You need to say it, Margaret. You need to say we're done." His voice was louder, rougher due to hurt and anger.

She remained silent and refused to utter the words that would finish them for good.

Gabriel grabbed her, careful not to manhandle her even though he was royally pissed off. A huge part of him wanted to hurt her as she was hurting him. But he wouldn't. Couldn't. However, he did cradle her head between both his palms and forced her to address him directly.

"Look at me," he commanded. "Look me in the eye and say it. Tell me to go and never come back. If you do, I'll leave you alone."

He knew what she thought and why she believed it to be true. But her mistrust was suffocating him. It made it impossible to explain whoever was on that video wasn't him. Although Gabriel swore he hadn't cheated, the doctored video the hacker had sent, proved differently.

Margaret firmed up her resolve, and Gabriel saw the exact moment she made the decision to end them. He wanted to throw back his head and wail like a wild wolf in a steel trap. Instead, he shut down. The old fallback of cold indifference from years of dealing with his father settled within him.

"Say the damned words, Margaret. Let's get this farce over with," he demanded harshly.

She opened her previously frozen lips and uttered the one thing guaranteed to make him go forever. "You need to leave and not come back, Gabriel. Whatever this..." She broke. Her last words arrived on a sob. "...W-whatever this was, it's over. I d-don't want y-you."

"This..." He copied her gesture and pointed back and forth between them. "...*This* was love. Whether you want to admit it or not. But it doesn't matter now because I'm done trying to prove myself to you. Even if we got past this, you would find another reason to destroy what we could have. It's your nature, isn't it?" He couldn't resist a final dig. "Inside, you're a scared little girl. Too frightened to take a risk. But I'll grant your final wish, and leave you alone to wallow."

The tears free-falling down her cheeks gutted him, and Gabriel didn't want to react. He mustered everything he had inside not to haul her close and soothe her hurt. To declare his undying devotion —*again*. But he needed to remember she didn't want him. Her pain was no longer his concern. Nursing his own wounds would be his number one priority from here on out.

"I want to be able to tell you that I hope you have a happy life, but I'm not that big a person. I want you to be miserable without me. I want you to suffer my loss as I'm going to suffer yours," he rasped out. "Goodbye, Margaret."

Walking away, putting one foot in front of the other and moving toward the back door, was the singular hardest thing Gabriel had ever done in his life. It would have been easier for him had she ripped his heart from his chest and hacked it to smithereens with an ax right in front of him. But, no. She had to leave that useless organ in place. Battered, bruised, and aching.

The pounding of dread and residual adrenaline reverberated in his ears until it was all he could hear. The mad drumming filled his mind and drove him insane from the pulsing rhythm. Was that a crack he heard? *Perhaps.* His heart certainly felt broken into a million pieces.

"Gabriel!"

For the briefest of seconds, he thought Margaret had called him back. But standing in her place was Kaley. The devastated look on her face caused a second crack.

"Don't go, Gabriel. *Please.* She doesn't know what she's saying. She's just being hateful."

Kaley's tearful entreaty nearly obliterated what was left of his heart, and he rushed to her. He bent his knees enough to be eye level. A grimace twisted up his mouth. What could he say in that moment? How could he make sure she didn't blame Margaret for what he suspected Don had done? He couldn't. But Gabriel could assure her he would always be there for her.

"Kaley, listen to me. Whatever's between your mom and me isn't for you to judge. She's doing what she thinks is best for her. But please know, if you ever need anything, I will be there for you and your brothers. You have my number. Whatever you need. Okay? Promise."

Gabriel waited an eternity for her to speak. He expected a "whatever" or a "fuck you, asshole," but what he got in return was a nod, and the tearful fifteen-year-old threw herself into his arms to cry her heart out.

As he looked over Kaley's purple-colored hair to Margaret, he noted her stony resolve.

Jesus, she was cold.

At that moment, he hated her.

There she stood, destroying what could've been a perfect family unit, because of some ass-wipe of a man and the games the little snake had played. How could she be so damned blind?

"Kaley, *enough!*" Margaret snapped. "He needs to leave. *Now!*"

Her daughter's head whipped around to stare at her in shock. Margie could almost predict the thoughts running through Kaley's mind. *How could her mother be so cruel?* Next, it would be her shouting how much she hated her.

None of it mattered.

Kaley's verbal jabs would be a fight for another day.

Right now Margie needed Gabriel gone. If he didn't leave soon, she would throw away her pride and beg him to stay. Eventually, she'd curse herself for being a weak fool. For loving him despite the cheating and lying. How many times would she have to turn her back on the indiscretions? How many times had she done it with Scott to keep her family intact?

As for Gabriel, how could she, a frumpy artist with a handful of kids and a boring existence, expect to keep him when he was so virile and every woman's fantasy?

Better to cut ties now.

Forever wasn't in their cards. It never had been. Fate had always destroyed their love one way or another in the centuries past. Why

216

fight it anymore? Sudden exhaustion struck her, and Margie wanted off this merry-go-round.

Squeezing her eyes tight, she dug deep to drum up an apology. Her daughter's hurt wasn't something to be dismissed lightly. "I'm sorry, Kaley. Take whatever time you need for your goodbyes."

Margie pushed past the two of them, ran for the front door, and grabbed her purse from a peg in the hall before fleeing.

Where she intended to go, she had no clue. Oddly, the person she most wanted to talk to was Sammy. She wished her sister wasn't tucked in some mental facility, suffering from her own devastation and loss, because Margie desperately needed a friend to talk this over.

Her mother would be on Gabriel's side. And why wouldn't she? Violet adored him. Annie wasn't an option, because she would still be inundated with the rash of feelings and emotions Margie was experiencing, and it would be too painful for an empath. The only remaining person was Jamie, and he'd want to beat the shit out of Gabriel for cheating if he knew the full truth.

It upset her more than she could say because she had no real friends to turn to. Why had she never cultivated close female relationships? To borrow Kaley's term, why did she have to be such a bitch to everyone around her?

Flagler Beach beckoned. The ocean would be a safe haven for the immediate future. A place for her to come to grips with the situation and hopefully center herself to face Kaley when she returned home.

The mild March sun beat down on her as she walked along the shoreline, occasionally bending to toss a shell into the dark waters that rushed toward her and washed across her toes. By the time she'd wandered past where the die-hard, early-morning sun worshipers lounged on their towels or chairs and where the fishermen stood with their multiple poles stuck in the sand, Margie had reached a decision.

The time to leave Palm Coast had arrived.

Scott didn't have much to do with the children. The boys were young enough to start over in another town and would make friends easily in another school. Kaley would be a problem because she still had another three years left of high school and she wouldn't want to go. If it were only her senior year left, Margie would be willing to let her move in with her grandmother for the year, but Kaley was still too young to leave behind. As it was, Margie would face resistance because it would be traumatic for her daughter not to graduate with her friends.

More positive than she'd felt in a long while, Margie whipped out her phone and dialed her mother. She needed to talk to someone about her decision, and her mother was it.

"Mom? Hi. It's Margie."

"Hi, honey. What's going on?" Violet had clear concern in her voice.

Margie focused on the horizon where the water met the sky. Her ability to speak vanished once she heard Violet's voice. Had she called because she needed her mother to fix things like when she was a small child? When had her life become such a mess she couldn't manage it on her own?

"Margaret? You're scaring me. What's wrong? Is it one of the kids?"

Violet's anxiety forced words from Margie's lips. "No, Mom. The kids are fine. I... it's me. I..."

"You and Gabriel broke up."

The quiet understanding from her mother almost broke her. Sobs wracked her body. There was no strength left to keep her standing, and Margie dropped to the sand. Fisting her right hand, the ground received the continued impact of her rage and hurt.

"Why? Why did he have to cheat on me? What is wrong with me that men can't seem to be faithful?" she wailed.

"I don't know, honey. Scott was an all-out ass. But Gabriel? Are you positive he did what you are accusing him of doing?"

"Someone gave me a video. Gabriel was getting a blow job." She closed her eyes against the embarrassment of discussing sex with her mother, especially something so personal.

"I'm sorry."

"Mom, I want to leave Palm Coast. Go somewhere and start over."

Silence greeted her declaration.

"Mom?"

"I'm still here." Another long pause filled the airwaves between them. "Are you sure this is what you want to do?"

"I'm sure. I can't be here anymore. Living next to Gabriel, seeing him on a daily basis, and then eventually watching him bring women back to his house...it will kill me. I love him so damned much."

"What about the kids? Do you think it is fair to them to remove them from school to start over? They've lived here all their lives."

"No. I know it isn't fair. But the boys will adjust. Kaley, I'm not so sure about." Margie dusted her palm down the length of her shirt. "I don't want to uproot her one year into high school, but what choice do I have? Maybe she should live with you and Dad for the next few years."

"Oh, Margaret. Have you even talked to Kaley about this?"

"Not yet. I just decided."

"You think she'll rebel." It wasn't a question.

"I do. Mom, Kaley is devastated by my breakup with Gabriel. She blames *me*. Again." Margie closed her eyes against the pain. "We'd finally gotten on solid footing, and now this."

"She's a teenager. When she grows up and has relationship issues of her own, she'll understand," Violet consoled her. "For now, know that every parent embarrasses their child from about the age of thirteen to twenty-three. You only have about eight more years of her contempt."

Margie snorted, caught between amusement and despair. "I love you, Mom. I'm so sorry if I put you through anything like that."

"Oh, you did. You were my know-it-all child. But look how well you turned out?" Violet laughed. "And, because I love you, I'd do it all again in an instant."

"Thank you."

"You're welcome. And, honey? The fault isn't with you. It's with the men you pick. There is absolutely nothing wrong with you. Do you understand me?"

"Yes," Margie whispered.

"What? I didn't hear you."

Margie rolled her eyes. Of course, her mother had heard her. Violet was simply trying to infuse Margie's spine with steel. She cleared her throat and tried again. *"Yes!"*

"Good. That's my girl. I'm glad to see you have your backbone in place." Violet sighed on her end of the line. "I'm not convinced you leaving is the right thing to do, but I will support you in any decision you make."

"Have I told you I think you are the best mother on the planet?"

"Yes, but I don't mind hearing it again."

After she hung up, Margie sat, arms hugging her knees, and stared out to sea. She knew uprooting her daughter might cause a breach in their relationship they might never get beyond. Yet finding a resolution right then was beyond her capability.

A text from Gabriel flashed across the screen of her phone.

"Where are you? Kaley is packing and talking about leaving. I think you should get home. I'm trying to stall her."

After typing out she was on her way, Margie stood and dusted the sand from the seat of her shorts. An echo of some long-buried instinct triggered a warning, and the hair on the back of her neck lifted.

"Margie."

Startled by the voice, she pivoted to see who'd addressed her.

The satisfied smirk on Don's face confused her. Before she could reason how he knew she had come to this stretch of beach, he lifted his arm toward her. The current from the taser knocked her flat. As she lay there, helpless, Margie felt a pinprick on her bicep.

Pure terror choked her, causing her heart to beat a rapid tattoo in her chest and a throbbing to start in her head. It felt like she was stroking out. Her urge to fight was strong, but whatever he'd injected her with made it impossible to move. She opened her mouth to scream and found that impossible, too.

"Don't bother. You should be out in three, two, ah. Right on time."

Blackness descended.

CHAPTER 24

$\mathcal{G}$abriel was worried. Margaret should've been home hours ago. Whatever her faults, whatever was broken between them, she wouldn't ignore her daughter's attempt to run away just to avoid seeing him. With a little luck and a whole lot of tap dancing, he'd been able to help Kaley see reason. But Margaret didn't know that. It was impossible to believe she wouldn't have rushed back.

The first three calls he made were to her cell. Each effort went straight to voicemail. The fourth was to the police department to make sure there hadn't been an accident. The fifth, to the hospital, yielded nothing. The sixth call, he directed to Grey to garner help in the search for Margaret. The last call, he asked Kaley to dial for him so he could speak to her grandparents.

Even as the phone on the other end rang, his anxiety level grew closer to requiring a tranquilizer.

"Violet? It's Gabriel. Have you heard from Margaret today?"

"I did. She called me from the beach about three hours ago. I haven't heard from her since. Why? What's going on?"

"Maybe nothing. I don't want to worry you, but I sent her a message around that same time. She texted me to say she was on her way home." He sighed in frustration. "She never arrived, and she's not answering her phone or texts."

"Do you think something happened to her?"

The concern coming through the speaker convinced him as nothing else would that Violet wasn't covering for Margaret.

"I don't know. The police department hasn't reported any accidents. Do you suppose you or Martin can come stay with the kids? I need to actually do something. Need to be out looking for her. Sitting here is driving me crazy."

"Of course. I'm leaving right now," Violet paused for the space of three heartbeats before continuing. "Gabriel? Thank you for caring enough about my daughter and her children to do this."

"I love her," he told her simply.

"Thank you for that, too. I'll see you soon."

He'd forgotten Kaley was in the same room until she touched his arm. The worry in her large, blue eyes had to mirror his own.

"Do you think something happened to Mom?"

"I don't know what to think, kid. It's not like her."

"If something happened to her, it's my fault," she cried.

This must be what Margaret was like as a teenager. Sassy and rebellious one moment, and heartbreakingly sweet the next. Both mother and daughter took on the world's problems as if they were their own.

"No, Kaley. Your mother walking out today had nothing to do with you and everything to do with the two of us. If anyone is to blame here, it's me. I let a misunderstanding fester into something bigger between us."

"She loves you, Gabe. I heard her telling my Aunt Annie."

Having Kaley reassure him when the situations should've been reversed, moved him. He'd always had a soft spot for Margaret's oldest child, but at that moment, he loved her as if she were his own. If he needed to lay his life down for hers, without question, he would.

DON HAD HAD ALMOST TWO YEARS TO CONSTRUCT MARGIE'S abduction. Each day, he laid one more brick in the foundation of his plan toward the ultimate goal of carrying her away to his cabin. A few trial runs with other women had assured him his strategy to nab her was a viable one.

Once Gabriel had shown up and captured Margie's interest, Don was forced to up his game. The man was determined to ruin everything, and if their relationship had moved any faster, Don wouldn't have had the opportunity to get to her.

Every night, Don dreamed of making love to Margie as she screamed his name and begged for more—just as she had done for that asshole Gabriel. Black rage clouded his mind, and he swerved into the next lane. A vicious honking horn brought him back to himself.

Margie had had her chance to do this the proper way, but she'd rejected Don's overtures again and again. Now she would need to pay for her betrayal. He'd devised punishments to fit each infraction. There had been plenty of those as well. He kept all those indiscretions of hers on a digital recording and watched them on a continuous loop. Careful to commit each detail to memory. Yes, she had done a lot of whoring, but he was here to help her learn the error of her ways. Before long she would be pleading with Don to forgive her.

As he passed the Florida/Georgia line on the I95 interstate, he allowed himself to breathe easier. If his involvement in taking her hadn't been discovered by this point, it probably would take a great while for anyone to connect him to her disappearance.

A high-pitched giggle escaped his lips.

He was smarter than the lot of them combined. No one had come close to proving his connection to the break-ins, and although Gabriel strongly suspected, he couldn't prove a damned thing. Palm Coast was still behind the bigger cities on crime-scene advancements. Investigations took a great deal of chance to solve if no fingerprints were found on the scene, and Don was always careful to erase the proof of his presence.

He shot a quick look over his right shoulder to be sure Margie still lay unconscious in the rear seat. She was. *Good.* It would make transport easier. Locking her up, too, when the time came. Not long now, and he'd reach the cabin he'd set up for his needs, then his constant itch to touch her would be satisfied.

"GODDAMNIT! WHERE IS SHE?" THE HELPLESSNESS JAMES WAS FEELING had given way to fear. And because none of the Holt family did fear well, he raged.

Gabriel wanted to have a meltdown right along with him.

Margaret's vehicle had been found parked in the dunes off the Atlantic Highway by North 22nd Street in Flagler Beach. Her purse had been shoved under the driver's seat. The only thing that appeared to be missing was Margaret, her phone, and her keys.

"James, calm down." Margaret's father, Martin, looked as ragged as the rest of them, but he seemed to be the voice of reason at this point. "Flying off the handle isn't going to help anyone right now. We need to concentrate on finding your sister."

The shrill ring of the house line caused everyone to jump. Initially in surprise, and then to grab for the receiver.

Gabriel managed to get to it first. "Hello? Margaret? Love? Is that you?"

"Gabe? Gabe, it's Sammy. Why are you answering Margie's home phone? I've been trying her cell all day. What the hell?"

"Sammy? How... I..." No words could convey what needed to be said. Helplessly, he stared at the counter. Shaking his head, unable to speak, he shoved the phone into James's waiting hands. Long, swift strides carried Gabriel out to the deck.

He dragged his hands up and down his face then gripped his hair. Every ounce of control he had, went into holding back the guttural yell working its way up from his tortured soul.

Margaret was gone, and no one knew where.

Fuck! Fuck! Fuck! Fuck! *Fuck!*

A gentle hand on his low back startled him.

Violet.

"Quite the extensive language you have there, Gabriel."

Apparently he hadn't done so well keeping his internal screaming at bay.

He snorted and shook his head. "Do you think the whole neighborhood heard?"

"I'm pretty sure all of Palm Coast heard," she said dryly.

"How are you so calm, Violet? What aren't you telling me?"

Her eyes widened.

He'd guessed correctly; she was hiding something.

Gabriel waited her out, keeping his steady gaze trained on her. The tactic worked well with his clients and courtroom opponents alike. She avoided looking at him, and instead, her eyes trailed into the line of woods beyond where they stood.

Lightning lit the sky in the distance. It created a sharp contrast between the bright night sky and the pines towering over the backyard. Even nature was restless tonight.

"Violet, tell me. *Now.*"

"Margie called me from the beach. I told you as much." She paused for a heavy sigh and to rub her arms. "I'm sure it was the heat of the moment, but she said she intended to leave town. Permanently."

She turned to him, a wary look on her face.

Did she assume he'd fly into a rage? Perhaps he refrained because her words didn't surprise him. If he were being honest with himself, he'd never expect Margaret to continue to live next door to him after what had transpired. It would be torture for the both of them. However, had she bothered to ask, he would have told her there was no need for her to go. He intended to trade Grey the house for his old condo. There were no memories of Margaret there, and Gabriel might have a chance in hell of getting through each day without losing his mind.

"It doesn't explain why you are so calm. If she *had* run away— and I don't believe she did—she would've taken the kids. Or, at the very least, made arrangements with you or Scott to get them. Did she?" He inhaled a deep breath. "And why would she leave her purse in her car? For that matter, why not take her car? It doesn't make sense."

Violet shrugged and shook her head. "She did say she intended to take the children, but she needed to talk to Scott first. Kaley's rebellion and hatred were a big concern for her. Margaret did mention the possibility of Kaley living with Martin and me to avoid the strife."

Worry had crept into her voice, and Gabriel suspected the reality of the situation was about to strike. He watched as her eyes widened in horror. A hand came up to her mouth as the other reached toward someone behind him.

He spun in time to see Kaley's face crumble. Hurt and betrayal shone from her baby blues. *Fucking great!* Now the kid thought her mom didn't want her. He recognized the look. Between himself and his two brothers, one of them wore it constantly while growing up.

Taking the four steps to reach her, Gabriel hugged her. She struggled to be free. Her small fists stuck him in the back, one after the other, for a full minute. He refused to let go. Refused to let her escape and wallow in her pain alone, to hide out like a wounded animal. Because he'd done that, too. It led to no place good.

"Kaley, stop!" he commanded. He had to control his jaw drop when she did.

Inch by inch, he pulled back, ready to grab her if she bolted. The energy drained from her a little at a time until nothing was left. He had the fleeting thought that the poor kid was almost dead on her feet.

Gabriel guided her to the two-person lounger and eased her down beside him. "When it came down to it, she would never have left you, kid."

"You don't know that!"

"I *do*. Believe me, I do."

Kaley studied his face, looking for signs of dishonesty. Gabriel let her see all the pent up pain and hurt he'd been so careful to keep hidden from his brothers.

"Who left you?"

"My dad. He was a mean sonofabitch, and it was no great loss."

"What makes you so sure my mom didn't leave us? She's always threatening to."

"How so?"

"Aaron burned a hole in the living room carpet yesterday. She said she doesn't know why she puts up with our shit. Said if she was smart, she would dump us in an orphanage and join a circus."

A snort of amusement burst from him. Yes, it sounded like something she'd say. "That was your mother being melodramatic. When have you ever known an adult to join the circus? I mean seriously. Can you see any of us learning the flying trapeze at our age?"

Kaley shook her head, a tentative smile forming on her lips.

"What about working with the elephants? She'd love that," piped in a young voice to the left of him. Gabriel smiled and opened his arms wider to allow Aaron to snuggle up with them.

"Talk about putting up with shit. There would be a mountain of it."

"Language," another voice scolded. Gabriel scooted right and made room for Scotty. Of the three, the oldest boy tended to parrot the adults and follow the rules more than the other two.

"I apologize," Gabriel said with wry humor. He met Violet's tearful stare.

Her hand still rested against her lips, barely containing her worry and fear.

The desire to ease her guilt from hurting Kaley compelled him to add, "Now you see why I don't think she left you three little punkasses? It's less work taking care of you than to clean up after elephants and to work out muscle knots from learning a trapeze routine. Your grandmother can tell you."

Violet rushed to the lounger and perched on the edge. Gabriel released Kaley to her grandmother's embrace.

"It's true. Your mom would never leave you, no matter what she threatened. She—"

"Mom." James's voice cut across whatever else she intended to say. "I need to talk to you and Gabe."

"If it's about my mom, I want to know." Kaley challenged James with a stare.

"It's not open for discussion, Kaley. Take Aaron and Scotty into the family room. Now."

Gabriel didn't care for James's attitude, but the urgency behind it communicated a deeper need to speak privately. Margaret's brother had important news.

"Do me a favor, kid. Listen to your uncle. If there's anything to report, I'll let you know. I promise to keep you in the loop. Okay?" He hoped his smile transmitted reassurance. From his side, it felt stiff and unnatural.

She must have seen something to put her mind at ease because she ushered her brothers inside.

"Spill," Gabriel barked at James. Rising from the recliner, he wrapped an arm around Violet's shoulders. Part of him had the sneaking suspicion they would both need the support.

"As you know, that was Sammy. She's been trying to reach someone all day." James uncrossed his arms and ran a hand through his already mussed up hair. A harsh laugh and a slight tilt of his head indicated he was still attempting to wrap his head around whatever Sammy had told him.

"Jesus, man. Spit it out already!" If James didn't spill the news soon, Gabriel wouldn't be responsible for his own actions.

"Yeah, about that... Sammy claims Margie's been taken."

CHAPTER 25

*A*s consciousness crept back in, Margie became aware of her surroundings. She was shivering from the cold, and her head ached something fierce. As she reached for her throbbing skull, she came up short. Wide, metal shackles surrounded her wrists like ugly goth bracelets. A tug caused thick links to clank and echo throughout the room, and she winced at the noise.

Dear God! She was chained!

Terror writhed snake-like in her belly and cleared the last of the fuzziness from her brain as reality set in.

Again, she tugged at her chains. With each forward motion of her arm, she was met with resistance. Panting sobs tore from her throat. She tried to twist to see where the metal met the wall, but the length of chain was too short on either arm, effectively locking her in place with her back to the cool stone. The feel of the rough rock on her skin made her aware of another fact—*she was naked!*

The horror of the situation triggered her gag reflex. And as she struggled to control her urge to vomit and to wrap her mind around her current situation, her lungs labored with each breath she took.

She was at the mercy of a deranged person.

Memory came roaring back.

Not just *any* deranged person. *Don Acker!* He'd tased, drugged, and locked her up.

A long, loud guttural cry conveyed her rage and fear. The sound hurt her own ears, but she screamed again and again, until her voice was almost gone and she was spent. She sagged as far as the iron manacles would allow.

Margie used her remaining strength for one last hoarse yell. "You'd better pray to God I never get loose, you bastard! I swear to all that I hold dear, I'll rip you limb from limb."

The two-faced coward didn't answer her. Not that she expected he would, but she sure as hell hoped he heard her and knew she'd fight until her dying breath.

With nothing left to do, she surveyed her surroundings.

Cameras were in every corner of the room. Even with her lack of tech knowledge, she could tell they were the top of the line. The lights around the lens of the closest one showed red and left her in little doubt he was watching her even now.

A snarl curled her lips as she glared before she turned her head in the opposite direction. When her eyes lit on the bed in the corner of the room, her horror grew to epic proportions.

He'd recreated her bedroom!

Paint, pictures, bedspread… down to the exact throw pillows.

She shuddered.

Did he intend to keep her here indefinitely?

The desk across from her drew her notice. It didn't belong in her house, but there was something vaguely familiar about the style, and she struggled to recall where she'd seen it before. What did he plan with an office desk?

Static came across a small speaker in the far corner of the room, followed immediately by Don's voice. "Do you recognize it, Margie? You should. It's the desk Gabriel James bent you across."

Sweat beaded along her upper lip. Nausea followed. Only deep breaths and determination kept her vomit at bay.

What twisted game was Don playing?

She didn't have to wait long to find out.

"You seemed to enjoy it so much, I decided you and I will give it a try."

This time, there was no stopping the eruption from her distressed stomach. Her throat burned from the bile, and hot tears raced down her cheeks. If that smarmy dung beetle thought she would allow him to touch her, he had another think coming. She'd kill him first.

"Rot in hell, you rat bastard!" she cried hoarsely.

"You'll come around. They always do."

Her face went numb.

They? Did that mean he'd done this to other women? Dull, amenable Don Acker was a serial kidnapper and rapist? She wondered how many women, and what had happened to them when he was done with them. Gabriel had tried to tell her Don was dangerous, and only in recent months, had she begun to believe it.

Margie started to shake uncontrollably. Her teeth chattered, and not an inch of her flesh wasn't covered in goose bumps. Should she try to appeal to whatever human part of that fucker remained? Maybe this was what he'd meant when he said those ominous words. Perhaps unable to withstand the cold, his victims would trade a favor for a robe.

Disgust curled her lip at the idea of sex with the little weasel-faced puss pocket. Hypothermia would take her before she begged.

She squeezed her eyes shut and thought of the one thing that would warm her—Gabriel's love. She'd been so stupid. It only took being held prisoner and chained to a rock wall for all of five minutes for her to realize the tapes had to have come from Don, and he must've found a way to doctor them. He'd caught her at a low point and played on her uncertainty. Like a dumbass, she fell for it.

Another, older memory pushed to the forefront of her mind. Don. They'd known each other before. It had to have been at least two hundred years ago. London.

She struggled to recall his name. Ronald? Roland?

Richard.

During her first season, he'd developed a fascination with her, becoming completely obsessed after only a handful of social gatherings.

She shuddered when she recalled the events of the past.

He'd abducted her then, too, but Gabriel, in his incarnation as Hugh Markham, had saved her. Dueling with and running Richard through in the process.

No wonder the two men hated each other!

Even without the ability to remember, animosity sometimes remained. Because the shadow of hate had lived between them before, it would linger and feel like a living, breathing thing between them in every lifetime.

Gabriel had been her savior then. How could she have been so foolish to believe he would ever betray her? He never had—not in *any* lifetime. He'd been loyal and her staunchest supporter. *Always.*

If she ever made it out of this prison, she'd apologize for ever doubting him.

Margie shivered.

The cold brought her back to the present and to thoughts of escape. She supposed she could play on Don's ego and try to con him into believing she cared about him. But she'd have to play it perfectly or risk him wondering why she went from cursing him to fawning in a short time span.

Another possibility was to find a way to utilize one of her siblings' gifts. Annie would be the best bet for feeling Margie's terror and physical discomfort. Sammy might be able to get a vision of where she was being held, but Margie didn't hold out hope her sister would be lucid enough to act on any premonitions.

More recently, Margie had discovered Jamie possessed the ability to speak to spirits. She could try to beseech Don's past victims seek her brother out, but it would be impossible to know if it worked since she didn't have Jamie's gifts.

All she knew was Gabriel couldn't save her this time.

Her eyes burned with unshed tears.

Her situation was hopeless. Any ideas were far-fetched and a pipe dream at this point. Margie would need her own plan because the reality of being found by anyone else was slim to none.

She could only recall feeling this horrendously cold and powerless once before. In another life, the night she sat huddled on a lifeboat with her sister.

APRIL 1912 -

Lucy and Rosie, sandwiched among others, shared a blanket and a prayer for a miracle. Entreating God to somehow, someway, save Sebastian and Andrew from the sinking vessel in the distance.

Her bones ached from the freezing temperature, and she gritted her teeth in an effort to stop them clanking together. Her sister's tears froze where they rolled off the sides of her devastated face. But Lucy couldn't cry. She sat wide-eyed and disbelieving of the maritime disaster she was witnessing.

Titanic had gone dark. Screams of pain and people's pleas echoed across the open air. Even those were growing fainter. The horrific creaking and shuddering sounds as the ship broke in half were not ones she'd forget.

Somewhere on that ship, a man she loved with all her heart was trapped.

Rosie begged the crew to return, but they studiously ignored her. As if by not making eye contact, they wouldn't have to acknowledge and consider her heart-wrenching pleas.

Lucy knew going back for survivors risked their lifeboat capsizing from those who would attempt to save themselves. For this reason, Sebastian and Andrew wouldn't have a true chance of survival. The suction of the sinking ship would drag them down. Should they miraculously make it off alive and get clear of the watery vacuum, the frigid sea would surely kill them.

Never before had Lucy considered death. But her heart was shattering in her chest, and she wondered what it would be like to slip over the side of the craft they were on. To let the icy water suck her under. To join Sebastian in his watery grave. Right now, it was impossible to consider going on without him. She didn't want to.

The bitter cold permeated the blanket and the coat she wore under-neath. A mere taste of what Sebastian and Andrew must be experiencing.

Lucy lifted her eyes to survey the shell-shocked expressions of her lifeboat companions. Molly Brown sat, facing her. Dark splotches of red were the only color on her pale skin. Earlier, she'd been kind to them and had taken charge, helping Lucy and Rosie secure a seat on the lifeboat. Now, her eyes were as haunted and horrified as the rest of the passengers around them.

"Can't we go back? Please?" Rosie cried. "Andrew might be alive."

Lucy couldn't disconnect her tortured gaze from Molly. They both knew the chances were slim. But a firm resolve entered Molly's eyes, and she made a case for going back to search for survivors. Besides Lucy and Rosie, no one else was willing to take the risk.

Molly's strident tones could be heard echoing over the expanse of water as she cursed those around her for the cowards they were. The other occu-pants of the lifeboats around them turned their heads away as she argued the boats weren't filled to capacity. Molly tried to shame the crew into turning their boat toward where the bodies of their fellow passengers now bobbed in the water.

The cries for help grew fewer and further between. Within twenty minutes, all but a handful of voices were silenced forever. The commander of lifeboat fourteen pulled alongside and urged survivors to transfer into other boats.

In her urgency to comply, Lucy slipped and forcefully crashed into the solid edge. Pain, sharp and savage, radiated from her rib cage, and it became difficult to breathe in any other way than a shallow pant. To complain was out of the question when the dying bobbed in the icy sea surrounding them.

Later, she discovered only four men were rescued. None were Sebastian or Andrew.

It wasn't until Lucy was on the RMS Carpathia, being treated for her injury, that she allowed her tears to finally fall.

CHAPTER 26

argaret had been gone for almost a complete day. Twenty-three long, torturous hours. The one thing playing over and over in Gabriel's mind was what James had later revealed to them. Not only had Margaret been taken, but Sammy swore she was chained to the wall in her bedroom in a basement-cave. What that even meant, Gabriel had no clue. Most likely nothing. But he couldn't dismiss the idea Margaret had been abducted.

Don Acker was the only suspect who came to mind.

Police reports were filed, by the female officer who'd responded to Margaret's attack. In her eyes was resignation and a gentle understanding. Without a doubt, she'd seen this type of thing before. Gabriel couldn't bring himself to ask how those other incidents had played out. He was a criminal attorney, and he'd seen too much. Way too many similar situations to hold out any hope.

Don had disappeared. His alarm-company employees had sworn they hadn't seen him in days and had no knowledge of his whereabouts. One female employee had gotten up the courage to complain about his high creep factor and how he'd insisted on being alerted to any activity on one particular account—Margaret Holt's.

Gabriel hated himself for not considering this outcome. They'd all played right into his hands, and the realization Don had outsmarted them didn't sit well.

"We know there are no basements or caves in this area. Are you sure that's what Sammy said? A basement-cave?"

James cast him a weary look and nodded.

It wasn't like Gabriel hadn't had him clarify the question multiple times, but he still couldn't wrap his head around this madness. "Where does that leave us?"

Margaret's brother continued to dig into his plate of eggs and sausage, and the smell turned Gabriel's stomach. He couldn't recall when he'd last eaten. Of course, he must've because Grey had been quietly preparing meals for him and Margaret's family since this whole nightmare began.

James swallowed before answering. "North? Georgia maybe. I don't think he'd want to risk driving a long way with her. I'd say five to eight hours max. Otherwise, he takes a chance of needing to stop for bathroom breaks, gas, things of that nature."

"I agree. So we start looking in Georgia. Perhaps see if we can find property in Don's name in any of the counties closest to the state line. Somewhere the ground might support a cave and still be stable enough to build a basement."

"I'll talk to a few contractors I know. They may be able to tell us where a home can be built into or against a mountain. Sammy said 'cave,' but it could be a simple stone wall."

"Christ, this is hopeless, isn't it?"

"No," James said sharply. His expression softened marginally. "Not for us. Not for the gifts we possess. Opal wants me to tell you to stay strong."

Gabriel took an involuntary step back and cast a wary glance around, unsure if he expected to see his aunt or not. "I still find it difficult to wrap my head around your family's 'gifts.'"

"No one has an inkling but those closest to us. It's not like we advertise. But they're real, Gabe. As surely as I'm sitting here." He gave a half smile. "The false bottom drawer in the dresser didn't prove it?"

"Lucky guess," Gabriel retorted, although they both knew it wasn't. "So my aunt can't tell us the who, what, where of what happened to Margaret?"

James cocked his head and seemed to be listening. "She said you know who and why. But she can't tell us where. That's for us to discover."

"Why? Why not?" Gabriel slapped his hand on the table and glared his frustration. "This is Margaret's life we're talking about. Our life. The lives of her children."

"I get it." James looked as annoyed as he felt. "But she doesn't know, Gabe. Whatever happened, this has to play out." His gaze shifted to the space next to Gabriel. "She said when we find Margie, we need to be loving and understanding. Opal says to not give up."

His head came up, and he pinned James with a hard stare. "When we find her? So we will?" His voice cracked, but he wasn't embarrassed.

"Opal believes it to be true."

Gabriel could've wept his relief. But doubts soon crept in.

Stephen had assured him the man they were dealing with wasn't rational. Don was sick. The average person didn't enact a crime this terrible, especially against someone they claimed to care about. No, Don had most likely fixated on Margaret years ago, and Gabriel's arrival on the scene had been a catalyst to force the other man's hand.

"I'm worried what her mental state will be when we get her back. I also find it highly probable she won't want anything to do with me."

"I think by the time this is over, she'll realize either Don, or someone he hired, was the one who doctored the video, Gabe." The compassion in James's voice nearly closed Gabriel's throat. His eyes burned, but he refused to give in to his overly emotional response. When they had Margaret back where she belonged, he could lose it. Until then, he had her children's welfare to see to, along with heading up the search to find her whereabouts.

Grey entered the meeting room followed by Gordon. His

brothers brought coffee and fresh croissants. Other than to whip up breakfast for James this morning, Grey's restaurant remained closed due to their family emergency.

"Grey, you don't have to keep your place shut down."

"Be quiet. I'm not arguing this again. It's just for a few days, most of my regulars will understand. I've given my staff paid leave for the duration. We're good."

Gabriel squeezed his little brother's wrist in gratitude.

James pushed aside his plate and reached for one of the four coffees. As he added cream and sugar to his drink, he gave Grey and Gordie a rundown of their earlier conversation and the message from Opal.

Both of Gabriel's brothers stiffened and cast a cautious look around, and he almost laughed at the similarity in their reactions. A ghostly Opal was a bit much to take in.

"I want to give the children the opportunity to remain at home, James." Gabriel rolled his shoulders and reached for a coffee. "According to Stephen, they need the security of their standard routine."

"I don't see where that's a problem. I can bring Sammy's dog over and crash there."

"I thought I'd stay there, too. To show a united front and maybe ease their minds. They have to be feeling uncertain and scared."

James gave him a half smile. "Kaley adores you, man. I'm sure she'll be thrilled if you stick around."

"I didn't want it to be weird, but I need..." Gabriel broke off when the sentiment clogged his throat and threatened to choke him. What he couldn't seem to voice was, yes, he wanted to be there for the children, but he needed them just as much. Needed any small connection to Margaret.

They all glanced away to allow him time to compose himself.

"First things first, Gabe. You're going home, and you're going to try to sleep." Grey, the damned mother hen, held up his hand and shook his head to stave off the impending argument. "You've hardly slept since the party and your fight with Margie, have you? I know for a fact you haven't since she disappeared."

"I'll sleep when she's back."

"You aren't doing her any good this way," Gordie said, adding his two cents. As the middle child, he tended to be quieter. Or maybe it was the artist in him. Either way, when he spoke, he intended to be heard. "I'm driving you home."

Gabriel lifted his coffee. "As if I'll sleep after this."

"It was decaf."

"Fine." He scowled his irritation at his brothers and climbed to his feet.

James made a point to catch his eye. "I'll have that list of locations by the time you wake up. Count on it."

"Thank you," Gabriel said gruffly. "Let's go, Gordie."

"And eat something." Grey bundled two croissants in a cloth napkin and tossed it to him.

His stomach rumbled its agreement.

GABRIEL FELL INTO A FITFUL SLEEP. IMAGES OF MARGARET BEING tortured, of being cold and hungry, of lying in a pool of her own blood, all took turns haunting his dreams. He woke drenched in sweat with a hoarse scream on his lips.

As he lay there, staring at the evening shadows collecting on his ceiling, he tried to drum up the energy to go next door and check on Kaley and the boys. But he couldn't. Their grandparents were with them, so he wasn't overly worried.

Instead, he rolled over and surrendered to the uncontrollable urge to cry. He bit his pillow to muffle the noise, so if anyone was in the other room, they wouldn't hear.

A whiff of vanilla and orange blossoms drifted to him, and he put the pillow to his nose. Margaret's unique scent flooded his senses, and Gabriel closed his eyes, trying to recall the last time they were happy together, before everything went drastically wrong.

He rubbed his cheek against the pillowcase and tried to pretend it was her silky soft hair. But he couldn't play make-believe when she was scared and alone in the clutches of a madman. Pain seared his insides and made taking a deep breath difficult. The only hope he held was Opal's assurance Margaret would be found.

He dozed off again.

This time, his dreams were just as tragic, but Margaret wasn't the victim.

APRIL 1912 -

Sebastian trailed off his conversation with the attendant who'd escorted him into the dining room. The dark-haired woman in royal blue, captured his attention immediately and refused to let it go. He'd been positively poleaxed by her beauty and shy innocence from the moment he saw her walk aboard the Titanic earlier. She simply captivated him, and he couldn't look away.

Even before meeting her at their dining table, he'd experienced a strong wave of déjà vu, as if he knew exactly how she'd respond to his every teasing comment or hot glance. The sense of familiarity refused to be dismissed. When he discovered, in passing, she was on her honeymoon, he wanted to howl his grief. Convinced he was a fool, but unable to help himself, he'd arranged to be seated at the same table each evening.

It didn't take long to discover hers was merely a marriage of convenience, and from the moment he'd learned it, he planned his seduction. When they landed in America, he fully intended to steal her away. To help her obtain a divorce so the two of them could be together, because they shared one soul.

Their one brief moment of dissension came when Lucy believed he'd gotten cozy with her sister. Convincing Lucy that Rosalie held no appeal for him after he'd set eyes on her wasn't easy, but she finally came around. It was the same night her sister disappeared, and Lucy begged Sebastian to help with her search.

Hours had passed, and still, they found no sign of the foolish girl. Lucy was beside herself, and she badgered the ship's staff to help in their search.

As the evening grew later, Sebastian suggested Lucy go rest, promising he would continue the search even if it took all night.

"No, I'll never be able to rest until she is found. I want to go with you, Sebastian."

Reluctantly, he agreed. "All right. But we are heading down to the third-class decks. It is the only place left." A niggling doubt plagued him, leaving him with a bad feeling and a question of what they'd find.

The two of them descended into the steerage section in a last-ditch effort to find Lucy's wayward sister. At one point, they'd felt the ship's impact with the iceberg and, after speaking with a handful of the crew, weren't oblivious to the dire straits the Titanic found herself in. However, their unease was second to their pressing need to find Rosalie.

As one hour flew into another, their search proved fruitless. Panic had set in for the passengers, and the White Star employees were feeling the strain. Sebastian refused to let Lucy remain with him any longer.

"If you don't go back to your suite, don a flotation vest, and find a lifeboat to take you to safety, I'll abandon this damned search for Rosie and put you on the bloody boat myself."

"Please, Sebastian. I can't leave you down here. Come back with me. We can gather more help," Lucy begged. She held his lapels in a death grip, claiming fear for him should he venture into the bowels of the ship.

"I promised you I would find her, love. Go locate Andrew and send him to help me if you must, but you will get off this ship if the opportunity presents itself. That is the one thing you can promise me."

As Lucy studied his face, her sapphire eyes turned solemn. She reached up and smoothed his mussed hair back from his brow. "I promise. Please, be careful."

They shared one last bittersweet kiss before he provided the exact directions to the suite she shared with her husband. She'd laughed at his attention to detail the first night, but he knew it would save her now.

He made her repeat the directions twice before he felt confident she would find her way. Lucy paused at the top of the staircase, giving him one last, long look.

Sebastian had a general idea of the layout of this beast of a ship. He had created a mental grid and marked off sections they'd already visited.

The problem, as he saw it, was Rosalie herself. That girl was impulsive, and he doubted she would stay in one place long enough for him to locate her. Therein lay his dilemma.

He strode to a crewman preparing to lock the last gates for the lower levels. Apprehension gripped Sebastian. Even if he found Rosie, would he be able to get them back topside? Damn that girl! Throwing caution to the wind, he charged down the stairs. The alarmed cry of the crew member ringing in his ears.

"Sir! We be locking these gates, sir. If ye go down there, ye'll be stuck."

"Is there another way up?"

"No, sir. This is the last gate."

"Don't lock it. Stand guard until I come back."

"I can't do that."

"Then hand me the bloody key and be done with it already, man. I have no more time to spare."

Shockingly, the wiry little man delivered the metal key into Sebastian's hand.

"God be with ye, sir."

A brisk nod sent the Irishman on his way, and Sebastian turned a grim eye to the rising water level. He plunged into the bitterly cold seawater, hissed, and swore a blue streak. Without another thought to his personal safety, he traversed the corridor and checked each unlocked room.

After a thorough search of the immediate area, Sebastian returned to the original stairwell where he'd last seen the Irishman. Back resting against the wall, he looked down at his cold, pale hands with their dark red fingers and purple nail beds. It was bloody freezing, and these damned hands of his refused to function properly. He'd pull the key from his pocket to save himself if he could.

"Hey, old man. Do you need some assistance?"

The mildly amused voice belonged to Andrew Hale.

"Actually, I do. However, I fear you probably wish to leave me to my fate," Sebastian countered.

"I came to find you. Rosie is safe, as is Lucy. Now tell me, how are we supposed to unlock this wretched gate without a key?"

"Funny you should ask. I happen to be in possession of such a key."

The two men grinned at each other.

"What are you waiting for? Let's have it!" Andrew demanded.

"Yes, well, I find my hands are refusing to cooperate enough to remove it from my vest," Sebastian told him, a wry smile playing on his lips.

"Hmm, yes. I can see where that would be a problem. Come closer. Which pocket?"

Sebastian gestured, and Andrew reached through the accordion-like bars to fumble around. He produced the key with a flourish and went about trying to unlock the gate.

"Damned thing's stuck," he muttered.

A gurgle sounded behind Sebastian, alerting both men to the danger.

"Bloody hell! Work faster, Hale!"

Motivated by the rising tide, Andrew accomplished the task in record time, but not before a surge of water swept Sebastian into the barrier. When he righted himself, blood dripped from his now-broken nose.

"Goddammit! This is that batty girl's fault," he snapped.

"Rosie?" queried Andrew, choking down his laughter.

"Yes! She is a menace."

Sebastian was sure Andrew would have taken umbrage that Rosalie was, indeed, a menace if the man hadn't already vocalized it the previous evening. Instead, he wedged a shoulder under Sebastian's arm and encouraged him to "get his arse moving."

Their breathing became labored with each step as they trudged through the icy saltwater. The freezing temperature stole the air from their lungs whenever the ship shifted and doused them with the rising tide. The corridors were dark now, and the Titanic offered up groans, pops, and creaks as if to bemoan her fate.

By the time they made their way to what Sebastian thought would be freedom, he came to the sickening conclusion they were too late. All the lifeboats were gone.

"Well, of all the damned luck," Andrew swore.

"Damned is correct," muttered Sebastian.

They leaned against the outer wall for support, teeth chattering, gulping in the frosty night air.

The ship rested at a forty-five-degree angle from the water's edge, making their footing precarious. Sebastian barely make out the safety boats dotting the horizon. Hair-raising screams could be heard as passengers lost their grip and plunged toward death in the icy depths of the unforgiving ocean. But he was now friendly comrades with Andrew in the last moments of their lives, and Sebastian appreciated he acted as if they didn't have a care in the world. It took away the true horror of their circumstances.

"I don't suppose we are going to be escaping this little adventure alive."

Andrew's comment startled a laugh from Sebastian. When he would have offered up a sarcastic retort, an unexpected melody cut through the shouting and weeping. "Bugger me! Is that music I hear playing?"

His companion cocked his head to listen then laughed with delight.

"I expect we should go enjoy it while it lasts, old man."

"Capital idea. Do you suppose we can find some brandy to warm us on the way?"

"I'll keep my eye out for a server," Andrew quipped.

GABRIEL WOKE FROM THE DREAM, STUNNED TO REALIZE ROSALIE WAS the spitting image of Sammy and Andrew Hale resembled her Michael. It explained the covert glances the two had shared during meals, and all the many times Andrew overlooked Lucy's flimsy excuses to go off on her own.

He snorted his disbelief. Surely, he'd imagined it all. When his eyes fell to the sketch Margaret had insisted he frame, he had a harder time writing off the dream as a flight of fancy. She'd said she knew him and they'd been together in every lifetime. Oddly, he believed her.

If they were indeed fated mates—soulmates, she'd called them— then he'd find her. He'd be with her again. Any other outcome was unimaginable.

CHAPTER 27

To Margie's shame, it only took nine hours of cold to break her resolve. The voices of the women held captive before her all encouraged her to be reasonable. To fool Don into believing he'd subdued her will until help arrived. She was convinced she'd either channeled James's gift, or she'd lost her stinking mind. Her money was on the latter.

Don initially ignored her when she'd swallowed her anger and pride to beg for a blanket. Thirty minutes later, he offered her the trade of a blanket in exchange for a kiss. When she gagged into his mouth, he stomped off in a fury, leaving the thin cover out of her reach to taunt her. An hour later, he offered it again for the opportunity to touch her breasts. She nodded her agreement without making eye contact.

And so it went. If she wanted food, a drink of water, the use of the bathroom, or to shower, she traded favors. After a day, she hated him with a passion. After two, she despised herself more. After three, she plotted his death—even if it meant her own.

She'd been allowed to transition to the bedroom area of her prison toward the end of the first week. By then, she'd have done almost anything to be able to sleep on a bed instead of against a hard wall with the weight of the shackles making her joints and muscles ache, and the sharp stone ridges cutting into her back.

Today, the door cracked open, and Don entered with a wide smile and a tray of food. With hatred in her soul and a fervent wish she had a sharp knife for plunging into his black heart, she pasted a pleasant expression on her face. Or as pleasant as a prisoner could conjure.

In the beginning, she'd been suspicious of anything he fed her, but he didn't need to drug her after the abduction. He had the bone-chilling room temperature and her gnawing belly on his side.

"Here you are, my love. Fresh fruit and coffee, just the way you like it."

She fucking hated fresh fruit and coffee now. If she ever got out of here, she'd become a total tea convert. His chipper attitude was souring hers, but she forced a smile anyway. "Thank you, Don."

As she ate, he checked the iron cuff attached to her ankle, a dark frown drawing his brows together. "Did you try to pick this lock?"

"Yes. It's chafing my skin, and it hurts." There was no point in lying since he had only to pull up footage of the last day.

He studied her for signs of falsehood, and she met his look with a defiant one of her own. Black rage flooded his features, and she had her first moment of true terror since waking. With a hard blow to the underside of the tray, Don flipped it onto the bed. The coffee scalded where it splashed her exposed flesh, and she hissed against the pain.

Tears came unbidden and trailed down her cheeks as she cradled her injured arm. Oddly, it was the sight of her reddened skin that reined in Don's temper. He ran for supplies to treat the burn, apologizing the entire time he pressed the ice to her forearm.

"It's okay, Don. You didn't do it on purpose," she said, giving him an understanding smile. In reality, she wanted to smash the coffee mug into his fucking face until the shards were embedded deep into his eye sockets and his nose was crushed, cutting off his ability to breathe.

His fingers fluttered along her jaw—the exact way Gabriel had touched her before making love—and she had to swallow the urge to sever his fingers with her teeth.

Don must've studied Gabriel's every move, because he employed them at each turn.

Margie's stomach was in a constant state of rebellion, and her mind shied away from existing memories.

"May I call my children today?" She detested the strong swell of pleading in her voice. "They'll be worried."

"No," he snapped. "Do you think I'm stupid, Margaret? Do you think I don't know you are trying to alert someone to where you are?"

"I don't know where I am, Don. How the hell can I alert someone?" she retorted. "I'm in a goddamned cave in fucking Afghanistan for all I know. Tell me how I can relay a location."

He backhanded her, and she tasted blood. A tentative touch of her lip told her he'd split it. She pressed the back of her hand to the spot in an attempt to stem the blood flow.

"Now look what you made me do!" He jumped up to pace. "You push and push until I get angry. Do you like being punished, Margaret? *Do you?*"

No, she couldn't say she did. She especially hated that he'd started calling her by her full name the way Gabriel always did. Thoughts of Gabriel brought rebellion, and Margie had to shove the instinct to fight deep enough to appear meek.

"Don, it's been a month. Please." She kept her head bowed and sniffed. It wasn't like she had to pretend to cry. Thoughts of her children brought her low. Early on, she'd tried tears and pleading, serving only to enrage him further. Now, if he was in a magnanimous mood, she could manipulate him with a tragic sniff and soulful eyes, which he tolerated a little better.

"*No.* Not another word."

He walked to the monitor on the far wall and turned it on. Always out of reach, she had no choice but to watch or listen to the video he played. The current entertainment was a replay of Gabriel's and her time in his office.

She remembered the day.

She'd shown up in nothing more than a trench coat and sexy red heels to thank him for helping Sammy. He'd gestured her forward and indicated she should unbutton her coat. Things quickly became heated. It had ended with Gabriel swiping the items off his desk and setting her atop to feast on her body. First, her breasts then lower. Finally, turning her to take her from behind as he pressed her to the cool glass surface. He'd rocked her world that day.

"Tonight we'll do this one," Don said. "Study the moves, Margaret. I want to get it right."

The eagerness in his voice made spots dance along the periphery of her vision. She knew from past experience if she didn't do what he said, she'd be nude and chained against the wall before she could blink. Even if they had to enact this particular scene more than once, she'd play her part. And her soul would die a little more.

The desire to weep returned. One more beautiful memory he would destroy, one more treasured moment with Gabriel removed. Her eyes burned as she stared at the monitor, but she swallowed the emotion. If she survived, she'd cry, but until that time, she wouldn't give Don the satisfaction of breaking her completely.

"Gabe, James Holt is on your private line." His assistant knew to answer his personal extension if he was tied up with a client or another call. He'd given her a rundown on the situation with Margaret and explained any calls on this designated number were a priority.

"Thanks, Jenny."

He closed his eyes and prayed for good news. Taking a deep breath, he lifted the receiver and pressed the button to answer. "James?"

"Hey, Gabe."

Gabriel rubbed the spot between his brows. "No news then?"

The defeated note in James's voice clued him in, but he needed it confirmed.

"No news. The police are... they..."

"It's okay."

It wasn't, and they both knew it, but the police had other pressing issues after three months without a lead.

"She's still alive, Gabe. I know she is."

James's positivity grated on Gabriel's nerves. As much as he wanted Margaret to be found alive and well, he worried for her mental stability should she survive. These long months in the hands of a twisted sonofabitch like Don would strain anyone's mind past the breaking point. Along the way, they'd all come to the conclusion he was behind Margaret's abduction, because he'd disappeared at the same time without a trace as to his whereabouts.

Gabriel tried not to let images of Don touching Margaret consume his thoughts because, when they did, he was unable to reason and he fell into a dark pit of despair.

Every day, he got up, downed his coffee, and came to work. Every night, he studied the grid he and James had created to search the fifty-seven thousand square miles of Georgia, looking for and eliminating potential sites for Don's hideout. And every weekend, he and James would drive to possible locations to physically search.

Gabriel sighed his frustration. "What else?"

"Huh?"

"You didn't just call to tell me there was no news. What else?"

"Scott filed for full custody on the belief Margie is missing, presumed dead."

Gabriel swore loud and long.

Jenny's head whipped around and peered at him through the open doorway. Without needing to tell her, she jumped up and closed the door.

He made a mental note to give her a raise in appreciation for her training and intuitiveness.

"It isn't enough that their mother is missing, he's going to try to take the kids away from all of you? That prick!" Gabriel was ready to spit nails—*right in Scott's fat face.*

"What do we do?"

"I have a friend. I'll give her a call when I get off the phone with you. Do you have a copy of the paperwork, or should I have Jenny obtain one?"

They discussed their options for another few minutes, eventually growing silent as they ran out of things to say.

"Is Opal still hanging around?" he heard himself ask.

"Here or there."

"She's still silent as to where..." Gabriel swallowed and blew out a breath. "She's still can't help?"

"Yes."

The suffocating feelings of loss and despair were difficult for him to overcome, but he did his best not to show it. "Leave the dickhead to me. Scott won't get custody while I'm breathing."

James signed off not long after.

Gabriel didn't know how long he sat, processing the last few months without Margaret. He rubbed his hand over the spot where his heart used to reside. Now, it was just a large gaping hole. Or so it felt.

As Gabriel sat in silence, staring at the spot where she had disrobed and stood in all her beautiful glory, wearing nothing but a pair of red heels designed to short-circuit his brain, his private line rang.

Believing it was James again, he hesitated before picking up. "Yeah?"

A voice sobbed his name.

"Violet? What's wrong?" It had to be dire if she was this upset.

"She's been found, Gabriel! Margie's been found!"

"Is she..." A hot tear dripped on his hand, and he stared at it in confusion.

"She's alive," Violet confirmed gently.

"I'm on my way!" He threw down the phone and ran for the

door. Four steps past Jenny's desk, he remembered his keys and wallet. "Reschedule the day," he barked on the return trip past her.

"Is it Margaret?" Jenny jumped up, and her hand fluttered to her throat.

"She's been found. I'll fill you in as soon as I know anything." He took another long stride then pivoted back. "Better cancel the next few days. I don't know what shape she's in," he admitted past the frog in his throat.

"Go, Gabe. I'll take care of everything."

"I was blessed the day I hired you, Jen."

"Yeah, you were. Now go."

Twenty minutes and a raging headache later, Gabriel arrived at Violet's home. James rushed out to greet him, elation and fear warring for dominance on his face. The same emotions Gabriel was experiencing, too.

"What do you know?"

"Right as I got off the phone with you, Mom got a call from the Georgia State Police. They received a call of a woman driving erratically along the highway. Turns out it was Margie." James ran a shaking hand through his dark hair. "Some guy said she pulled off the road, but when he tried to help her, she freaked the fuck out on him. He called the police, thinking she might be on drugs or something."

"She's alive? Really alive?"

"Yes."

Gabriel fell to his knees as relief took over, and his body began to shake. After all this time, she was coming home. James knelt in front of him and wrapped him in a hug. Together, they wept.

CHAPTER 28

"One of my brothers can stay with the kids if you want to fly with us. I'd offer, but I'm going," Gabriel stated gruffly.

Violet placed her hand on his arm. "I appreciate the offer, but I think the children need stability right now. You and James go. Please bring my daughter home."

"I will." He'd come to love her as much as he loved Margaret and her kids. Violet was his family now. Reaching over, he hugged her tightly and took comfort in the contact. Finally, he released her to head home and pack.

Within three hours, he and James were at the Jacksonville airport, ready to board a flight. A few hours later, they met up with Annie at the Atlanta airport, and she drove them to the hospital where Margaret had been admitted.

"How is she?" James asked the austere woman behind the desk at the nurse's station.

"When can we see her?" Gabriel asked, speaking over him.

The RN attempted to allay their fear, but Gabriel knew he wouldn't rest until he touched Margaret and saw with his own eyes she was alive and well.

Ignoring their impatience, the no-nonsense woman turned to Margaret's sister. "Are you Annie?"

"I am."

"She said you'd arrive, and she wants to see you first."

"All right." Annie frowned and cast a sidelong glance at James and Gabriel.

He began to follow, but she turned around and held up a hand. "Give us time, Gabe. We all have a good idea what happened. I suspect she's in a fragile state."

Knowing she was right didn't make hanging back any easier. "Go."

He paced the hall outside Margaret's room, a caged tiger waiting for the lock to be sprung. James, on the other hand, sat still as a statue, absorbed by the generic landscape across from him.

"What the hell is taking her so long?" Gabriel wanted to know. James simply shrugged, never taking his eyes from the stupid painting. "How are you so calm, James? *You*, of all people?"

"My sister is alive, Gabe. That's all I care about right now, not my own selfish need to see her."

The censure lacerated him, but Gabriel would be damned if he'd apologize for caring.

A lifetime and a few thousand gray hairs later, Annie returned and nodded to James. "She said you can go in, Jamie. Not Gabe, though."

All the air escaped Gabriel's lungs, and he struggled to inhale again.

"She doesn't want to see you," Annie stated as kindly as she was able. "She's been through a lot."

"*No!* Screw that. I need to see with my own eyes that she's all right." He hated that his voice went from forceful to begging. He cleared his throat and tried again. "I intend to see her."

"What's going on, Annie?" James demanded.

Helplessness, irritation, and then resolve flew across her face in rapid succession. "Don't make me the bad guy here, fellas. She's not up to visiting with *anyone* right now, but she's agreed to talk to you, Jamie, knowing you'll muscle your way in regardless."

"Why?" Though he suspected, Gabriel needed it spelled out for him.

"She's been abused. She doesn't want you seeing her in her current condition," Annie said simply.

Dear God!

Abused was the nicest possible way of saying violated. Gabriel went cold all over. In the back of his mind, he'd known it was a probability. But he'd shunned the idea. Sammy and James had implanted the image of her being chained in his mind, and the visual had been bad enough. Sweat broke out on his forehead, and his butt managed to hit the chair behind him when his knees failed to support him any longer.

Annie offered up a bottled water without comment. The understanding in her eyes was painful.

"I need to see her, Annie. *Please,*" he croaked.

Anguish lit the eyes she cast toward James.

Gabriel knew she hated keeping him at bay as much as he hated her doing it. Her indecision was all the time he needed to dart past her and storm into Margaret's room. The sight of her brought him up short. There she was, his forever love. Gaunt. Bruised. Frail looking. But she was still the most beautiful woman he'd ever known.

"Margaret." It came out like the barest whisper, yet it was still loud enough to gain her attention.

The eyes she turned his way weren't the sparkling ones he remembered. There was no love, no happy recognition, no emotion whatsoever. They were cold, flat, and completely lifeless. All moisture left his mouth, and anything he intended to say dried up.

"I told Annie you were to stay away." Her tone was colorless and that of a perfect stranger.

He stepped farther into the room. "I couldn't, love."

"I don't want you here."

Her words were a solid iron fist to his gut. He didn't know what he would have said, because James distracted them both.

"Good Christ!" James cursed when he saw the condition his sister was in. He rushed to her side, and she raised a pale, shaking hand to ward him off.

"*Don't!* Don't touch me, Jamie."

Hot tears filed one after the other down Gabriel's cheeks, gaining volume and speed. He could feel them soaking the neckline of his shirt. His anguish was matched by both of Margaret's siblings. They all wanted to hold her, to comfort, to assure themselves she was real, but touching was the last thing she'd tolerate. He was afraid she'd shatter if any of them tried.

Jamie and Annie lingered on either side of the bed while Gabriel crossed to the window, unable to walk away but trying to allow the Holts their privacy.

Lightning flashed in the distance, a network of jagged white lines across the horizon. As he stared out at the darkening Georgia sky, he wondered if he was making it worse for everyone. No one spoke, and the air around them grew heavy.

Sensing eyes on him, he glanced over his shoulder.

Margaret's stare was unwavering. "I'd like to talk to you alone."

Gabriel frowned because, mere minutes before, she'd wanted him gone. Perhaps he was off base, but the hard look in Margaret's eyes gave him the distinct impression their upcoming conversation had nothing to do with their relationship and everything to do with legal issues.

Annie rose and gestured to Jamie. "We'll get some coffee."

Margaret winced, and her face turned a sickly shade.

"Are you okay?" Gabriel asked her softly.

"Yes."

He'd be damned if she was, but he nodded absently and crossed to the foot of the bed, knowing instinctively she wanted him no closer.

Neither spoke until Annie and James cleared the door.

"I'm sorry I accused you of cheating." She studied her trembling hands. "Don confessed to doctoring the video."

Gabriel remained silent.

"I killed him," she whispered.

Time stopped along with his heart. "Did you confess that to the police?" *Please, God, no!*

A ghost of a smile touched her chapped lips and disappeared. "I was the girlfriend of a criminal attorney. I had enough sense not to admit to murder."

Good, he could work with that. Closing his eyes, he pinched the bridge of his nose.

Think, Gabriel! Think!

When his heart resumed its regular pace, he strode to the door and closed it. Forcefully transitioning to lawyer mode, he approached the bed. "I don't want you to say anything to anyone about his death until I can get you a good attorney, Margaret."

She winced when he said her name, a reaction similar to when Annie mentioned coffee.

Gabriel watched her closely, unsure how to proceed.

"Will you help me?" Margaret's voice only wavered slightly before she lifted her chin and met his steady gaze.

How did she even need to ask?

He'd die for her.

Gabriel shoved down his personal feelings and did a mental run-through of what it would take to help her. He was going to do everything in his power to make this go away, but he needed to be honest with her regarding the law.

"Margaret, I'd defend you if I could, but I'm not licensed in the state of Georgia. I promise we'll find you the best. In the meantime, I can petition the court to allow me pro hac vice if this goes to trial."

"What does that mean?"

"Some states make an exception and will allow an attorney licensed in another state to work a case. There may be conditions applied, like I'm second chair or I'll have to work closely with a local firm."

She nodded. Wringing her hands, she said, "I don't know where I was held or how long I drove. I just grabbed his keys and took off, praying to God I'd find help."

"The police can try to use reverse GPS on the vehicle you were driving. If they can't, they can try to determine a location based on how far you traveled and a number of other things. They'll find him." He took a deep breath in preparation of his next question. "Do you want to tell me what happened?"

"No."

"You'll need to if I'm to defend you, Margaret."

Again, she winced.

"Why does it bother you if I say your name?"

Her head came up, and in her eyes, he saw revulsion.

For him?

His stomach flipped.

WITNESSING HIS PAIN, MARGIE FOUND IT DIFFICULT TO FEEL anything. She'd turned off the feeling part of herself months ago. She'd had to in order to survive. With the minor exception of worry for her children's welfare, the only thing she'd allowed herself to feel was cold, hard logic and the ingrained knowledge that she'd have her revenge on Don—*one way or another.*

"Maybe for the immediate future, you should call me something else," she suggested, avoiding his stricken gaze.

"Like a made-up name?" he tried to joke. The strain around his eyes and mouth told her it was a supreme effort.

"Margie's fine. Just not... not..." She could do it. She could say her damned name. "Margaret. Not Margaret," she gritted out. "And I'll tell you what happened if or when I need to. Not before."

He frowned at her hard tone, but she shrugged it off. This was about *her* recovery. *Her* ability to cope. Not his. Not right now.

"Have you seen my children?"

"Yes. I've been in touch with them almost daily."

"H-how are they?" She could sense he was weighing his words. "Just tell me, Gabe."

His brows clashed together, and Margie assumed it was at the abbreviated use of his name. She'd never called him anything but Gabriel since they'd met. Perhaps because Opal had always used his full name, she'd done the same. But since her captivity, Margie had had to compartmentalize names, relationships, the whole works. Especially regarding him.

"I imagine they're going to be happy to have their mother returned to them," he said.

"Pfft. That's a generic statement if I've ever heard one."

His mouth quirked in a quicksilver half smile, but it dropped just as quickly.

They stared at each other. His rawness and her reticence on display.

Shutters came down, and he did his best to hide his reaction from her. Circling the side of the bed, he sat on the edge. "May I?"

Margie stared at his outstretched hand, trying to decide if touching him was wise. She hadn't freaked out when the doctor examined her, but this was Gabriel. This was the man she'd once confused with Don —and Don with him—as she lay fevered during her captivity.

As he started to withdraw, she tentatively placed her palm in his. He did no more than entwine his fingers with hers, but panic began to brew in her chest, and she jerked her hand away.

"I'm sorry," he whispered.

"Don't blame yourself, okay?" She leaned forward, looking deeply into his glistening eyes and trying to ease a little of his suffering. "It's me, Gabe. It's all me."

"We're going to get through this. Together," he promised.

She didn't have the heart to say they never would. "The kids?"

His severe look said he didn't miss her avoidance. "Kaley took it harder than Scotty and Aaron. She blamed herself because of your argument the day you... disappeared."

"She would." Love for her eldest filled her heart. Margie almost sighed her relief to be able to experience some semblance of deeper emotion. "And now?"

"Stephen has been working with her as a favor to me. Helping her see this really had nothing to do with her." Gabriel toyed with the blanket by Margie's fingers, as if he fought the urge to touch her again. "He actually counseled all the children."

"Good. That's good." She crossed her arms to remove the temptation of her hand.

He rubbed the back of his neck, and she sensed he was struggling over whether he should tell her more or not.

"Just say it, Gabe."

"James told me earlier today Scott filed for sole custody."

"*Over my fucking dead body,*" she growled.

Another half smile twisted his lips. "Yeah, those were the grounds."

"I guess he'll have to amend his paperwork since I'm still breathing."

A commotion at the door caught their attention. Two police detectives entered with James and Annie fast on their heels.

Margie knew the time of reckoning was upon her for slicing Don's throat.

CHAPTER 29

*T*he detectives asked an ungodly number of questions, and Margie looked at Gabriel before answering each one. He would give a subtle nod or shake of his head to indicate what she should or shouldn't reply to.

"There were other women there," she said softly. "Before me. I don't know what became of them, but I have a good guess."

James cast her a sharp look.

She returned it with a pleading one of her own. "If those women can be identified and their families notified, then it should be done, Jamie."

The detective in charge noted their exchange and asked about it.

"I'm a... psychic medium," James finally confessed, ill at ease. Usually, speaking to anyone about their gifts brought ridicule, but her brother knew the difference between right and wrong, and wrong was to let those victims continue to go missing without at least attempting to find their remains.

One of the cops snorted, and the other appeared intrigued.

"Ramirez, don't tell me you're buying into this crap."

"I won't rule anything out."

Margie glanced down at the skeptical detective's nameplate.

Jones. If she needed to have any future dealings with the police, she'd be sure to ask for Ramirez if he was available.

"Did you find the cabin? How far is it from here?" James asked, already rubbing the back of his neck in anticipated aggravation.

"We did. Thirty miles. Give or take a few," Ramirez replied. His attention snapped to Annie, who seemed like she was trying to blend with the drywall. "Are you psychic too?"

"No. Not in the way you think."

"But you have a gift." His voice lowered on the word "gift."

Margie knew a believer when she saw one, and Ramirez had readily accepted the idea Jamie was able to talk to the dead.

Annie's sickly pallor worried Margie. She wondered if perhaps the detective's avid curiosity was making Annie ill at ease.

The two of them locked gazes, and finally, Annie spoke. "I'm an empath. I get the occasional premonition. I can't talk to spirits like Jamie or get images of impending events like our sister Sammy."

"Wait. Are you saying your entire family can do these things?" Jones demanded.

There was a distinctive sneer residing on his face, and Margie found her irritation spiking.

"Yes. Our entire family has some sort of ability," she snapped. "Open your mind, and you just might discover there is a world beyond your small little scope."

Gabriel snorted his amusement. "Welcome back, love. I was wondering when that fighting spirit was going to strike out."

She lifted a brow and narrowed her eyes, but refused to dignify his comment with an answer.

"What's yours?" Ramirez wanted to know.

"I have total recall of the lives I've lived before."

His dark eyes took on a speculative light, and Margie imagined he'd stay and ask questions all night if he could. She dubbed him Spock, anticipating he'd say words like "fascinating" or "interesting" in response to her answers.

"When can you meet to accompany us to the site, Mr. Holt?"

James shrugged. "First thing tomorrow? We're tired from the flight and need to catch a few hours' sleep."

"That should allow the medical examiners and investigators time to finish." Ramirez nodded as he jotted James's number on his silver clipboard. "I was told the hospital intends to keep you overnight, Ms. Holt. May I stop back in the early afternoon with any further questions?"

Margie turned to Gabriel.

"That will be fine," he said on her behalf. He pulled a card from his wallet and handed it to Ramirez. "You can also call me for follow up. We're happy to cooperate in any way we can."

"I'm sorry you were put through this, ma'am," Jones had the grace to say. All disbelief was suspended as he offered sympathy for what she'd been through. "We'll wrap this up as quickly as we can."

Compressing her lips tightly together, she nodded. The quicker, the better as far as she was concerned. She never wanted to hear Don's name again as long as she lived.

James escorted the detectives from the room as Margie, Gabriel, and Annie all shared a speaking glance.

"How much trouble is Margie in, Gabe?"

"It's hard to say. If they rule Don's death self-defense or an opportunity to save herself, they'll go easier and it will be simpler to defend." He rested back against the windowsill and shoved his hands in his jeans pockets. "With any luck, James will help them discover what happened to the other victims. If Don *did* murder them, this is pretty open-and-closed."

Margie appreciated Gabriel speaking in layman's terms. Neither she nor Annie were well-versed with the law.

"You don't mind hanging around a bit longer?" Margie hated to ask when she knew it would torture them both.

His mouth tightened, and a fine white line appeared around his lips.

Annie placed a hand on his bicep and rubbed briskly. "She didn't mean it as an insult, Gabe. We appreciate your help."

The warning glare from her mild-mannered sister almost made

Margie laugh. Almost. Maybe at another time, it would've, but right now, she was mentally exhausted. "I'm tired," she murmured, shifting to present her back to them.

Closing her eyes, she regulated her breathing, as she'd done many times during the weeks she'd been captive. Pretending sleep had been her one true escape, until she did.

WHEN NEXT MARGIE WOKE, THE DARKENED ROOM AND THE LACK OF sound in the hallway told her it was after visiting hours. She sensed the presence before she looked up.

Gabriel.

He dwarfed the visitor's chair with his large frame. The thin blanket covering him couldn't have provided much by way of warmth. She was able to look her fill while he was sleeping, and she registered the fatigue on his face. Usually, he looked younger in sleep, but not this time. The ravages of the last few months were evident.

"I dreamed of us," he said quietly, his eyes still closed. The warmth of his voice caressed her insides where she didn't want to feel anything.

"What did you dream?" she asked, equally as soft.

"Our time on the ship. We were searching for your sister. You and I at first, then me alone. Michael, or rather Andrew, saved me from belowdecks after I was locked in."

She inhaled sharply. "I never knew, but I often wondered."

"We made it topside, but the last of the lifeboats were gone."

"It must've been terrifying."

"It was. But I was more sad than anything." Finally, he opened his eyes, and in those silvery depths, she saw a fierce love. "Sad because you and I never had a real chance."

Biting her lip, she nodded as the remembered sorrow permeated her soul. "I recall feeling that, too."

"Was Michael really Andrew and Sammy really Rosie? Or was that all my imagination?"

"That's how I recalled it."

"They were in love even then."

"Yes."

Gabriel sat up and swung the blanket around his shoulders to ward off the chill of the room. "It's odd how love transcends death. How it follows us from lifetime to lifetime." He scrubbed a hand along the stubble of his jaw. "When I saw you for the first time, in your hammock, it was as if my soul sighed. As if I recognized you. You hold a fascination for me I can't seem to shake, Margar—uh, Margie."

"Why are you here now, Gabe?"

"Why do you call me Gabe instead of Gabriel like you used to?" The question came across as mild, but it wasn't. His burning desire to discover what had happened to her was easy to discern.

She shrugged and looked out at the blackened night sky. For three months, she'd gone without seeing anything but that damned cave. A shudder shook her, and she met his steady stare. "Isn't it funny that someone who has the ability to see the past no longer has the desire to?" she said softly. "I'm forced to move forward."

He leaned forward, eyes intent. "We can do that together."

"No," she said, weary to the marrow of her bones. "No, we can't."

"I know you're going to require help, love. We'll get you whatever we need, but please don't shut me out."

Shutting him out was the only option.

GABRIEL HAD NEVER SEEN ANYONE SO VOID OF EMOTION, AND HE'D defended a lot of people without a conscience. Witnessing this behavior was like dealing with a perfect stranger.

"What did he do to you?" His voice cracked; he couldn't prevent it. "Tell me, Margaret."

"*No.* Let it go. Let *me* go." Her hardness startled him. It shouldn't have, because she'd been detached since the moment he'd stepped into her hospital room. But this behavior wasn't the woman he knew and loved, and Gabriel had a difficult time reconciling it.

"I'm staying."

"Do what you want." She pulled the covers around her neck. "You always do," she muttered.

"You said you know I didn't cheat on you. How about you tell me what else it is you think I've done?"

"Jesus Christ, Gabe," she snapped, sitting up and throwing a pillow in his direction. "Stop! Just stop! This isn't about *you*."

"Obviously, to an extent, it is. You're saying my name differently. I'm not allowed to call you Margaret, and you can hardly stand to *look* at me."

All her anger seemed to evaporate, and she gave him a pitying look. "You've done nothing wrong, but I need you to leave me be, okay? I need you to run, not walk, as far and as fast as you can without looking back, because I'll never be normal again. And this..." She gestured between them. "... this is gone. Over. I don't love you anymore."

Cold washed over him, followed by a burning humiliation. Suddenly, he was a little boy again and his father was sneering at him, telling him to grow up. Oh, how he wanted to delve deeper and find the root cause of her disdain, but he wouldn't. Not now.

"How many times does someone have to tell you you're not worthy, boy?" The words of his father echoed inside his brain, and the old self-hatred rose to choke him.

"Gabe?" He lifted his eyes to Margaret's. Her concern for him was evident, and he wondered why she bothered. "You're pale. Are you—"

"I'm fine," he bit out. His body felt like that of a ninety-year-old man as he stood up and folded the blanket. "Get some sleep. I'm going to find coffee."

She winced, covering it with a strained half smile. "You should go back to the hotel and a real bed. The chair can't be comfortable for someone your size."

He nodded and headed for the door.

"Gabriel." His name on her lips was dripping with regret. "I'm sorry."

"For what, not loving me? Please, don't sweat it. I'm a big boy."

He rushed out of the room and down the corridor, but he wasn't able to outrace his demons. They were hot on his heels and taunting him all the way to the vending machine. Scrounging around inside his wallet, he pulled out a five-dollar bill and inserted it. He wasn't sure how long he stared at the digital display when a pretty blonde nurse tapped him on the shoulder.

"There's better stuff in the nurse's lounge. I could take you there."

Looking down at her, he could see she was interested in more than sharing a cup of coffee. Some people were up for fast, furious sex with strangers. For all of five seconds, he considered giving her what she sought, just to feel the comfort of another person's arms around him and ward off the chill permeating his soul as a result of Margaret's words.

He shook his head, knowing any random hook-up would be pale in comparison to what he once shared with Margaret. Despite the fact she'd given him his walking papers, not once, but twice, Gabriel couldn't begin to entertain the idea of being with another woman. "I'm good. Just trying to decide how much sugar I need to keep me awake."

"Do you have a family member here?"

"My fiancée," he lied. Turning back to the machine, he blindly plugged in a number.

Her disappointed "oh" didn't make him feel guilt in the least.

"Excuse me," he murmured as he moved around her to leave.

"If you change your mind about the better... coffee, my name is Elise."

"I won't."

Gabriel found James stretched out on the couch in the waiting room. Seemed he, too, had a hard time leaving the hospital. He snorted. Margaret was going to get sick of the two of them playing bodyguard real soon. Living in a state of limbo, half out of their minds with worry, made it difficult to pretend everything was normal now. Impossible to pretend she was in the hospital with nothing more than a mild sickness when they knew she'd been starved, dehydrated, and abused. So they would stay—if only to ease their own minds.

"My sister kick you out?" James asked. His eyes were still closed, and his voice was husky from sleep. Not waiting for a reply, he said, "I'm not surprised."

"Why's that?" Gabriel sipped his coffee and grimaced. Maybe he should have agreed to accompany Elise to her break room just for the better brew.

James yawned and stretched before sitting up. "Annie. She was feeling all kinds of varying emotions radiating off Margie. Humiliation. Coldness. Isolation. Hopelessness." He shrugged. "It's not surprising she's trying to shove us all away."

"Yeah, well, has she told any of you she doesn't love you anymore?" The snark in his own voice made Gabriel cringe. "Sorry."

"Don't be. And she's lying."

"You didn't see her face."

"Gabe." James waited until Gabriel met his steady gaze. "She's lying."

"We'll see."

CHAPTER 30

*B*ecause Gabriel needed to know more about what Margaret had gone through and because she refused to be forthcoming with anyone, he went with James to Don's cabin. Once he stepped through the door, he wished he hadn't.

Evilness seemed to hang in the air around them, and even someone without the Holts' abilities could sense it. His skin crawled. A simple glance showed the eerie sensation wasn't only messing with him.

Skin pale, James was focused on something neither Gabriel nor Ramirez could see. "Margie was right," he said quietly. "There are spirits here."

"How many? Can you identify them?" the detective asked.

"Give me a little bit." James turned left and faced a blank wall. He nodded his head thoughtfully, turned slightly to his right, and nodded again. "Ramirez, do you have a notebook for the names?"

The detective produced a pen and pad for James. The fascination on his face meant Margie's brother had a fan for life.

"When?" James asked the phantom in front of him as he scribbled on the paper. He held up a hand. "One at a time, please."

There were a total of seven names when he was finished, and

beside them were dates going as far back as twenty years ago. Ages, addresses, and various detailed incidents were noted as well.

"Seven women?" Gabriel asked, mouth drier than dirt. "Seven women died here?"

"Yes," James replied grimly. The longer he listened to the women, the more ashen he'd become, and now, he refused to meet Gabriel's eyes.

"What did they tell you?" he demanded.

James shook his head and rushed from the room.

"If it was anything like what we found for his sister, those other women suffered," Ramirez told Gabriel.

"What do you mean?"

"It's still a crime scene down there, but from what I've seen, I don't understand how your client didn't lose her damned mind."

Client. Right. They didn't know she was so much more.

Shoving by him, Gabriel headed for the stairs. His way was blocked by Detective Jones. "Let me by."

"No, sir."

"I want to see..." He swallowed and closed his eyes. "I need to."

"No, sir, you don't. Want to, that is." Jones had lost all the previous night's attitude. "No normal person does something like what that sonofabitch did. It's too bad he didn't die when your friend slit his throat."

The blood rushed from Gabriel's head, and he swayed. "What?"

"Yeah, I hope he doesn't get some smarmy lawyer who finds a loophole. Damned criminal attorneys..." He trailed off as if suddenly remembering Gabriel was one of their ilk. "Sorry."

"Are you telling me Don Acker survived?"

"Yes. When they found him, he was barely alive. But the officer guarding him told me Acker pulled through surgery."

"Surgery?" Gabriel was having a difficult time wrapping his brain around what the detective said. "Where?"

"Memorial."

"That's where Margaret is!" Redundant because Jones knew that, but Gabriel needed to stress it anyway.

"We have a guard on him, and Acker's in recovery. He's not going anywhere."

Gabriel wanted to punch the smug confidence off the guy's face.

"Margaret is in that hospital," he said slowly as if talking to a moron, of which, he wasn't convinced Jones wasn't. "Don is *obsessed* with her."

Spinning on his heel, he raced for the door. He noted with a grim satisfaction that at least Ramirez took the threat seriously. Outside, James was pacing with his head cradled between his palms, as if by pressing hard enough, he could crush the horrendous images in his mind.

"James!"

Gabriel's tone was enough to prompt Margie's brother into action. The men raced for the car as Ramirez spoke into his radio.

EVEN IN DREAMS, MARGIE STILL COULDN'T SEEM TO SHAKE DON. Ugliness and hatred burned brightly in the fanatical eyes glaring down at her.

"Look what you did to me, you bitch!" His voice was low and hoarse, not at all like how it had been when he was alive. But the same evil intent saturated the air around her.

He tore away the bandage and exposed his throat. Margie somewhat expected to see exposed muscle, tendons, and blood, or at the very least a raw, gaping hole. To see the three-inch gash stitched with perfect precision threw her.

His icy fingers caressed her throat. "Now you'll know what it's like to taste death, Margaret. To feel what I felt when you left me on the cold floor, gasping for breath." Wrapping his fleshy hands around her neck, he began to squeeze.

The monitor to her right went haywire, registering her elevated stress. She strove to wake from this vivid, heart-stopping dream, but couldn't. No amount of fighting, of telling herself this wasn't real, could rouse her. As the fingers closed off her airways and she tugged at his thick, hairy wrists, the realization struck this was no dream.

Drawing her legs up, she attempted to wedge her knees between them. The leverage briefly broke his hold, but his strength far surpassed hers, and he latched onto her throat a second time. The promise of death was in the eyes boring into hers. The ones burning with a loathing so great, her terror escalated.

As she gasped for air, black spots danced on the outskirts of her vision, rapidly closing in. Panicked, she scrounged for a weapon with one hand as she clawed at his face with the other. Her wrist knocked the rail, and the blow to the IV underneath her skin sent a sharp pain radiating up her arm. In a last-ditch effort, she ripped the needle from its vein. Working her forearm between them, she used what strength she had left and jabbed him in his eye socket.

His agonized howl coincided with copious amounts of clear fluid flowing from the hole. Don's shrill scream sent up an alarm, and from what felt like a long distance, Margie heard running and shouting.

The one remaining hand on her throat spasmed, and she lost the last of her ability to fight. As her eyes were drifting shut for the final time, she saw Annie slam a flower vase down on Don's balding head. Margie wanted to scream. To warn her sister to run like hell. To say there was no stopping him now, because he was possessed and determined to finish this once and for all.

Don swayed on his feet but spun toward the new threat. Annie kicked him squarely in the giblets, and if Margie had it in her to cheer, she would've. But the lights were fading, and she knew no more.

"SHE'S COMING AROUND."

Margie's first thought was her throat ached like a bitch. It was as if she had strep, tonsillitis, and a wedge of cheese lodged all in one spot together. Her second thought registered the oxygen mask, covering two-thirds of her face. The edges applied pressure across the bridge of her nose, down her cheeks and along the line of her jaw, sealing it to her skin. The cool flow of air was forced into her airways. She lifted a hand to explore the device, and she frowned her confusion.

Annie grasped her wrist and, with gentle but firm pressure, tugged it down. One look into her swollen eyes, and Margie knew someone had died. Her sister wasn't prone to emotional outbursts or crying jags, because they sapped her energy too much.

Margie trailed the fingers of her opposite hand along Annie's purpling cheekbone. Her desire to speak was curtailed by the oxygen mask, but her sister understood what she wanted to know.

"Don attacked you, Margie."

Remembered fear and panic caused Margie's body to jerk, and she glanced wildly about. Although he shouldn't still be in the room, her brain couldn't quite come to grips with logic.

"He's dead, Margaret."

Gabriel's flat comment shocked her.

She tugged at the mask, but he resettled it in place and sandwiched her hand between both of his.

"Your oxygen levels took a nose-dive, love. You have to leave this in place for a little while."

"What happened?" she rasped. The words came out garbled, and she wanted to scream her frustration. Trying to vocalize anything immediately brought to mind sword-swallowing acts gone wrong. Instead of going for the respirator, she used her fingers to explore her throat.

The last thing she recalled was Don glaring down at her.

Gabriel and Annie shared a long look. Her sister gave him a subtle nod.

"When Don attacked you..." He shook his head once and tried again. "When Don attacked you, you stabbed him in the eye with your IV needle." He ran trembling hands through his mussed hair.

Annie cast him an understanding half smile and took over the explanation. "I was returning to see you, Margie, and was in the elevator when a premonition struck. I arrived as he was choking you." Her tormented gaze dropped below Margie's chin. "All I could think to do was hit him. You'd just jabbed his eye, and I thought between the two of us, we'd stopped him." Annie touched her bruised cheek. "He punched me after I kicked him in the ballsack."

Margie's distressed cry was more of a croak.

"I'm okay. They've already checked it all out," Annie assured her. "After Don knocked me across the room, he turned back to finish what he started. But he dropped like a stone. One second, he was reaching for you, the next, he was on the floor."

"The doctor ruled it an aneurysm," Gabriel concluded as he moved sideways to allow the nurse to attend Margie. "But he's gone, love. For good, this time."

She knew she should feel relief, but the emptiness inside was like a black hole swallowing all her emotions. Fatigue struck, and sleep's siren call couldn't be ignored. She gave in rather than try to process everything they'd told her.

As Gabriel watched Margaret's eyes flutter closed, he once again thought about how close they'd come to losing her. If Annie hadn't arrived when she did... *Jesus!*

"Why don't you go join Jamie and get something to eat, Gabe? I'll wait with her."

"I'm good. You should, though. I'll be here for when she wakes again."

"How are you holding up?"

"Twice that sonofabitch hurt her, and twice I was too late to help. I don't know how I feel."

"You couldn't have known."

"The first time, I strongly suspected he was off. I don't have your gifts, but everything about him was wrong, you know?"

"I do."

"Then he set us up for failure with that damned video."

Annie remained quiet.

"After Margie disappeared, I thought about all the things I never got to say to her. Every night, I dreamed of her in some small way. In my waking hours, I imagined the horrors she must've undergone." He shook his head. "They didn't even come close if what the officers inferred is true."

"You aren't twisted like he was. There's no way you could've come close to imagining what he'd do."

His head came up, and he pinned her with a stare. "Do you know? Did you see?"

Gabriel didn't know how to begin to breech Margaret's walls or ultimately help her if he couldn't understand what she'd been through. And he desperately wanted to ease her suffering if he could.

"I don't know all of it, but I won't betray her trust, Gabe." Her lips tightened, and she glanced down at her sleeping sister. "If she wants you to know, she'll tell you."

"No." He gingerly eased a strand of Margaret's dark hair away from her sweat-dampened brow. "No, she won't. Don't ask me how I know, but I do."

CHAPTER 31

A crash and a curse rang out from the area of Margie's pool deck. Even knowing it couldn't be Don, knowing that nightmare would never play out in real life again, her heart accelerated to heart-attack speed.

Post Traumatic Stress Disorder.

Dr. Stephen Montgomery had been counseling her for weeks now and had warned her PTSD would be an issue. It would strike at odd times, paralyzing her from taking action—as it was now. For all she knew it was a damned raccoon, but her mind automatically assumed intruder, and her body reacted accordingly.

"Mom?" Kaley rubbed the sleepiness from her eyes. "What was that noise?"

Mama Bear kicked in. "Grab your phone and lock yourself in with the boys. Try not to wake them if you don't have to, but be on alert."

Her daughter's blue eyes flared wide, and her hand flew to her throat. "Is someone trying to break in? We should call nine-one-one."

Another crash and curse sounded from the other side of the

slider. This time Margie recognized the voice. "Never mind. It's Gabe. Go back to bed."

"Gabriel? At two in the morning?"

"Apparently." Anger bloomed. The careless disregard he exhibited had scared her and Kaley both. Of all the boneheaded moves for him to make, terrifying Kaley after all those torturous months was right up there.

"You sure it's him?"

Kaley's life had altered drastically this last year. First, with the death of Michael. Second, when her beloved aunt was admitted to Brookhaven. And then again when Margie had disappeared. Trauma had forced her to grow up faster than a teenager should've had to.

Margie flipped on the floodlights.

Gabriel's large body was sprawled across the hammock, face-down. A grimace twisted her lips. How many times had he done this now? Five? Ten? Maybe more. Certainly only when he got piss drunk, which seemed more frequent of late.

"I'm sure. Go back to bed, sweetheart."

"Okay."

Margie keyed in the new alarm code. She was careful to change it monthly. Something simple for the family, but still a challenge for anyone to figure out. Easing open the slider, she stepped out onto the deck and crossed to where Gabriel began to snore.

"Gabe." She shook his foot. "Gabriel, wake up and go home."

He grunted and attempted to roll onto his back, dislodging himself from his nest and landing hard on the concrete. *"Fuck!"*

Biting her lip to abort a laugh, she offered a hand to help him up. He ignored her gesture and stayed where he was, head in hands.

"I failed you." The raggedness and pain in his voice made Margie want to gather him close.

She wouldn't.

Touching him opened a can of worms she wasn't able to deal with.

Instead, she sat cross-legged on the ground across from him. "No, you didn't."

"*I did!*" His head came up, and the tortured look on his face chipped off another piece of her fractured heart. "I did, Margaret. I failed to protect you."

"It was never your job to protect me, Gabriel."

"Yes. Because I love you, and that's what you do. You protect the ones you love."

He'd once told her about his past and all he'd been through. Time and time again, he'd taken the brunt of his father's abuse to save his brothers a beating. Gabriel was the model big brother. He was the perfect everything because he'd had to be. Seeing him not so perfect like this was awful, but not because she required him to be flawless. This departure from who he normally was and tried so hard to be, was killing him. He was conflicted, filled with pain, and *that* was the saddest part.

Ignoring her trepidation and giving into instinct, she placed a hand on his knee. "Listen to me. Neither of us knew how sick Don was. We had no idea he'd planned what he had. It was impossible to predict he'd..." Her throat went dry. "It doesn't matter. He was a fucking deviant, and you're not to blame for this. You need to stop torturing yourself."

"I can't seem to," he whispered, turning away to stare at the deep end of the pool.

"I've had an offer on the house."

His head whipped back around. "You're really leaving?"

"It's for the best. You need to get on with your life, and this..." She gestured to his slumped shoulders. "... this isn't helping either of us."

"What can I do or say to make you stay? If it's this place, you and the kids can come live with me."

The earnestness in his face caused her heart to spasm. Without a doubt, he'd haul them next-door this minute if she said yes. But the ability to agree wouldn't come. First, he'd need to know what had happened in that basement, yet every single time she thought about telling him, her throat locked up.

This was no different.

"Talk to me, Margaret. *Please.*"

"You need to get on with your life, Gabriel. You can't show up here at night and give me a heart attack whenever you knock into the furniture." She rose to her feet and purposely hardened her expression. "There is no more us. I thought I made it clear. The sooner you realize it, the better."

"I can't walk away without knowing why." He staggered to his feet and swayed as he leaned over her. "Hell, even if I did know why, I couldn't walk away."

"You can't even walk, period," she muttered. There was no way she was going to get him back home by herself. She glanced at Gabriel's darkened house, doubting Gordie was in residence during touring season.

Her couch would have to be Gabriel's bed for the night.

Steeling herself, she placed his arm across her shoulders and hers around his waist. Beads of sweat popped out on her upper lip, and her skin turned clammy. But it wasn't from the exertion of helping him toward her door. The mere act of him touching her made Margie want to hurl.

With small, controlled breaths, she guided him into the house.

They made it into the living room with a lot of grunting on both their parts. Right when she would've left him to settle onto the sofa, he twisted and cupped her face.

Her heart began to hammer, and she clawed his skin, trying desperately to remove his hands from her person. "Don't touch me! Don't touch me!" she whimpered. "Don't touch me!"

"Jesus! I'm not, Margaret. I'm not." All drunkenness drained from his face, and he held his hands up and out from his sides. "Please, love, calm down. I'm not."

It took roughly ten seconds for reason to penetrate her brain. On the heels of her hysteria came embarrassment. "Ohmygod, Gabriel! I'm so sorry. I..." Sobs came from the deepest part of her soul and broke from her lips. "I'm... s-so sorry... I'm s-sorry... I... c-can't... can't."

Never, in the weeks since she'd been home, had she cried. All the residual terror and emotion left over from her abduction had been shoved so far down, it was never supposed to see daylight again. She'd had to be strong for her children. Strong for her family. Strong for Gabriel. Margie wasn't allowed to break down. But that's exactly what she did.

Collapsing on the floor, she continued to weep. Continued to struggle to draw a breath from her overworked lungs. Gasping and choking, she cried on.

Thin arms wrapped around her from behind. Somewhere within the depths of her mind, she registered it was Kaley and tried not to react negatively to her touch. Freaking the fuck out on her child wasn't good.

"Go away!" Scotty screamed at Gabriel, punching at his stomach, arms, and any body part he could reach. "Go away! You're making her cry. You promised you'd never hurt her. *You promised!*"

As Gabriel shifted to go, Margie latched onto his leg and rested her forehead against his thigh. Her children grew still, and Kaley's arms dropped away as Gabriel knelt down beside her. Finally, Margie was able to contain herself, but only enough to meet his tormented, gray eyes. "It's not... your... f-fault, Gabriel."

His desire to hold her was written on every line of his body, and Margie had to grant him this one last favor. Inching forward, she caressed his face with her fingertips. If this was goodbye, he couldn't go with the memory of terrorizing her.

"I d-do love y-you," she whispered past the ache in her throat.

Taking his hands in hers, she guided them to her waist, flinching only slightly and praying he didn't feel the movement. She feared he did because he started to draw away. More firmly, she pressed his hands to the flat area of her back then wrapped her arms around his neck. "Please hold me, Gabriel. Just this once."

His breath gushed out, and he drew her into his embrace, inch by inch, with such tenderness, such reverence, Margie nearly began sobbing again. Frantically, she blinked away the tears.

When his arms were fully around her and her head rested on his shoulder, she closed her eyes and inhaled the smell of sunshine and love.

Gabriel. Her beloved Gabriel.

She didn't want to lift her head, but in her peripheral, she could see her children hovering. "It's all right, Kaley. You and Scotty go back to bed, okay?"

THE CHILDREN WERE RELUCTANT TO LEAVE THEIR MOTHER, AND Gabriel understood their reticence because he'd have felt the same.

In the cradle of his arms, Margaret remained stiff as a board, unable to relax, and his heart knew true sorrow. It would be the last time she'd allow this. She believed she was too damaged for him to love, and he couldn't bridge the distance or convince her otherwise.

If he had one wish, it would be to resurrect Don and kill that sonofabitch by his own hand, but much slower and with a lot more pain to make his passing sheer agony. It was no less than he deserved.

"Margaret?"

"Yes?"

"Will you tell me what happened?"

Gabriel would've sworn it wasn't possible for her to stiffen more than she was, but she did.

"No."

"Stephen keeps telling me to give you time, but he won't say why you've decided I'm the enemy."

She drew away and slumped against the edge of the couch. The dead eyes she turned on him were crushing. "It's not his place to tell you what happened."

"I agree. It's yours. Please. Talk to me."

She stared at him the longest time, and Gabriel was positive she'd reject him yet again. When he thought he might not be able to bear another moment of her silence, Margaret rose to her feet slowly, as if she were a hundred years old. "Come. I don't want the children to overhear."

He placed his palm within her proffered hand, pathetically grateful she permitted this small contact. They strolled out to the pool deck, and she shut the door so curious kids couldn't overhear.

They each settled into separate loungers. Margaret sitting with her legs out in front of her, and Gabriel perched on the edge of one chair, facing her. He rested his forearms on his knees and clasped his hands together in an effort to keep them to himself instead of pulling her into his arms again. His need for contact continually tried to override his reason. And all the alcohol he'd consumed made that reason sketchy at best.

"Are you sure you want to know, Gabriel? Once you do, you can't go back to blissful ignorance. It will forever mar your memories."

"I'm sure."

Her eyes dulled, and she nodded.

Was he doing her a disservice by insisting? Stripping away her last thread of dignity? He almost changed his mind, but his overactive brain would continue its relentless imaginings until he knew what had transpired.

"I was on the beach when Don arrived. It was the secluded spot you and I had chosen for lunch." She inhaled sharply. "I was trying to sort through my feelings and reconcile the man begging for a second chance with the man in the video, getting a blow job from another woman."

"I swear on Opal's grave, it wasn't me. I don't know what Don did to—"

She held up a hand. "I know, Gabriel. He confessed to splicing the video footage together. Apparently, Don was excellent at photoshopping." She shook her head. "I think part of me knew it back then, too. But that's neither here nor there. I'm trying to tell you what happened."

Gabriel scrubbed his hands up and down his face, then through his hair. "Sorry."

"I heard a noise behind me and turned around. He tased me before I ever registered what he had in his hand."

The air left his lungs in a whoosh, and he couldn't catch his breath. *"Jesus!"*

"If you keep interrupting, I won't get through this."

"Right. Sorry."

"I was unconscious the entire trip. Apparently, he'd stopped at rest areas along the way to dose me with some drug or another."

Margaret closed her eyes, and Gabriel forced himself to remain silent. Inside, his blood boiled. If he did nothing else with his life, he intended to see animals like Don put away for life from here on out.

"When I came to, I was chained to a wall."

A strangled cry escaped him. "Sammy's vision was correct."

"Sammy?"

"She managed to call here the day you went missing. She spoke to James, but he didn't tell her you were missing. No one wanted to add to her trials."

"I see." And perhaps she did because she didn't seem surprised by the information. Margaret rubbed her hands along her upper arms. "He'd built a basement into the side of a mountain, and I remember thinking the space was enormous." She shook her head as if irritated by the errant thought. "Don had constructed various platforms. Each one represented a different room. There was a duplicate of my bedroom, yours, your office..."

"What?" Gabriel couldn't wrap his mind around what she was saying. "Why?"

"He thought by recreating what you and I... by copying us..." Pressing the heels of her palms to her eyes, she swallowed audibly.

"You don't have to tell me anything else, love," he said quietly. As much as he wanted to know, he didn't need her to relive the horror of her time there. Plus, his imagination was thrust into overdrive, and everything he was envisioning was wreaking havoc on his mind.

"No. You asked. Now you'll listen."

Her tone was cold and brittle, and Gabriel tried to reconcile this hard woman with the warm, caring Margaret of the past.

"Don forced me to recreate what you and I shared. Every moment spent in your home or mine, in your office. With him." With a steadying breath, she stared out at the illuminated aqua pool, her expression lifeless. "All in the belief I'd fall in love with him."

Nausea churned in Gabriel's gut, and he rushed for the screen door. All the alcohol he'd consumed emptied from his stomach onto the base of the azalea bushes by the pool enclosure. Over and over, he heaved until nothing remained.

Good God! No wonder she couldn't stand to have him touch her. In her mind, she must've confused the two of them. Hands braced on his legs, he knelt, shaken to his very core and unable to move. He lost track of time as image after image of their most intimate moments replayed like a movie in his brain. All tainted by the actions of a psycho.

A washcloth appeared before him, and he accepted it without comment.

"I had that same, exact reaction while I was there," she said, her voice barely above a whisper. Her fingers brushed the back of his head as she stroked his hair. "The shock and horror of him continually watching us until he perfected the setting. Perfected your actions. Then the... rest." She cleared her throat. "He would get angry when he couldn't get the same response you did. Those were the times he withdrew food or blankets until I caved, or pretended." Her voice trembled when she said, "I was so hungry and cold."

He wanted to retch again but pressed the wet cloth to his mouth. Her time in captivity was so much worse than he'd imagined. She sounded as if she were trying to justify surrendering to Don's demands. Gabriel tried to tell her she had nothing to be ashamed of. In those conditions, no one could hold out. Yet when he tried to speak, his vocal cords were frozen.

Margaret didn't need him to act magnanimous or pave the way for her to forgive herself for not being a superwoman. She didn't need him to understand a damned thing. What had happened, happened, and now they were left to deal with the fallout.

"I never blamed you, Gabriel. But you can see why you and I are impossible, right?"

He twisted to stare up into her bleak countenance. "We can make new memories, away from here. We can move somewhere else and buy all new things. We—"

"No." The pitying look nearly did him in. "He ruined us. Ruined *me*." So saying, she bent and kissed the crown of his head then walked back inside, locking the screen door. "Don't come back, Gabriel. For *both* our sakes."

CHAPTER 32

The speed at which her house sold astounded everyone. With mixed emotions, Margie allowed the three James men to help her brother load her boxes and furniture into the moving van.

Wanting to make herself scarce in order to avoid Gabriel's dejected looks, she took the kids to the beach.

As she stood on the spot where she'd been abducted, she tried to make her panicky inner self understand it was the crime, not this particular location, she had a problem with. Prior to Don, this had been her favorite place to come.

She gazed out over the churning waters of the Atlantic. Wave after wave crashed along the shore as the sky above her darkened. If she were being fanciful, she'd have believed she conjured the gathering storm to match her mood. But it was Florida, and afternoon storms weren't unusual.

Her eyes wandered to where she and Gabriel had played on the shoreline. The remembered teasing brought a small, bittersweet smile to her lips. The one memory Don hadn't been able to steal, because he'd never known about it. The one she'd treasure always.

Gabriel had temporarily switched residences with Grey to avoid running into her. The only time he couldn't prevent it, was her little sister's release from Brookhaven a few days past.

Stephen had actually thrown them both under the bus after belting out Karaoke with Sammy onstage. Margie still chuckled when she thought of Gabriel's and her performance. They'd actually been booed off because they were both horrid singers. He'd graciously accepted all the blame for the song choice. She shook her head, awed by his caring and consideration. Was there ever a man so perfect? If there was, he'd be impossible to find.

Of course, their little bit of fun changed nothing, but she decided to write a letter to add to the gift basket she intended to give him tonight. One more final goodbye, with the added benefit of being able to thank him on paper for the joy he'd brought to her life because she couldn't in person.

Her future stretched out in front of her like a barren, desert wasteland, but maybe Gabriel could find the oasis in the sand. He didn't have to subscribe to her craptastic life. The issues she faced were hers alone. And if she woke some nights reaching for him, no one ever needed to know.

As the wind increased and whipped grit into her eyes, she raised a protective hand to her face. Frowning, she realized the moisture on her cheeks was from crying, and not from the salty spray.

Looking around, she spotted the boys kicking water at one another. Kaley, on the other hand, hovered only a few feet away, watching her with cautious longing.

Margie widened her eyes and blinked a few times to dispel her lingering grief. With a tight smile, she joined her daughter and wrapped an arm around her thin shoulders.

She frowned. "Have you lost weight, sweetheart?" Dieting fads were the norm for teenagers, and she hoped Kaley didn't fall victim to the trend. All sorts of complications could arise because of body image.

"I'm not dieting, Mom."

Margie nodded. "But you didn't have much of an appetite while I was gone?"

"Right."

"We're going to be okay, sweetheart. I promise."

Kaley's skinny arm inched around Margie's waist. "I want to believe that."

"Me, too." She kissed her daughter's temple. "I don't want you to worry, though. I'm back and have no intention of going anywhere."

"I'm scared all the time, Mom."

She drew back to study Kaley's somber face. "What are you afraid of?"

"You."

The one word had the power to steal the air from her lungs.

Seeing her horrified reaction, Kaley was quick to clarify. "Not *of* you, but *for* you. I don't want you to be alone and sad."

Margie rubbed her upper arms and ran her tongue along the outside of her teeth. After a pregnant pause to gather her thoughts, she said, "No one knows what the future holds, Kaley. Not you, not me. I'll be honest, I went through some serious shit, and before you ask, no. You don't get to know the details, because you shouldn't be burdened with them." Turning her face to the sky, she filled her lungs with the scent of the salt air. "But you should know I talk to Stephen twice a week in my efforts to put this behind me. One day, the sadness will be gone, and I'll find ways to enjoy life again." Looking down into eyes so like her own, she said, "I want you to promise to do the same. To be young and carefree while you can. To not take on my problems as your own. Can you do that?"

Tears streamed down her daughter's pale cheeks, and the sight was agonizing.

"I can try," Kaley whispered.

"Good. That's good." Margie opened her arms wider and tried not to wince when Kaley gave her a fierce hug. Tolerating physical affection from her children shouldn't pose such a serious problem, and she'd be damned if she'd let them see how badly a simple touch affected her.

She silently counted to ten, trying not to hold her breath. Trying to apply enough pressure to be an active participant in the hug. To be convincing.

As Kaley pulled back, she gave Margie a wry grin. "You're going to need to work on your poker face, Mom."

Stunned stupid, she stared at her kid.

Kaley actually snorted a laugh. "If you think I can't feel the difference, you're losing it."

"Here I thought I should get an Oscar nod for my performances," Margie quipped. Suddenly, she couldn't joke about it. "I'm sorry, honey. Please know it isn't you. Please—"

"Mom, I get it." Compassion filled Kaley's young, beautiful face. "You don't have to pretend with me, okay? I'd prefer you didn't. You can keep your secrets, but don't lie."

"I love you very much. That's the God's honest truth. It's the physical part I'm having a difficult time with, but I don't want to. My deepest wish is to be able to hold you or your brothers without breaking into a cold sweat. To accept *my* mother's comfort. To not seem like a cold fish."

"To be with Gabriel?" Kaley asked quietly.

"Please, don't press me about him." Margie hated the pleading quality in her own voice. For weeks, she'd been dodging questions from everyone, and she was at her wits' end.

"I won't. I mean, I still don't understand it. But I won't."

"Thank you." This time, she was able to clasp Kaley's hand in hers. She lifted it to drop a kiss on the back then gently tugged her daughter in the direction Scotty and Aaron had scampered down the beach. "Let's round up your beastly brothers and grab a bite to eat."

"Only if you release my hand. It's not cool to be seen like this with your mom."

Margie laughed—honest to goodness laughed—at Kaley's bored-teenager act. "Thanks for trying to let me save face, but we're holding hands until I say so."

"Or I could race you?"

Because it was the better option and Margie knew her daughter was trying her best to be helpful, she took her up on it. "Fine. But I'm older than you by a goodly number of years, and I get a head—"

Kaley fleet-footed it across the sand without a "by your leave" or a "ready, set, go."

"Little cheating shit!" Margie hollered, taking off after her mischievous daughter. A giggle floated back to her and made her genuinely laugh a second time.

"I'M NOT GOING TO HUG YOU, SO GET THAT RIGHT OUT OF YOUR head," Gabriel told Margaret, a small smile forming on his lips. Yeah, it was all for show, but he wanted her to go without guilt or the feeling she was leaving behind a shell of a man.

She grinned even as the fading daylight caught the sheen of tears she fought to contain. "Of all the times to keep your hugs to your-self... pfft!"

"I'm selfish that way." He smacked a hand on the back of the moving van. "Well, this is where my part in your moving adventure ends. It's best I don't know where you're going, so I'm not tempted to show up drunk and hang out on your pool deck."

Margie's white teeth worried her lower lip, and Gabriel was reminded of the first day they met. He wanted to kiss her as badly now as he had that day.

"Smart," she agreed.

"James, Grey, and Gordie have it covered." Why he was prolonging the goodbye and torturing them both was anyone's guess.

She nodded, and even though it was sweltering outside, she rubbed her upper arms. "I have something for you."

"Oh?"

With a gesture toward his porch, she shrugged. "It's a small gift for all you've done."

"Margie—"

"Margaret," she corrected softly. "You can call me Margaret, Gabriel."

His heart pinged. Drawing a ragged breath, he began again. "Margaret, everything I've done was because I love you. You've made my life brighter for the short time we spent together. Please never think you have to thank me for anything. I should be thanking you."

With compressed lips, she nodded. Breaking eye contact was impossible for both of them, it seemed.

"Ahem."

Gabriel smiled wryly as Grey tried to delicately get their attention. "One more sec, man." Rolling his eyes, he shook his head. "My brothers. You'd think at some point they'd learn it's bad form to interrupt a poignant moment."

Margaret laughed as he hoped she would. With a suddenness that stole his wits, she flung herself against his chest. "You're wrong, Gabriel. I *do* need to thank you."

Oh, how he wanted to crush her within his embrace, but he curbed his impulse and only touched a hand to her hip as he stroked her hair with the other. "Goodbye, Margaret Holt. You have the best life possible, okay?"

"You, too." The breaking of her voice echoed the breaking of his heart.

THE NEXT EVENING, AS HE SAT ON HIS PORCH, NURSING A LUKEWARM beer, Gabriel stared at Margaret's empty house. All the lights were dark, and there was an eerie stillness to the night air. He could pinpoint the exact moment it all went wrong, and he wished like hell he'd been able to prevent it. But he couldn't reverse time. All he knew was there would be an aching loneliness he'd be unable to ease for the remainder of his days.

He'd read the letter she left him. More than once. So many times, in fact, he could recall the exact location of each of her teardrop stains and what sentences they enhanced. She'd left him in no doubt that she loved him, but apparently not enough to try. A bitter pill to swallow. For sure he understood her reasons, and it was never a question of diminishing what she'd gone through.

With Margaret's strength and Stephen's counsel, Gabriel had no doubt she'd survive this and recover to the highest degree a victim could. Yet when she was ready to love again or explore a relationship, *he* wanted to be the one she turned to. Her refusal to let him in, to let him help her so they could both heal together, was destroying him.

He sipped his beer and grimaced at the taste. Everything was dull and dark, like her house currently was. And like the beer, he wondered if his life would grow flatter with each passing minute.

CHAPTER 33

FOUR MONTHS LATER...

The click of heels echoed off the pavement behind him, and believing it might be his dinner companion, Allison Jennings, Gabriel stopped at the entrance to Grey's restaurant. With his hand on the door, he turned with the beginning of a smile. It froze when his brain registered the sight.

Margaret and Sammy.

When the former recognized him, she halted, and her deep sapphire eyes became wary. In those eyes, he witnessed such sadness his heart wept. She glanced between him and Sammy as if trying to determine if they'd set her up.

Trying to keep his greeting as impersonal as possible, he gave a short nod. "Ladies." The huskiness in his voice gave away his deeper feelings. He cleared his throat and opened the door for them.

Before they reached him, Allison arrived.

"I'm sorry I'm late, Gabe. I was just... oh, sorry!" Her light rush of laughter indicated she sensed the awkwardness around the four of them. "Am I interrupting?"

"No." Margie's forcefulness added to the tension of the moment.

"No," Gabriel echoed softly, his gaze locked with Margaret's. He opened the door wider. "Have a nice evening."

Margaret entered first, but Sammy paused and placed a hand on his arm. "I'm sorry. About everything." She frowned down at where her fingers were touching the bare skin of his forearm. Her mouth opened and closed in one quick motion, and he wondered what she saw because, if he wasn't mistaken, she'd had a vision.

But he wouldn't ask.

He didn't want to know how bleak his future was going to be.

With a shake of her head, she said, "It's good to see you again, Gabe."

"You, too." He allowed the door to close behind her so he could regain his equilibrium.

"Are you okay?"

Looking into the sympathetic eyes of his future business partner, he gave a self-deprecating smile. "I will be."

David Jennings, Allison's brother, had been Gabriel's best friend during their college years. For explanation as to why he needed a change, he'd given David a brief rundown of his woes without revealing Margaret's abduction.

Now, he was left to wonder if he was a pitiful mess, with his emotions on display for all to see, or if David had told his sister about his angst.

"Would you rather go somewhere else?" The compassion in her voice was embarrassing for him.

Gabriel withdrew his man card at the same time he tucked his emotional baggage away. "It's strictly up to you, but Grey makes the best burgers around. If our negotiation goes well, I imagine I won't get back here much after I move to Jacksonville. I should take advantage while I still can."

"Burgers, it is."

They were seated at a table across the room from the Holt sisters, and Gabriel wished his chair faced the opposite direction from the women. If he had to continually stare at Margaret while trying to hammer out his new contract with Allison, he'd probably settle for pennies on the dollar and give Jennings, Jennings, and Norris Law Offices the upper hand regarding his employment.

Grey approached their table with a bottle of wine and a menu. Beyond his shoulder, Gabriel could see Margaret down her third shot. He shared a concerned look with Sammy. Reminding himself it was no longer his business, he averted his gaze and met his brother's solemn-eyed stare.

"While I know my burgers are the best, maybe taking your date elsewhere tonight would be best, Gabe."

Rage rippled underneath Gabriel's skin. *Where the hell did his brother get off, reprimanding him in front of a virtual stranger?* All for a woman who had rejected him time and time again. All for a woman who had called it quits by confusing him with a serial rapist and murderer. Sure, he'd grown more bitter with time, but he was trying to be a bigger person. Leaving this freaking town in his rearview mirror was the only way forward.

"Grey, I'd like you to meet Allison Jennings. She's a senior partner in a Jacksonville firm I'm considering going to work for. Allison, my interfering brother, Greyson."

Gabriel rose to his feet, removed the menu from Grey's hand, and placed it in front of Allison. "I'll be right back. Please, take your time deciding." He faced his brother. "Grey, may I see you in your office?"

Neither spoke until the door was shut.

"You don't get to look down on me for trying to move on with my life, Grey. I'm doing the best I can. And I had no idea Margaret would be here tonight."

"She lives in Seminole Woods now and visits regularly with Sammy." Grey sat on the edge of his desk. The censure in his eyes did nothing to calm Gabriel's rising temper. "Margie doesn't normally drink, and she's out there, killing her liver because you're here with another woman, Gabe."

"No, it's not because of me. But even if it is, that's on *her*, not me. You don't know the whole story, and you sure as hell don't know how hard I tried… after." He began to pace. "You want the truth of it? She gave me my walking papers, literally, in the form of a letter the day we helped her load up the moving van. I die inside every time I have to look at the strangers on her pool deck or on her lawn or in her driveway. So do us both a favor, and *stay the fuck out of it*."

"I can't do that. Not when I see you *both* hurting this badly."

Gabriel closed his eyes against the wave of pain seeing Margaret had brought. "Nothing you or I can do will change her mind, Grey. Believe me." His voice was as raw as his nerves and hollowed-out heart. The desire to cry or rage or both rose up to the surface, but he ruthlessly tamped it down again. After all was said and done, and when he finally packed up his home for the last time, he'd allow himself a breakdown. And when the following day rolled around, he'd pick up the pieces and start fresh in his new life. But until that day came, he had to hold it together.

"I'm sorry, Gabe. Truly." Grey surprised him with a tight hug, and Gabriel worried he might not be able to let go or he'd shatter.

"I know. Do me a favor and start watering down Margaret's drinks. I don't imagine she's used to anything stronger than a glass of wine, and she doesn't need the horrendous hangover tomorrow."

"I can't do that if she's paying for drinks."

"Tell her they're on the house and bill my card."

MARGIE HAD ALMOST REACHED THE RESTROOM WHEN A DOOR IN THE hallway was jerked open. Not expecting to see Gabriel, she gasped as he filled up the narrow space.

He was heartbreakingly handsome. He wore a black button-down shirt with the sleeves rolled up to his elbows, and his hair was slightly rumpled—as if he'd run his hands through it a few times. The look made him mouthwateringly approachable and less godlike in appearance. The intensity in his eyes hadn't diminished, but the ever-present teasing twinkle was long gone.

"Gabriel. How are you?" she asked, her voice sounding breathy and uncertain to her own ears.

"Do you want an honest answer, or do you want me to lie, Margaret?"

Her insides shriveled. "Sorry. I was making polite conversation."

If she thought he'd been irritated a second before, it was nothing compared to the thundercloud expression he now wore. "If it's come to that, I'd rather you didn't bother at all, okay?"

He spun on his heel to leave.

"Gabriel." She winced at the desperate thread in her voice, but those couldn't be their last words.

He didn't turn around, but he paused long enough to listen.

"You d-deserve to be happy. I n-need you to b-be."

He didn't respond for the longest time. "Right."

Left alone in the hallway, she stared at his retreating back and swallowed the desire to cry. As she turned to continue her journey to the restroom, she caught sight of Grey lingering quietly in the shadow of his office.

"He's planning on leaving."

His words struck like a mule kick to her ribs. She gasped and pressed her fists to her chest. Grey seemed to expect an answer, but nothing she could say would change Gabriel's mind or make things right with his family.

"He won't tell me what happened after you returned, only that you ended things." Grey stepped into the light of the hall. "I've never seen him so broken, Margie."

"I can't fix him, Grey. I can't even fix myself." She hiccuped a sob. "I wish I could. I'm sorry."

He opened his arms, and she hesitated only a second because she could use the unassuming comfort offered by a friend. As if he understood her new claustrophobic feeling while being held, he kept his arms loose and gently stroked her shoulder.

"He wants me to water down your drinks so you don't have a hangover tomorrow," he confessed.

She snorted at the dryness in his tone. "Same old Gabriel, always feeling compelled to control a situation."

"Doesn't he just?"

"Thank you for not hating me, Grey," she whispered.

"None of us do, babe. Not even Gabe. We know you went through hell. It's harder to understand why you pushed him away, though."

"Maybe someday I'll find it easier to talk about and I'll explain, but I need more time."

"You don't have to share your secrets with me. I'm sure you've had enough people pry."

Pulling back, she looked up into his kind steel-blue eyes. "Thank you."

"Go on, or Sammy's going to think you fell in."

Her first real laugh of the night bubbled up. It felt good to share a light moment with someone. "Okay, but fair warning. Don't you dare water down my drinks. I have no kids tomorrow, and I intend to make the most of it."

"You got it. I'll also give you a sure-fire hangover recipe." His grin was an exact replica of Gabriel's, and her heart stuttered.

"Much appreciated."

Five minutes later, she joined Sammy and was happy to see their food had arrived. For the first time in forever, she felt a stirring of hunger.

"You've been crying."

Margie grimaced. "Only a little."

"Over Gabriel?"

"Only a little," she repeated.

"So what caused the majority of your tears?" Sammy looked up from shifting her food around her plate so it didn't touch.

"My feelings of inadequacy and knowing I hurt Gabriel as badly as I did."

Sammy reached for her hand across the table. When they connected, her sister's eyes went blank and she was mentally transported to another time and place. A minute later, she shook free of her trance. "Sorry."

"You have nothing to apologize for, Sammy. I'm sure you don't always have control over your gift."

"I mostly do. I'm getting stronger since my time in Brookhaven." She shrugged and popped a fry in her mouth.

"Do you want to talk about it?" Margie never felt she had the right to ask before now. For the most part, she was a horrid big sister. "I'm here for you."

"Oh, sissy. You're still dealing with your own problems. You don't need to pile mine on top. Besides, after eight months in the mental pokey, I'm talked out."

Margie giggled. "'The mental pokey'? Does Stephen know you refer to his hospital that way?"

"You'd be surprised what I torture him with."

The sisters shared a laugh, and years fell off Margie's shoulders. She deconstructed her burger, added condiments, and put it together the way it should be. From the corner of her eye, she saw Grey frown when Sammy did the same.

Trying hard not to smirk, Margie gave a subtle nod in his direction. "I think we are seriously offending Grey by doctoring our burgers."

Her sister held hers up, made eye contact with him, and took a large bite. Margie snorted. Only Sammy could get away with such cheekiness.

"Will you tell me what you saw?"

Sammy set down her burger and wiped her hands, a mirrored image of Margie's own movements. "I had an image of you and Gabriel, happy together. You were hiking with the kids and laughing at something he said. At one point, he pulled you behind a tree to lay one on you." She gave her a stern look. "I'm not sure why you gave up a man who steals scorching-hot kisses like that. Seems like he knows the business end of making love."

Margie choked on her margarita. The coughing lasted forever, and when she could draw a breath without fire coating her throat, she threw a fry at Sammy's head. "You almost killed me." She was about to take another bite of her burger when her sister's words registered. "Wait. Hiking? Are you sure? Where?"

"I don't know where you've gone in the past. You would know better than me. All the trees and trails look the same."

Her body went cold, and she dropped her food on her plate. "But it was definitely a walk through the woods?"

"Sissy? What's wrong?"

"Gabriel and I have never been hiking. *Not ever.*"

The import of the moment sunk in, and they shared a wide-eyed look. Sammy's vision hadn't been of the past, but of a future event.

Her sister took a sip of her drink, and her eyes zeroed in on Gabriel across the room. "I touched his arm when we arrived tonight. I saw him in a tuxedo about to get married."

The urge to vomit struck Margie. *"Oh, God!"*

"I didn't mention it, because I didn't want to hurt you. But what if it's *your* wedding? To him? To Gabriel?" Sammy sounded as stunned as Margie felt.

"What if?" danced about in her brain, and she found Gabriel's reflection in the bar mirror. He happened to glance up, and their gazes connected in the glass.

Coward that she was, she broke eye contact. "You're wrong," she croaked.

"I'm sorry, Margie." Sammy's softly spoken words shredded her.

"It's okay. But can we change the subject now? Please?"

CHAPTER 34

*M*argie lurched from the back of the Uber with slurred instructions for the driver to wait. The blueberry-colored house with the white trim and the cheery yellow door, loomed large in the dark. Not a single light shone from any of the windows, and she felt like a damned fool.

What if Gabriel wasn't home? What if he'd decided to take the sexy blonde woman up on her come-fuck-me eyes? Despite what Grey had told her about Allison Jennings only being with Gabriel for a business meeting, the woman was seriously into him. What was to stop him from taking her up on her blatant flirting? *Nothing.*

Sick to her stomach—unsure if it was the booze or her nerves—Margie wondered, not for the first time, if her sister was wrong.

She scolded herself for her foolishness and bent to scoop up a handful of pebbles from Gabriel's flower bed. After weaving her way around the back of the house, she stopped shy of carrying through on her ill-conceived plan. Agonizing over images of him and Allison wrapped around each other in the bed he'd shared with *her.*

How long Margie stared at his darkened bedroom window, she didn't know. It felt like forever for her to work up her nerve. The pebbles began to feel like lead weights in her hand, and with a silent prayer that she was doing the right thing, she chucked one.

The clink of stone on glass was louder than she expected, and she pivoted her head back and forth to make sure she hadn't woken the neighbors. A wave of dizziness hit her, and she put her hand on the stucco wall to prevent falling over. With grim determination, she lifted her arm to throw another.

All the rocks from her hand slapped the window at once, and Margie gasped her horror as the noise ricocheted off the walls and filled the space between the houses.

The brightness of the floodlights froze her in place. Were they sensored, or had Gabriel woken at the sound of the rocks hitting his window? When nothing more happened, she bent to retrieve another pebble and tossed it.

Again, silence.

She swore under her breath and frowned her irritation.

Gabriel didn't sleep that heavily. He probably knew she was here and was purposely ignoring her.

In the distance, Margie heard a car start up.

She staggered around the corner in time to see the Uber drive away.

Her purse was in the car!

Taking three steps after the retreating taillights, she decided she'd never catch him and cursed her suck-ass luck.

"Goddammit!"

As she turned back, a large shadow detached itself from the side of the house. She reacted with a bloodcurdling scream, and lights in the neighboring house came on.

"One of us is going to be in jail before the night is up if you keep up this racket, Margaret," Gabriel said dryly.

Putting her hand to her racing heart, she bent over and sucked in air. Her pleasant buzz was officially a thing of the past.

"Jesus, Gabriel. You gave me a heart attack."

He held out her purse. "I thought you might need this."

"You sent him away?"

"I figured you were here for a reason. If you want to leave, I can drive you or call another car."

"Right." She stared at her bag as if it were a snake ready to strike.

"You can message him to come back," he said softly.

Taking a deep breath, she lifted her gaze to meet his. The gentle understanding gutted her. Even now, he was trying to give her what she needed. "No. I came to break you out. It occurred to me you might be lonely."

He grinned.

Margie's heart was instantly lighter. It thrilled her to see the twinkle return to his eyes.

"Did you now?"

She gave a jerky nod. "I've been so self-absorbed, Gabriel. I don't want to do this without you."

"This?"

"The future."

He remained silent.

Drawing her courage from somewhere around her big toe, she asked, "Will you forgive me for shutting you out?"

"Of course he forgives you. Now will you two suck face and make up so the rest of us can get some damned sleep?" Gordon's grumpy voice, coming from the other side of the screen, sent Margie careening into Gabriel's embrace from sheer fright. How she never heard the window open was beyond her.

"You're way too jumpy, love," Gabriel murmured next to her ear, with a light rub of his palms on her shoulders.

"You knew he was there, didn't you?" she said in disgust, giving his chest a light smack.

"We were up, having a beer. I just turned the lights off when we heard the car pull up." He gave a small shrug. "I've been out here the whole time you were trying to decide whether to throw those rocks. The floodlights must've been my brother's warped sense of humor."

"Pebbles," she corrected. "Why didn't you say anything?"

All amusement abandoned his face. "You had an important decision to make."

She caressed his jaw, running her index finger along his lower lip. "I made it." When he didn't say anything but continued to stare, her nerves got the better of her. "Am I too late?"

"No, I'm waiting for you to take Gordie's suggestion to suck face. I thought I'd let you take the lead."

"Who says 'suck face' anymore?" She laughed even as tears of relief burned her eyes.

Rising up on tiptoes, she planted her mouth on his. When their lips connected and when he didn't press for more than this light contact, she sighed. The simple, clinging touch was like coming home. The faint taste of beer and love greeted her, and she smiled. She'd been wrong to think Don had ruined what she could have with Gabriel.

She drew back and met his burning silver gaze. "I love you."

"Thank God!" He closed his eyes and swallowed. "I never thought I'd hear you say those words again." His voice was raspy and packed with pain. "I love you, too, Margaret. More than I can ever say."

When he lifted his lids again, he touched his nose to hers and clasped her hand to lead her to the front porch. He sat down in one of the Adirondack chairs and eased her into his lap, again, careful of her reaction.

"From the beginning, one of my biggest fears was this life ending in disaster like all the others," she told him in a low voice. "When I was chain—uh, being held prisoner, my fear was confirmed. I thought I was going to die, Gabriel."

His arms spasmed, but he remained quiet.

"Then Don systematically destroyed every memory I had of us. There was no hope. Nothing to cling to as I tried to keep my mind intact all those long months." She felt his shuddering breath and paused to give him a chance to process. "I didn't know how to deal with all those tainted memories. To bridge the gap between what happened and the future."

"But now you can? What changed?"

His question was legitimate. She'd have asked the same.

"Stephen helped. Mostly." Embarrassment snaked through her. Her therapy would be ongoing for a long while, because as much as she needed to, she wasn't ready to discuss everything. "Also, Sammy. Tonight at the bar, she had a vision of us together. More than one, actually."

He stiffened.

"What is it?" she asked.

"You didn't come here on your own? You came because Sammy prodded you?"

"*No!* No, Gabriel, it wasn't like that." But maybe it was a little. "She told me what she saw and encouraged me to speak to you. But this? Coming here tonight, this was my idea."

"Is this choice one you're going to regret in the morning when you're completely sober?"

"I'm not some twenty-something girl who's drunk-texting an ex," she snapped. "And if I wasn't sober when I got here, the fright I got from both you and your brother did the trick."

The tension eased from his body, and he drew her to settle against his chest. "Sorry, love. The idea of you doing an about-face in the morning freaked me out."

"There will be no more about-faces. Not from me. I promise."

"Marry me, Margaret. Say you'll marry me and complete my life."

"What about the Jacksonville move? Did you take the job *Allison* offered?" She couldn't keep the cattiness from her voice. The woman wanted Gabriel, and if he committed to working for her firm, the two of them would surely have a future problem.

His deep chuckle rumbled in his chest. "Sounds like you might be a little jealous of my dinner companion tonight."

"Damned straight." She poked his chest.

"I didn't take the job. They promised me everything I could ever want, including partner, but I couldn't seem to sever my last link to you."

"What link?"

"Moving meant giving up this house. It's where some of my best memories of us are."

She went cold inside. For her, those memories had become nightmares.

"But I will," he gently assured her. "Gordie can have this place, and we can build one of our own. Something new where there aren't any ghosts between us."

"I'm worried, Gabriel. Worried we'll make love and I'll freak the fuck out on you. I don't want to hurt you or make you feel worse." She inched back to look at him. "What if I really am too broken?"

He processed her words, and it was a moment before he spoke. "Don't borrow trouble, Margaret. We'll take it as slow or as fast as you need. And if we have to go to couples counseling to find a way past this, we will. I'll do whatever it takes."

"And if I never fully recover?" she pushed the question past the lump in her throat, her mouth bone dry.

"Then I suppose we deal with it if the time ever comes. Right now, I'm content with the fact you love me and want to try."

"Maybe we should shelve any major commitments until *after* I've put the abduction behind me?"

GABRIEL KNEW IT MIGHT NEVER HAPPEN. KNEW THAT MARGARET WAS still struggling six months after the fact. Yet she was willing to take a risk, and it mattered that she was.

"I think yours is a reasonable plan," he said gruffly. "Can I hug you, or is this all you can manage right now?"

"I'd like a hug. I'm not sure how I'm going to react to it, though."

Tightening his embrace, he drew her down on his chest and kissed the top of her head. She remained stiff in the circle of his arms, and after fifteen seconds, he dropped one hand to her hip and stroked the top of her thigh in a light figure-eight pattern. Within a minute, the rigid tension left her body, and after another few, she tilted her head back to look at him.

"I missed this," she said. "Simply being with you. No pressure to talk or be anyone but myself."

"These are the moments I love best when we're together," he confessed. "It's as if we're of one mind and one soul. Corny, I know, but—"

Margaret placed an index finger over his mouth. "No. Not corny, and I totally get it. I feel exactly the same."

He bit her finger, and she released a breathless laugh. When their gazes connected, a deeper understanding passed between them. Perhaps he was being fanciful, but he felt it to his toes.

"I will never stop loving you, Margaret. Not in this life, the next, or the one after. If we don't make it this time around—and it's my sincerest hope we do—but should we go our separate ways, then I'll look for you first, next time."

"You said that before." She smiled, more of a mischievous smirk. "More than once."

"Well, I did a piss-poor job of it, didn't I? We both did by marrying someone else first. But it feels as if we got it right now."

"I hope so." She stood up and reached for her purse. "It's getting late. I should go."

"Stay." Before she could protest, he settled a light kiss on her forehead. "Only to sleep."

"I'm afraid I'll have a meltdown if I wake... here... because of the room Don created... I... the nightmares still disorient me."

Her uncomfortableness was painful to witness.

"Then I'll drive you home. Let me get my keys."

"Will you stay with me? At my house?"

He could tell it cost her everything to ask. "If that's what you want."

"I do." Relief flooded her face.

"Come on. Let me pack an overnight bag." He held out his hand and inwardly cheered when she clasped it.

"A weekend bag," she corrected.

He grinned. "A weekend bag."

LATER THAT NIGHT, AFTER SHE'D WOKEN SCREAMING HIS NAME, Gabriel soothed her as best he could. He carried her to the couch, bundled her in a blanket, and raided the freezer for the ice cream he knew he'd find. After grabbing a spoon, he sprawled next to her on the new sectional.

In an attempt at normal, Gabriel gestured to the L-shaped sofa. "I like this, by the way. It's long enough that my legs don't stick off the end."

"I may have purchased it with you in mind." She smiled around the bite of mint, chocolate chip he offered her.

Surprised, he looked around the room. "Why? You sent me packing after you assured me we were over."

Her eyes dropped, and she cleared her throat.

"That wasn't a criticism, love. I'm curious what made you consider a couch to accommodate my size."

"I figured even if you and I could never be together, I could still dream." Her voice broke as she spoke, and Gabriel was sure he could hear his heart echo the sound.

He shoved the spoon into the ice cream and placed it on the end table. Sitting up, he shifted to face her more fully and tugged on a loose strand of her hair.

"That's the most heartbreaking thing I've ever heard. And also the sweetest." He sighed when she ducked her head to lay a butter-fly-light kiss on his jaw. She rearranged herself to lean into his chest and grabbed the ice cream again. They took turns sharing. After a few minutes of savoring the feel of her—relaxed—in his arms, he broke the silence. "What was the vision Sammy saw?"

"Us, a few years down the road."

"Care to elaborate?"

"We were hiking—you, me, and the kids. She said you stopped and tugged me behind a tree to sneak a kiss."

He nodded. "Sounds like me. And when she described the scene, you knew it was our future."

"Yes."

"This is how she convinced you to give us another chance?"

"Yes and no. She suggested I should after I confessed we'd never been hiking. But it was the idea we could be normal again that got me most."

"It was a vision of hope."

She twisted to stare at him, wonder lighting up her face. "Yes! Exactly."

"Here." He handed her the ice cream. "Let's do something truly normal and watch a movie like an old married couple."

"Yeah, you're going to have to drop the word 'old' from your vocabulary if you plan to stick around," she warned.

"Duly noted. But you're going to have to get over our age gap one day." His eyes dropped to her ice-cream-slick lips. "Do you suppose we can try something else normal?"

She tilted her head and tentatively offered her mouth. The creamy sweetness of the Häagen-Dazs blended with Margaret's unique flavor, and he loved that her tongue was cool against the warmth of his. The second she grew uncomfortable from their extended contact, he sensed it. Giving her a light bite on her lower lip, he stole the utensil from her hand.

"Stop being a hog, Margaret."

Her breathy laughter made him grin around a spoonful of ice cream. He winked and picked up the remote. They would be okay.

He'd make sure of it.

FROM THE AUTHOR...

Thank you for taking the time to read *THIS TIME YOU!*

Be sure to join my mailing list for news on current releases, potential sales, new-to-you author introductions, and contests each month. But if it gets to be too much, you can unsubscribe at any time. Your information will always be kept private. No spam here! tmcromer.com/newsletter

Join my Facebook Reader Group. I have created a group for fans who like to interact. This group entitles readers to "fan page only" contests, as well as an exclusive first look at covers, excerpts and more. Cromer's Carousers is the most fun way to follow yet! bit.ly/tmc-readers

ALSO BY T.M. CROMER

RETURN HOME

ONE WISH

CPSIA information can be obtained
at www.ICGtesting.com
Printed in the USA
LVHW051153250522
719694LV00010B/744

9 780996 572057